Emir promised plea~~sure~~ forgetfulness and, f~~or~~ the prospect of that ~~seemed preferable right~~ now to doing battle endlessly on every front.

How would it feel to have this big man hold her and have those strong hands bring her pleasure? She must have swayed toward him, for the next thing she knew he was holding her in front of him.

"Why, Britt," he said. "If I'd known, we could have arranged something before the meeting."

He was blunter than she had ever been, blunter than she was prepared for, and breath shot out of her lungs as he dipped his head to brush her lips with his. Incredibly, she was instantly hungry, instantly frantic, for more pressure, more intimacy, and for everything to happen fast.

He felt so good…so very good…

She wanted this. She needed it and she forgot everything the moment his hands caressed her breasts. She wanted this—wanted him. She wanted, just for once in her life, to feel that she didn't have to be the leader, the fighter, but that just this one time she could be a woman.

All about the author…
Susan Stephens

SUSAN STEPHENS was a professional singer before meeting her husband on the tiny Mediterranean island of Malta. In true Harlequin Presents style they met on Monday, became engaged on Friday and were married three months later. Almost thirty years and three children later, they are still in love. (Susan does not advise her children to return home one day with a similar story as she may not take the news with the same fortitude as her own mother!)

Susan had written several nonfiction books when fate took a hand. At a charity costume ball there was an after-dinner auction. One of the lots, "Spend a Day with an Author," had been donated by Harlequin Presents author Penny Jordan. Susan's husband bought this lot, and Penny was to become not just a great friend but a wonderful mentor who encouraged Susan to write romance.

Susan loves her family, her pets, her friends and her writing. She enjoys entertaining, travel and going to the theater. She reads, cooks and plays the piano to relax, and can occasionally be found throwing herself off mountains on a pair of skis or galloping through the countryside.

Visit Susan's website, www.susanstephens.net. She loves to hear from her readers all around the world!

Other titles by Susan Stephens available in ebook:

Harlequin Presents®

GRAY QUINN'S BABY *(The Untamed)*
THE UNTAMED ARGENTINIAN
THE ARGENTINIAN'S SOLACE
TAMING THE LAST ACOSTA*

*a 2-in-1 release with the previously published title
ITALIAN BOSS, PROUD MISS PRIM

Susan Stephens

DIAMOND IN THE DESERT

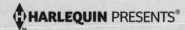
HARLEQUIN PRESENTS®

Recycling programs
for this product may
not exist in your area.

ISBN-13: 978-0-373-13155-6

DIAMOND IN THE DESERT

Copyright © 2013 by Susan Stephens

This edition published by arrangement with Harlequin Books S.A.

For questions and comments about the quality of this book,
please contact us at CustomerService@Harlequin.com.

Printed in U.S.A.

DIAMOND IN THE DESERT

For all my wonderful readers who love the mystery of the desert and the romance of a sheikh.

CHAPTER ONE

MONDAY SEVEN A.M. on a cold, foggy day in London a breakfast meeting was being held by a powerful consortium set up to acquire the world's biggest diamond mine. The group of three men was led by Sheikh Sharif al Kareshi, a leading geologist otherwise known as the Black Sheikh, thanks to his discovery of vast oil lakes beneath the desert sands of Kareshi. Concealed lighting was set at the perfect level for reading the fine print on a contract, and the surroundings were sumptuous as befitted the ruling Sheikh of Kareshi in his London home. Seated with the sheikh at the table were two men of roughly the same age, that was to say, thirty-two. One was a Spaniard, and the other owned an island off southern Italy. All three men were giants in the world of commerce, and heartbreakers in the game of life. Colossal sums of money were being bandied about. The atmosphere was tense.

'A diamond mine beyond the Arctic circle?' the darkly glamorous Count Roman Quisvada remarked.

'Diamonds were discovered in the Canadian Arctic some years back,' Sharif explained, leaning back. 'Why not the European Arctic, my friend?'

All three men had been friends since boarding school in England, and, although they had all gone on to make individual fortunes, they were bound by friendship and trusted each other implicitly.

'My first pass over the findings suggests this discovery by Skavanga Mining could be even larger than we suspected,' Sharif went on, pushing some documents across the table to the other two men.

'And I hear that Skavanga boasts three sisters who have become known as the Skavanga Diamonds, which in itself intrigues me,' the dangerous-looking Spaniard commented as he peeled a Valencia orange with a blade as sharp as a scalpel.

'I'll tell you what I know, Raffa,' the sheikh promised his friend, better known as Don Rafael de Leon, Duke of Cantalabria, a mountainous and very beautiful region of Spain.

Count Roman Quisvada also sat forward. Roman was an expert in diamonds, with laboratories that specialised in cutting and polishing high-value stones, while Raffa owned the world's largest and most exclusive chain of high-end retail jewellers. The Black Sheikh, the Italian count, and the Spanish duke had the diamond business sewn up.

There was just one loose end, Sharif reflected, and that was a company called Skavanga Mining. Owned by the three sisters, Britt, Eva and Leila Skavanga, along with the girls' absentee brother, Tyr, Skavanga Mining had reported the discovery of the largest diamond deposits ever recorded. He was on the point of going to Skavanga to check out these reports for himself.

While he was there he would check out Britt Skavanga, the oldest sister, who was currently running the company, Sharif mused as he drew a photograph towards him. She looked like a worthy opponent with her clear grey eyes, firm mouth and the tilt of that chin. He looked forward to meeting her. A deal with the added spice of down time in the bedroom held obvious appeal. There was no sentiment in business and he certainly wasted none on women.

'Why do you get all the fun?' Roman complained, frowning when Sharif told the other men about his plan.

'There are plenty to go round,' he reassured them dryly as the other two men studied the photographs of the sisters. Glancing at Raffa, he felt a momentary twinge of something close to apprehension. The youngest sister, whom Raffa was studying, was clearly an innocent, while Raffa was most certainly not.

'Three good-looking women,' Roman commented, glancing between his friends.

'For three ruthless asset strippers,' Raffa added, devouring the last piece of orange with relish. 'I look forward to stripping the assets off this one—'

Raffa's dark eyes blackened dangerously as Sharif gathered the photographs in. Sharif hardly realised that he was caressing the photograph of Britt Skavanga with his forefinger while denying Raffa further study of Leila, the youngest sister.

'This could be our most promising project to date,' the man known to the world as the Black Sheikh commented.

'And if anyone can land this deal, Sharif can,' Roman remarked, hoping to heal the momentary rift between his friends. He could only be thankful their interest wasn't in the same girl.

Raffa's laugh relaxed them all. 'Didn't I hear you have some interesting sexual techniques in Kareshi, Sharif? Silken ties? Chiffon blindfolds?'

Roman huffed a laugh at this. 'I've heard the same

thing. In the harem tents it's said they use creams and potions to send sensation through the roof—'

'Enough,' Sharif rapped, raising his hands to silence his friends. 'Can we please return to business?'

Within seconds the Skavanga girls were forgotten and the talk was all of balance sheets and financial predictions, but in one part of his mind Sharif was still thinking about a pair of cool grey eyes and a full, expressive mouth, and what could be accomplished with a little expert tutelage.

An absolute monarch, bred to a hard life in the desert, Sharif had been trained to rule and fight and argue at council with the wisest of men—women being notable by their absence, which was something he had changed as soon as he took over the country. Women in Kareshi had used to be regarded as ornaments to be pampered and spoiled and hidden away; under his rule they were expected to pull their weight. Education for all was now the law.

And who would dare to argue with the Black Sheikh? Not Britt Skavanga, that was for sure. Staring at Britt's photograph and seeing the steely determination so similar to his own in her eyes only reinforced his intention to check out all the assets in Skavanga personally. Britt possessed the generous, giving mouth of a concubine, with the unrelenting gaze of a Viking warrior. The combination aroused him. Even the severity of the suit she was wearing intrigued him. Her breasts thrusting against the soft wool stirred his senses in a most agreeable way. He adored severe tailoring on a woman. It was a type of shorthand he had learned to read many years ago. Severe equalled repressed, or possibly a player who liked to tease. Either way, he was a huge fan.

'Are you still with us, Sharif?' Raffa enquired with

amusement as his friend finally pushed Britt's photograph away.

'Yes, but not for long as I will be leaving for Skavanga in the morning, travelling in my capacity of geologist and advisor to the consortium. This will allow me to make an impartial assessment of the situation without ruffling any feathers.'

'That's sensible,' Raffa agreed. 'Talk of the Black Sheikh descending on a business would be enough to send anyone into a panic.'

'Have you ever *descended* on a tasty business prospect without devouring it?' Roman enquired, hiding his smile.

'The fact that this mysterious figure, conjured by the press and known to the world as the Black Sheikh, has never had a photograph published will surely be an advantage to you,' Raffa suggested.

'I reserve judgement until we meet again when I will be in a position to tell you if the claims that have been made about the Skavanga Diamonds are true,' Sharif said with a closing gesture.

'We can ask for no more than that,' his two friends agreed.

'Well, clearly, I must be the one to meet him,' Britt insisted as the three sisters sat round the interestingly shaped—if not very practical, thanks to the holes the designer had punched in it—blonde wood kitchen table in Britt's sleek, minimalist, barely lived-in penthouse.

'Clearly—why?' Britt's feisty middle sister, Eva, demanded. 'Who says you have the right to take the lead in this new venture? Shouldn't we all have a part in it? What about the equality you're always banging on about, Britt?'

'Britt has far more business experience than we have,' the youngest and most mild-mannered sister, Leila, pointed out. 'And that's a perfectly sensible reason for Britt to be the one to meet with him,' Leila added, sweeping anxious fingers through her tumbling blonde curls.

'Perfectly sensible?' Eva scoffed. 'Britt has experience in mining iron ore and copper. But diamonds?' Eva rolled her emerald eyes. 'You must agree the three of us are virgins where diamonds are concerned?'

And Eva was likely to remain a virgin in every sense if she kept on like this, Britt thought, fretting like a mother over her middle sister. Eva had been a glass-half-empty type of person for as long as Britt could remember and sadly there were no dashing Petruchios in Skavanga to prevent Eva from turning into a fully-fledged shrew. 'I'm going to deal with this—and with him,' she said firmly.

'You and the Black Sheikh?' Eva said scornfully. 'You might be a hotshot businesswoman here in Skavanga, but the sheikh's business interests are global— and he runs a country. What on earth makes you think you can take a man like that on?'

'I know my business,' Britt said calmly. 'I know our mine and I'll be factual. I'll be cool and I'll be reasoned.'

'Britt's very good at doing stuff like this without engaging her emotions,' Leila added.

'Really?' Eva mocked. 'Whether she can or not remains to be seen.'

'I won't let you down,' Britt promised, knowing her sisters' concerns both for her and for the business had prompted this row. 'I've handled difficult people in the past and I'm well prepared to meet the Black Sheikh. I realise I must handle him with kid gloves—'

'Nice.' Eva laughed.

Britt ignored this. 'We would be unwise to underestimate him,' she said. 'The ruler of Kareshi is known as the Black Sheikh for a very good reason—'

'Rape and pillage?' Eva suggested scathingly.

Britt held her tongue. 'Sheikh Sharif is one of the foremost geologists in the world.'

'It's a shame we couldn't find any photographs of him,' Leila mused.

'He's a geologist, not a film star,' Britt pointed out. 'And how many Arab rulers have you seen photographs of?'

'He's probably so ugly he'd break the camera,' Eva muttered. 'I bet he's a nerd with pebble glasses and a bristly chin.'

'If he is he would be easier for Britt to deal with,' Leila said hopefully.

'A ruler who has moved his country forward and brought peace sounds like a decent man to me, so, whatever he looks like, it doesn't matter. I just need your support. Fact: the minerals at the mine are running out and we need investment. The consortium this man heads up has the money to allow us to mine the diamonds.'

There was a silence as Britt's sisters accepted the truth of this and she breathed a sigh of relief when they nodded their heads. Now she had a chance to rescue the mine and the town of Skavanga that was built around it. That, together with all the fresh challenges ahead of her, made her meeting with the so-called Black Sheikh seem less of a problem.

She was feeling slightly less sanguine the following day.

'Serves you right for building up your hopes,' Eva said as the girls gathered in Britt's study after hearing her groan. 'Your famous Black Sheikh can't even be bothered to meet with you,' Eva remarked, peering over Britt's shoulder at the email message on the computer screen. 'So he's sending a representative instead,' she scoffed, turning to throw an I-told-you-so look at Leila.

'I'll get some fresh coffee,' Leila offered.

Eva's carping was really getting on Britt's nerves. She'd been up since dawn exchanging emails with Kareshi. It was practically noon for her, Britt reflected angrily as Leila brought the coffee in. Her sisters loved staying in the city with her, but sometimes they forgot that, while they could lounge around, she had a job to do. 'I'm still going to meet with him. What else am I going to do?' she demanded, swinging round to confront her sisters. 'Do you two have any better ideas?'

Eva fell silent, while Leila gave Britt a sympathetic look as she handed her a mug of coffee. 'I'm just sorry we're going back home and leaving you with all this to deal with.'

'That's my job,' Britt said, controlling her anger. She could never be angry with Leila. 'Of course I'm disappointed I won't be meeting the Black Sheikh, but all I've ever asked for is your support, Eva.'

'Sorry,' Eva muttered awkwardly. 'I know you got landed with the company when Mum and Dad died. I'm just worried about what's going to happen now all the commodities are running out. I do realise the mine's sunk without the diamonds. And I know you'll do your very best to land this deal, but I'm worried about you, Britt. This is too much on your shoulders.'

'Stop it,' Britt warned, giving her sister a hug. 'Whoever the Black Sheikh sends, I can deal with him.'

'It says that the man you're to expect is a qualified geologist,' Leila pointed out. 'So at least you'll have something in common.' Britt's degree was also in Geology, with a Master's in Business Management.

'Yes,' Eva agreed, trying to sound as optimistic as her sister. 'I'm sure it will be fine.'

Britt knew that both her sisters were genuinely concerned about her. They just had different ways of showing it. 'Well, I'm excited,' she said firmly to lift the mood. 'When this man gets here we're another step closer to saving the company.'

'I wish Tyr were here to help you.'

Leila's words made them all silent. Tyr was their long-lost brother and they rarely talked about him because it hurt too much. They couldn't understand why he had left in the first place, much less why Tyr had never contacted them.

Britt broke the silence first. 'Tyr would do exactly what we're doing. He thinks the same as us. He cares about the company and the people here.'

'Which explains why he stays away,' Eva murmured.

'He's still one of us,' Britt insisted. 'We stick together. Remember that. The discovery of diamonds might even encourage him to return home.'

'But Tyr isn't motivated by money,' Leila piped up.

Even Eva couldn't disagree with that. Tyr was an idealist, an adventurer. Their brother was many things, but money was not his god, though Britt wished he would come home again. She missed him. Tyr had been away too long.

'Here's something that will make you laugh,' Leila said in an attempt to lift the mood. Pulling the newspaper towards her, she pointed to an article in the newspaper that referred to the three sisters as the Skavanga Diamonds. 'They haven't tired of giving us that ridiculous nickname.'

'It's just so patronising,' Eva huffed, brushing a cascade of fiery red curls away from her face.

'I've been called worse things,' Britt argued calmly.

'Don't be so naïve,' Eva snapped. 'All that article does is wave a flag in front of the nose of every fortune-hunter out there—'

'And what's wrong with that?' Leila interrupted. 'I'd just like to see a man who isn't drunk by nine o'clock—'

This brought a shocked intake of breath from Britt and Eva, as Leila had mentioned something else they never spoke about. There had long been a rumour that their father had been drunk when he piloted the small company plane to disaster with their mother on board.

Leila flushed red as she realised her mistake. 'I'm sorry—I'm just tired of your sniping, Eva. We really should get behind Britt.'

'Leila's right,' Britt insisted. 'It's crucial we keep our focus and make this deal work. We certainly can't afford to fall out between us. That article is fluff and we shouldn't even be wasting time discussing it. If Skavanga Mining is going to have a future we have to consider every offer on the table—and so far the consortium's is the only offer.'

'I suppose you could always give the sheikh's representative a proper welcome, Skavanga style,' Eva suggested, brightening.

Leila relaxed into a smile. 'I'm sure Britt has got a few ideas up her sleeve.'

'It's not my sleeve you need to worry about,' Britt commented dryly, relieved that they were all the best of friends again.

'Just promise me you won't do anything you'll regret,' Leila said, remembering to worry.

'I won't regret it at the time,' Britt promised dryly.

'Unless he truly is a boffin with pebble glasses—in which case I'll just have to put a paper bag over his head.'

'Don't become overconfident,' Eva warned.

'I'm not worried. If he proves difficult I'll cut a hole in the ice and send him swimming. That will soon cool his ardour—'

'Why stop there?' Eva added. 'Don't forget the birch twig switches. You can always give him a good thrashing. That'll sort him out.'

'I'll certainly consider it—'

'Tell me you're joking?' Leila begged.

Thankfully, Britt's younger sister missed the look Britt and Eva exchanged.

CHAPTER TWO

BRITT WAS UNUSUALLY nervous. The breakfast meeting with the Black Sheikh's representative had been arranged for nine and it was already twenty past when she rushed through the doors of Skavanga Mining and tore up the stairs. It wasn't as if she was unused to business meetings, but this one was different for a number of reasons, not least of which was the fact that her car had blown a tyre on the way to the office. Changing a tyre was an energetic exercise at the best of times, enough to get her heart racing, but the circumstances of this meeting had made her anxious without that, because so much depended on it—

'I'll show myself in,' she said as a secretary glanced up in surprise.

Pausing outside the door to the boardroom, she took a moment to compose herself. Eva was right in that when their parents were killed Britt had been the only person qualified to take over the company and care for her two younger sisters. Their brother was... Well, Tyr was a maverick—a mercenary, for all they knew. He had been a regular soldier at one time, and no one knew where he was now. It was up to her to cut this deal; there was no one else. The man inside the boardroom could save the company if he gave a green light to the consortium.

And she was late, an embarrassment that put her firmly on the back foot.

Back foot?

Forget that, Britt concluded as the imposing figure standing silhouetted against the light by the window turned to face her. The man was dressed conventionally in a dark, beautifully tailored business suit, when somehow she had imagined her visitor would be wearing flowing robes. This man needed no props to appear exotic. His proud, dark face, the thick black hair, which he wore carelessly swept back, and his watchful eyes were all the exotic ingredients required to complete a stunning picture. Far from the bristly nerd, he was heart-stoppingly good-looking, and it took all she'd got to keep her feet marching steadily across the room towards him.

'Ms Skavanga?'

The deep, faintly accented voice ran shivers through every part of her. It was the voice of a master, a lover, a man who expected nothing less than to be obeyed.

Oh, get over it, Britt told herself impatiently. It was the voice of a man and he was tall, dark and handsome. So what? She had a company to run.

'Britt Skavanga,' she said firmly, advancing to meet him with her hand outstretched. 'I'm sorry, you have me at a disadvantage,' she added, explaining that all she had been told was that His Majesty Sheikh Sharif al Kareshi would be sending his most trusted aide.

'For these preliminary discussions that is correct,' he said, taking hold of her hand in a grip that was controlled yet deadly.

His touch stunned her. It might have been disappointingly brief, but it was as if it held some electrical charge that shot fire through her veins.

She wanted him.

Just like that she wanted him?

She was a highly sexed woman, but she had never experienced such an instant, strong attraction to any man before.

'So,' she said, lifting her chin as she made a determined effort to pitch her voice at a level suitable for the importance of the business to be carried out between them, 'what may I call you?'

'Emir,' he replied, more aloof than ever.

'Just Emir?' she said.

'It's enough.' He shrugged, discarding her wild fantasy about him at a stroke.

'Shall we make a start?' He looked her up and down with all the cool detachment of a buyer weighing up a mare brought to market. 'Have you had some sort of accident, Ms Skavanga?'

'Please, call me Britt.' She had completely forgotten about the tyre until he brought it up, and now all she could think was what a wreck she must look. She clearly wasn't making an impression as an on-top-of-things businesswoman, that was for sure.

'Would you like to take a moment?' Emir enquired as she smoothed her hair self-consciously.

'No, thank you,' she said, matching his cool. She wasn't about to hand over the initiative this early in the game. 'I've kept you waiting long enough. A tyre blew on my way to the office,' she explained.

'And *you* changed it?'

She frowned. 'Why wouldn't I? I didn't want to waste time changing my clothes.'

'Thank you for the consideration.' Emir dipped his head in a small bow, allowing her to admire his thick, wavy hair, though his ironic expression suggested that

Emir believed a woman's place was somewhere fragrant and sheltered where she could bake and quake until her hunter returned.

Was he married?

She glanced at his ring-free hands, and remembered to thank him when he pulled out a chair. She couldn't remember the last time that had happened. She was used to fending for herself, though it was nice to meet a gentleman, even if she suspected that beneath his velvet charm Emir was ruthless and would use every setback she experienced to his advantage.

No problem. She wasn't about to give him an inch.

'Please,' she said, indicating a place that put the wide expanse of the boardroom table between them.

He had the grace of a big cat, she registered as he sat down. Emir was dark and mysterious compared to the blond giants in Skavanga she was used to. He was big and exuded power like some soft-pawed predator.

She had to be on guard at all times or he would win this game before she even knew it had been lost. Business was all that mattered now—though it was hard to concentrate when the flow of energy between them had grown.

Chemistry, she mused. And no wonder when Emir radiated danger. The dark business suit moulded his athletic frame to perfection, while the crisp white shirt set off his bronzed skin, and a grey silk tie provided a reassuring sober touch—to those who might be fooled. She wasn't one of them. Emir might as well have been dressed in flowing robes with an unsheathed scimitar at his side, for seductive exoticism flowed from him.

She looked away quickly when his black gaze found hers and held it. *Damn!* She could feel her cheeks blazing. She quickly buried her attention in the documents in front of her.

Britt's apparent devotion to her work amused him. He'd felt the same spark between them that she had, and there was always the same outcome to that. He generally relied on the first few minutes of any meeting to assess people. Body language told him so much. Up to now Skavanga had not impressed him. It was a grey place with an air of dejection that permeated both the company and the town. He didn't need the report in front of him to tell him that the mineral deposits were running out, he could smell failure in the air. And however good this woman was at running the business—and she must be good to keep a failing company alive for so long—she couldn't sell thin air. Britt needed to mine those diamonds in order to keep her company alive, and to do that she needed the consortium he headed up to back her.

The town might be grey, but Britt Skavanga was anything but. She exceeded his expectations. There was a vivid private world behind those serious dove grey eyes, and it was a world he intended to enter as soon as he could.

'You will relate our dealings verbatim to His Majesty?' she said as they began the meeting.

'Of course. His Majesty greets you as a friend and hopes that all future dealings between us will bring mutual respect as well as great benefit to both our countries.'

He had not anticipated her sharp intake of breath, or the darkening of her eyes as he made the traditional Kareshi greeting, touching his chest, his mouth and finally his brow. He amended his original assessment of Britt to that of a simmering volcano waiting to explode.

She recovered quickly. 'Please tell His Majesty that I welcome his interest in Skavanga Mining, and may I also welcome you as his envoy.'

Nicely done. She was cool. He'd give her that. His senses roared as she held his gaze. The only woman he knew who would do that was his sister, Jasmina, and she was a troublesome minx.

As Britt continued to lay out her vision of the future for Skavanga Mining he thought there was a touching innocence about her, even in the way she thought she would have any say once the consortium took over. Her capable hands were neatly manicured, the nails short and unpainted, and she wore very little make-up. There was no artifice about her. What you saw was what you got with Britt Skavanga—except for the fire in her eyes, and he guessed very few had seen that blaze into an inferno.

'You must find the prospect of mining the icy wastes quite daunting after what you're used to in the desert,' she was saying.

He returned reluctantly to business. 'On the contrary. There is a lot in Skavanga that reminds me of the vastness and variety of my desert home. It is a variety only obvious to those who see it, of course.' As much as he wanted this new venture to go ahead, he wanted Britt Skavanga even more.

As hard as she tried to concentrate, her body was making it impossible to think, but then her body seemed tuned to Emir's. She even found herself leaning towards him, and had to make herself sit back. Even then his heat curled around her. His face was stern, *which she loved,* and his scent, spicy and warm, sandalwood, maybe, it was a reminder of the exotic world he came from. Her sisters had already teased her mercilessly about Kareshi supposedly being at the forefront of the erotic arts. She had pretended not to listen to such nonsense, especially when they insisted that the people of Kareshi had a potion they used to heighten sensation. But she'd heard them. And now she was wondering if anything they'd said could be true—

'Ms Skavanga?'

She jerked alert as Emir spoke her name. 'I beg your pardon. My mind was just—'

'Wandering? Or examining the facts?' he said with amusement.

'Yes—'

'Yes? Which is it?'

She couldn't even remember the question. The blood rush to her cheeks was furious and hot, while Emir just raised a brow and his mouth curved slightly.

'Are you ready to continue?' he said.

'Absolutely,' she confirmed, sitting up straight. She was mad for this man—crazy for him. No way could she think straight until the tension had been released.

'There are some amendments I want to discuss,' he said, frowning slightly as he glanced up at her.

She turned with relief to the documents in front of her.

'I need more time,' she said.

'Really?' Emir queried softly.

She swallowed deep when she saw the look in his eyes. 'I don't think we should rush anything—'

'I don't think we should close any doors, either.'

Were they still talking about business? Shaking herself round, she explained that she wouldn't be making any decisions on behalf of the other shareholders yet.

'And I need to take samples from the mine before I

can involve the consortium in such a large investment,' Emir pointed out.

He only had to speak for alarm bells to go off in every part of her body, making it impossible to think about anything other than long, moonlit nights in the desert. Not once since taking over at Skavanga Mining had she ever been so distracted during a meeting. It didn't help that she had thought the Black Sheikh's trusted envoy would be some greybeard with a courtly air.

'Here is your copy of my projections,' she said, forcing her mind back to business before closing her file to signify the end of the meeting.

'I have my own projections, thank you.'

She bridled at that before reminding herself that just a murmur from the Black Sheikh could rock a government, and that his envoy was hardly going to be a push-over when it came to negotiations.

'Before we finish, there's just one here on the second page,' he said, leaning towards her.

'I see it,' she said, stiffening as she tried to close her mind to Emir's intoxicating scent. And those powerful hands…the suppleness in his fingers…the strength in his wrists…

He caught her staring and she started blushing again. This was ridiculous. She was acting like a teenager on her first date.

Exhaling shakily, she sat back in the chair determined to recover the situation, but Emir was on a roll.

'You seem to have missed something here,' he said, pointing to another paragraph.

She never missed anything. She was meticulous in all her business dealings. But sure enough, Emir had found one tiny thing she had overlooked.

'And this clause can go,' he said, removing it with a strike of his pen.

'Now, just a minute—' She stared aghast as Emir deconstructed her carefully drawn-up plan. 'No,' she said firmly. 'That clause does not go, and neither does anything else without further discussion, and this part of the meeting is over.'

He sat back in his chair as she stood up, which explained why she wasn't ready for him moving in front of her to stand in her way.

'You seem upset,' he said. 'And I don't want the first part of our meeting to end badly.'

'Bringing in investors is a big step for me to take—'

'Britt—'

Emir's touch on her skin was like an incendiary device, but the fact that his hand was on her arm at all was an outrage. 'Let me go,' she warned softly, but they both heard the shake in her voice. And surely Emir could feel her trembling beneath his touch. He must feel the heated awareness in her skin.

He murmured something in his own language. It might as well have been a spell. She turned to look at him, not keen to go anywhere suddenly.

'It seems to me we have a timing problem, Britt. But there is a solution, if you will allow me to take it?'

Emir's eyes were dark and amused. At first she thought she must have misunderstood him, but there was no mistake, and the solution he was proposing had been in her mind for some time. But surely no civilised businessman would be willing to enter into such a risky entanglement within an hour of meeting her?

As Emir's hand grazed her chin she moved into his embrace, allowing him to turn her face up to his. This was no meeting between business colleagues. This was a meeting between a man and woman who were hot for each other, and the man was a warrior of the desert.

Emir promised pleasure. He also promised a chance to forget, and, for however short a time, the prospect of that seemed preferable at this moment to doing battle endlessly on every front. How would it feel to have this big man hold her and bring her pleasure? She must have swayed towards him, for the next thing she knew he was holding her in front of him.

'Why, Britt,' he said with amusement. 'If I'd known how badly you wanted this I'm sure we could have arranged something before the meeting.'

Emir's blunt approach should have shocked her—annoyed her—but instead it made her want him all the more, and as he brushed her lips with his she found herself instantly hungry, instantly frantic, for more pressure, more intimacy, and for everything to happen fast.

But Emir was even more experienced than she had realised, and now he took pleasure in subjecting her to an agonising delay. As the clock ticked, the tension built and he held her stare with his knowing and faintly amused look. She guessed Emir knew everything about arousal, and could only hope it wouldn't be long before he decided she had suffered enough. She voiced a cry of relief when he cupped her face in his warm, slightly roughened hands, and another when her patience was rewarded by a kiss that began lightly and then brutally mimicked the act her body so desperately craved.

It was in no way subjugation by a powerful man, but the meeting of eager mates, a fierce coupling between two people who knew exactly what they wanted from each other, and as Emir pressed her back against the boardroom table and set about removing her clothes she gasped in triumph and began ripping at his.

He tossed her jacket aside. She loosened his tie and dragged it off, letting it drop onto the floor. As he ripped her blouse open she battled with the buttons on his shirt. She exclaimed with pleased surprise when he lifted her and she clung to him as he stripped off her tights and her briefs. Suddenly it was all about seeing who could rid themselves of any barriers first. She was mindless sensation—hot flesh brushing, touching, cleaving, in a tangle of limbs and hectic breathing, while Emir remained calm and strong, and certain. He felt so good beneath her hands…so very good—

Too good! You have never felt like this about a man before—

Danger! This man can change your life—

You won't walk away from this with a smile on your face—

Using sheer force of will, she closed off her annoying inner voice. She wanted this. She needed it. This was her every fantasy come true. Even now as Emir took time to protect them both she saw no reason not to follow her most basic instinct. Why shouldn't she? Emir was—

Emir was enormous. He was entirely built to scale. Was she ready for this?

He made her forget everything the moment he caressed her breasts. Moaning, she rested back and let him do what he wanted with her. Just this once she wanted to feel that she didn't have to lead or fight. Just this once she could be the woman she had always dreamed of being—the woman who was with a man who knew how to please her.

And I wonder what he thinks about you—

To hell with what he thinks about me, she raged silently.

To hell with you, don't you mean?

CHAPTER THREE

Britt was beautiful and willing and he had needs. Willing? She was a wild cat with a body that was strong and firm, yet voluptuous. Her breasts were incredible, up-tilted and full, and he took his time to weigh them appreciatively, smiling when she groaned with pleasure as he circled her nipples very lightly with his thumbnails. She was so responsive, so eager that her nipples had tightened and were thrusting towards him, pink and impertinent, and clearly in need of more attention. He aimed to please. Kissing her neck, he travelled down, part of him already regretting that they had wasted so much time. She shuddered with desire as he blazed a trail through the dust she had collected when she changed her tyre. 'You're clean now,' he said, smiling into her lust-dazed eyes.

She laughed down low in her throat in a way he found really sexy, and then weakened against him as she waited for him to continue his sensory assault.

'Shall I take the edge off your hunger?' he offered.

'Yours too,' she insisted huskily.

'If that's what you want, you tell me what you'd like.'

Her gaze flicked up and her cheeks flushed pink. She wasn't sure whether to believe him or not.

'I'm serious,' he said quietly.

'Please—'

As she appealed to him he decided that the time he had allowed for this visit to Skavanga wouldn't be enough. He ran his fingers lightly over her beautiful breasts before moving on to trace the swell of her belly. Lifting her skirt, he nudged her thighs apart. She made it easy for him, so he repaid her gesture by delicately exploring the heated flesh at the apex of her thighs. When she whimpered with pleasure it was all he could do to hold back. So much for his much-vaunted self-control, he mused, as Britt thrust her hips towards him, trying for more contact. He wanted nothing more than to take her now. Clutching his arms, she tilted herself back against the table, moaning with need. Opening her legs a little more for him, she showed him a very different woman from the one in the starchy photograph he had examined in London, but this was the woman he had suspected Britt was hiding all along.

'You're quite clinical about this, aren't you?' Britt panted in a rare moment of lucidity as he watched her pleasure.

Duty could do that to a man. He never let himself go. Growing up the second son of the third wife had hardly been to his advantage as a youth. He had been forced to watch the cruelty inflicted on his people by those closer to the throne than he was on a daily basis. So, yes, he was cold. He'd had to be to overthrow tyrants that were also his relatives. There was no room now in his life for anything other than the most basic human appetite.

'Don't make me wait,' Britt was begging him.

She needn't worry. His preference at this moment was to please her.

This was insane. Emir was cold, detached—and the

sexiest thing on two legs. He was frighteningly distant, but she was lost in an erotic haze of his making. She needed more—more pressure, more contact—more of him. The more aloof he was, the more her body cried out to him. The ache he'd set up inside her was unbearable. She had to have more of his skilful touches—

An excited cry escaped her throat when she felt the insistent thrust of his erection against her belly. She rubbed herself shamelessly against it, sobbing with pleasure as each delicious contraction of her nerve endings gave some small indication of what was to come. Emir's hard, warrior frame was even more powerful than she had imagined, and yet he used his hands so delicately in a way that drove her crazy for him. Lacing her fingers through his thick black hair, she dragged him close. He responded by cupping the back of her head to keep her in place as he dipped down and plundered her mouth. Sweeping the table clear, he lifted her and balanced her on the edge. Moving between her legs, he forced them apart with the width of his body. 'Wrap your legs around me,' he commanded, pushing them wider still.

She had never obeyed a man's instructions in her life, but she rushed to obey these. Resting her hands flat on the table behind her, she arched her spine, thrusting her breasts forward, while Emir reared over her, magnificent and erect.

Like a stallion on the point of servicing a mare?

With far more consideration than that—

Are you sure?

She was sure that any more delay would send her crazy. She was also sure that Emir knew exactly what he was doing.

'Tell me what you want, Britt,' he demanded fiercely.

'You know what I want,' she said.

'But you must tell me,' he said in low, cruel voice.

Her throat dried. The harsher he got, the more arousing she found it. No one had ever pushed her boundaries like this before. And she had thought herself liberal where sex was concerned? She was a novice compared to Emir.

She had also thought herself emotion-free, Britt realised, but knew deep in her heart that something had changed inside her. Even when she plumbed the depths of Emir's cold black eyes she wanted to be the one to draw a response from him—she wanted to learn more about him, and in every way.

'Say it,' he instructed.

Her face blazed red. No one spoke to her like that—no one told her what to do. But her body liked what was happening, and was responding with enthusiasm. 'Yes,' she said. 'Yes, please.' And then she told him exactly what she wanted him to do to her without sparing a single lurid detail.

Now he was pleased. Now she got through to him. Now he almost smiled.

'I think I can manage that,' he said dryly. 'My only concern is that we may not have sufficient time to work our way through your rather extensive wish list.'

On this occasion, she thought. 'Perhaps another time,' she said, matching him for dispassion. But then she glanced at the door. How could she have forgotten that it was still unlocked? Just as she was thinking she must do something about it, Emir touched her in a way that made it impossible for her to move.

'Don't you like the risk?' he said, reading her easily.

She looked at him, and suddenly she loved the risk.

'Hold me,' he said softly. 'Use me—take what you need.'

She hesitated, another first for her. No one had ever given her this freedom. She moved to do as he said and found it took two hands to enclose him.

'I'm waiting,' he said.

With those dangerous eyes watching her, she made a pass. Loving it, she made a second, firmer stroke—

Taking control, Emir caught the tip inside her. She gasped and would have pulled away, but he cupped her buttocks firmly in his strong hands and drew her slowly on to him. 'What are you afraid of?' he said, staring deep into her eyes. 'You know I won't hurt you.'

She didn't know him at all, but for some reason she trusted him. 'I'm just—'

'Hungry,' he said. 'I know.'

A sound of sheer pleasure trembled from her throat. She had played games with boys before, she realised, but Emir was a man, and a man like no other man.

'Am I enough for you?' he mocked.

She lifted her chin. 'What do you think?'

He told her exactly what he thought, and while she was still gasping with shock and lust he kissed her, and before she could recover he thrust inside her deeply to the hilt. For a moment she was incapable of thinking or doing, and even breathing was suspended. This wasn't pleasure, this was an addiction. She could never get enough of this—or of him. The sensation of being completely inhabited while being played by a master was a very short road to release.

'No,' he said sharply, stopping her. 'I'll tell you when. Look at me, Britt,' he said fiercely.

On the promise of pleasure she stared into Emir's molten gaze. She would obey him. She would pay whatever price it took for this to continue.

He was pleased with her. Britt was more responsive

than even he had guessed. She was a strong woman who made him want to pleasure her. He loved the challenge that was Britt Skavanga. He loved her fire. He loved her cries of pleasure and the soft little whimpers she made when he thrust repeatedly into her. What had started as a basic function to clear his head had become an exercise in pleasuring Britt.

'Now,' he whispered fiercely.

He held her firmly as she rocked into orgasm with a release so violent he trusted his strength more than the boardroom table and held her close, though he could do nothing about the noise she was making, which would probably travel to the next town, and so he smothered it with a kiss. When he let her go, she gasped and called his name. He held her safe, cushioning her against the hard edge of the table with his hands as he soothed her down. Withdrawing carefully, he steadied Britt on her feet before releasing her. Smoothing the hair back from her flushed, damp brow, he stared into her dazed eyes, waiting until he was sure she had recovered. The one thing he had not expected was to feel an ache of longing in his chest. He had not expected to feel anything.

'Wow,' she whispered, her voice muffled against his naked chest.

He liked the feeling of Britt resting on him and was in no hurry to move away. If she had been anyone else the next move would have been simple. He would have taken her back to Kareshi with him. But she was too much like him. There would be no diamond mine, no town, no Skavanga Mining, without Britt. Just as he belonged in Kareshi, she was tied here. But still he felt a stab of regret that he couldn't have this exciting woman.

'Are you okay?' he murmured as she stirred.

She lifted her chin to look at him, and as she did this

she drew herself up and drew her emotions in. As she pulled herself together he could almost see her forcing herself to get over whatever it was she had briefly felt for him.

'There are two bathrooms,' she informed him briskly. 'You can use the one directly off the boardroom. I have my own en suite attached to my office. We will reconvene this meeting in fifteen minutes.'

A smile of incredulity and, yes, admiration curved his lips as he watched her go. She walked across the room with her head held high like a queen. It might have seemed ridiculous had anyone else tried it, but Britt Skavanga could pull it off.

He showered down quickly in the bathroom she had told him about, and was both surprised and pleased by the quality of the amenities until he remembered that Britt had a hand in everything here. There were high-quality towels on heated rails, as well as shampoo, along with all the bits and pieces that contributed to making a freshen-up session pleasurable. Britt hadn't forgotten anything—at which point a bolt of very masculine suspicion punched him in the guts. Had she done this before? And if so, how many times?

And why should he care?

He returned to the boardroom to find Britt had arrived before him. She looked composed. She looked as if nothing had happened between them. She looked as she might have looked at the start of the meeting if she hadn't been forced to change a tyre first. She also looked very alone to him, seated beneath the portraits of her forebears, and once again he got the strongest sense that duty ruled Britt every bit as much as it ruled him.

They both imagined they were privileged and, yes, each was powerful in their own way, but neither of them could choose what they wanted out of life, because the choices had already been made for them.

She hated herself, *hated herself* for what she had done. Losing control like that. She hadn't even been able to meet her sex-sated reflection in the bathroom mirror. She had weakened with Emir in a way she must never weaken again. She put it down to a moment of madness before she closed her heart. But as her mind flashed back to what they'd done, and the remembered feeling of being close to him, for however short a time, she desperately wanted more—

She would just have to exercise more control—

'Is something distracting you, Britt?' Emir demanded, jolting her back to the present.

'Should there be something?' she said in a voice that held no hint that Emir was the only distraction.

'No,' he said without expression.

They deserved each other, she thought. But she was curious all the same. Did he really feel nothing? Didn't his body throb with pleasurable awareness as hers did? Didn't he want more? Didn't he yearn to know more about her as she longed to know more about him? Or was she nothing more than an entertainment between coffee breaks for Emir?

And rumour had it she was the hardest of the Skavanga Diamonds?

What a laugh!

Tears of shame were pricking her eyes. She could never make a mistake like this again—

'Hay fever,' she explained briskly when Emir glanced suspiciously at her.

'In Skavanga?' he said, glancing outside at the icy scene.

'We have pollen,' she said coldly, moving on.

She wasn't sure how she got to the end of the second half of their meeting, but she did. There was too much hanging on the outcome for her to spoil the deal with a clouded mind. So far so good, Britt concluded, wrapping everything up with a carefully rehearsed closing statement. At least she could tell her sisters that she hadn't been forced to concede anything vital, and that Emir was prepared to move on to the next stage, which would involve a visit to the mine.

'I'm looking forward to that,' he said.

There was nothing in his eyes for her. The rest of Emir's visit would be purely about business—

And why should it be anything else?

She hated herself for the weakness, but she had expected something—some outward sign that their passionate encounter had made an impression on him… but apparently not.

'Is that everything?' Emir said as he gathered up his papers. 'I imagine you want to make an early start in the morning if we're going to the mine.'

The mine was miles away from anywhere. The only logical place for them to stay was the old cabin Britt's great-grandfather had built. It was isolated—there were no other people around. Doing a quick risk-assessment of the likely outcome, knowing the passion they shared, she knew she would be far better off arranging for one of her lieutenants to take him…

But Emir would see that as cowardice. And was she frightened of him? Could she even entrust the task of taking him to the mine to anyone else? She should be there. And maybe getting him out of her system once and for all would allow her to sharpen up and concentrate on what really mattered again.

'I would like to make an early start,' she said, 'though I must warn you there are no luxury facilities at the cabin. It's pretty basic.' Somehow, what Emir thought about the cabin that meant so much to her mattered to her, Britt realised. It mattered a lot.

Emir seemed unconcerned. 'Apart from the difference in temperature, the Arctic is another wilderness like the desert.'

'My great-grandfather built the cabin. It's very old–'

'You're fortunate to have something so special and permanent to remember him by.'

Yes, she was, and the fact that Emir knew this meant a lot to her.

They stared at each other until she forced herself to look away. This was not the time to be inventing imaginary bonds between them. Better she remembered Eva's words about a true Nordic welcome to contain this warrior of the desert. It would be interesting to discover if Emir was still so confident after a brush with ice and fire.

CHAPTER FOUR

HE LEARNED MORE about Britt during the first few hours of their expedition than he had learned in any of the reports. She was intelligent and organised, energetic and could be mischievous, which reminded him to remain on guard.

She had called him at five-thirty a.m.—just to check he was awake, she had assured him. He suspected she hadn't slept after their encounter, and guessed she was hoping he'd had a sleepless night too. He gave nothing away.

It couldn't strictly be called dawn when her Jeep rolled up outside his hotel, since at this time of year in Skavanga a weak grey light washed the land for a full twenty-four hours. Only Britt coloured the darkness when she sprang down and came to greet him. He was waiting for her just outside the doors. Her hair gleamed like freshly harvested wheat and she had pulled an ice-blue beanie over her ears to protect them from the bitter cold. Her cheeks and lips were whipped red by the harshest of winds, and she was wearing black polar trousers tucked into boots, with a red waterproof jacket zippered up to her neck. She looked fresh and clean and bright, and determined.

'Britt—'

'Emir.'

Her greeting was cool. His was no more than polite, though he noticed that the tip of her nose was as red as her full bottom lip and her blue-grey eyes were the colour of polar ice. She gave him the once-over, and seemed satisfied by what she saw. He knew the drill. He might live in the desert, but he was no stranger to Arctic conditions.

'Was the hotel okay?' she asked him politely when they were both buckled in.

'Yes. Thank you,' he said, allowing his gaze to linger on her face

She shot him a glance and her cheeks flushed red. She was remembering their time in the boardroom. He was too.

She drove smoothly and fast along treacherous roads and only slowed for moose and for a streak of red fox until they entered what appeared to be an uninhabited zone. Here the featureless ice road was shielded on either side between towering walls of packed snow. She still drove at a steady seventy and refused his offer to take over. She knew the way, she said. She liked to be in control, he thought. Except when she was having sex when she liked him to take the lead.

'We'll soon be there,' she said, distracting him from these thoughts.

They had been climbing up the side of a mountain for some time, leaving the ice walls far behind. Below them was a vast expanse of frozen lake—grey, naturally.

'The mine is just down there,' she said when he craned his neck to look.

He wondered what other delights awaited him. All he could be sure of was that Britt hadn't finished with him yet. She liked to prove herself, so he was confident the test would include some physical activity. He looked forward to it, just as he looked forward to a return bout with her in the desert.

Emir seemed utterly relaxed and completely at home in a landscape that had terrified many people she had brought here. She knew this place like the back of her hand, and yet, truthfully, had never felt completely safe. Knowing Emir, he had probably trialled every extreme sport known to man, so what was a little snow and ice to him?

'Penny for them,' he said.

She made herself relax so she could clear her mind and equivocate. 'I'm thinking about food. Aren't you?'

She was curious to know what he was thinking, but as usual Emir gave nothing away.

'Some,' he murmured.

She glanced his way and felt her heart bounce. She would never get used to the way he looked, and for one spark of interest from those deceptively sleepy eyes she would happily walk barefoot in the snow, which was something Emir definitely didn't need to know.

'The food's really good at the mine,' she said, clinging to safe ground. 'And the catering staff will have stocked the cabin for us. The food has to be excellent when people are so isolated. It's one of the few pleasures they have.'

'I wouldn't be too sure about that,' he said dryly.

'There are separate quarters for men and women,' she countered promptly—and primly.

'Right.' His tone was sceptical.

'You seem to know a lot about it,' she said, feeling a bit peeved—jealous, maybe, especially when he said,

'It's much the same for people who work in the desert.'

'Oh, I see.'

'Good,' he said, ignoring her sharp tone and settling back. 'I'm going to doze now, if you don't mind?'

'Not at all.'

Sleep? Yeah, right—like a black panther sleeps with one eye open. There was no such thing as stand down for Emir.

Emir could play her at her own game, and play it well, Britt realised as she turned off the main road. She could be cool, but he would be cooler, and now there was no real contact between them as he dozed—apparently—which she regretted. He wanted her to feel this way—to feel this lack of him, she suspected.

'Sorry,' she exclaimed with shock as the Jeep lurched on the rutted forest track. The moment's inattention had jolted Emir awake and had almost thrown them into the ditch.

'No problem,' he said. 'If you want me to drive...?'

'I'm fine. Thank you.' She'd heard that the ruler of Kareshi was introducing change, but not fast enough, clearly. Emir probably resented her running the company too. He came from a land where men ruled and women obeyed—

She gasped as his hand covered hers. 'Take it easy,' he said, steadying the steering wheel as it bounced in her hands.

'I've been travelling these roads since I was a child.'

'Then I'm surprised you don't know about the hazards of melting snow.'

He definitely deserved a session in the sauna and a dip in the freezing lake afterwards, she concluded.

'We're nearly there,' she said.

'Good.'

Why the smile in his voice? Was he looking forward to their stay at the isolated cabin? She squirmed in her seat at the thought that he might be and then wondered angrily why she was acting this way. It was one thing bringing her city friends into the wilderness for a rustic weekend, but quite another bringing Emir down here when there could only be one outcome—

Unless he had had enough of her, of course, but something told her that wasn't the case. She'd stick with her decision to enjoy him and get him out of her system, Britt concluded, explaining that the nearest hotel was too far away from the mine to stay there.

'You don't have to explain to me, Britt. I like it here. You forget,' Emir murmured as she drew to a halt outside the ancient log cabin, 'the wilderness is my home.'

And now she was angry with him for being so pleased with everything. And even angrier with herself because Emir was right, the wilderness was beautiful in its own unique way, she thought, staring out across the glassy lake. It was as if she were seeing it for the first time. Because she was seeing it through Emir's eyes, Britt realised, and he sharpened her focus on everything.

'This is magnificent,' he exclaimed as they climbed down from the Jeep.

She tensed as he came to stand beside her. Her heart pumped and her blood raced as she tried not to notice how hot he looked in the dark, heavy jacket and snow boots. Emir radiated something more than the confidence of a man who was sensibly dressed and comfortable in this extreme temperature. He exuded the type of strength that anyone would like to cling to in a storm—

He looked downright dangerous, she told herself sensibly, putting a few healthy feet of fresh air between them. But the lake was beautiful, and neither of them was in any hurry to move away. It stretched for miles and was framed by towering mountains whose jagged peaks were lost in cloud. A thick pine forest crept up these craggy slopes until there was nothing for the roots to cling to. But it was the silence that was most impressive, and that was heavy and complete. It felt almost as if the world were holding its breath, though she had to smile when Emir turned to look at the cabin and an eagle called.

'I'll grab our bags,' he said.

As he brushed past her on his way to the Jeep she shivered with awareness, and then smiled as she walked towards the cabin. She was always happy here—always in control. There would be no problems here. She'd keep things light and professional. Here, she could put what had happened between them in the boardroom behind her.

Emir caught up with her at the door, and his first question was how far was it to the mine? With her back to him, she pulled a wry face. Putting what had happened behind her was going to be easier than she had thought. They hadn't even crossed the threshold yet and Emir's mind was already set on business.

Which was exactly what she had hoped for—

Was it?

Of course it was, but she wasn't going to pretend it didn't sting. Everyone had their pride, and everyone wanted to feel special—

Hard luck for her, she thought ruefully.

'So, how far exactly is it to the mine?' he said. 'How long will it take by road?'

'Depending on the weather?' She turned the key in the lock. 'I'd say around ten minutes.'

'Is there any chance we can take a look around today, in that case?' Emir asked as he held the door for her.

He was in more of a hurry than she'd thought. Well, that was fine with her. She could accommodate a fast turnaround. 'The mine is a twenty-four-hour concern. We can visit as soon as you're ready.'

'Then I'd like to freshen up and go see it right away—if that's okay with you?'

'That's fine with me.' She had to stop herself laughing at the thought that she had never met anyone quite so much like her before.

As she used to be, Britt amended, before Emir came into her life. Taking charge of her bag, she hoisted it onto her shoulders. 'Welcome,' she said, walking into the cabin.

'This is nice,' Emir commented as he gazed around.

He made everything seem small, she thought, but in a good way. The cabin had been built by a big man for big men, yet could be described as cosy. On a modest scale, it still reflected the personality of the man who had built it and who had founded the Skavanga dynasty. With nothing but his determination, Britt's great-grand-father had practically clawed the first minerals out of the ground with his bare hands, and with makeshift tools that other prospectors had thrown away. There was nothing to be ashamed of here in the cabin. It was only possible to feel proud.

'What?' Emir said when he caught her staring at him.

'You're the only man apart from my brother who makes me feel small,' she said, managing not to make it sound like a compliment.

'I take it you're talking about your brother, Tyr?'

'My long-lost brother, Tyr,' she admitted with a shrug.

'I can assure you the very last thing on my mind is to make you feel small.'

'You don't—well, not in the way you mean. How tall are you, anyway?'

'Tall enough.'

She could vouch for that. And was that a glint of humour in Emir's eyes? Maybe this wouldn't be so bad, after all. Maybe bringing him to the cabin wasn't the worst idea she'd ever had. Maybe they could actually do business with each other *and* have fun.

And then say goodbye?

Why not?

'Are you going to show me to my room?' Emir prompted, glancing towards the wooden staircase.

'Yes, of course. '

Ditching her bag, she mounted the wooden stairs ahead of him, showing Emir into a comfortable double bedroom with a bathroom attached. 'You'll sleep in here,' she said. 'There are plenty of towels in the bathroom, and endless hot water, so don't stint yourself— and just give me a shout if you need anything more.'

'This is excellent,' he called downstairs to her. 'Thank you for putting me up.'

'As an alternative to having you camp down the mine?' She laughed. 'Of course, there are bunkhouses you could use—'

'I'm fine here.'

And looking forward to tasting some genuine Nordic hospitality, she hoped, tongue in cheek, as she glanced out of the window at the snow-clad scene.

'Britt—'

'What?' Heart pounding, she turned. Even now with all the telling off she'd given herself at the tempting thought of testing out the bed springs, she hoped and smiled and waited.

'Window keys?' Emir was standing on the landing, staring down at her. 'It's steaming hot in here.'

Ah… 'Sorry.'

She stood for a moment to compose herself and then ran upstairs to sort him out. The central heating she'd had installed was always turned up full blast before a visit. She could operate it from her phone, and thoughts of turning it down a little had flown out of the window along with her sensible head thanks to Emir. 'I suggest you leave the window open until the room cools down.' Fighting off all feelings about the big, hard, desirable body so very close to her, she unlocked the window and showed him where to hang the key.

'This is a beautiful room, Britt.'

The room was well furnished with a thick feather duvet on the bed, sturdy furniture, and plenty of throws for extra warmth. She'd hung curtains in rich autumnal shades to complement the wooden walls. 'Glad you think so.'

Now she had to look at him, but she lost no time making for the door.

'Are these your grandparents?'

She did not want to turn around, but how could she ignore the question when Emir was examining some sepia photographs hanging on the wall?

'This one is my great-grandfather,' she said, coming to stand beside him. The photographs had been hung on the wall to remind each successive generation of the legacy they had inherited. Her great-grandfather was a handsome, middle-aged man with a moustache and a big, worn hat. He was dressed in leather boots with his heavy trousers tucked into them, his hands were gnarled and he wore a rugged jacket, which was patched at the elbows. Even the pose, the way he was leaning on a spade, spoke volumes about those early days. Family and Skavanga Mining meant everything to her, Britt realised as she turned to leave the room.

She had to ask Emir to move. Why was he leaning against the door? "Excuse me…'

Straightening up, he moved aside. Now she was disappointed because he hadn't tried to stop her. What was wrong with her? She had brought a man she was fiercely attracted to to an isolated cabin. What did she think was going to happen? But now she wondered if sex with Emir would get him out of her system. Would anything?

At the top of the stairs she couldn't resist turning to see if he was still watching her.

Something else for her to regret. And what did that amused look signify—the bed was just a few tempting steps away?

And now the familiar ache had started up again. They were consenting adults who made their own agenda, and, with the mine open twenty-four seven, it wasn't as if they didn't have time—

And if she gave in to her appetite, Emir would expect everything to be on his terms from hereon in—

'I'll take quick a shower and see you outside in ten,' she called, running up the next flight of stairs to her own room in the attic. Slamming the door, she rested back against it. Saying yes to Emir would be the easiest thing in the world. Saying no to him required cast-iron discipline, and she wasn't quite sure she'd got that.

She had to have it, Britt told herself sternly as she showered down. Anything else was weakness.

Britt's bedroom was one of three at the cabin. She

had chosen it as a child, because she could be alone up here. She had always loved the pitched roof with its wealth of beams, thinking it was like something out of a fairy tale. When she was little she could see the sky and the mountains if she stood on the bed, and when she was on her own she could be anyone she wanted to be. Over the years she had collected items that made her feel good. Her grandmother had worked the patchwork quilt. Her grandfather had carved the headboard. These family treasures meant the world to her. They were far more precious than any diamonds, but then she had to remember the good the diamonds could do—for Skavanga, the town her ancestors had built, and for her sisters, and for the company.

She had to secure Emir's recommendation to his master, the Black Sheikh, Britt reflected as she toyed with some trinkets on the dressing table. They were the same cheap hair ornaments she had worn as a girl, she realised, picking them up and holding them against her long blonde hair so she could study the effect in the mirror. She hadn't even changed the threadbare stool in front of the dressing table, because her grandmother had worked the stitches, and because it was a reminder of the girl Britt had been, like the books by her bedside. This was a very different place from her penthouse in the centre of Skavanga, but the penthouse was her public face while this was where she kept her heart.

And to keep it she must cut that deal to her advantage—

With a man as shrewd as Emir in the frame?

She had never doubted her own abilities before, Britt realised as she wandered over to a window she could see out of now without standing on the bed. Skavanga

Mining had meant everything to her parents, but they hadn't been able to keep it—

Because her father was a drunk—

She shook her head, shaking out the memory. Her parents had tried their best—

Leaving little time for Britt and her siblings.

So she had picked up a mess. Lots of people had to do that. And somehow she would find a way to cut a favourable deal with the consortium.

Staring out of the window drew her gaze to the traditional sauna hut, sitting squat on the shore of the lake. With its deep hat of snow and rows of birch twigs switches hanging in a rack outside the door, it brought a smile to her face as she remembered Eva's teasing recommendation—that she bring Emir into line here. There were certainly several ways she could think of to do that. If only there weren't a risk he might enjoy them too much…

Seeing Emir's shadow darkening the snow outside, she quickly stepped back from the window. Tossing the towel aside, she pulled out the drawers of the old wooden chest and picked out warm, lightweight Arctic clothing—thermals, sweater, waterproof trousers and thick, sealskin socks. She resented the way her heart was drumming, as if she were going out on a date, rather than showing a man around a mine so he could make vast sums of money for his master out of generations of her family's hard work. She also hated the fact that Emir had beaten her to it downstairs. She was endlessly competitive. Having two sisters, she supposed. Determined to seize back the initiative, she knocked on the window to capture his attention, and when she'd got his attention she held up five fingers to let him know she'd be down right away. Almost. She'd brush her hair and put some lip gloss on first.

Traitor.

Everyone likes to feel good, Britt argued firmly with her inner voice. This has nothing to do with Sharif.

He had the cabin keys as well as the keys to the Jeep, and was settled behind the wheel by the time Britt appeared at the door. Climbing out, he strolled over to lock the cabin. She held out her hand to take charge of the keys.

'I'll keep them,' he said, stowing them in the pocket of his lightweight polar fleece.

Britt's crystal gaze turned stony.

'I'm driving too,' he said, enjoying the light floral scent she was wearing, which seemed at complete odds with the warrior woman expression on her face.

She was still seething when she swung into the passenger seat at his side. 'I know where we're going,' she pointed out.

'Then you can guide me there,' he said, gunning the engine. 'I'll turn the Sat Nav off.'

She all but growled at this.

'Why don't you let me drive?' she said.

'Why don't you direct me?' he said mildly, releasing the brake. 'It doesn't hurt to share the load from time to time,' he added, which earned him an angry glance.

They drove on in silence down the tree-shrouded lane. He noticed she glanced at the sauna on the lakeside as they drove past. He guessed his trials might begin there. The sauna was all ready and fired up. She wasn't joking when she'd said the people at the mine looked after her. The consortium would have to work hard to win hearts and minds as well as everything else if they were going to make this project a success. Perhaps they needed Britt's participation in the scheme more than he'd thought at first.

The snow was banked high either side of the road. The tall pines were bowed under its weight. The air was frigid with an icy mist overhanging everything. Snow was falling more heavily by the time they reached the main road. It had blurred the tyre tracks behind them and kept the windscreen wipers working frantically. 'Left or right?' he said, slowing the vehicle.

'If you'd let me drive—'

He put the handbrake on.

'Left,' she said impatiently.

As he swung the wheel Britt tugged off her soft blue beanie and her golden hair cascaded down. If she had been trying to win his attention she couldn't have thought up a better ruse, he realised as the scent of clean hair and lightly fragranced shampoo hit him square in the groin. He smiled to himself when she tied it back severely as if she knew that he liked it falling free around her shoulders. The fact that Britt didn't want to flaunt her femininity in front of him told him something. She liked him and she didn't want him to know.

'You must be tired,' he said, turning his thoughts to the stress she was under. It wasn't easy trying to salvage the family business, as he knew only too well. Whether it was a town or a country made no difference when people you cared about were involved. Her thoughts were with all the people who depended on her, as his were with Kareshi.

'I'm not as fragile as you seem to think,' she said, turning a hostile back on him as she stared out of the window.

She wasn't fragile at all. And if Britt tired at any

point, he'd be there. Crazy, but somehow this woman had got under his skin—and he had more than enough energy for both of them.

CHAPTER FIVE

EMIR HAD WHAT was needed to take the mine to the next level summed up within the first half hour of him visiting the immense open-cast site. Digging down into the Arctic core would require mega-machines, as well as an extension to the ice road in order to accommodate them, and that would take colossal funding.

With such vast sums involved he would oversee everything. Second in command—second in anything—wasn't his way. Britt was beginning to wonder how Emir managed to work for the sheikh—until he handed over the car keys.

As she thanked him she couldn't have been more surprised and wondered if she had earned some respect down the mine? She had known the majority of the miners most of her life, and got on with everyone, and, though her brother Tyr would have been their first choice, she knew that in Tyr's absence the miners respected her for taking on the job. Some of them had worked side by side with her grandfather, and she was proud to call them friends. She would do anything to keep them in employment.

Emir broke the silence as she started the engine. 'Once I've had the samples tested, we can start planning the work schedule in earnest.'

'I'm sure you won't be disappointed with the result of the test. I've had reports from some of the best brains in Europe, who all came to the same conclusion. The Skavanga mine is set to become the richest diamond discovery ever made.' If they could afford to mine the gems, she added silently. But surely now Emir had seen the mine for himself he wouldn't pull back. *He mustn't pull back.*

She tensed as he stretched out his long legs and settled back. 'So what do you think of the mine now you've seen it? Will you put in a good report? I have had other offers,' she bluffed in an effort to prompt him.

'If you've had other offers you must consider them all.'

Emir had called her bluff and left her hanging. Who else did he think could afford to do the work? It was the consortium or nothing. 'I would have liked Tyr to be involved, but we haven't seen him for years.'

'That doesn't mean he isn't around.'

'I'll have a word with our lawyers when we get back—to see if they can find him. I imagine you'll need to consult with your principal before making the next move?' She glanced across, but the only fallout from this was a heart-crunching smile from Emir. She turned up the heating, but there was ice in her blood. The fact remained that only three men had the resources to bring the diamonds to the surface.

'Why don't you stop by the sauna?' Emir suggested as she shivered involuntarily.

She was shivering, but at the thought of all the battles ahead of her.

Battles she hadn't looked for in a job she didn't want—

No one must know that. No one would *ever* know

that. She had accepted responsibility for the mine because there was no one else to do so, and had no intention of welching on that responsibility now. 'The sauna sounds like a good idea. I'm sure you'll enjoy it—'

'I'm sure I will too.'

It would be interesting to see if Emir felt quite so confident by the time they left the sauna.

Shock at the sudden dramatic change in temperature as they climbed out of the Jeep rendered them both silent for a few moments. The sky was uniform grey, though the Northern Lights had just begun to sweep across the bowl of the heavens as if a band of giants were waving luminescent flags. It was startling and awe-inspiring and they both lifted their heads to stare. The air was frigid, and mist formed in front of their mouths as they stood motionless as the display undulated above them.

The ice hole was probably frozen solid, Britt realised as the cold finally prompted them to move. They kept a power saw at the hut and that would soon sort it out. The sauna hut looked like a gingerbread house with a thick white coat of snow. It was another of her special places. Taking a sauna was a tradition she loved. It was the only way to thaw out the bones in Skavanga. And it was a great leveller as everyone stripped to the buff.

'No changing rooms?' Emir queried.

'Not even a shower,' she said, wondering if he was having second thoughts. 'We'll bathe in the lake afterwards.'

'Fine by me,' he said, gazing out across the glassy skating rink the lake had become.

As his lips pressed down with approval her attention was drawn to his sexy mouth. There wasn't much about Emir that wasn't sexy, and she couldn't pretend

that she wasn't looking forward to seeing him naked.
So far their encounters had been rushed, but there was
no rushing involved in a traditional sauna. There would
be all the time in the world to admire him.

She left him to open the locked compartment where
the power saw was kept, but Emir wasn't too happy
when she started it up. She turned, ready to give him a
lecture on the fact that she had been cutting holes in the
ice since she was thirteen, and stalled. That man could
take his clothes off faster than anyone she knew. And
could cause a ton of trouble just by standing there. How
was she supposed to keep her gaze glued to his face?

'I'll cut the ice. You go inside. The sauna's been lit
for some time. It should be perfect. Just ladle some more
water on the hot stones—'

She hardly needed steam at this point, Britt reflected
as Emir pushed through the door and disappeared. He
was a towering monument to masculinity.

*And she was going to share some down time with
him?*

She'd always managed to do so before with people
without leaping on top of them—

And they all looked like Emir?

None of them looked like Emir.

Having cut the hole in the ice, she stripped down
ready for the sauna. She kept her underwear on. She'd
never done that before. Not that it offered much protection, but she felt better. And maybe it sent a message.
If not, too bad; for the first time she could remember
ever, she felt self-conscious, so the scraps of lace helped
her, if no one else.

She found Emir leaning back on the wooden bench,
perfectly relaxed, and perfectly naked as he allowed

the steam rising from the hot stones on the brazier to roll over him.

She sat down in the shadows away from him, but couldn't settle.

'Too hot?' he asked as she constantly changed position.

Try, overheating…

And that was something else he didn't need to know. Emir's eyes might be closed, but she suspected he knew everything going on around him. If she needed proof of that, his faint smile told her everything. And as if she needed any more provocation with those hard-muscled legs stretched out in front of him, and his best bits prominently displayed—should she be foolish enough to take a look. She transferred her gaze to his face. His eyelashes were so thick and black they threw crescent shadows across his cheekbones, while his ebony brows swept up like some wild Tartar from the plains of Russia…

Or a sheikh…

Waves of shock and faintness washed over her, until she told herself firmly to give that overactive imagination of hers a rest. 'I'm going outside to cool off.'

Emir went as far as opening one eye.

'I'm going for a swim in the swimming hole—'

'Then I'm coming with you—'

'No need,' she said quickly, needing space.

Too late. Emir was already standing and taking up every spare inch in the hut. Regret at her foolishness replaced the shock and faintness. They should have said goodbye in Skavanga. She could have sent a trusted employee to the mine.

Could you trust anyone else to do this deal but you?

Whatever. There had to be an easier way than this.

'You can't go swimming in an ice lake on your own,' Emir said firmly, as if reading her.

'I've been swimming in the lake since I was a child.'

'When you were supervised, I imagine.'

'I'm old enough to take care of myself now.'

'Really?'

Emir's mockery was getting to her. And what did he think he was looking at now?

Oh... She quickly crossed her arms over her chest.

'I'm coming anyway,' he said, still with a flare of amusement in his eyes.

So be it, she thought, firming her jaw. In fairness, the golden rule at the cabin was that no one *ever* went swimming in the frozen lake alone. But did Emir have to tower over her to make his point?

He grabbed a towel on his way out, which he flung around her shoulders. 'You'll need it afterwards,' he said.

She gave him a look that said she didn't need his help, especially not here, and then gritted her teeth as she thought about the icy shock to come.

Running to the lake, she tossed her towel away at the last minute and jumped in before she had chance to change her mind.

She might have screamed. Who knew what she did or said? Once the icy water claimed her, rational thought was impossible. She was in shock and knew better than to linger. She was soon clambering out again—only to find Emir standing waiting for her with a towel.

'You didn't need to do that.'

He tossed the towel her way without another word, and then dived into the lake before she could stop him. She ran to the edge, but there was no sign of him— just loose ice floating. Panic consumed her, but just as she was preparing to jump in after him he emerged. Laughing.

Laughing!

Emir had barely cracked a smile the whole time he'd been in Skavanga, and *now* he was laughing?

She repaid the favour by tossing him a clean towel, which he wrapped around his waist. She didn't wait to see how securely he fixed it. She just pelted for the sauna and dived in. Emir was close behind and shut the door.

'Amazing,' he said, like a tiger that, finding itself in the Arctic, had played with polar bears and found it fun.

He shook his head, sending tiny rainbow droplets of glacier flying around the cabin like the diamonds they were both seeking.

'You enjoyed it, I see?' she said as the spray from him hissed on the hot stones.

'Of course I enjoyed it,' he exclaimed. 'I can think of only one thing better—'

She could be excused for holding her breath.

'Next you rub me down with ice—'

Before it melted? She doubted that was possible.

'I definitely want more,' he said, glancing through the window.

Oh, to be a frozen lake, she thought.

As Emir settled back on the wooden bench and closed his eyes she realised she was glad he had embraced her traditions, which led on naturally to wondering about his. She had to stop that before her thoughts took a turn for the seriously erotic.

'You love this place, don't you?' he said.

'It means a lot to me,' she admitted, 'as does the cabin.'

'It's what it represents,' Emir observed.

Correct, she thought.

'If I lived in Skavanga, I'd come here to recharge my batteries.'

Which was exactly what she did. She sometimes came to the cabin just for a change of pace. It helped her to relax and get back in the race.

And it was high time she stopped finding points of contact between them, Britt warned herself, or she'd be convincing herself that fate was giving her a sign. There was no sign. There was no Emir and Britt. It seemed they got on outside sex and business, but that was it.

'What are you thinking?' he said.

She was resting her chin on her knees when she realised Emir was staring at her.

'Why don't you take your underwear off?' he suggested. 'You can't be comfortable in those soggy scraps.'

'They'll soon dry out,' she said, keeping her head down.

Out of the corner of her eye she saw him shrug, but his expression called her a coward. And he was right. She was usually naked before she reached the door of the sauna—and she'd had sex with this man. Plus, she was hardly a vestal virgin in the first place. But somehow with Emir she felt exposed in all sorts of ways, and her underwear was one small, tiny, infinitesimal piece of armour—and she was hanging onto it. 'I'm going outside,' she announced.

'Excellent. I'm ready for my ice rub, Ms Skavanga.'

'Okay, tough guy, bring a towel. And don't blame me if this is too hard core for you.' Her grand flounce off was ruined by the sight of Emir's grin.

She had used to swim through the snow when she was a little girl—or pretend to—and so she plunged straight in. It wasn't something you stopped to think about. The shock was indescribable. But there was pleasure too as all her nerve endings shrieked at once. The soft bed of snow was cold but not life threatening. It was invigorating, and wiped her mind clean of any concerns she had—

But where was Emir?

She suddenly realised he wasn't with her. Springing up, she looked around. Nothing—just silence and snow. She called his name. Still nothing.

Had he gone back to the hut?

She ran to the window and peered in. It was empty.

The lake—

Dread made her unsteady on her feet as she stumbled towards the water, but then she gusted with relief…and fury as his head appeared above the surface. 'You're mad,' she yelled. 'You never go swimming in the lake on your own. What if something had happened to you?'

'You stole my line,' he said, springing out. 'I'm flattered you'd care.'

'Of course I'd care,' she yelled, leaning forward hands on hips. 'What the hell would I tell your people if I lost you in a frozen lake? Don't you dare laugh at me,' she warned when Emir pressed his lips together. 'Don't you—'

'What?' he said sharply. Catching hold of her arms, he dragged her close, but she saw from his eyes that he was only teasing her. 'Didn't I tell you I wanted more?' he growled.

His brows rose, his mouth curved. She could have stamped on his foot—much good it would do her in bare feet. They stared at each other for a long moment, until finally she wrestled herself free. 'You're impossible! You're irresponsible and you're a pig-headed pain in the neck.'

'Anything else?'

'You deserve to freeze to death!'

'Harsh,' he commented.

Wrapping both towels around her, she stormed off.

'You're a liability!' she flashed over her shoulder, unable to stare at the gleaming lake water streaming off his naked body a moment longer.

'Come back here. You haven't fulfilled your part of the bargain.'

She stopped at the door to the sauna. Emir's voice was pitched low and sent shivers down her spine. This was another of those 'what am I doing here?' moments…

And as soon as she turned she knew. There was nowhere else on earth she'd rather be. 'My part of the bargain?' she queried.

'Ice,' he said, holding her gaze in a way that shot arousal through her.

'I can't believe you haven't had enough yet.'

'I haven't had nearly enough.'

Those black eyes—that stare—that wicked, sexy mouth—

'You asked for this,' she said, scooping up a couple of handfuls.

She was right about ice melting on Emir. Even now, fresh from the lake, he was red hot, and as the ice scraped across his smooth, bronzed skin it disappeared beneath the warmth of her hands, leaving her with no alternative but to explore the heat of his body.

'That's enough,' she said, stepping back the instant her breathing became ragged. She had been wrong to think she could do this—that she could play with this man—toy with him—amuse herself at his expense. Emir was more than a match for her, and the strength she'd felt beneath her hands had only confirmed her thoughts that his body was hard, while hers was all too soft and yielding.

She didn't need to see his face to know he was smiling again as she went back to the sauna hut. Her hands were trembling as she let herself in, and hot guilt rushed through her as she curled up on the bench with her knees tucked under her chin and her arms wrapped tightly round them. By the time Emir walked in, she had put safety back at the top of her agenda. 'Let me know if you plan any more solo trips in the lake. Forget the sheikh—I don't even have a contact number for your next of kin.'

'Your concern overwhelms me,' Emir said dryly as he poured another ladle of water onto the hot stones.

'Where are you going now?' she said as he turned for the door.

'To choose which birch switch I would like to use,' he said as if she should have known. 'Would you care to join me?'

Talk about a conversation stopper.

CHAPTER SIX

SHE WAS TWISTED into a ferment of lust. Her heart was beating like a drum as she watched Emir selecting a birch twig switch. She loved that his process of elimination was so exacting. She loved that he examined each bunch before trying them out on his muscular calves. Each arc through the air…each short, sharp slap against his skin…made her breath catch. Her head was reeling with all sorts of erotic impressions, though she couldn't help wondering if he ever felt the cold. She had grabbed a robe and fur boots before exiting the hut and was well wrapped up.

He started thrashing his shoulders. This was like an advanced lesson in how to watch, feel and suffer— from the most intense frustration she had ever known.

'What do you think?' His dark eyes were full of humour.

'I think I'll leave you to it,' she said, shaking her head as if to indulge the tourist in him.

'Why so prudish, suddenly?' Emir challenged as she turned to go.

Yes. Why was she so strait-laced with Emir when thrashing the body with birch twigs was a normal part of the traditional sauna routine in Skavanga?

'Don't you want to try it?' Emir called after her with amusement in his voice.

She stopped, realising that however high she raised the bar he jumped over it and raised it yet more for her.

Where would this end?

'I can do it any time,' she said casually. He didn't need to know she was shivering with arousal rather than cold as she headed for the door. She swung it open and the enticing warmth with the mellow scent of hot wood washed over her.

'It's not like you to run away from a challenge, Britt.'

She hadn't closed the door yet. 'You don't know anything about me.'

'Are we going to debate this while our body temperatures drop like a stone?'

His maybe. 'You could always join me in the sauna...' she suggested.

'Or you could join me with the birch twigs.' As Emir laughed she made her decision.

'In your dreams. And you might want to put some clothes on,' she added, heading for the sauna hut.

Slamming the door behind her, she leaned back against it, exhaling shakily. Damn the man! Did nothing faze him? She had dreamed of meeting her match, but now she'd met him she wasn't so sure it was such a good idea. They were too similar—too stubborn—too set on duty—too competitive—too everything.

It was too exhausting!

Flopping down on the bench, she closed her eyes, but that didn't help to blank out the fact that a connection of some sort, that wasn't sex, was growing between them. Crashing into the hut in a blast of energy and frigid air, Emir exclaimed, 'Make room for me,' before she could progress this thought.

'Close the door!'

'Wuss,' he murmured in a way that made her picture his sexy mouth curved in that half-smile.

'I don't like the cold,' she muttered, hugging her knees and burying her face so she didn't have to look at him.

'You could have fooled me! But I guess you'd love the desert,' he said.

She went very still and then forced herself to reach for the ladle so she didn't seem too impressed by this last comment.

'You can't still be cold?' Emir commented as she ladled water onto the hot stones. 'That's enough!'

The small hut was full of steam. She had been ladling the water on autopilot, trying not to think about the possibility of travelling to the desert with Emir, and in doing so was threatening to steam them alive. 'Sorry.' She lifted her shoulders in a careless shrug. 'I got carried away.'

'You certainly did,' Emir agreed as he towelled down.

'It's a long time since I've done the whole sauna ritual thing. I'd forgotten—'

'What fun it was?' Emir interrupted.

'How cold you get,' she argued, picking up the ladle again.

He laughed and took it from her. 'That's enough,' he said as their hands brushed. 'Sit down.' He towered over her, blocking out the light. 'If you want to raise the temperature, just ask me.'

'Very funny.' She glanced up.

Emir shrugged and smiled faintly, making her glad she was wearing a towel. He had no inhibitions, and, in fairness, most people went naked in the sauna, but that only worked if they had no sexual interest in each other.

'How about I build a fire in the fire pit outside?' Emir suggested. 'You don't want to be cooped up in here much longer.'

She had always enjoyed sitting round a blazing fire surrounded by snow and ice, and it would be one heck of a lot safer than this intimate space. 'That's a great idea.'

'I'll call you when I'm ready.'

You do that, she thought, banking Emir's sexy smile.

Her heart thumped on cue when he rapped on the door. Sliding off the bench, she went outside to join him. Emir had built an amazing fire...roaring hot and set to last.

'Nights in the desert can be freezing,' he explained. 'And in some parts a fire is essential to keep mountain lions away. We have amazing wildlife,' he added as she sat down and stretched her feet out. 'Kareshi is a country of great contrasts. We have big modern cities as well as a wilderness where tribal traditions haven't changed in centuries.'

Why was he telling her this? Was he serious about her visiting Kareshi? They were staring at each other again, Britt realised, turning away to pretend interest in the fire. There was no point in getting any closer to Emir when their relationship, such as it was, wasn't going anywhere. Lifting his chin, he stared at her as if he were expecting her to say something. Who knew that Britt Skavanga, lately hotshot businesswoman, as her sisters liked to teasingly call her, could feel so awkward, even shy?

Maybe you should get out of the office more often.

Maybe she should, Britt thought wryly, lacking the

energy for once to argue with her contrary inner voice.
Emir had gone quite still, she noticed.

'Do you see them?' he said, looking past her into
the trees.

'The deer? Yes,' she murmured. A doe and a fawn
were watching them from the safety of the undergrowth.
'They're so beautiful,' she whispered, hardly daring to
breathe. 'I always feel close to nature here,' she con-
fided in another whisper.

'As I do in the desert,' Emir murmured back.

There was that connection thing again. It was there
whether she liked it or not. And now she stiffened, remembering the warning her mother had given her when
Britt was a child. Now she understood why her mother
had said the things she had, but as a little girl she had
thought her father loud rather than violent, and playful,
rather than bullying. Now she knew he'd been a drunk
who had prompted her mother to warn all her daugh-
ters that men kept you down. Her girls were going to
be warriors who went out into the world and made their
own way. Britt had grown up with the determination
that no man would ever rule her engraved on her heart.
And Emir was a forceful man...

His touch on her arm made her flinch, but then she
realised he was pointing to the deer watching them. The
animals were considering flight, and she wondered if it
was Emir's inner stillness holding them. Their brown
eyes were wide in gentle faces, and though Emir had
moved closer to her he kept space between them, which
made her feel relaxed. He had that sort of calming
aura—which didn't mean she wasn't intensely aware
of him. It was a special moment as they watched the
deer watching them. It was as if humans and animals
had come together briefly.

'What an amazing encounter,' she breathed as the deer turned and picked their way unhurriedly back through the maze of trees into the depth of the forest.

'Now I'm certain you'd love the desert,' Emir said, turning to smile at her. 'Many think it's just a barren space—'

'But we know better?'

He huffed a laugh, holding her gaze in a way that said he was glad she had understood.

'Maybe one day I'll make it to the desert,' she said, trying not to care too much.

'I'll make sure of it,' Emir said quietly. 'If this deal goes through I'll make sure you visit Kareshi.'

'I'd love to,' she exclaimed impulsively.

How much longer are you going to wear your heart on your sleeve? Britt wondered as Emir flashed her an amused glance and raised a brow. But she could see that a whole world of possibility was opening up, both for her and for Skavanga, and she couldn't pretend that the thought of visiting an emerging country where the vigorous young ruler had already done so much for his people didn't excited her.

'I want you to see what the money from the diamonds can accomplish,' Emir remarked.

Yes, there were benefits for both their countries. 'I will,' she said, more in hope than expectation. 'I think you miss Kareshi,' she added in an attempt to shift the spotlight onto him.

'I love my country. I love my people. I love my life in Kareshi. I love my horses—they're a real passion for me. I breed pure Arabs, though sometimes I strengthen the line of my breeding stock with Criolla ponies from the Argentine pampas.'

'You play polo?'

'Of course, and many polo players are my friends. You will have heard of the Acosta brothers, I'm sure.'

She had heard of the Acosta brothers. Who hadn't? 'I learned to ride at the local stable,' she admitted. 'Just old nags compared to the type of horses you're talking about, but I loved it all the same. I love the sense of freedom, and still ride whenever I get the chance.'

'Something we have in common,' he said.

Something else, she thought, inhaling steadily. Friendships were founded on sharing a passion for life, and there was no doubt that they were opening up to each other. So much for her mother's warning. And, yes, it was dangerous to reveal too much of yourself, but if you didn't, how could you ever get close to anyone?

She had to face facts. Once he had collected the information he needed, Emir would go home—and inviting her to Kareshi was probably just talk. Making her excuses, she stood up to go. Emir stood too.

'No birching?' he asked wryly.

She gave him a crooked smile. 'I'm warm enough, thanks to you.'

'That's right,' he called after her as she walked away. 'You probably deserve a good birching—probably even want it. But you're not getting it from me—'

Britt shook her head in wry acceptance, but Emir didn't turn around as she huffed a laugh. He didn't need to. There was a new sort of ease between them—an understanding, almost.

He caught her at the door of the hut, and, lifting a switch from the rack, he shot her a teasing look. 'Are you quite sure?'

'Certain,' she said, but there was laughter in both their eyes.

Laughter that died very quickly when Emir ran the

switch of twigs very lightly down between her breasts
and over her belly to the apex of her thighs. She was instantly aroused and couldn't move, even had she wanted
to. She remained motionless as he increased the pressure just enough, moving the bunched twigs with exactly the right degree of delicacy. Her breath came out
in a noisy shudder, and all this time Emir was holding
her gaze. His eyes told her that he knew exactly what
she wanted him to do. Her breathing stalled when he
used the switch to ease her legs apart.

'Why deny yourself, Britt?'

'Because I need to get inside where it's warm,' she
said lightly, pulling herself together.

Physically, she yearned for everything Emir could
give her, Britt realised as she quickly shed her underwear, while emotionally she was a wreck. She felt such
a strong connection to him, and knew she would never
be able to ignore those feelings—

Better she end this now.

He joined her in the hut. That was a foregone conclusion. The stag didn't abandon the doe when it was cor-
nered. The stag knew what the doe wanted and tracking
it was part of the game. They sat opposite each other
with the hot stones sizzling between them, and, leaning back, Emir gave her a look—just a slight curve at
the corner of his sexy mouth.

'What?' she said, knowing he could hardly have
avoided noticing that she was naked.

'Now we get really hot,' he said.

CHAPTER SEVEN

As Emir's familiar warmth and scent flared in her senses and his arms gathered her in, Britt felt a new energy flooding through her. She even spared a foolish moment to wish it could always be like this—that he was really hers, and that these strong arms and this strong body would sometimes take over so she could take time out occasionally. But that was so ridiculous she had no difficulty blanking it out. She took one last look at a world where desire for a man could grow into friendship, and where that friendship could grow into love. That was just childhood fantasy. She'd settle for lust.

Holding her face between his hands, Emir made her look at him. Gazing into the burning stare of a man who knew so much about her body made it easy to forget her doubts. Her face must have shown this transition, because he brushed her lips with his. And from there it was an easy slide into a passionate embrace that ended with Emir manoeuvring her into a comfortable position on the bench—which just happened to be under him.

'Is there any part of this you don't like?' he said, smiling down at her.

She liked everything—too much—and at what risk to her heart? Right now she didn't care as another part of Britt Skavanga, warrior woman, chipped off and floated away. At one time sex was little more than a normal function for her, like eating or sleeping, but now...

Now that wasn't nearly enough.

But Emir's hands were distracting her, and as he traced the line of her spine she embraced the feelings inside her. They were so strong she could hardly ignore them. She wanted this man. She wanted him so badly. She wanted to be one with him in every way. Unfortunately, Emir's approach to sex was much like hers had used to be, and being on the receiving end of that was very different from doling it out. But then her mind filled with pleasure as his lips caressed her neck. He knew just how to work her hot spots until she softened against him and relaxed. She had always taken the lead in the past—she had been the one who knew what she was doing and where she was going, the one who was completely in control—but with Emir there was no control. She was his.

'I love your body,' he said as she writhed beneath him.

'I love yours too.' How could she not?

Emir was built on a heroic scale. She doubted she had ever met a bigger man. There wasn't a spare inch of unnecessary flesh on his hard, toned body, and each muscle was clearly delineated after his strenuous physical exercise in the lake. He was every bit the soldier, the fighter, the leader, yet he had the most sensitive hands. She groaned as he massaged her scalp with his fingertips.

'What do you want, Britt?' he murmured.

'Do you really need me to answer that?'

'I like you to tell me,' he said.

Emir's voice had the power to arouse her almost as

much as the man himself. Raising her chin, she took a deep breath and then told him what she wanted.

'So open your legs wider,' he said.

Her first thought was, No. I can't do that—not while you're looking down at me.

'Wider,' he said.

She wanted this. He excited her—

'Wider still...'

'I can't—you're merciless—'

'Yes, I am,' he agreed in the same soft tone.

'Enough,' she begged him, reaching out. She needed human contact. She needed closeness more than anything. She needed a kiss—a tender kiss. She still longed for the illusion that they were close in every way, Britt realised, feeling a pang of regret for what could never be.

He had never seen anything more beautiful than Britt at this moment, when every part of her was glowing and aroused. His desire to be joined to her was overwhelming, but something as special as this could not be rushed. It must be appreciated and savoured. One of the so-called erotic secrets of Kareshi was nothing more than this lingering over pleasure. Making time for pleasure was a so much a national pursuit he had been forced to persuade the Kareshi people to balance their country's business needs against it, but he would never wish these old traditions to die out. In fact, he had every intention of fostering them, and as Britt reached for him he took her wrists in a firm grip. 'Not yet,' he whispered.

'Don't you want me?' she said, arching her back as she displayed her breasts to best advantage.

She had no idea how much.

He held her locked in his stare as she sat up. He even

allowed her to lace her fingers through his hair, binding him to her. Britt was easy to read. She was already on the edge. Intuition had always helped him in the past— in all sorts of situations, and now this. With Britt he mastered his own desires by channelling his thoughts into all the things that intrigued him about her.

'How can you bear to wait?' she complained.

'I bear it because I know what's best for you,' he said. 'I know what you need and I know the best way to give it to you.'

'How do you know?' she said, writhing with impatience.

On the sexual front that was all too obvious, but knowing Britt wasn't so hard. She was the oldest child, always trying to do her best, the lab-rat for her sisters, the one who would have been given the strictest upbringing by her parents. Britt was used to bearing the weight of responsibility on her shoulders, and with duties at home and then duties in the business she hadn't had much time to explore life, let alone discover the nuances of sex and how very good it could be.

'So, how did you like our Nordic traditions?' she murmured against his mouth.

Distracted, he brushed a kiss against her lips. 'I like them a lot. I'd like to know more. I'd like to know more about you—'

The look of surprise on her face almost broke the erotic spell for him, and then she said with touching honesty, 'I'd like to know more about you and your country.'

'Maybe you will.'

Closing his eyes, he inhaled her wildflower scent, and realised then that the thought of never smelling it again was unthinkable. He was still on guard, of course.

There was still a business deal to do and it would be unwise to underestimate Britt Skavanga. She was everything he had been warned to expect…and so much more.

When Emir kissed her she was glad of his arms supporting her, because he didn't just kiss her breath away, he kissed her thoughts away too. It felt so good to drop her guard and lose herself in sensation, shut out the business robot she had become. It was good to feel sensation spreading in tiny rivers of fire through her veins, and even better to feel Emir's erection resting heavily against her thigh, because that said he wanted her as much as she wanted him. She groaned with anticipation when he nudged her thighs apart. Moving between them, he started teasing her with delicate touches until she thought she would go mad for him.

'Wrap your legs around me,' he instructed, staring deep into her eyes.

'Don't make me wait,' she warned, but in a way she was glad when he soothed her with kisses and caresses first. She cried out and urged him on. There were no certainties other than the fact that she was being drawn deeper into a dangerous liaison with him.

As if sensing her unease, he took her face in his big, warm hands and drugged her with kisses. Gentle to begin with, they grew deeper and firmer as the embers inside her sparked and flared. She loved it when he took possession of her mouth, and loved it even more when he took possession of her body. She loved being held so firmly. She loved the powerful emotions inside her.

'Have you changed your mind?' he said as she tried to rein them in.

She denied this, and then he did something so amazing she couldn't have stopped him if she had tried. A shaking cry escaped her throat as he sank slowly deep inside her. She could never be fully prepared for Emir. The sheer size of him stole the breath from her lungs. He was such an intuitive lover. He understood every part of her and how she responded. He knew her limits and never stepped over them, while his hands and mouth worked magic. Today he was using the seductive language of Kareshi—soft and guttural, husky and persuasive—to both encourage and excite her. It must have succeeded because she found herself pressing her legs wide for him with the heel of her palms against her thighs.

'Good,' he approved, thrusting even deeper.

She cried out his name repeatedly as he moved rhythmically and reliably towards the inevitable conclusion. But suddenly some madness overcame them, and control was no longer possible as they fought their way to release.

She was still shuddering with aftershocks minutes later. Her internal muscles closed around him gratefully, to an indescribably delicious beat.

Neither of them spoke for quite a while. They had both experienced the same thing—something out of the ordinary, she thought as Emir stared down at her. At last his eyes were full of everything she had longed to see.

'I take it you enjoyed that?' he murmured, and, withdrawing gently, he helped her to sit up.

'And you?' she said, resting her cheek against his chest.

'I have one suggestion—'

She glanced up.

'Next time we try a bed.'

His grin infected her. 'Now there's a novel thought,'

she agreed, but after she had rested on him for a moment or two harsh reality intruded and she remembered who she was, who he was, and the parts they played in this drama.

Lifting her chin, she put on the old confident face. 'Don't get ahead of yourself, mister. I sleep alone.'

'Who mentioned sleeping?' Emir argued.

'Do you always have to show such perfect good sense?'

'With you, I think I do,' he said, smiling, unrepentant.

Emir was probably the one man she was prepared to take instruction from, Britt concluded as she showered down later in her en-suite bathroom at the cabin, if only because the pay-off was so great. And she wasn't just thinking about the sexual pay-off, but the pay-off that was making her sing and waltz around the bathroom like a fruit-loop—the pay-off that made her feel all warm and fuzzy inside—and optimistic about the future—about everything. She felt suddenly as if anything could happen—as if the boundaries of Skavanga and her job had fallen away, leaving a world full of possibility. And the desert kingdom of Kareshi was definitely the stand out country in that world waiting to be discovered.

Of course, she must visit Emir's homeland as he had suggested. If the deal went through it would be wrong to accept the consortium's investment without wanting to know as much as she possibly could about the benefits the diamonds would bring to both countries. Perhaps there could be reciprocal cultural and educational opportunities—anything was possible. She longed to get stuck into it—to get out of the office and meet people at last. Her mind was blazing with ideas. No dream seemed too far-fetched.

Showering down after his unique encounter with Britt, Sharif's thoughts were arranged in several compartments. The first was all to do with Britt the businesswoman. She was meticulous and had held the company together when many would have failed. Her attention to detail was second to none—as he had learned when it had taken him several hours, rather than the usual five minutes, to pore over her first agenda and find a hole. She was clear-headed and quick-thinking in her business life—

And an emotional mess when it came to anything else.

Her life was tied up in duty, but she wanted it all. He guessed she heard the clock ticking, but she didn't know how to escape from her work long enough to find the fulfilment she craved—the satisfaction of raising her own family and extending her sphere of influence in the workplace too. She did everything she could to support her sisters while they studied and campaigned for this and that, but they didn't seem to stop and think that Britt deserved some fulfilment too.

And neither should he, he reminded himself. He had one duty, one goal, and one responsibility, which was to the men who had come in with him on this deal. Business always came first, because business fed improvements in Kareshi, and only then could he afford to pause to wonder if there was anything missing from his life—

Britt?

Any man would be missing a woman like Britt in his life. She was exceptional. She was an intriguing mix of control and abandonment, and it seemed to him that the only time Britt let go was during sex, which made cutting the best deal possible a challenging prospect, but not impossible.

Business, always business, he thought, towelling down. He liked that Britt was part of that business. He had always loved a challenge and Britt was a challenge. Securing the towel around his waist, he picked up his razor to engage in the one battle he usually lost. His beard grew faster than he could shave it off, but at least the ritual soothed him and gave him time to think.

Shaking his head as if that could shake thoughts of Britt out of it, he rinsed his face and raked his thick, unruly hair into some semblance of order. The deal was a tantalising prospect and he would bring it in. Between them he and his friends had the means and the skill and the outlets necessary to transform dull, uncut diamonds into sparkling gems that would shimmer with fire as they shivered against a woman's skin. Britt believed she held all the cards, and could cut the better deal, but he held the joker.

Stepping into jeans, he tugged on a plain back top, and fastened his belt before reaching for the phone. Some decisions were harder to take than others, and this was harder than most. Britt had all the instincts of a man inside the body of a woman, but she had a woman's emotions, which held her back when it came to clear thinking in a deal like this where family was involved. He wished he could protect her from the fallout from this call, but his duty was clear. This wasn't for him alone, but for the consortium, and for Kareshi. In the absence of her brother, Britt led her tribe as he did, making her a worthy adversary. He just had to hope she could handle this new twist in the plot as competently as she had coped with other obstacles life had thrown at her.

He drummed his fingers impatiently as he waited for the call to connect. Three rings later the call was answered. He hesitated, which was definitely a first for him, but the die had been cast on the day he had sat down to research the share structure of Skavanga Mining and had discovered that the major shareholder was not in fact the three sisters, but their missing brother, Tyr Skavanga. More complicated still was that, for reasons of his own, Tyr didn't want his sisters to know where he was. Having given his word, Emir would have to keep that from Britt even though Tyr's long-distance involvement in the deal would swing the balance firmly in the consortium's favour.

'Hello, Tyr,' he said, settling down into what he knew would be a long call.

CHAPTER EIGHT

HE WAS PACKING? *Emir was packing?* She had come downstairs after her shower expecting to find him basking in front of a roaring fire—which he would have banked up, perhaps with a drink in hand and one waiting for her on the table. She had anticipated more getting-to-know-you time. That was what couples did when they'd grown closer after sex…

And they had grown closer, Britt reassured herself, feeling painfully obvious in banged-up jeans, simple top and bare feet. She felt as if, in this relaxed state, all her feelings were on display. And all those feelings spoke of closeness and intimacy with Emir. She had dressed in anticipation of continuing ease between them. She had dressed as she would dress when her sisters were around. And now she felt vulnerable and exposed. And utterly ridiculous for having let her guard down so badly.

How could she have got this so wrong?

She watched him from the doorway of his bedroom as Emir folded his clothes, arranging them in a bag that he could sling casually over his shoulder. He must have known she was standing there, but he didn't say a word. The chill seemed to creep up from the floor and consume her. Even her face felt cold.

What had gone wrong?

What was wrong was that Emir didn't care and she had refused to see that. He had come here to do a job and his job was done. He had taken samples for analysis and had seen the mine for himself. He had weighed her up and interviewed her colleagues. His only job now was to pack up and leave. What had she been? An unexpected bonus on the side? She had no part to play in Emir's plans, he'd made that clear. Why had she ever allowed herself to believe that she had? All that talk of Kareshi and the desert was just that—talk.

Her throat felt tight. Her mouth was dry. She felt numb. Anything she said in this situation would sound ridiculous. And what was the point of having a row when she had no call on this man? She had enjoyed him as much as he had enjoyed her. Was it his fault if she couldn't move on?

All this was sound reasoning, but reason didn't allow for passion, for emotion—for any of the things she felt for Emir. And out of bitter disappointment at his manner towards her—or rather his lack of…anything, really—came anger. What had he meant by staring into her eyes and suggesting they should take sex to the bedroom next time? Was that concern for her? Or was Emir more concerned about getting grazes on his knees? She had laughed with and trusted this man. Everything had changed for her, because she'd thought… Because she'd thought…

She didn't have a clue what she'd thought, Britt realised. She only knew she had given herself completely to a man, something she'd never done before, and now, just as her mother had predicted, she was paying the price. But she would not play the role of misused mistress and give him the chance to mock.

'You're leaving?' she said coolly. 'Already?'

'My job here's done,' Emir confirmed, straightening up. He turned to face her. 'My flight plan is filed. I leave right away.'

When did he file his flight plan? Immediately after making love to her?

'Do you have transport to the airport?' She wasn't so petty she would let him call a cab. She would take him to the airport if she had to.

'My people are coming for me,' he said, turning back to zip up his bag.

Of course. 'Oh, good,' she said, going hot and cold in turn as she chalked up the completeness of his plan as just one more insult to add to the rest. He'd had sex with her first and then had called his people to come and get him. He'd used her—

As she had used men in the past.

Her heart lurched as their eyes met. Mistake. Now he could see how badly she didn't want him to go.

'I have to report back to the consortium, Britt,' he said, confirming this assumption.

'Of course.' She cleared her throat and arranged her features in a composed mask. She had never been at such a disadvantage where a man was concerned. But that was because she had never known anyone like Emir before and had always prided herself on being able to read people. She had not read him. They were like two strangers, out of sync, out of context, out of time.

She stood in embarrassed silence. With no small talk to delay him, let alone some siren song with which to change his mind, she could only wait for him to leave.

'Thank you for your hospitality, Britt,' he said, shouldering the bag.

Her hospitality? Did that include the sex? Her face

was composed, but as Emir moved to shake her hand she stood back.

Emir didn't react one way or the other to this snub. 'I'll wait for test results on the samples, and if all goes well you will hear from my lawyers in the next few weeks.'

'Your lawyers?' Her head was reeling by now, with business and personal thoughts hopelessly mixed.

'Forgive me, Britt.' Emir paused with his hand on the door. 'I meant, of course, the lawyers acting for the consortium will be in touch with you.'

Suddenly all the anger and hurt inside her exploded into fury, which manifested itself in an icy question. 'And what if I get a better offer in the meantime?'

'Then you must consider it and we will meet again. I should tell you that the consortium has been in touch with your sisters, and they have already agreed—'

'You've spoken to Eva and Leila?' she cut in. He'd done that without speaking to her? She couldn't take any more in than she already had—and she certainly couldn't believe that her sisters would do a deal without speaking to her first.

'My people have spoken to your sisters,' Emir explained.

'And you didn't think to tell me?' *They didn't think to tell me?* She was flooded with hurt and pain.

'I just have.' A muscle flicked in his jaw.

'So all the time we've been here—' Outrage boiled in her eyes. 'I think you'd better go,' she managed tensely. Suddenly, all that mattered was speaking to her sisters so she could find out what the hell was going on.

Meanwhile, Emir was checking round the room, just to be sure he hadn't forgotten anything, presumably. He didn't care a jot about her, she realised with a cold rush of certainty. This had only ever been about the deal. How convenient to keep her distracted here while the consortium's lackeys acted behind her back. How very clever of Emir. And how irredeemably stupid of her.

'If you've left anything I'll send it on,' she said coldly, just wanting him to go.

How could her heart still betray her when Emir's brooding stare switched to her face?

'I knew I could count on you,' he said as her stupid heart performed the customary leap.

Emir's impassive stare turned her own eyes glacial. 'Well, you've got what you wanted from me, so you might as well go. You'll get nothing else here.'

The inky brows rose, but Emir remained silent. She just hoped her barb had stabbed home. But no.

'This is business, Britt, and there is no emotion in business. I wish I could tell you more, but—'

'Please—spare me.' She drew herself up. 'Goodbye, Emir.'

She didn't follow him out. She wouldn't give him the satisfaction. She listened to him jog down the stairs, while registering the tenderness of a body that had been very well used, and heard him stride across the main room downstairs where they had been so briefly close. It was as if Emir were stripping the joy out of the cabin she loved with every step he took, and each of those departing steps served as a reminder that she had wasted her feelings on someone who cared for nothing in this world apart from business.

Apart from her sisters and Tyr, that had been how she was not so very long ago, Britt conceded as the front door closed behind Emir.

She hadn't even realised she had stopped breathing

until she heard a car door slam and she drew in a desperate, shuddering breath.

There were times when he would gladly exchange places with the grooms who worked in his stables and this was one of them, but harsh decisions had to be made. He thought he could feel Britt's anguished stare on his back as he held up his hand to hail the black Jeep that had come to collect him. His men would take him back to the airport and his private jet. His mind was still full of her when he climbed into the passenger seat and they drove him away. It was better to leave now before things became really complicated.

Her sense of betrayal by Emir—and, yes, even more so by her sisters—was indescribable. And for once both Eva and Leila were out of touch by phone. She had tried them constantly since Emir had left, prowling around the cabin like a wounded animal, unable to settle or do anything until she had spoken to them. Even her beloved cabin had let her down. It failed to soothe her this time. She should never have brought Emir here. He had tainted her precious memories.

Not wanting to face the fact that she had been less than focused, she turned on every light in the cabin, but it still felt empty. There was no reply from her sisters, so all she could do was dwell on what she'd seen through the window when he'd left—Emir climbing into a Jeep and being driven away. She'd got the sense of other big men in the vehicle, shadowy, and no doubt armed. Where there were such vast resources up for grabs, no one took any chances. She had been kidding herself if she had thought that bringing investors in would be easy to handle. She was up against a power-

ful and well-oiled machine. She should have known
when each man in the consortium was a power in his
own right, and she was on her own—

So? Get used to it! There was no time for self-pity.
This was all about protecting her sisters, whatever
they'd done. They weren't to blame. They had no idea
what it took to survive in the cut-throat world of business—she didn't want them to know. She would protect
them as she always had.

She nearly jumped out of her skin when the phone
rang, and she rushed to pick it up. Mixed feelings when
she did so, because it was Eva, her middle and least
flexible sister, calling. 'Eva—'

'You rang?' Eva intoned. 'Seven missed calls, Britt?
What's going on?'

Where to begin? Suddenly, Britt was at a loss, but
then her mind cleared and became as unemotional as
it usually was where business was concerned. 'The
man from the consortium just left the cabin. He said
you and Leila signed something?' Britt waited tensely
for her sister to respond, guessing Eva would be doing
ten things at once. 'So, what have you signed?' Britt
pressed, controlling her impatience.

'All we did was give permission for the consortium's
people to enter the offices to start their preliminary investigations.'

'Why didn't you speak to me first?'

'Because we couldn't get hold of you.'

And now she could only rue the day she had left Skavanga to show Emir the mine.

'We thought we were helping you move things on.'

Britt could accept that. The sooner the consortium's
accountants had completed their investigations, the
sooner she could bring some investment into Skavanga

Mining and save the company. 'So you haven't agreed to sell your shares?'

'Of course not. What do you take me for?'

'I don't want to argue with you, Eva. I'm just worried—'

'You know I don't know the first thing about the business,' Eva countered. 'And I'm sorry you got landed with it when our parents died. I do know there are a thousand things you'd rather do.'

'Never mind that now—I need to help people at home. I'm coming back—'

'Before you go, how did you get on with him?"

'Who?' Britt said defensively.

'You know—the man who was at the mine with you—the sheikh's man.'

'Oh, you mean Emir.'

'What?'

'Emir,' Britt repeated.

'Well, that's original,' Eva murmured with a smile in her voice. 'Did the Black Sheikh come up with any more titles to fool you, or just the one?'

Britt started to say something and then stopped. 'Sorry?'

'Oh, come on,' Eva exclaimed impatiently. 'I guess he was quite a man, but I can't believe your brain has taken up permanent residence below your belt. You know your thesaurus as well as anyone: emir, potentate, person of rank. Have I rung any bells yet?'

'But he said his name was—' Hot waves of shame washed over her. She was every bit as stupid as she had thought herself when Emir left, only more so.

'Since when have you believed everything you're told, Britt?' Eva demanded.

Since she met a man who told her that his name was Emir.

She had to speak to him. She would speak to him, Britt determined icily, just as soon as she had finished this call to her sister.

'You haven't fallen for him, have you?' Eva said shrewdly.

'No, of course not,' Britt fired back.

There was a silence that suggested Eva wasn't entirely convinced. Too bad. Whatever Britt might have felt for Emir was gone now. Gone completely. Finished. Over. Dead. Gone.

'You should have taken him for a roll in the snow so you could both cool down.'

'I did,' she admitted flatly. 'He loved it.'

'Sounds like my kind of guy—'

'This isn't funny, Eva.'

'No,' Eva agreed, turning serious. 'You've made a fool of yourself and you don't like it. Turns out you're not the hotshot man-eater you thought you were.'

'But I'm still a businesswoman,' Britt murmured thoughtfully, 'and you know what they say.'

'I'm sure you're going to tell me,' Eva observed dryly.

'Don't get mad, get even.'

'That's what I was afraid of,' Eva commented under her breath. 'Just don't cut off your nose to spite your face. Don't screw this deal after putting so much effort into it.'

'Don't worry, I won't.'

'So what are you going to do?' Eva pressed, concern ringing in her voice.

For betraying her—for allowing his people to approach her sisters while Britt and he were otherwise engaged?

'I'm going to follow him to Kareshi. I'm going to track him down. I'm going to ring his office to try and find out where he is. I'll go into the desert if I have to. I'm going to find the bastard and make him pay.'

CHAPTER NINE

KARESHI...

She was actually here. It hardly seemed possible. For all her bitter, mixed-up thoughts when it came to the man she had called Emir and must now learn to call His Majesty Sheikh Sharif al Kareshi, Britt couldn't help but be dazzled by her first sight of the ocean of sand stretching away to a purple haze following the curve of the earth. She craned her neck, having just caught sight of the glittering capital city. It couldn't stand in greater contrast to the desert.

Just as her thoughts of the man the world called the Black Sheikh couldn't have stood in starker contrast to the universal approval the man enjoyed. How could he fool so many people? How could he fool her?

That last question was easily answered. Her body had done that for her, yearning for a man when it should freeze at the very thought of him—if she had any sense.

As the city came into clearer view and she saw all the amazing buildings she got a better picture of the Black Sheikh's power and his immense wealth. It seemed incredible that she was here, and that His Majesty Sheikh Sharif had been her lover—

That she had been so easily fooled.

'The captain has switched the seat-belt sign on.'

'Oh, yes, thank you,' she said glancing up, glad of the distraction. Any distraction to take her mind off that man was welcome.

Having secured her belt, she continued to stare avidly out of the window. Her life to date hadn't allowed for much time outside Skavanga, and from what she could see from the plane Kareshi couldn't have been more different. The thought of exploring the city and meeting new people was exciting in spite of all the other things she had to face. An ivory beach bordered the city, and beyond that lay a tranquil sea of clear bright blue, but it was the wilderness that drew her attention. The Black Sheikh was down there somewhere. His people had told her this in an attempt to put her off. They didn't know her if they thought she would be dismayed to learn His Majesty was deep in the desert with his people. She would find him and she would confront him. She had every reason to do so, if only to learn the result of the trials on the mineral samples he had taken from the mine. She suspected he would agree to see her. His people were sure to have told him that she had been asking for him and, like Britt, the Black Sheikh flinched from nothing.

Another glance out of the window revealed a seemingly limitless carpet of umber and sienna, gold and tangerine, and over this colourful, if alien landscape the black shadow of the aircraft appeared to be creeping with deceptive stealth. The desert was a magical place and she was impatient to be travelling through it. Would she find Sheikh Sharif? The ice fields of Skavanga were apparently featureless, but that was never completely true, and where landmarks failed there was always GPS. Tracking down the ruler of Kareshi would be a challenge, but not one she couldn't handle.

* * *

Shortly after she reached the hotel Britt received a call from Eva to say that one of their main customers for the minerals they mined had gone down, defaulting on a payment to Skavanga Mining, and leaving the company dangerously exposed. It was the last thing she needed, and her mind was already racing on what to do for the best when Eva explained that the consortium had stepped in.

'I think you need to speak to the sheikh to find out the details.'

'That's my intention,' Britt assured her sister, feeling that the consortium's net was slowly closing over her family business.

As soon as she ended the call she tried once again to speak to a member of the sheikh's staff to arrange an appointment as a matter of urgency. Audience with His Majesty was booked up for months in advance, some snooty official informed her. And, no, His Majesty had *certainly not* left any message for a visitor from a *mining* company. This was said as if mining were some sleazy, disreputable occupation.

So speaks a man who has probably never got his hands dirty in his life, Britt thought, pulling the phone away from her ear. She had been placing calls non-stop from her bedroom for the past two hours—to Sharif's offices, to his palace, to the country's administrative offices, and even to her country's diplomatic representative in the city.

Okay. Calm down, she told herself, taking a deep breath as she paced the room. Let's think this through. There was a number she could call, and this really was a wild card. Remembering Emir telling her about his love of horses, she stabbed in the number for His Majesty's stables.

The voice that answered was young and female and it took Britt a couple of breaths to compute this, as her calls so far had led Britt to believe that only men worked for the sheikh and they all had tent poles up their backsides.

'Hello,' the pleasant female voice said again. 'Jasmina Kareshi speaking…'

The Black Sheikh's sister! Though Princess Jasmina sounded far too relaxed to be a princess. 'Hello. This is Britt Skavanga speaking. I wonder if you could help me?'

'Call me Jazz,' the friendly voice on the other end of the line insisted as Jazz went on to explain that her brother had in fact been in touch some time ago to warn her that Britt was due to arrive in the country.

'How did he find out?' Britt exclaimed with surprise.

'Are you serious?' Jazz demanded.

Jazz's upbeat nature was engaging, and as the ruler of Kareshi's sister proceeded to tell Britt that her brother knew everything that was going on in Kareshi at least ten minutes before it happened Britt got the feeling that in different circumstances Jazz and she might have been friends.

'As he's not here, I'm supposed to be helping you any way I can,' Jazz explained. 'I can only apologise that it's taken so long for the two of us to get in touch, but I've been tied up with my favourite mare at the stables while she was giving birth.'

'Please don't apologise,' Britt said quickly. She was just glad to have someone sensible to talk to. 'I hope everything went well for your horse.'

'Perfectly,' Jazz confirmed, adding in an amused

tone, 'I imagine it went a lot better for me and my mare than it did for you without a formal introduction to my brother's stuffy staff.'

Diplomacy was called for, Britt concluded. 'They did what they could,' she said cagily.

'I bet they did,' Jazz agreed wryly.

This was really dangerous. Not only had she fallen for the Black Sheikh masquerading as Emir, but now she was starting to get on with his sister.

'My brother's in the desert,' Jazz confirmed. 'Let me give you the GPS—'

'Thanks.'

Jazz proceeded to dispense GPS coordinates for a Bedouin camp in the desert as casually as if she were directing Britt to the local mall. Britt was able to draw a couple of possible conclusions from this. Sharif had not wanted his staff to know about the connection between them—possibly because as she was a woman in a recently reformed and previously male-dominated country they wouldn't treat her too well. But at least he had entrusted the news of her arrival to Jazz. She'd give him the benefit of the doubt this one time. Just before signing off, she checked with Jazz that the car hire company she had decided on had the best vehicles for trekking in the desert.

'It should be the best,' Jazz exclaimed. 'Like practically everything else in Kareshi, my brother owns it.'

Of course he did. And he thought Skavanga Mining was in the bag too. Not just an investment, but a takeover. There was no time to lose. Having promised to keep in touch with Jazz, she cut the line.

She had a moment—a fluttering heart, sweaty palms moment—when she knew it would have been far safer to deal with the Black Sheikh from a distance, preferably half a world away in Skavanga. Sharif was too confident for her liking, telling his sister about Britt's arrival in Kareshi as if he knew all her arrangements. According to Jazz it was very likely that he did, Britt reasoned, more eager than ever to get into the desert to confront him. And this time she would definitely confine their talks to business. She might be a slow learner, but she never made the same mistake twice.

He wasn't surprised that Britt had decided to track him down in the desert. He would have been more surprised if she had remained in Skavanga doing nothing. He admired her for not taking anything lying down. Well, almost anything, he mused, a smile hovering around his mouth. He did look forward to taking her on a bed one day.

Stretching out his naked body on the bank of silken cushions in the sleeping area of his tent, he turned his thoughts to business. Business had always been a game to him—a game he never lost, though with Britt it was different. He wanted to include her. He knew about the customer going bankrupt leaving Skavanga Mining in the lurch. He also knew there was nothing Britt could have done about it even had she been in Skavanga, though he doubted she would see it that way. He had been forced to get in touch with Tyr again to fast-track the deal, and with Britt on her way to the desert maybe he would get the chance to put her straight. He didn't like this subterfuge Tyr had forced upon him, though he could understand the reasons for it.

He rose and bathed in the pool formed by an underground stream that bubbled up beside his sleeping quarters. Donning his traditional black robes, he ran impatient hands through his damp black hair. Jasmina had contacted him to say that Britt had landed safely and would soon be joining him. Not soon enough, he thought as one of the elders of the tribe gave a discreet cough from the entrance to the tent to attract his attention.

A tent was a wholly inadequate description for the luxurious pavilion in which this noble tribe had insisted on housing him, Sharif reflected as he strode in lightweight sandals across priceless rugs to greet the old man. A simple bivouac would have been enough for him, but this was a palatial marquee fitted out as if for some mythical potentate. It was in fact a priceless ancient artefact, full of antique treasures, which had been carefully collected and preserved over centuries by the wandering tribesmen who kept these sorts of tents permanently at the ready to welcome their leader.

The elder informed him that the preparations for Britt's arrival were now in place. Sharif thanked him with no hint of his personal thoughts on his face, but it amused him to think that an experienced businesswoman like Britt had shown no compunction in attempting to throw him off stride by introducing him to a variety of Nordic delights. It remained to be seen how she would react when he turned the tables on her. How would she like being housed in the harem, for instance?

The elderly tribesman insisted on showing him round the harem tent set aside for Britt. It was a great deal more luxurious than even Sharif's regal pavilion, though admittedly it was a little short on seating areas. The large, luxuriously appointed space was dominated by an enormous bank of silken cushions carefully arranged into the shape of a bed enclosed by billowing white silk curtains. The harem tent had one purpose and one purpose only—a thought that curved his lips in a smile, if only because Britt would soon realise where she was staying, and would be incensed. Teasing her was one of his favourite pastimes. How long was it going to take her to realise that?

Thanking his elderly guide, he ducked his head and left the tent. Pausing a moment, he soaked in the purposeful bustle of a community whose endless travels along unseen paths through a wilderness that stretched seemingly to infinity never failed to amaze him. He didn't bring many visitors to the desert, believing the change from their soft lives in the city to the rigours of life in an encampment would be too much for them, but Britt was different. She was adventurous and curious, and would relish every moment of a challenge like this.

Spending time with his people was always a pleasure for him. It gave him a welcome break from the constant baying of the media—to see his face, to know his life, to know him. And, more importantly, it gave him the chance to live alongside his people and understand their needs. On this visit the elders had asked for more travelling schools, as well as more mobile clinics and hospitals. They would have them. He would make sure of it.

No wonder he was passionate about the diamond deal, Sharif reflected as some of the children ran up to him, clustering around a man who, in their eyes, was merely a newcomer in the camp. He hunkered down so they were all on eye level, while the children examined his prayer beads and the heavily decorated scabbard of his *khanjar*, the traditional Kareshi dagger that he wore at his side.

This was his joy, he realised as he watched the children's dark, inquisitive eyes, and their busy little hands as they examined these treasures. They were the future of his country, and he would allow nothing to put a dent in the prospects of these children. He had banished his unscrupulous relatives with the express purpose of allowing Kareshi to grow and flourish, and he would support his people with whatever it took.

He was still the warrior Sheikh, Sharif reflected as the children were called away for supper. His people expected it of their leader, and it was a right that he had fought for, and that was in his blood. But he did have a softer side that he didn't show the world, and that side of him longed for a family, and for closeness and love. He hadn't known that as a child. He hadn't even realised that he'd missed it until he spent more time here in the desert with his people. What he wouldn't give to know the closeness they shared...

He stopped outside the tent they had prepared for Britt, and felt a rush of gratitude for the heritage his people had so carefully preserved. As he fingered the finely woven tassels holding back the curtains over the opening his thoughts strayed back to Britt. They had never really left her.

It wasn't as if she hadn't changed a tyre before—

Famously, she had changed one on the very first day she had met Sharif. But that had been on a familiar vehicle with tools she had used before, and on a hard surface, while this was sand.

As soon as she raised the Jeep on the jack, it slipped and thumped down hard, narrowly missing her feet. Hands on her hips, she considered her options. It was a beautiful night. The sky was clear, the moon was bright, and she had parked in the shadow of a dune where she was sheltered from the wind. It was lovely—if she could just calm down. And, maybe she shouldn't have set out half cock with only the thought of seeing Emir/Sharif again in her head. But she was where she was, and had to get on with it.

She had never seen so many stars before, Britt realised, staring up. What a beautiful place this was. There was no pollution of any kind. A sea of stars and a crescent moon hung overhead. And there was no need for panic, she reasoned, turning back to the Jeep. She had water, fuel, and plenty of food. The GPS was up and running, and according to that she was only around fifteen miles away from the encampment. The best thing she could do was wait until the morning when she would try again to wedge the wheels and stop them slipping. As a sensible precaution, and because she didn't want Jazz to worry, she texted Sharif's sister: *Flat tyre. No prob. I'll sleep 4WD then change it am and head 2 camp.*

A reply came through almost immediately: *I hve yr coordinates. Do u hve flares? Help o—*

The screen blanked. She tried again. She shook the phone. She screamed obscenities at it. She banged it on her hand and screamed again. She tried switching it off and rebooting it.

It was dead.

So what had Jazz meant by that last message? Help was on its way? Or help off-road in the middle of the desert at night was out of the question?

Heaving a breath, she stared up, and blinked to find the sky completely changed. Half was as beautiful as the last time she looked, which was just a few seconds ago, while the other half was sullen black. A prickle of unease crept down her spine. And then a spear of fright when she heard something…the rushing sound of a ferocious wind. It was like all her childhood nightmares come at once. Something monstrous was on its way—

what, she couldn't tell. The only certainty was that it was getting closer all the time.

Her hands were trembling, Britt realised as she buttoned the phone inside the breast pocket of her shirt. Not much fazed her, but now she wished she had a travelling companion who knew the desert. Sharif would know. This was his home territory. Sharif would know what to do.

The elders had invited him to eat with them around the campfire. The respect they showed him was an honour he treasured. Here in the wildest reaches of the desert he might be their leader, but he could always learn from his people and this was a priceless opportunity for him to speak to them about their concerns. They talked on long into the night, and by the time he left them he was glad he could bring them good news about renewed investment and the realisation of their plans. He didn't go straight back to his tent. He felt restless for no good reason other than the fact that the palm trees seemed unnaturally still to him, as if they were waiting for something to happen. He had a keen weather nose and tonight the signs weren't good. He stared up into the clear sky, knowing things could change in a few moments in the desert.

He paced the perimeter of the camp and found himself back at the harem tent where Britt would be housed when she arrived. His mood lightened as he dipped his head to take a look inside. He could just imagine her outraged reaction when she realised where she was staying. He hoped she would at least linger long enough to enjoy some of the delights. The surroundings were so sumptuous it seemed incredible that they could exist outside a maharaja's palace, let alone in the desert. Like his own pavilion, hers had been cleverly positioned around the underground stream. The water was clear and warm and provided a natural bathing pool in a discreetly closed off section of the tent. Solid gold drinking vessels glinted in the mellow light of brass lanterns, while priceless woven rugs felt rich and soft beneath his sandaled feet. The heady scent of incense pervaded everything, but it was the light that was so special. The candles inside the lanterns washed the space with a golden light that gave the impression of a golden room. It certainly wasn't a place to hold a business meeting. This tent was dedicated entirely to pleasure, a fact he doubted Britt would miss. He tried not to smile, but there was everything here a sheikh of old might have required to woo his mistress. The older women of the tribe had heard a female visitor was expected and had approached him with their plan; he couldn't resist.

Would their Leader's friend be pleased to experience some of the very special beauty treatments that had been passed down through generations?

Absolutely, he had replied.

Would she enjoy being dressed in one of the precious vintage robes they had lovingly cleaned and preserved; a robe they carried with them in their treasure chest on their endless travels across the desert?

He didn't even have to think about that one. He was sure she would.

And the food...Would she enjoy their food? Could they make her sweetmeats like the old days; the sort of thing with which the sheikhs of old would tempt their... their...

Their friends? he had supplied helpfully.

'I'm sure she would,' he had confirmed. He had yet to meet a woman who would refuse a decent piece of cake.

His acceptance of all these treats for Britt had put smiles into many eyes, and that was all he cared about.

Their final assurance was that if their sheikh would honour them by entertaining a female visitor in their camp, they would ensure he did so in the old way.

Perfect, he had said, having some idea of what that might entail. He couldn't think of anything his visitor would enjoy more, he had told them.

Imagining Britt's expression when she was treated as a prized concubine was thanks enough, but there was a serious element to this mischief. The older women guided the young, and it was imperative to have them onside so they embraced all the educational opportunities he was opening up to women under his rule. Kareshi would be different—better for all in the future, and on that he was determined.

The peal of the phone distracted him from these musings. It was his sister Jasmina, calling him to say that Britt had decided not to wait until the morning to travel into the desert, but with all the confidence of someone who believed she knew the wilderness—every wilderness—Britt had insisted on setting out by road, just a couple of hours ago.

Issuing a clipped goodbye to his sister, he went into action. No wonder he'd felt apprehensive. Here with tents erected against the shield of a rock face people were safe, but if the weather worsened out in the desert, and Britt was lost—

All thoughts of Britt in connection with the harem tent shot from his mind. She knew *her* wilderness, not his!

Striding back into the centre of the camp, he was already securing the headdress called a *howlis* around his face and calling for his horse, while his faithful people, seeing that he meant to leave the camp, were gathering round him. They had no time to lose. If a sandstorm was coming, as he suspected, and Britt was alone on treacherously shifting sand, all the technology of a modern age wouldn't save her.

Calling for a camel to carry the equipment he might need, he strode on towards the corral where they were saddling his stallion. Springing onto its back, he took the lead rope from the camel and lashed it to his tack. He wasted no time riding away from the safety of the camp at the head of his small troupe, into what Britt would imagine was the most beautiful and tranquil starlit night.

Where had the romance of the desert gone? She had almost been blasted away in a gust of sand in a last attempt to change the tyre. What was it about her and tyres? And this wasn't fun, Britt concluded, raking her hand across the back of her neck. Sand was getting everywhere. Eddies of sand were exfoliating her face while more sand was slipping through the smallest gap in her clothes.

Did she even stand a chance of being found? Britt wondered, gazing around, really frightened now. Visibility was shrinking to nothing as the wind blew the sand about, and the sky was black. She couldn't even see the stars. She had never felt more alone, or so scared. Battling against the wind, she made it to the back of the Jeep and locked her tools away. Shielding her eyes, she opened the driver's door and launched herself inside. The wind was so strong now it was lifting the Jeep and threatening to turn it over. She had never wished for Sharif more. She couldn't care less about their differences right now. She just wanted him to find her.

She had checked the weather before setting out, but could never have imagined how quickly it could change. There was nothing to see out of the window. She changed her mind about Sharif finding her. It was too dangerous. She didn't want him to risk his life. But she just couldn't sit here, helpless, waiting to buried, or worse… She had to remain visible. If the Jeep were buried she would never be found.

There was a warning triangle in the boot—and a spade handle. And the very last thing she needed right now was a bra. She could make a warning symbol. And there were flares in the boot.

Downside? She would just have to brave the storm again.

The wind was screaming louder than ever and the sand was like an industrial rasp. But she was determined—determined to live, determined to be seen, and determined to do everything in her power to ensure that happened.

Once she had managed to get everything out of the back of the Jeep, securing the warning triangle to the handle of the spade with her bra was the easy part. Finding a way to fix it onto the Jeep wasn't quite so simple. She settled for wedging it into the bull bars, and now she had to get back into the shelter of the vehicle as quickly as she could or she would be buried where she stood.

Closing the door, she relished the relative silence, and, turning everything off, she resigned herself to the darkness. She had to conserve power. There was nothing more she could do for now but wait out the storm and hope that when it passed over she would still be alive and could dig her way out.

CHAPTER TEN

DISMOUNTING, SHARIF COVERED his horse's face with a cloth so he could lead it forward. Attached to his horse by a rope was the camel loaded down with equipment. The camel's eyelashes provided the ultimate in protection against the sand, while he had to be content with narrowing his eyes and staring through the smallest slit in his *howlis*. His men had gathered round him, and so long as he could see the compass he was happy he could lead them to Britt's Jeep. When all else failed magnetic north saved the day.

As they struggled on against the wind he sent up silent thanks that Jasmina had been able to text him Britt's last coordinates, but a shaft of dread pierced him when he wondered if he would reach her in time.

He *had* to reach her in time. He had intended to test Britt as she had tested him in Skavanga when she arrived in the desert, but not like this.

What would she think when he appeared out of the storm? That a bandit was coming for her? It only occurred to him now that she had never seen him in robes before. That seemed so unimportant. He just prayed he would find her alive. He had left the encampment battening down for what was essentially a siege. Custom dictated the tribe pitch their tents at the foot of a rock face to allow for situations like a sandstorm. The best he could hope for where Britt was concerned was that she'd had enough sense to stay inside her vehicle. She wouldn't stand a cat in hell's chance outside.

The scream of the wind was unbearable. It seemed never ending. It was as if a living creature were trying every way it knew how to reach her inside the Jeep. Curled up defensively with her hands over her ears, she knew that the electrics were shot and the phone was useless. The sand was already halfway up the window. How much longer could she survive this?

What a rotten end, she thought, grimacing at the preposterous situation in which she found herself. She could only feel sorry for the person who had to drag her lifeless body out of the Jeep—

She Would Not Die Like This.

Throwing her weight against the driver's door, she tried to force it open, but it wouldn't budge—and even if it had, where was she going?

Flares were her last hope, Britt reasoned. She had no idea now if it was day or night, and before she could set off a flare she needed something to break the window.

Climbing over the seats, she found everything she needed. The vehicle was well equipped for a trek in the desert. There were flares and work gloves, safety goggles, a hard hat, and heavy-duty cutters, as well as a torch and a first-aid kit. Perfect. She was in business.

He had almost given up hope when he saw the flare flickering dimly in the distance. Adrenalin shot through his veins, giving him the strength of ten men and the resolve of ten more. He urged his weary animals on and his brave men followed close behind him. He couldn't be sure it was Britt who had let off the flare until he saw the warning triangle she had fixed onto the top of a spade handle with a bra, and then he smiled. Britt was ever resourceful, and any thought he might have had about her setting off into the desert at night without a proper guide seemed irrelevant as he forged on, his lungs almost exploding as he strained against the wind. Nothing could keep him back. Sharp grains of sand whirled around him, but the robes protected him and the *howlis* did its job. Just thinking about Britt and how frightened she must be made his discomfort irrelevant. His only goal was to reach her—to save her—to protect her—to somehow get her back to the camp—

If she were still alive.

He prayed that she was, as he had never prayed before. He prayed that he could save her as he sprang down from his horse, and started to work his way around the buried Jeep. The vehicle was buried far deeper than he had imagined, and, worse, he couldn't hear anything against the wind. Was she alive in there? With not a moment to lose he yanked at the windscreen with his men helping him. Britt had already loosened it to let off the flare—

And then he saw her. Alive! Though clearly unconscious. She had managed to free the rubber seal on the glass and had forced it out far enough to let off the flare, but in doing so had allowed sand to pour in and fill the vacuum, almost burying her. He waved his men back. It wasn't safe. Too many of them and the Jeep might sink further into the sand or even turn over on top of them, killing his men and burying Britt. He would not let anyone else take the risk of pulling her out.

He dug with his hands, and with the spade he had freed from the bull bars of the Jeep. He was desperate to reach her—frantic to save her. It was the longest hour of his life, and also his greatest triumph when he finally sliced through Britt's seat belt with the *khanjar* at his side, and lifted her to safety in his arms.

To say she was bewildered would be putting it mildly. She had woken up to find herself transported from a nightmare into a Hollywood blockbuster, complete with sumptuous Arabian tent and billowing curtains, with not a grain of sand to be seen. Added to which, there were women clustering around what passed for her bed. Dressed in rainbow hues, they looked amazing with their flowing gowns and veils. At the moment they were trying to explain to her in a series of mimes that she had been barely conscious when their leader carried her into the camp. At which point it seemed they had to pause and sigh.

She must have been asleep for ages, Britt realised, staring around. The bed on which she was reclining was covered in the most deliciously scented cushions, and was enclosed by billowing white curtains, which the women had drawn back. She felt panicked for a moment as she tried to take it all in. Was this the encampment Jazz had told her about—or was she somewhere else?

And then it all came flooding back. The terrifying storm— The sickening fear of being buried alive. Her desperate attempt to set off a flare, not knowing if anyone would see it—

Someone had. She squeezed out a croak on a throat that felt as if it had been sandpapered, and the women couldn't understand a word she said, anyway, so the identity of her rescuer was destined to remain a mystery.

The women were instantly sympathetic and rushed to bring her drinks laced with honey, and one of them indicated an outdoor spa, which Britt could now see was situated at the far end of the tent.

And what a tent! It was more of a pavilion, large and lavishly furnished with colourful hangings and jewel-coloured rugs covering the floor. Burnished brass lanterns decorated with intricate piercing cast a soft golden glow, while the roof was gathered up in the centre and had been used to display a number of antique artefacts. She was still staring up in wonder when the women distracted her. They had brought basins of cool water and soft towels, and, however much she indicated that she could sort herself out, they insisted on looking after her and bathing all her scratches and battle wounds.

It was a nice feeling to be made so welcome. Thanking the women with smiles, she drank their potions and accepted some of their tiny cakes, but she couldn't lie here all day like some out-of-work concubine. She was badly in need of a sugar rush to kick her into gear. And those little cakes were delicious. She was contentedly munching when she suddenly remembered Jazz. Sharif's sister must be out of her mind with worry—

Thank goodness she had a signal. She quickly stabbed in: *safe @camp. sorry if i frightnd u! lost a day sleeping! talk soon* J

A message came back before she had chance to put the phone away: *relieved ur safe. Look fwd 2 mtg u b4 long!* ☺

Britt smiled as she put the phone down again. She looked forward to that meeting too. And now the women were miming that she should come with them. She hesitated until they pointed towards the spa again, but the thought of bathing in clean, warm water was irresistible.

She was a little concerned when the women started giggling as they drew her out of the bed and across the rugs towards the bathing pool, especially when they started giggling and then sighing in turn. Were they preparing her for the sheikh? Was she to be served up on a magic carpet with a honey bun in her mouth?

Not if she could help it.

She asked with gestures: 'Did your sheikh bring me here?' She tried to draw a picture with her hands of a man who was very tall and robed, which was about all she could remember of her rescuer—that and his black horse. She must have kept slipping into unconsciousness when he brought her back here. 'The Black Sheikh?' she suggested, gazing around the golden tent, hoping to find something black to pounce on. 'His Majesty, Sheikh Sharif al Kareshi…?'

The women looked at her blankly, and then she had an idea. She sighed theatrically as they had done.

Exclaiming with delight, they smiled back, nudging each other as they exchanged giggles and glances.

She left a pause to allow for more sighs while her heart thundered a blistering tattoo. So it was very likely that Emir or Sharif, or whatever he was calling himself these days, had rescued her. Her brain still wasn't functioning properly, but it seemed preferable to be in the tent of someone she knew, even if that someone was the Black Sheikh.

She allowed the women to lead her into the bathing pool. She didn't want to offend them and what was the harm of refreshing herself so she could start the new day and explore the camp? The women were keen to pamper her outer self with unguents, and her inner self with fresh juice. One of them played a stringed instrument softly in the background, while the scent rising from the warm spring water was divine. Relaxing back in the clear, warm water, she indulged in a little dream in which she was a young woman lost in the desert who had been rescued by a handsome sheikh—

She *was* a young woman lost in the desert who had been rescued by a handsome sheikh!

And however she felt about him, the first thing she had to do was thank Sharif for saving her life. She had to forget all about who had done what to whom, or how angry she had been about his people's interference in the business, and start with that. She could always tell him what she thought about his high-handed ways afterwards. Sharif had risked his life to save her. Compared to that, her pride counted for nothing.

The women interrupted her thoughts, bringing her towels, which they held out like a screen so she could climb from the pool with her modesty intact. They quickly wrapped her, head to foot, and she noticed now that the sleeping area had already been straightened, and enough food to feed an army had been laid out.

Was she expecting visitors?

One visitor?

Her heart thundered at the thought.

As they led her towards the bed of cushions she caught sight of the lavender sky, tinged with the lambent gold of a dying sun. The women insisted she must lie down on a sheet while they massaged her skin with soothing emollients to ease the discomfort of all the cuts and bruises she had sustained during her ordeal. The scent of the cream was amazing and she couldn't ever remember being indulged to this extent. Being prepared for the sheikh indeed…

She was a little concerned when, instead of her own clothes, the women showed her an exquisite gown in flowing silk. 'Where are my clothes?' she mimed.

One of the women mimed back that Britt's clothes were still wet after having been washed.

Ah… 'Thank you.'

She bit her lip, wondering how the rest of this night would play out, but then decided she would just have to throw herself into the spirit of generosity being lavished on her by these wonderful people. And the gown was beautiful, though it had clearly been designed for someone far more glamorous than she was. In ice blue silk, it was as fine as gossamer, and was intricately decorated with silver thread. It was the sort of robe she could easily imagine a sheikh's mistress wearing. But as there were no alternatives on offer…

One of the women brought in a full-length mirror so Britt could see the finished effect. The transformation was complete when they draped a matching veil over her hair and drew the wisp of chiffon across her face, securing it with a jewelled clip. She stood for a moment staring at her reflection in amazement. At least she fitted in with the surroundings now, and for perhaps the first time ever she felt different about herself and didn't long for jeans or suits. She had never worn anything so exotic, or believed she had the potential to project an air of mystery. I could be the Sheikh's diamond, she thought with amusement.

She tensed as something changed in the tent…a rustle of cloth…a hint of spice…

She turned to find the women backing away from her.

And then she saw the man. Silhouetted with his back against the light, he was tall and powerful and dressed in black robes. A black headdress covered half his face, but she would have known him anywhere, and her body yearned for her lover before her mind had chance to make a reasoned choice.

'So it was you…' Even as she spoke she realised how foolish that must sound.

His Majesty, Sheikh Sharif al Kareshi, the man known to the world as the Black Sheikh, and known to her before today as Emir, loosened his headdress. Every thought of thanking him for saving her life, or condemning him for walking out on her without explaining why, faded into insignificance as their stares met and held.

'Thank you for saving my life,' she managed on a throat that felt as tight as a drum.

She was mad with herself. The very last thing she had intended when she first set out on this adventure was to be in awe of Sharif. She had come to rail at him, to demand answers, but now she was lost for words and all that seemed to matter was that they were together again. 'You risked your life for me—'

'I'm glad to see you up and well,' he said, ignoring this. Removing his headdress fully, he cast the yards of heavy black silk aside.

'I am very well, thanks to you.'

Dark eyes surveyed her keenly. 'Do you have everything you need?'

As Sharif continued to hold her stare her throat seemed to close again. She felt horribly exposed in the flowing, flimsy gown and smoothed her hands self-consciously down the front of it.

'Relax, Britt. We're the same people we were in Ska-vanga.'

Were they? Just hearing his voice in these surroundings seemed so surreal.

'You've had a terrible ordeal,' he pointed out. 'Why don't you make the most of this break?'

'Your Majesty, I—'

'Please—' he stopped her with the hint of a smile '—call me Sharif.' He paused, and then added, 'Of course, if you prefer, you can call me Emir.'

The laughter in his eyes was quickly shuttered when she drew herself up. 'There are many things I'd like to call you, but Emir isn't one of them,' she assured him. 'This might not be the time to air grievances—after all, you did save my life—'

'But you're getting heated,' he guessed.

'I am curious to know why you found it necessary to deceive me.'

'I conduct my business discreetly.'

'Discretion's one thing—deception's another.'

'I never deceived you, Britt.'

'You didn't explain fully, did you? I still don't know why you left in such a hurry.'

'Things moved faster than I expected, and I wasn't in a position to explain them to you.'

'The Black Sheikh is held back? By whom?'

'I'm afraid I can't tell you that.'

'Isn't that taking loyalty too far?'

'Loyalty can never be taken too far,' Sharif assured her. 'Just be satisfied that your sisters were not involved and that everything I've done has been for the sake of the company—'

'And your deal.'

'Obviously, the consortium is a consideration.'

'I bet,' she muttered. 'I'm glad you find this amusing,' she added, seeing his eyes glinting.

'I don't find it in the least amusing. When a company defaults on a payment risking the livelihoods of families who have worked for Skavanga Mining for generations, I did what I could to put things right as fast as I could, and while you were still in the air flying to Kareshi to see me.'

She knew this was true and blushed furiously beneath her veil. She was used to being on top of things—at work and with her sisters. She was also used to being told all the facts, and yet Sharif was holding something back for the sake of loyalty, he had implied—but loyalty to whom?

It hardly mattered. He wasn't going to tell her, Britt realised with frustration. 'Okay, I'm sorry. Maybe I did overreact, but it still doesn't explain why you couldn't have said something before you left the cabin.'

'I'm not in the habit of explaining myself to anyone.'

'You don't say,' she murmured.

'It's just how I am, Britt.'

'Accountable to no one,' she guessed.

The Black Sheikh dipped his head.

'Well, whatever you've done, or haven't done, thank you—' She was on the point of thanking him again for saving her life, when Sharif held up his hands.

'Enough, Britt. You don't have to say it again.' Glancing towards the curtained sleeping area, he added, 'And you should take a rest.'

Her mind had been safely distracted from the sumptuous sleeping area up to now, and she stepped back, unconsciously putting some distance between herself and Sharif. She needed time to get her thoughts in order. Better do something mundane, she decided, drawing back the curtains. Task completed, she turned to face Sharif, who made her the traditional Kareshi greeting, touching his chest, his mouth and finally his brow.

'It means peace,' he said dryly. 'And you really don't have to stand in my presence, Britt.'

'Maybe I prefer to—'

'And maybe, as I suggested, you should take a rest.'

Now was not the time to argue, so she compromised, sitting primly on the very edge of one of the deep, silk-satin cushion. 'I apologise for putting you to so much trouble,' she said, gesturing around. 'I had no idea a storm was coming, or that it would close in so quickly. I did do my research—'

'But you couldn't wait to come and see me a moment longer?' he suggested dryly.

'It wasn't like that.' It was like that, Britt admitted silently.

She watched warily as Sharif prowled around the sleeping area, his prayer beads clicking at his waist in a constant reminder that she was well out of her comfort zone here. She stiffened when he came to sit with her—on the opposite side of the cushions, true, but close enough to set her heart racing. And while she was dressed in this flimsy gown, a style that was so alien to her in every way, she couldn't help feeling vulnerable.

'The women gave me this gown to wear while they were washing my clothes,' she felt bound to explain.

'Very nice,' he said.

Very nice was an understatement. The gown was gloriously feminine and designed to seduce—which she could have done without right now. Her sisters would laugh if they could see her. Britt Skavanga backed into a corner, and now lost for words.

CHAPTER ELEVEN

'I AM GLAD you have been given everything you need,' Sharif said, glancing round the sumptuous pavilion.

'Everything except my clothes.' Britt was becoming increasingly aware that the gown the women had dressed her in was almost sheer. 'I believe my own clothes will soon be here.' She had no idea when they were arriving, or even if they would ever arrive. She only knew that her body burned beneath Sharif's stare as his lazy gaze roved over the diaphanous gown—she had never longed for a business suit more.

Sharif's lips tugged a little at one corner as if he knew this.

Turning away, she ground her teeth with frustration at the position she found herself in. Of course she was grateful to Sharif for saving her, but being housed in the harem at the sheikh's pleasure was hardly her recreation of choice—

She had to calm down and accept that a lot had happened in the past twenty-four hours and she was emotionally overwrought. The temptation to do exactly as Sharif suggested—relax and recline, as he was doing—was overwhelming, but with his familiar, intoxicating scent washing over her—amber, patchouli and sandalwood, combined with riding leather and clean, warm man—she couldn't be answerable for her own actions if she did that. Business was her safest option. 'If I'd seen a photograph of you before you came to Skavanga, I wouldn't have mixed you up with Emir and maybe we could have avoided this mess, and then you wouldn't have been forced to risk your life riding through the storm to find me.'

'I don't make a habit of issuing photographs with business letters. And as it happens, I did see a photograph of you, but it wasn't a true representation.'

'What do you mean?' she asked.

'I mean the photograph showed one woman when you are clearly someone very different.'

'In what way?'

Sharif smiled faintly. 'You're far more complex than your photograph suggests.'

She pulled a face beneath the veil, remembering the posed shot. She had been wearing a stiff suit and an even stiffer expression. She hated having her photograph taken, but had been forced to endure that one for the sake of the company journal.

'Well, I haven't seen a single photograph of you in the press,' she countered.

'Really?' Sharif pretended concern. 'I must remedy that situation immediately.'

'And now you're mocking me,' she protested.

He shrugged. 'I thought we agreed to call a truce. But if there's nothing more you need—'

'Nothing. Thank you,' she said stiffly as he turned to go. Her body, of course, had other ideas. If she could just keep her attention fixed on something apart from Sharif's massive shoulders beneath his flowing black robe, or those strong tanned hands that had given her so much pleasure—

'I'll leave you to rest,' he said, getting up.

'Thank you.'

And now she was disappointed?

He was leaving while her body was on fire for him.

Yes. And she should be glad, Britt told herself firmly. A heavy pulse might be throbbing between her legs, but this man was not Emir—and Emir had been dangerous enough—this man was a regal and unknowable stranger, who could pluck her heart from her chest and trample it underfoot while she was still in an erotic daze. She stood too and, lifting her chin, she directed a firm stare into his eyes. Even that was a mistake. Lust ripped through her, along with the desire to mean something to this man. For a few heady seconds she could think of nothing but being held by him, kissed by him, and then, thankfully, she pulled herself round.

'This is wonderful accommodation and I can't thank you enough for all you've done for me. Your people are so very kind. They let me sleep, they tended to my wounds, they—'

'They bathed you?' Sharif supplied.

The way his mouth kicked up at one corner sent such a vivid flash of sensation ripping through her she almost forgot what she was going to say. 'I...I had a bath,' she admitted in a shaking voice that was not Britt Skavanga at all.

'They spoiled you with soothing emollients, and that's so bad?'

'They did,' she agreed, wishing he would look anywhere but into her eyes with that dark, mocking stare. And every time she nodded her head, tiny jewels tinkled in a most alluring way—she could do without that too!

'The women have dressed you for their sheikh,' Sharif observed.

And now she couldn't tell if he was joking or not. Her chest was heaving with pent-up passion thanks to her desire deep down to be angry—to have a go. *He can't talk to you like that!* She wasn't a canapé to whet his appetite—a canapé carefully prepared and presented to the sheikh for him to sample, then either swallow or discard.

'They have prepared you well,' Sharif said, showing not the slightest flicker of remorse for this outrageous statement. 'Would you rather they had brought you something ugly to wear?' he demanded when her body language gave away her indignation. 'Moral outrage doesn't suit you, Britt,' he went on in the same mocking drawl. 'It's far too late for that. But I must say the gown suits you. That shade of blue is very good with your eyes…'

So why wasn't he looking into her eyes?

Straightening up, she wished her jeans and top were dry so she could bring an end to this nonsense.

And yet…

And yet she was secretly glad that Sharif's gaze was so appreciative. Why else would she stand so straight? Why were her lips parted, and why was she licking them with the tip of her tongue? And why, for all that was logical, was she thrusting her breasts out when her nipples were so painfully erect?

'It's a very pretty dress,' she agreed coolly.

'Our desert fashions suit you,' Sharif agreed.

She shivered involuntarily as he reached out to run the tip of his forefinger down the very edge of her veil. There was still a good distance between them, but no distance could be enough.

And now her thoughts were all erotic. Perhaps Sharif saving her life had added a primitive edge to her feelings towards him. The desire to thank him fully, and in the most obvious way, was growing like a madness inside her. Thank goodness for the veil.

'I'll call back later—when you've had a rest,' he said.

She watched without saying anything as Sharif drew the gauzy curtains around the sleeping area. She reminded herself firmly that she might be dressed like the sugar plum fairy, but she had no intention of dancing to his tune. She was here for business, and business alone. She had to be wary of this man. Sharif had spoken to her sisters without telling her. He had taken mineral samples from the mine, and yet he hadn't had the courtesy to share the results of the tests with her. This might be a seductive setting, she reasoned angrily as the curtains around the sleeping area blew in the warm, early evening breeze, and Sharif was certainly the most seductive of men, but, grateful or not, she still wanted answers, and he had a lot of explaining to do.

He was back? She tried not to care—not to show she cared. She must have failed miserably as breath shot out of her when he dragged her close. This was not even the civilised businessman—this was the master of the desert. There was no conversation between them, no debate. And there was quite definitely no thought of business in Sharif's eyes. There was just the determination to master her and share her pleasure.

'Well, Britt?' Sharif demanded, holding her in front of him. 'You had enough to say for yourself in Skavanga. You must have something to say to me now. Why did you really come to Kareshi when you could have wired your test results and I could have done the same? When you could have laid out your complaints against me in an email message without making this trip?'

Why had she listened to Eva? Eva was hot-headed

and impetuous, and was always getting herself into some sort of trouble, while Britt was cool and meticulous, and never allowed emotion to get in the way.

How had this happened?

'Why are you really here?' Sharif pressed mercilessly, smiling grimly down into her eyes. 'What do you need from me?'

He knew very well what she needed from him. She needed his hands on her body, and his eyes staring deep into hers. She needed his scent and heat to invade her senses, and his body to master hers—

His senses raged as Britt pressed her body against his. This was his woman. This was the woman he remembered and desired. This was the fierce, driven woman he had first met in Skavanga, the woman who took what she wanted and rarely thought about it afterwards.

'Sharif?'

Could it be possible that he didn't want that part of her? he marvelled as Britt spoke his name. Did that wildcat bring out the worst in him? Loosening his grip on her arms, he let her go. When he had first entered the pavilion he had seen the tender heart of a woman he had started to know in Skavanga—the vulnerable woman inside the brittle shell—the woman he had walked away from before he could cause her any hurt.

'Sharif, what is it?'

He stared down and saw the disappointment in her eyes. And why shouldn't Britt expect the worst when he had walked out on her before?

Everything had been so cut and dried in the past. He'd fed his urges and moved on, but he had never met a woman like this before. He had never realised a woman could come to mean so much to him. The feelings raging inside him when he had found Britt alive were impossible to describe. All he could think was: she was still in the world, and thank God for it. But he had a country to rule and endless responsibilities. Did he make love to her now, as he so badly wanted to do, or did he save her by turning and walking away?

'It's not like you to hesitate,' she murmured.

'And it's not like you to be so meek and mild,' he countered with an ironic smile. 'What shall we do about this role reversal?'

'You're asking me?' she queried, starting to smile.

He closed his eyes, allowing her scent and warmth and strength to curl around his core, clearing his mind. He prided himself on his self-control, but there was will power and then there was denial, and he wasn't in the mood to deny either of them tonight. He wanted Britt. She wanted him. It was that simple. Above all, he was a sensualist who never ate merely because he was hungry, but only when the food was at its best. Britt thought she knew everything about men and sex and satisfaction, but it would be his pleasure to teach her just how wrong she was.

'What are you doing?' she said as he led her back through the billowing curtains.

Settling himself on the silken cushions, he raised a hand and beckoned to her.

'What the hell do you think this is?' she said.

'This is a harem,' he said with a shrug. 'And if you don't like that idea you might want to step out of the light.'

'I'll stand where I like,' she fired back.

His shrugged again as if to say that was okay with him. It was. There wasn't one inch of Britt that wasn't beautifully displayed or made even more enticing by the fact that she was wearing such an ethereal gown and standing in front of the light. He let the silence hang for a while, and then, almost as if it were an afterthought, he said, 'When the women brought that gown, didn't they bring you any underwear?'

Her gasp of outrage must have been heard clearly in Skavanga.

'You are totally unscrupulous,' she exclaimed, wrapping the flimsy folds around her.

'I meant no offence,' he said, having difficulty hiding his grin as he eased back on the cushions. 'I was merely admiring you—'

'Well, you can stop admiring me right now.'

'Are you sure about that?'

'Yes, I'm sure. I feel ridiculous—'

'You look lovely. Now, come over here.'

'You must be joking.'

'So stand there all night.'

'I won't have to,' she said confidently, 'because at some point you'll leave. At which time I will settle down to sleep on *my* bed.'

Britt looked magnificent when she was angry. Proud and strong, and finely bred, she reminded him of one of his prized Arabian ponies. And this was quite a compliment coming from him. Plus, a little teasing was in order. Hadn't she put him through trials by fire and ice in Skavanga? Britt had done everything she could think of to unsettle him while he was on her territory, but now the tables were turned she didn't like it. 'Come on,' he coaxed. 'You know you want to—'

'I know I don't,' she flashed. 'Just because you saved my life doesn't give you droit de seigneur!'

'Ah, so you're a virgin,' he said as if this were news to him. 'When did that happen?'

Her look would have felled most men. It suggested she would like to bring the curtains and even the roof down on his head. She was so sure he had styled himself on some sheikh of old, she couldn't imagine that beneath his robes he was the same man she had met in Skavanga. He should get on with proving that he was that man, but he was rather enjoying teasing her. Helping himself to some juice and a few grapes, he left Britt to draw back a curtain to scan the tent, no doubt searching for another seating area. She wouldn't find one, and he had no intention of going anywhere.

'There's nowhere else to sit,' she complained. 'Until you go,' she added pointedly.

He shrugged and carried on eating his grapes. 'Formal chairs are not required in the harem—so there is just this all-purpose sleeping, lounging, pleasuring area, where I'm currently reclining.'

'Don't remind me! I don't know what game you're playing, Sharif, but I'd like you to leave right now.'

'I'm not going anywhere. This is my camp, my pavilion, my country—and you,' he added with particular charm, 'are my guest.'

'I treated you better than this when you were my guest.'

He only had to raise a brow to remind Britt that she had treated him like a fool, and was surprised when he had turned the tables on her at the lake.

'I came to do business with you,' she protested, shifting her weight from foot to foot—doing anything rather than sit with him. 'If you had stuck around long enough for us to have a proper discussion in Skavanga, I wouldn't even be here at all.'

'So that's what this is about,' he said. 'It still hurts.'

'You bet it does.'

He had left at the right time and, though he wouldn't betray Tyr's part in the business, he wanted to reassure her. 'Well, I'm sorry,' he said. 'It seems I must learn to explain myself in future.'

'Damn right you should,' she said, crossing her arms. 'I'm just so glad you're here—and in one piece.'

'Thank you for reminding me,' she said wryly. 'You know I can't be angry with you now.'

They were both in the same difficult place. They wanted each other. They both understood that if you laid the bare facts on the table theirs was not a sensible match. The only mistake that either of them had made was wanting more than sex out of this relationship.

'So maybe we can be friends?' she said as if reading his mind. 'Except in business, of course,' she added quickly.

'Maybe,' he said. 'Maybe business too.'

After a long pause, she said, 'So, tell me about the tent. Do your people always provide you with a harem tent—just in case?'

'In case of what?' he prompted, frowning.

'I think you know what I mean—'

'Come and sit with me so I can tell you about it. Or don't you trust yourself to sit close to me?' he added, curbing his smile.

She chose a spot as far away from him as possible. Again he was reminded of his finely bred Arabian ponies, whose trust must be earned. Britt was as suspicious as any of them. 'Remember the deer,' he said.

'The deer?' she queried.

'Remember the deer in Skavanga and how relaxed we were as we watched them?'

'And then you'll tell me about the tent?'

'And then I'll tell you about the tent,' he promised.

She hardly knew Sharif, and they sat in silence until—yes, she remembered the deer—yes, she began to relax.

'This pavilion is a priceless artefact,' he said. 'Everything you see around you has been carefully preserved—and not just for years, but for centuries by the people in this camp and by their ancestors. It is a treasure beyond price.'

'Go on,' she said, leaning forward.

'You may have guessed from the lack of seating that this pleasure tent is devoted to pursuits that allow a man or a woman to take their ease. Pleasure wasn't a one-sided affair for the sheikhs. Many women asked to be considered for the position of concubine.'

'More fool them.'

'What makes you say that?' he asked as she removed the veil from her hair.

She huffed. 'Because I would never be seduced so easily.'

'Really?'

'Really.'

'It's a shame your nipples are such a dead giveaway.'

She looked down quickly and, after blushing furiously, she had to laugh.

'Shall I go on?'

'Please…'

'After yet another day of struggles beneath the merciless sun,' he declaimed as if standing in an auditorium, 'fighting off invaders—hunting for food—the sheikh would return…'

'Drum roll?'

He laughed. 'If you like.'

'How many women did he return to?'

'At least a football team,' he teased. 'Maybe more.'

'Sheikhs must have been pretty fit back then.'

'Are you suggesting I'm not?'

She met his eyes and smiled and he thought how attractive she was, and how overwhelmingly glad he would always be that he'd found her in time to save her. He went on with his storytelling. 'Or, maybe there could be just one special woman. If she pleased the sheikh one woman would be enough.'

'Lucky her!' Britt exclaimed. 'Until the sheikh decides to increase his collection of doting females, I presume?'

She amused him. And he liked combative Britt every bit as much as her softer self. 'Your imagination is a miraculous thing, Britt Skavanga.'

'Just as well since it allows me to anticipate trouble.'

'So, what's the difference between my story and the way you have treated men in the past? You think of yourself as independent, don't you? You're a woman who does as she pleases?'

'You bet I am.'

'No one forced any of the sheikh's women to enter the harem. They did so entirely of their own accord.'

'And no doubt considered it an honour,' she agreed, flashing him an ironic look.

'But surely you agree that a woman is entitled to the same privileges as a man?'

'Of course I do.'

Where was this leading? Britt wondered. Why did she feel as if Sharif was backing her into a corner? Perhaps it was his manner. He was way too relaxed.

'So if you agree,' he said with all the silky assurance of the desert lion she thought him, 'can you give me a single reason why you shouldn't take your pleasure in the sheikh's pavilion…like a man?'

Her mouth opened and closed again. The only time

she was ever lost for words was with Sharif, Britt realised with frustration. He was as shrewd as he was distractingly amusing, and was altogether aware of how skilfully he had backed her into that tight little corner. He was in fact a pitiless seducer who knew very well that, where he might have failed to impress her with the fantasy of the harem tent, with its billowing curtains and silken cushions, or even the rather seductive clothes they were both wearing, he could very quickly succeed with fact. She had always been an ardent believer in fact.

CHAPTER TWELVE

SHE COULD HARDLY believe that Sharif had just given her a licence to enjoy him in a room specifically created for that purpose. Crazy. But not without its attraction, Britt realised, feeling her body's eager responses. But she would be cautious. She had heard things about Kareshi. And she liked to be in control. What if she didn't like some of these pleasures Sharif was hinting at? Her gaze darted round. She started to notice things she hadn't seen before. They might be ancient artefacts, as Sharif described them, but they were clearly used for pleasure.

She drew in a sharp, guilty breath hearing him laugh softly. 'Where are you now, Britt?' he said.

Caught out while exploring Planet Erotica, she thought. 'I'm in a very interesting tent—I can see that now.'

'Very interesting indeed,' Sharif agreed mildly, and he made no move to come any closer. 'So I have laid you bare at last, Britt Skavanga?'

'Meaning?' she demanded, clutching the edges of her robe together.

'Have I challenged your stand only to find it has been erected on dangerously shifting sand?' Sharif queried with a dangerous glint in his eyes. 'I've offered you the freedom of the harem—the opportunity to take your pleasure like a man—and yet you are hesitating?'

'Maybe you're not as irresistible as you think.'

'And maybe you're not being entirely truthful,' he said. 'What do you see around you, Britt? What do your prejudices lead you to suppose? Do you think that women were brought here by force? Do you look around and see a prison? I look around and see a golden room of pleasure.'

'That's because you're a sensualist and I'm a modern woman who's got more sense.'

'So quick sex in a corner is enough for you?'

'I deplore this sort of thing.'

The corner of Sharif's mouth kicked up. 'You're such a liar, Britt. You have an enquiring mind, and even now you're wondering—'

'Wondering what?'

'Exactly,' he said. 'You don't know.'

'That's no answer to that.'

'Other than to say, you're wondering if there can be pleasure even greater than the pleasure we have already shared. Why don't you find out? Why don't you throw your prejudices away? Why don't you open your mind to possibility and to things we *modern-thinking* people may not have discovered if they hadn't been treasured and preserved by tribes like this.'

'There can't be much that hasn't been discovered yet,' she said, gasping as she snatched her hand away when Sharif touched it.

'Did you feel that?' he said.

Feel it? He had barely touched her and her senses had exploded.

'And this,' he murmured, lightly brushing the back of her neck.

Her shoulders lifted as she gave a shaky gasp. 'What is that? The sensation's incredible. What's happening to me?'

'This is happening to you.' Sharif explained, gesturing towards the golden dish of cream the women had used to massage her skin. 'This so-called magic potion has been passed down through the generations. Not magic,' he said, 'just a particular blend of herbs. Still…'

They had a magical effect, Britt silently supplied. The scratches she had acquired during her ordeal in the desert had already vanished, she realised, studying her skin. She shivered involuntarily as Sharif's hand continued its lazy exploration of the back of her neck, moving through her hair, until she could do no more than close her eyes and bask in the most incredible sensation.

'They put lotion on your scalp as well as on your body, and that lotion is designed to increase sensation wherever it touches.'

And they touched practically every part of her, she remembered, though the women had taken great care to preserve her modesty. She looked at Sharif, and saw the amusement in his eyes. So he thought he'd won again.

She stood abruptly, and became hopelessly entangled in her gown.

'I've heard of veils being used as silken restraints and even as blindfolds,' Sharif remarked dryly, 'but why would you need those when you can tie yourself in knots without help from anyone? Here—let me help you…'

She had no alternative but to rest still as Sharif set about freeing her.

She wasn't prepared for him being so gentle with her, or for her own yearning to receive more of this care. She wanted him—she had always wanted him.

She was still a little tense when he unwound the fine

silk chiffon gown—exposing her breasts, her nipples, her belly, her thighs, with just a wisp of fabric covering the rest of her. She concentrated on sensation, glad that Sharif was in no rush. Everything he did was calculated to soothe and please her. He took time preparing her, which she loved. She loved his lack of haste, and his thoroughness, and knew she could happily enjoy this for hours. Sharif's hands were such delicate instruments of pleasure, and so very knowing where she was concerned.

'And now the rest of you,' he said in a tone of voice that was a husky sedative.

Each application of cream brought her to a higher level of arousal and awareness, so that when he slipped a cushion beneath her hips, she understood for the first time what they were for, and applauded their invention. And when he dipped his hands in the bowl of cream a second time, warming it first between his palms...

And when he touched her...

'Good?' he murmured.

'Do you really need me to answer that?'

And at last he touched her where she was aching for him to touch, but his attention was almost clinical in its brevity.

'Not yet,' he soothed when she groaned in complaint.

He sat back, and she heard him washing his hands in the bowl of scented water and then drying his hands on a cloth. 'You need time to appreciate sensation, and I'm going to give you time, Britt.'

She sucked in a shocked breath. Words failed her. Being on the ball in the office was very different from being...on the sheikh's silken cushions.

'Why confine yourself to once or twice a night?' Sharif said, his eyes alive with laughter.

She didn't know whether to be outraged or in for the journey. When would she ever get another chance like this, for goodness' sake? And with Sharif's dark gaze drawing her ever deeper into his erotic world, and the knowing curve of his mouth reassuring her, there was only one reality for her, and that was Sharif.

'And now you have a job to do,' he said, breaking the dangerous spell. Removing the cushions, he carefully eased her legs down.

'What?' she said, wondering if this was the moment to admit to herself that she would walk on hot coals if that was what it took to have Sharif touch her again.

She followed his gaze to the dish of cream.

Desert robes were intended to come off with the least amount of trouble, Britt discovered as she loosened the laces on the front of Sharif's robe. As it dropped away to reveal his magnificent chest she realised that she might have found the sight of such brute force intimidating had she not known that Sharif was subtle rather than harsh and, above all, blessed with remarkable self-control.

She was glad when he turned on his stomach and stretched out. She wasn't sure she was ready for the whole of naked Sharif just yet. This warrior of the desert was a giant of a man with a formidable physique. Using leisurely strokes, she massaged every part of him, though had to stop herself paying too much attention to his buttocks. They might be the most perfect buttocks she had ever seen on a man, buttocks to mould with your hands—to sink your teeth in—but there was only so much cream to spare, she reflected wryly as he turned. 'Did I say you could move?'

'Continue,' he murmured, settling onto his back.

Okay, so she could do this—and with Sharif watching, if she had to. Hadn't they both seen each other naked in the snow? And was she going to turn her back on Sharif's challenge? Because that was what this was. She had acted big-time girl-around-town, and now he'd called her bluff as she'd called his at the ice lake. He'd come through that with flying colours—flying them high and proud.

How could she ever forget?

She took her time scooping up more cream in her hands and spent ages warming it until she really couldn't put off what had to be done any longer. She began with his chest, loving the sensation as she spread the cream across his warm, firm flesh. She moved on down his arms, right to his fingertips where she spent quite a lot of time lavishing care and attention on hands that were capable of dealing the most extreme pleasure—and gasped with shock when Sharif captured her hands and guided them down. They exchanged a look: his challenging and hers defiant.

He won.

Thank goodness.

Sharif had creamed her intimately and she would do the same for him...

Maybe they both won.

She took her time to make certain that every thick, pulsing inch of him was liberally coated with the cream. She was breathless with excitement at the thought of having all of that inside her—

'So, Britt,' he said, distracting her momentarily. 'You're beginning to see the benefit in delay.'

'And what if I am?' she said carelessly.

'Don't pretend with me,' Sharif warned, stretching out, totally unconcerned by his nudity.

As well he might be, she thought, admiring him in silence.

'So what do you think of my golden room of pleasure?' he demanded.

'Not bad,' she agreed. She'd come across perks in business before, but none like this.

'So you like it?' he said with amusement.

'It's fascinating,' was as far as she was prepared to commit. 'Okay, so it's fabulous,' she admitted when he gave her a look.

'But?' he queried.

'It's got such a vibe of forbidden pleasure—how can anyone be here without feeling guilty?'

'Do you feel guilty?'

Actually, no. The cream was beginning to do its work. 'It's just that this is the sort of place where anything could happen...'

'What are you getting at, Britt?'

Her throat tightened. 'I'd like to hear about all the possibilities,' she said.

And so Sharif told her about the various uses of the hard and soft cushions, and the feathers she had been wondering about. She blushed at his forthright description.

'What about your sauna in Skavanga?' Sharif countered, seeing her reaction to his explanation. 'What about your birch twig switches?'

'They are used for health reasons—to get the blood flowing faster.'

She wasn't going to ask any more questions, because she wasn't sure she was ready to hear Sharif's answers.

'Ice and fire,' he murmured, staring at her.

They held that stare for the longest time while decisions were being made by both of them. Finally, she knelt in front of him, and, reaching up, cupped his face in her hands. That thanks she had intended to give him for saving her life was well overdue. Leaning forward, she kissed him gently on the lips.

Sharif's lips were warm and firm. They could curve with humour or press down in a firm line. Both she loved, but now *she* wanted to both tempt and seduce. She increased the pressure and teased his lips apart with his tongue, but just as she began kissing him more deeply Sharif swung her beneath him and pinned her down.

'All that trouble I've gone to with you, Britt Skavanga,' he complained, smiling against her mouth, 'and all you really want is this—'

She let out a shocked cry as Sharif lodged one powerful leg between her thighs, allowing her to feel just how much he wanted it too.

'All you want is the romance of the desert and the sheikh taking you. Admit it,' he said.

'You are impossible.'

'And you are incredible,' he murmured, drawing her into his arms.

'I do want you,' she admitted, still reluctant to give any ground.

'Well, isn't that convenient?' Sharif murmured. 'Because I want you too.'

This teasing was all the more intense because she knew where it was leading. She knew Sharif wouldn't pull back, and nor would she. Somehow her legs opened wider for him, and somehow she was pulling her knees back and pressing her thighs apart and he was testing her for readiness, and catching inside her—

And she was moving her hips to capture more of him, only to discover that the cream had most definitely done its work. One final thrust of her hips and she claimed him completely. When Sharif took her firmly to the hilt, she lost control immediately. She might have called his name. She might have called out anything. She only knew that when the sensation started to subside he took her over the edge again and again.

They were insatiable. No thrust was too deep or too firm, no pace too fast, or too deliciously slow. Her cries of pleasure encouraged Sharif and he made her greedy for more. He never seemed to tire. He never seemed to tire of drawing out her pleasure, either, and each time was more powerful than the last, until finally she must have passed out from exhaustion.

'Welcome to my world, Britt Skavanga,' was the last thing she heard him say before drifting contentedly off to sleep.

CHAPTER THIRTEEN

HE WATCHED BRITT sleeping, knowing he had been searching for a woman like this all his life. *And now he'd found her, he couldn't have her?* Britt would never agree to be his mistress. And when he married—

When he married?

Yes, Sharif's thoughts where Britt was concerned were every bit as strong as that. Selfishly, he hoped she felt the same way about him. But he had always believed when he married it should be for political reasons, for the good of his country. He'd never been much interested before. His council had pressed him into giving advantageous matches consideration, but he'd never had an appetite for the task. He wanted a woman who excited him—a woman like Britt.

Warm certainty rushed through him as he brushed a strand of hair away from Britt's still-flushed face. He would find a way. The Black Sheikh could always find a way. He would never ask Britt to give up her independence. No one knew better than he that privilege came with a price, and that price was freedom to do as he pleased, but with a woman like Britt anything was possible.

Or, was it? Britt was exceptional and could do great things in life. She deserved the chance to choose her own path, while his was cast in stone. And then there was Skavanga Mining, and all the subterfuge with her brother...

He exhaled heavily as business and personal feelings collided. The consortium needed Britt's expertise in the mining industry as well as her people skills, but would she stay with the company when the consortium took over? She had been running the company up to now, so it would take some fine diplomacy on his part to keep Britt on board. Could he find something to soften the blow for her?

His dilemma was this: while he cared deeply for Britt, his loyalty could only be fixed in one direction, and his was firmly rooted in the consortium.

The phone flashing distracted him. It was Raffa to say he had been forced to move money into Skavanga Mining on the recommendation of their financial analysts. Britt could only see this as another plot, when in fact what Raffa had done had saved the company.

'Our money men are already swarming on Skavanga Mining, and we need you on the ground to reassure everyone that the changes don't mean catastrophe,' Raffa was saying.

'What about Tyr?' And the grand reunion he had been planning for Britt.

'Tyr can't be there—'

'What do you mean, Tyr can't be there?' He cursed viciously. Having Tyr in Skavanga in person would have softened the blow for Britt when she discovered Tyr's golden shares had swung the ownership of the company into the hands of the consortium. But now—how was he going to explain Tyr's absence without betraying Britt's brother as he had promised faithfully not to do?

He had to get back to Skavanga Mining right away to sort this out—and he could only do that without Britt's newly discovered emotions getting in the way, which meant returning to Skavanga without her. Thankfully, his jet was always fuelled. 'I'll be there in fourteen hours,' he said, ending the call.

Glancing at Britt, he knew there was no time to waste, and by the time he had woken her and explained as gently as he could about Tyr coming into the equation it could all be over in Skavanga. This was one emergency she would definitely want to be part of, but it was better if he prepared the ground first, and then sent the jet back for her.

She woke cautiously and her first thought was of Sharif. She didn't want to wake him as it was barely dawn. The first thin sliver of light was just beginning to show beneath the entrance to the tent. She stretched luxuriously, and, still half asleep, reached out to find him...

The empty space at her side required she open one eye. The initial bolt of surprise and disappointment was swiftly replaced by sound reasoning. He must have gone riding. It was dawn. It was quiet. It was the perfect time of day for riding. Groaning with contentment, she rolled over in the bed of soft silken cushions, and, clutching one, nestled her face into it, telling herself that it still held Sharif's faint, spicy scent. He'd held her safe through the night, and the pleasure they'd shared was indescribable. The closeness between them was real, and she was content, a state she couldn't claim very often. This encouraged her to dream that one day they might work side by side to create something special, something lasting, and not just for Skavanga, but for Kareshi too.

She stilled to listen to the muffled sounds of the encampment coming to life for another day. She could hear voices calling somewhere in the distance and cooking vessels clanking against each other, and then there was the gentle pop and fizz of the water in her bathing pool as it bubbled up from its warm underground source. Everything was designed to soothe the senses. Everything was in tune with her sleepy, mellow mood. She wasn't too warm or too cold, and her body felt deliciously well used by a man who made every day a special day, an exciting day.

Yes, she was a contented woman this morning, Britt reflected as she stretched languorously on her silken bed, and she couldn't ever remember feeling that way before—

She jumped up when the phone rang.

'Leila?'

She sat bolt upright. When her younger sister called it was invariably good news. Leila didn't have a grouchy bone in her body and had to be one of the easiest people in the world to get along with, and Britt was bursting to share the news about her growing closeness with Sharif. 'It's so good to hear your voice—'

An ominous silence followed.

'Leila, what's wrong?' Britt realised belatedly that if it was dawn in the desert it was the middle of the night in Skavanga.

'I don't know where to start.' Leila's voice was soft and hesitant. 'We're in trouble. You have to come home, Britt. We need you.'

'Who's in trouble? What's happened?' Britt pressed anxiously. Her stomach took a dive as she waited for Leila to answer.

'The company.'

As Leila's voice tailed away Britt glanced at the empty side of the bed. 'Don't worry, I'm coming straight home.'

She was already off the bed and launching herself through the curtains with her brain in gear. 'Hang on a minute, Leila.' Grabbing a couple of towels from the stack by the pool, she wrapped them around her and ran to the entrance of the pavilion where she saw a passing girl and beckoned her over. Smiling somehow, she gestured urgently for her clothes, before retreating back into the privacy of the pavilion.

'Okay, I'm here,' she reassured her sister. 'So tell me what's going on.'

The pause at the other end of the line might have been a few seconds, but it felt like for ever. 'Leila, please,' Britt prompted.

'The consortium has taken over the company,' Leila said flatly.

'*What?*' Britt reeled back. 'How could they do that? I had the confidence of all the small shareholders before I left.'

'But we don't have enough shares between us to stave off a takeover, and they've bought some more from somewhere.'

'The consortium's betrayed our trust?' Which meant Sharif had betrayed her. 'I don't believe it. You must have got it wrong—'

'I haven't got it wrong,' Leila insisted. 'Their money men are already here.'

'In the middle of the night?'

'It's that critical, apparently.'

While she was in a harem tent in the desert!

Had nothing changed? Had she learned nothing? Sharif had walked away from her again—distracted her again. And this time it all but destroyed her. For a moment she couldn't move, she couldn't think.

'I'm sorry if I shocked you,' Leila said.

Shock?

'I'm sorry that you've had to handle this on your

own,' Britt said, forcing her mind to focus. 'I'll be there just as soon as I can get a flight.'

She had been stupidly taken in, Britt realised. Sharif had betrayed her. By his own admission, nothing was signed off without the Black Sheikh's consent. He must have known about the share deals all along.

'There's one thing I don't get,' she said. 'How can the deal be done when the family holds the majority shareholding? You didn't sell out to him, did you?'

'Not us,' Leila said quietly.

'Who then?'

'Tyr…Tyr has always had more shares than we have. Don't you remember our grandmother leaving him the golden shares?'

Shock hit her again. Their grandmother had done something with the shares, Britt remembered, but she had been too young to take it in. 'Is Tyr with you? Is he there?' Suddenly all that mattered was seeing her brother again. Tyr had always made things right when they were little— Or was that just her blind optimism at work again? She couldn't trust her own judgement these days.

'No. Tyr's not here, Britt. Neither Eva or I has seen him. The only thing I can tell you is that Tyr and the Black Sheikh are the main forces behind this deal,' Leila explained, hammering another nail into the coffin of Britt's misguided dream. 'The sheikh has got his lawyers and accountants swarming all over everything.'

'He didn't waste any time,' Britt said numbly. While she had been in bed with Sharif, he had been seeing the deal through and speaking to her brother. This had to be the ultimate betrayal, and was why Sharif hadn't been at her side when she woke this morning. He was already on his way to Skavanga. What could she say to Leila— to either of her sisters? Sorry would never cover it.

'It's such a shock,' Leila was saying. 'We still can't believe this is happening.'

There was no point regretting things that couldn't be changed, Britt reasoned as she switched quickly to reassuring her sister. 'Don't worry about any of this, Leila. Just stay out of it until I get back. I'll handle it.'

'What about you, Britt?'

'What about me?' She forced a laugh. 'Let me go and pack my case so I can come home.'

She had been betrayed by her feelings, Britt realized as she ended the call. She was to blame for this, no one else. And now it was up to her to make things right.

She spun around as the tent flap opened, but her hammering heart could take a break. It was the smiling women with her clothes. And whatever type of man their master was, these women had been nothing but kind to her. Greeting them warmly, she explained with mime that although she would love to spend more time with them, she really couldn't today.

It was as if she had never been away, Britt reflected as the cab brought her into the city from the airport. But had the streets always been so grey? The pavements were packed with ice and with low grey cloud overhead everything seemed greyer than ever. After the desert, she reasoned. This was her home and she loved it whatever the climate might be. This harsh land was where she had been born and bred to fight and she wasn't about to turn tail and run just because the odds were against her. Nothing much frightened her, she reasoned as the cab slowed down outside the offices of Skavanga Mining. Only her heart had ever let her down.

Her sisters were waiting for her just inside the glass entrance doors. Whatever the circumstances she was always thrilled to see them. Knowing there was no time to lose, she had come straight to the office from the airport with the intention of getting straight back in the saddle. Thank goodness she'd had a non-crease business suit and stockings in her carry-on bag. She needed all the armour she could lay her hands on.

'Together we stand,' Britt confirmed when they finally pulled apart from their hug.

'Thank God you're here,' Eva said grimly. 'We're overrun by strangers. We have never needed to show a united force more.'

'Not strangers—people from the consortium,' Leila reassured her. 'But he's here,' Leila added gently. 'I just thought you should know.'

'Tyr's here?' Britt's face dropped as she realised from Leila's expression who her sister was talking about. 'You mean Sharif is here,' she said softly. Better she face him now than later, Britt determined, leading her sisters past Reception towards the stairs. 'With his troops,' Eva added as a warning.

Britt made no response. Troops or not, it made no difference to her. She would face him just the same. She could only hope her heart stopped pounding when she did so.

How the hell had he got here ahead of her?

His private jet, of course—

Get your head together fast, Britt ordered herself fiercely. She was strong. She could do this. She had to do this. She had always protected her sisters and the people who worked for Skavanga Mining. That was her role in life.

Without it what was she?

Nothing had changed, she told herself fiercely.

'Don't worry,' she said. 'I can handle this.'

Eva was right. The first-floor lobby was bustling with people Britt didn't know. Sharif's people—the consortium's people—Sharif had moved them in already. Her temper flared at the thought. But she had to keep her cool. She had lost the initiative the moment she allowed her emotions to come into play, and that must never happen again.

So, Tyr definitely wasn't coming. Sharif had tried to persuade him, but now he put his phone away. Their conversation had been typical of the type Sharif had come to expect from the man who was a latter day Robin Hood. If a worthy cause had to be fought Tyr would drop everything and swing into action. He couldn't blame the man, not with everything that was going on in Tyr's life, but his presence here today would have softened the blow for Britt, whose arrival was imminent. Britt's campaign to save the company was on track, but a happy reunion with the brother she hadn't seen for years was not on the cards. So now she would just be bewildered by what she would see as Tyr's betrayal and his.

He pulled away from the window when he saw Britt's cab arrive. However angry she was he had to keep her on board. Skavanga Mining needed her—

He needed her—

He would protect her from further distress the only way he knew how, which was to say nothing about Tyr, just as he had promised, and allow the blame to fall on the ruthless Black Sheikh instead. He would live up to his reputation. Better she hated him than she blamed Tyr for throwing in his lot with the consortium. Tyr had seen it as the only way to save the company in a hurry, and Tyr was right, though Sharif didn't expect Britt to be so understanding; and with Tyr and the other two men in the consortium tied up half a world away, it was up to him to handle the takeover. There had been time to leave a brief message for Britt with the women at the encampment, and he hoped she'd got it. If not he was in for a stormy ride.

'Britt.' He turned the instant she entered the room. His response to her was stronger than ever. She lit up the room—she lit up his life. She forced him to re-evaluate every decision he had ever made, and he always came to the same conclusion. He would never meet another woman like her, but from her expression he guessed she hated him now. 'Wait for me outside,' she told her sisters in a cold voice that confirmed his opinion.

'Are you sure?' the youngest asked anxiously.

'I'm sure,' Britt said without taking her eyes off him.

She looked magnificent—even better than he remembered. A little crumpled from the journey, maybe, but her bearing was unchanged, and that said everything about a woman who didn't know the meaning of defeat. He'd made a serious error leaving her behind in Kareshi. He should have brought her with him and to hell with the consequences. He should have known that Britt was more than ready for whatever she had to face. Her steely gaze at this moment was unflinching.

'Please sit down,' she said, and then she blinked as if remembering that he was in charge now.

'Thank you,' he said, making nothing of it.

Crossing to the boardroom table, he held out the chair for her and heard the slide of silk stockings as she sat down and crossed her legs. He was acutely aware of her scent, of her, but, despite all those highly feminine traits that she was unable to hide, she was ice.

He chose a chair across the table from her. They both

left the chairman's chair empty, though if Britt felt any
irony in sitting beneath portraits of her great-grandfather, who had hacked out a successful mining company
from the icy wastes with his bare hands, or the father
who had pretty much lost the business in half the time
it had taken his own father to build it up, she certainly
didn't show it. As far as Britt was concerned, it was
business as usual and she was in control.

Even now she felt a conflict inside her that shouldn't
exist. She had entered the room at the head of her sisters, determined to fight for them to the end. But seeing Sharif changed everything. It always did. The man
beneath that formal suit called to her soul, and made
her body crave his protective embrace.

So she might be stupid, but she wasn't a child, she told
herself impatiently. She was a grown woman, who had
learned how to run this company to the best of her ability
when it was thrust upon her, whether she wanted it or not.
And nothing had changed as far as she was concerned.
'I called the lawyers in on my way from the airport.'

'There's no point in rushing to do that,' he said,
'when I can fill you in.'

'I prefer to deal with professionals,' she said.

He couldn't blame Britt for the bite in her tone. The
way that things had worked out here meant she could
only feel betrayed by him.

She searched his eyes, and found nothing. What would
he find in hers? The same? If her eyes contained only
half the anger and contempt she felt for him, then that
would have to do for now. She could only hope the hurt
and bewilderment didn't show at all.

'I'd be interested to hear your account of things,' she
said coldly. 'I believe my brother's involved in some

way.' For the first time she saw Sharif hesitate. 'Did you think I wouldn't find out?'

'In an ideal world I would have liked things to take their course so you could get used to the idea of Tyr's involvement. As it was he stepped in to prevent a hostile takeover from any other quarter.'

'And this isn't a hostile takeover?'

'How can it be when Tyr is involved?'

'I wouldn't know since I haven't heard from him.'

'He is still on his travels.'

'So I believe. I heard he took the coward's way out—'

'No one calls your brother a coward in my hearing,' Sharif interrupted fiercely. 'Not even you, Britt.'

Sharif's frown was thunderous and though she opened her mouth to reply something stopped her.

'You realise Tyr and I go back a long way?'

'I don't know all his friends,' she said. 'I still don't,' she added acidly.

Ignoring her barb, Sharif explained that Kareshi was one of the countries Tyr had helped to independence.

'With his mercenaries?' she huffed scathingly.

He ignored this too. 'With your brother's backing I was able to protect my people and save them from tyrants who would have destroyed our country.' He fixed her with an unflinching stare. 'I will never hear a wrong word said against your brother.'

'I understand that from your perspective, my brother has done no wrong. Tyr knows how to help everyone except his own family—'

'You're so wrong,' Sharif cut in. 'And I'm going to tell you why. If Tyr had added his golden shares to those you and your sisters own, the company would still go down. Add those shares to the weight of the consortium and the funds we can provide—not some time in the

future, but right now—and you have real power. That's
what your brother's done. Tyr has stepped in to save,
not just you and your family, but the company and the
people who work here.'

'So why couldn't he tell me that himself?'

'It's up to Tyr to explain when he's ready.' Sharif
paused as if he would have liked to say something
more, but then he just said quietly, 'Tyr's braver than
you know.'

She felt as if she had been struck across the face.
There was no battle to fight here. It had already been
won.

'A glass of water?' Sharif enquired softly.

She passed an angry hand over her eyes, fighting for
composure. She felt sick and faint from all the shocks
her mind had been forced to accept. The structure of
the business had changed—Tyr was involved, but he
still wasn't coming home. And mixed into all this were
her feelings for this man. It was too much to take in
all at once.

Thrusting her chair back, she stood.

Sharif stood too. 'We want to keep you, Britt—'

'I need time—'

'The consortium could use your people skills as well
as the mining expertise you have. At least promise me
that you'll think about what I've said.'

'Ten minutes,' she flashed, turning from the table.
She had to get out of here—now.

*One foot in front of the other—how hard could that
be?*

That might be easy if she didn't know she had let everyone down. She allowed herself to become distracted
and everything had changed. The company might have
been thrust upon her, but she had given it all she'd got,

and had intended to continue doing so for the rest of her working life. So much for that.

Bracing her arms against the sink in the restroom, she hung her head. She couldn't bear to look at her reflection in the mirror. She couldn't bear to see the longing for Sharif in her eyes. Everything he'd said made sense. He wasn't even taking over and booting her out. They wanted her to stay on, he'd said. And she wanted Sharif in every way a woman could want a man. She wanted them to have a proper relationship that wasn't just founded on sex. She had run the gamut of emotions with him, and had learned from it, but this was the hardest lesson of all: the man they called the Black Sheikh would stop at nothing to achieve his goal—even recruiting Britt's long-lost brother, if that got him where he wanted to be. And Sharif didn't even want the part of her she wanted to give, he wanted her people skills. The only way she could survive knowing that was to revert to being the Britt who didn't feel anything.

Sluicing her face down in cold water, she reached for a towel and straightened up. Now she must face the cold man in the boardroom whom she loved more than life itself, and the only decision left for her to make was whether or not she could stay on here and work for Sharif.

She could stay on. She had to. She couldn't abandon the people who worked here, or her sisters. And if that meant her badly bruised heart took another battering, so what? She would just have to return it to its default setting of stone.

CHAPTER FOURTEEN

BRITT RETURNED TO the boardroom to find Sharif pacing. Caught unawares, he looked like a man with the weight of the world on his back. For the blink of an eye she felt sorry for him. Who shared the load with Sharif? When did he get time off? And then she remembered their time in the desert and her heart closed again.

'There is a problem,' he said, holding her stony gaze trapped in his.

'Oh?' She felt for the wall behind her as wasted emotions dragged her down. She could fix her mind all she liked on being tough and determined, and utterly sure about where she wanted this to go, but when she saw him—when she saw those concerns she couldn't know about furrowing his brow and drawing cruel lines down each side of his mouth—she wanted to reach out to him.

She wanted to help him, and, even more than that, she wanted to stand back to back with Sharif to solve every problem they came across, and she wanted him to feel the same way she did.

'I've had to make some changes to my plans.'

'Trouble in Kareshi?' she guessed.

'A troublesome relation who was banished from the kingdom has returned in my absence and is trying to rally support amongst the bullies who still remain. It's

a basic fight between a brighter modern future for all
and a return to the dark days of the past when a privileged few exploited the majority. I must return. I promised my people that they would never be at the mercy
of bullies again, and it's a promise I intend to keep.'

Sharif really did have the weight of the world on his
shoulders. 'What can I do?' Britt said. Whatever had
led them to this place was irrelevant compared to so
many lives in jeopardy.

'I need your agreement to stay on here. I need you
to do my job for me while I'm away. I need you to ease
the transition so that no one worries about change unnecessarily. Will you do that for me, Britt?'

Sharif needed her. The people here needed her. And
if he didn't need her in the way she had hoped he would,
she still couldn't turn her back on him, let alone turn
her back on the other people she cared about.

'I really need you to do this for me, Britt.'

Her heart hammered violently as Sharif came closer
to make his point, but he maintained some distance
between them, and she respected that. Her heart responded. Her soul responded. She could no more refuse this man than she could turn and walk away from
her duties here. But there was one thing she did have to
know. 'Am I doing this for you, or for the consortium?'

'You're doing it for yourself, and for your people,
Britt, and for what this company means to them. Hold
things together for me until I get back and we can get
this diamond project properly under way and then you'll
see the benefits for both our people.'

'How long will you be away?' The words were out
before she could stop them, and she hated herself for
asking, but then reassured herself that, as this concerned
business, she had to know.

'A month, no more, I promise you that.'

The tension grew and then she said, 'I noticed a lot of new people were here when I arrived. Will you introduce me?'

Sharif visibly relaxed. 'Thank you, Britt,' he said. 'The people you saw are people I trust. People I hope you will learn to trust. They moved in with the approval of your lawyers and with your own financial director alongside them to smooth the path—'

'Of your consortium's takeover of my family's company,' she said ruefully.

'Of our necessary intervention,' Sharif amended. 'I hope I can give you cause to change your mind,' he said when he saw her expression. 'This is going to be good for all of us, Britt—and you of all people must know there's no time to waste. Winter in the Arctic is just around the corner, which will make the preliminary drilling harder, if not impossible, so I need your firm answer now.'

'I'll stay,' she said quietly. 'Of course, I'll stay.'

How ironic it seemed that Sharif was battling to keep her on. He was right, though, she could handle anything the business threw at her, but when it came to her personal life she was useless. She had no self-belief, no courage, no practice in playing up to men, or making them see her as a woman who hurt and cared and loved and worried that she would never be good enough to deserve a family of her own to love, and a partner with whom she shared everything

'And when you come back?' she said.

'You can stay or not, as you please. You can still have an involvement in the company, but you could travel, if that's what you want to do. I have business interests in Kareshi that you are welcome to look over.'

A sop for her agreement, she thought. But a welcome one—if a little daunting for someone whose life had always revolved around Skavanga. 'I'd be like you then, always travelling.'

'And always returning home,' Sharif said with a shrug. 'What can I tell you, Britt? If you want responsibility there is no easy way. You should know that. You have to take everything that comes along.'

'And when Tyr comes home?'

'I'm not sure that your brother has any interest in the business—beyond saving it.'

She flushed at misjudging her brother when she should have known that Tyr would have all their best interests at heart.

'And now I've got a new contract of employment for you—'

'You anticipated my response.' But she went cold. Was she so easy to read? If she was, Sharif must know how hopelessly entangled her heart was with his.

Sharif gave nothing away as he uncapped his pen. 'Your lawyers have given it the once-over,' he explained. 'You can read their letter. I've got it here for you. I'll leave you in private for a few moments.'

She picked it up as Sharif shut the door behind him. Her nerves were all on edge as she scanned the contents of the letter. 'This is the best solution,' jumped out at her. So be it. She drew a steadying breath, knowing there wasn't time for personal feelings. There never had been time. She had consistently fooled herself about that where Sharif was concerned.

Walking to the door, she asked the first person she saw to witness her signature and two minutes later it was done. She issued a silent apology to her ancestors. This was no longer a family firm. She worked for the consortium now like everyone else at Skavanga Mining.

Sharif returned and saw her face. 'You haven't lost anything, Britt. You've only gained from this.'

That remained to be seen, she thought, remembering Sharif leaving her in Kareshi and again at the cabin.

'I left a message for you in Kareshi,' he said as if picking up on these thoughts. 'Didn't you get it? The women? Didn't they come to find you?' he added as she slowly shook her head.

And then she remembered the women trying to speak to her before she left. She'd been in too much of a hurry to spare the time for them. 'They did try to speak to me,' she admitted.

'But you didn't give them chance to explain?' Sharif guessed. 'Like you I never walk away from responsibility, Britt. You should know I would always get a message to you somehow.'

And he was actually paying her a compliment leaving Skavanga Mining in her care. It was a compliment she would gladly park in favour of hearing Sharif tell her that he couldn't envisage life without her—

How far must this self-delusion go before she finally got it into her head that whatever had happened between them in the past was over? Sharif had clearly moved on to the next phase of his life. Why couldn't she?

'Welcome on board, Britt.'

She stared at his outstretched hand, wondering if she dared touch it. She was actually afraid of what she might feel. She sought refuge as always in business. 'Is that it?' she said briskly, turning to go. 'I really should put my sisters out of their misery.'

'They already know what's going on.'

'You told them?'

'Like you, I didn't want them to worry, so I told them what was happening and sent them home.'

'You don't take any chances, do you, Sharif?' She

stared into the dark, unreadable eyes of the man who had briefly been her lover and who was now her boss.

'Never,' he confirmed.

A wave of emotion jolted her as she walked to the door. Sharif's voice stopped her. 'Don't leave like this,' he said.

She turned her face away from him, unwilling to meet his all-seeing stare. The last thing she wanted now was to break down in front of him. Sharif must be given no reason to think she wasn't tough enough to handle the assignment he had tasked her with.

'Britt,' he ground out, his mouth so close to her ear. 'Please. Listen to me—'

She tried to make a joke of it and almost managed to huff a laugh as she wrangled herself free. 'I think I've listened to you enough, don't you?'

'You don't get it, do you?' he said. 'I'm doing this for you—I rushed here for you—to save the company. This isn't just for the consortium. Yes, of course we'll benefit from it, but I wanted to save your company for you. Can't you see that? Why else would I leave my country when there's trouble brewing?'

'I don't know,' she said, shaking her head. 'Everything's happened so fast, I just don't know what to think. I only know I don't understand you.'

'I think you do. I think you understand me very well.'

She would not succumb to Sharif's dark charm. She would not weaken now. The urge to soften against him was overpowering, but if she did that she was lost. She might as well pack up her job and agree to be Sharif's mistress for as long as it amused the Black Sheikh. 'I need to go home and see my sisters.'

'You need to stay here with me,' Sharif argued.

She wanted his arms around her too badly to stay. She

still felt isolated and unsure of herself. She, who took pride in standing alone at the head of her troops, felt as if the ground had been pulled away from her feet today.

'Are you frightened of being alone with me, Britt?' Cupping her chin, Sharif made her look at him and she stared back. He was a warrior of the desert, a man who had fought to restore freedom to his country, and who could have brushed her aside and taken over Skavanga Mining without involving her.

So why hadn't he?

'I asked you a question, Britt? Why won't you answer me?'

Sharif's touch on her face was so seductive it would have been the easiest thing in the world to soften in his arms. 'I'm not frightened of you,' she said, speaking more to herself.

'Good,' he murmured. 'That's the last thing I want.'

But if he could know how frightened she was of the way she felt about him, he would surely count it as a victory. And the longer Sharif held her like this, close yet not too close, the more she longed for his warmth and his strength, and the clearer it became that, for the first time in her life, being Britt Skavanga, lone businesswoman, wasn't enough.

'I've got an idea,' Sharif said quietly as he released her.

'What?' she said cautiously.

'I'd like you the think about working in Kareshi as well as Skavanga— Don't look so shocked, Britt. We live in a small world—'

'It's not that.' Her heart had leapt at the thought, but she still doubted herself, doubted her capabilities, and wondered if Sharif was just saying this to make her feel better.

'It's not that—' Her heart had leapt at the thought, even as doubt crowded in that for some reason Sharif just wanted to make her feel better.

'I have always encouraged people to break down unnecessary barriers so they can broaden their horizons in every way. I'm keen to develop talent wherever I find it, and I'd like you to think about using your interpersonal skills more widely. I know you've always concentrated on Skavanga Mining in the past, and that's good, but while I'm away— Well, please just agree to think about what I've said—'

'I will,' she promised as Sharif moved towards the door.

'One month, Britt. I'll send the jet.'

Anything connected with Sharif was a whirlwind, Britt concluded, her head still reeling as he left the room. He ruled a country— He was a warrior. He was a lover, but no more than that. But Sharif had placed his trust in her, and had put her back in charge of Skavanga mining where she could protect the interests of the people she cared about.

A month, he'd said? She'd better get started.

He had to give her time, he reasoned. He would see Britt again soon—

A month—

He consoled himself with the thought that in between times he could sort out his country and his companies—

To hell with all of it!

Without Britt there was nothing. He'd known that on the flight when every mile he put between them was a mile too far. Without Britt there was no purpose to any of this. What was life for, if not to love and be loved?

CHAPTER FIFTEEN

A MONTH WAS a long time in business, and Britt was surprised at how many of the changes were good. With new blood came new ideas, along with fresh energy for everyone concerned to fire off. The combination of ice and fire seemed to be working well at Skavanga Mining. The Kareshis brought interesting solutions for deep shaft mining, while nothing fazed workers in Skavanga who were accustomed to dealing with extreme conditions on a daily basis. Drilling was already under way, and even Britt's sisters had been reassured by how well everyone was getting on, and how much care, time and money the consortium was putting into preserving the environment. They had always taken their lead from Britt where business was concerned and so when she explained Sharif's plan to them, they were all for her trip to Kareshi—though their teasing she could have done without.

'Oh, come off it,' Eva insisted in Britt's minimalist bedroom at the penthouse, where the sisters were helping Britt to pack in readiness for the arrival of Sharif's jet the following day. 'We've seen him now. Don't tell me you're not aching to see your desert sheikh again.'

Aching? If a month was a long time in business, it was infinity when it came to being parted from Sharif.

'He isn't *my* desert sheikh,' she said firmly, ignoring the glances her sisters exchanged. 'And, for your information, this is a business trip.'

'Hence the new underwear,' Leila remarked tongue in cheek.

Business trip?

Business trip, Britt told herself firmly as the limousine that had collected her from the steps of the royal flight, no less, slowed in front of the towering, heavily ornamented golden gates that led into the courtyard in front of Sheikh Sharif's residence in his capital city of Kareshi. She had read during the flight that the Black Sheikh's palace was a world heritage site, and was one of the most authentically restored medieval castles. To Britt it was simply overwhelming. The size of the place was incredible. It was, in fact, more like a fortified city contained within massive walls.

It was one month since she had last seen Sharif. One month in which to prepare herself for pennants flying from ancient battlements, alongside the hustle and bustle of a thriving modern city—but she could never be properly prepared, if only because the contrast was just too stark. And those contrasts existed in the Black Sheikh himself. Respectful of traditional values, Sharif was a forward-thinker, always planning the next improvement for his country.

Excitement wasn't enought to describe her feelings. There was also apprehension. Until she saw Sharif's expression when he saw her again, she couldn't relax. She was prepared for anything, and was already steeling her heart—the same heart that was hammering in her ears as she wondered if Sharif would be wearing his full and splendid regalia—the flowing black robes of the desert king? Or would he be wearing a sombre tailored suit to greet a director of what he had referred to in the press as his most exciting project yet?

Exhaling shakily, she hoped the problems he had referred to in Kareshi had been resolved, because she was bringing him good news from the mine. They were ahead of schedule and there was a lot to talk about. Ready for their first business meeting, she had changed into a modest dress and jacket in a conservative shade of beige on the plane.

Her heart bounced as the steps of the citadel came into view. Somewhere inside that gigantic building Sharif was waiting.

Not inside.

And not wearing black robes, either, she realised as the limousine drew to a halt.

Sharif was dressed for riding in breeches, polo shirt and boots...breeches that moulded his lower body with obscene attention to detail...

'Welcome to my home,' he said, opening the car door for her.

His face was hard to read. He was smiling, but it could easily have been a smile of welcome for a business associate, newly arrived in his country. Forget business—forget everything—her heart was going crazy. 'Thank you,' she said demurely, stepping out.

He was just so damn sexy she couldn't think of anything else to say. Her mind was closed to business, and her wayward body had tunnel vision and could only see one man—and that was the sexy man who knew just how to please her. There was only one swarthy, stubble-shaded face in her field of vision, and one head of unruly, thick black hair, one pair of keenly assessing eyes, one aquiline nose, one proud, smooth brow, one firm, sexy mouth—

Pull yourself together, Britt ordered herself firmly as Sharif indicated that she should mount the steps ahead of him.

There were guards in traditional robes with scimitars hanging at their sides standing sentry either side of the grand entrance doors and she felt overawed as she walked past them into the ancient citadel. Every breath she took seemed amplified and their footsteps sounded like pistol shots in the huge vaulted space. Everything was on a grand scale. It was an imposing marble-tiled hall with giant-sized stained-glass windows. There were sumptuous rugs in all the colours of the rainbow, and the beautifully ornamented furniture seemed to have been scaled for a race of giants. She felt like a mouse that had strayed into the lion's den. The arched ceiling above her head seemed to stretch away to the heavens, and she couldn't imagine who had built it, or how the monstrous stone pillars that supported it had been set in place.

Attendants bowed low as Sharif led her on. Even when he was dressed in riding gear, authority radiated from him. He was a natural leader without any affectation, and—

And she was going there again, Britt realised, reining her feelings in. Each time she saw Sharif she found something more to admire about him, yet his insular demeanor irritated the hell out of her too, even if she accepted that hiding his feelings must be an essential tool of kingship.

'Do you like it?' he said, catching her smile.

She jolted back to full attention, realising that Sharif had been watching her keenly the whole time. 'I think it's magnificent,' she said as a group of men in flowing robes with curving daggers in their belts and prayer beads clicking in their hands bowed low to Sharif.

A hint of cinnamon and some other exotic spices cut the air, a timely reminder of just how far away from home she was, and how they still had quite a few issues to address. She wondered if Sharif would hand her over to some underling soon, leaving their discussions until later. She almost hoped he would to give her chance to get used to this.

'What's amusing you?' he said.

'Just taking it all in,' she said honestly. 'I'm a historic building fanatic,' she admitted, thinking that a safe topic of conversation. 'And this is one of the best I've seen.'

'The main part of the citadel was built in the twelfth century—'

As he went on she realised that Sharif really did mean to be her tour guide. She had no complaints. He was an excellent teacher, as she knew only too well.

He took her into scented gardens while her heart yearned for him to a soundtrack of musical fountains.

'We have always had some of the greatest engineers in the world in Kareshi,' he explained.

And some of the greatest lovers too, she thought. And what else but love could this exquisite courtyard have been designed for? Everything spoke of romance—the intricate mosaic patterns on the floor, the songbirds carolling in the lemon trees, and the tinkling water features. Surely it was the most romantic place on earth?

And as such was completely wasted on her, Britt concluded, as Sharif indicated that they should move on. 'I'll have someone show you your room,' he said.

So that was it. Tour over. Her heart lurched on cue as he raked his wild, unruly hair into some semblance of order. He probably couldn't wait to pass her over to someone else.

'Freshen up and then meet me in ten,' he said.

Oh…

'Unless you're too tired after your journey?'

'I'm not tired.'

'Good. Put something casual on. Jeans—'

She held back on the salute as a group of women clothed in flowing gowns in a multitude of colours appeared out of nowhere. She turned to look over her shoulder as they ushered her away, but Sharif had already gone.

'These are your rooms,' an older woman, who seemed in charge of the rest, explained as Britt gazed around in wonder.

'All of them?' she murmured.

'All of them,' the smiling woman explained. 'My name is Zenub. If you need anything you only have to ask—or call me.' And when Britt looked surprised, she added, 'This is an ancient building, but we have a very modern sheikh. There is an internal telephone system. This room leads into your dressing room and bathroom,' she explained, opening an arched fretted door that might have been made of solid gold, for all Britt knew. The door was studded with gems that seemed real enough, and probably were, Britt concluded, since Sharif had explained that every original feature inside the citadel had been faithfully restored to its former glory.

She was excited to discover that she had her own inner courtyard, complete with fountain and songbirds. The scent from a cluster of orange trees decorated with fat, ripe fruit was incredible while the fretted walls and covered walkways kept everything cool. It was just the type of place to invite exploration—the type of place to linger and to dream. Perhaps it was just as well she didn't have time.

'There are clothes in the wardrobe, should you need them,' Zenub told her as she ushered the other women out. 'And your suitcase is over here,' she added, indicating a dressing room with yet another glorious display of fresh flowers on one of the low-lying, heavily decorated brass tables. 'Please don't hesitate to call me if you need anything else.'

Britt smiled. 'I will—thank you. And thank you for everything you've done to make me so welcome.'

Amazing didn't quite cover this, Britt reflected as the women left her alone in what amounted to the most fabulous apartment. Every item must have been a priceless treasure, and it was only when she walked into the bathroom and smiled that she saw Sharif's hand in the restoration. The bathroom was state of the art too. There were the high-quality towels on heated rails, as well as fabulous products lined up on the shelves. If the harem pavilion in the desert had been a place of pure pleasure, this was sheer indulgence. It was just a shame she didn't have time to indulge. Another time, she mused ruefully, stepping into the shower.

She showered down quickly and dried off. Tying back her hair, she thought, Sharif stipulated casual, so she tugged on her jeans. A simple white tee and sneakers completed the outfit. A slick of lip gloss and a spritz of scent later and she was ready—for anything, she told herself firmly, leaving the room.

Except for the sight of Sharif wearing a tight black top that sculpted his muscular arms to perfection, and snug-fitting jeans secured by a heavy-duty belt, holding heaven in its rightful place.

And why had she never noticed he had a tattoo before? *She'd been otherwise engaged, possibly?*

'Hello,' she managed lamely, while her thoughts ran crazy stupid wild.

'Britt.' He looked her over and seemed pleased. 'You fulfilled the brief.'

'Yes, I did, boss.' She raised her chin and met the dark, appraising stare with a challenging grin.

'Shall we?'

She glanced at the imposing doors, either side of which stood silent guards whose rich, jewel-coloured robes and headdresses reminded her that this was an exciting land full of rich variety and many surprises. But not half as many surprises as the man standing next to her, Britt suspected as they jogged down the steps together. She stopped at the bottom of the steps and did a double take. 'A motorbike?'

Sharif raised a sexy, inky brow. 'I take it you've seen one before?'

'Of course, but—'

'Helmet?'

'Thank you.' She buckled it on.

And yes, there were outriders. And yes, there was an armoured vehicle that might have contained anything from a rocket launcher to a mobile café, but it wouldn't have mattered, because none of the following posse could keep up with Sharif.

Riding a bike was hot without any additional inducements, like jean-clad sheikhs she had to cling to. Sharif was a great rider. She felt safe and yet in terrible danger—in the most thrilling way. By the time he stopped the big machine outside the university he could have had her on the street.

Fortunately, Sharif had more control than she had

and led her through the beautifully groomed grounds, explaining that he wanted to talk to her before he introduced Britt to the students.

'You've got another idea,' she guessed.

'You know me so well,' he said, his dark eyes glinting.

I wish, she thought as Sharif ruffled his hair. 'So, what's it about?'

'We've talked about this before, in a way,' he said, perching on a wall and drawing her down beside him. 'If you agree, I'd like you to start thinking about plans to bring our two countries together by arranging exchange trips between students.'

'Is that why you've brought me here?'

'That's one reason, yes. I want you to see where your diamonds are going.'

She couldn't pretend she wasn't excited. Her world had always revolved around Skavanga, but now Sharif was offering her more—so much more and her heart soared with hope.

'You're the best person for the job,' he said. 'You'll be reporting to me, of course—'

'Oh, of course.' She tried to keep it light.

'Don't mock,' he warned.

He touched her cheek as he said this, and stared deep into her eyes. It was impossible to feel nothing. Impossible, but she tried not to show it.

'Your first task is to work on a way for our people to learn about each other's culture.'

And now the dam finally burst and she laughed. 'Birch twig switches and harem tents? That should go down well with the students—'

'Britt—'

'I know. I'm sorry. I think it's a wonderful idea.' And

she could tell that it meant a lot to Sharif. This wasn't a whim on his part; this was a declaration of sorts—and maybe the only one she would ever get. But they were close. Deep down she knew this. And she wasn't fooling herself this time, because Sharif was sharing some of the things closest to his heart with her, and when he squeezed her hand and smiled into her eyes, she knew how much this meant to Sharif and was honoured to be a part of it.

'You would have to come back to Kareshi, of course,' he said, frowning.

'Of course,' she said thoughtfully.

'Once the changes have been implemented in Skavanga and everything has settled down here, I want you to tour our universities and colleges with me—art galleries, concert halls and museums. I want to share everything with you, Britt.'

'For the sake of the exchange scheme,' she clarified, still lacking something on the confidence front.

'Absolutely,' Sharif agreed. 'We have some fascinating exhibits in the museums. You might even recognise some of them.'

'But you don't expect me to explain those to students, I hope?'

'I don't think they need any explanation, do you?'

She stared into Sharif's laughing eyes, remembering everything in the fabulous pavilion where she had lost her heart. It had never occurred to her that Sharif might have lost his too.

Or was she just kidding herself again?

CHAPTER SIXTEEN

HE STOOD BACK to watch Britt, wanting to remember every single detail as she met and mingled with the students for the first time. He wished then that he had been less preoccupied and more open from the start, so he could have showered her with gifts and told her how he felt about her. But he had been like Britt—all duty, with every hour of every day filled. They had both changed. He had maybe changed most of all when he had discovered that a month away from Britt was like a lifetime. He'd realised then how much she meant to him and had concluded that it must never happen again.

He wondered now if he'd ever seen her truly relaxed before. Britt Skavanga unmasked and laughing was a wonderful creation. She genuinely loved people and would be wasted behind a desk in an office.

They ate together with a crowd of students who swarmed around Britt. He was almost jealous. Their table was the noisiest, but she still got up and went around every table in the refectory, introducing herself and explaining the scheme she was already cooking in her head. It was as if there had never been a misunderstanding between them, he thought as she glanced over to him and smiled as if wanting to reassure him that she was enjoying this. One of the students commented that Britt came from a cold country, but she had a warm heart.

Cheesy, but she'd warmed his heart. How long had he been in love with her? From that first crazy day, maybe? He just hadn't seen it for what it was. But one of the nice things about being a sheikh was that he could pretty much follow his instinct, and his instinct said, don't let this woman go. He had everything in a material sense a man could want, but nothing resonated without Britt. He saw things differently through her eyes. She made every experience richer. He wanted her in his life permanently and that meant not half a world away. He wanted them to do more than plan an exchange scheme or run a company. He was thinking on a much wider scale—a scale that would encompass both their countries. A life together was what he wanted. He knew that now, and that could only benefit the people who depended on them, and for the first time he thought he saw a way to do it.

'Are you ready to go?' he whispered to Britt discreetly.

'Not really,' she admitted with her usual honesty, gazing round at all the people she hadn't had chance to meet yet.

'You can come back,' he promised. 'Remember—I've asked you to run this project, so you're going to be seeing a lot of these people.'

'But—'

As he held her stare she saw with sudden clarity exactly what he was thinking. Her own eyes widened as his gaze dropped to her mouth.

They were never going to make it back to the citadel. He lost the outriders a few streets away from the university and the security van went off radar in a maze of side-turnings in the suburbs. Britt yelled to ask him what he was he doing when he pulled into a disused parking lot earmarked for development.

'What do you think?' he yelled back, skidding to a halt.

The scaffolding was up and a few walls were built, but that was it. More importantly, no one was working on the site today. Dismounting, he propped the bike on its stand and lifted Britt out of the saddle.

'Is this safe?' she demanded when he backed her against a wall.

'I thought you loved a bit of danger?'

'I do,' she said, already whimpering as he kissed her neck.

He couldn't wait. Neither could she. Pelvis to pelvis with pressure, waiting was impossible. Fingers flying, they ripped at each other's clothes. Blissful relief as Britt's legs locked around his waist and her small strong hands gripped his shoulders. Anything else was unimportant now. They were together. She was ready for him—more than. Penetration was fast and complete. There was a second's pause when they both closed their eyes to savour the moment, but from then on it was all sensation. He cupped her buttocks in his hands to prevent them scraping on the gritty wall, as he kissed her. He groaned and thrust deep, dipping his knees to gain a better angle. Britt was wild, just as he liked her. He wanted to shout out—let the world know how he felt about this woman— How he'd felt without her, which was empty, lost, useless— And how he felt now—exultant. Nothing could ever express his frustration at how long it had taken him to realise that if they wanted each other enough, they would find a way to be together. And that it had to happen here in a parking lot—

'Sharif?' she said.

She was giving him a worried look he'd seen before; he knew she couldn't hold on. 'Britt...'

He smiled against her mouth, loving the tension that always gripped her before release. And now it was a crazy ride, hands clawing, chests heaving, wild cries, until, finally, blessed release. The best. It wasn't just physical. This was heart and soul. Commitment. He was committed to this woman to the point where even the direction his future took would depend on what she said now.

'Marry me,' he said fiercely. 'Marry me and stay with me in Kareshi.'

'Yes,' she murmured groggily in a state of content- ment, resting heavily against him. '*What?*' she yelped, coming down to earth with a bump.

'Stay with me and be my queen.'

'You *are* joking?'

'No,' he said, brushing her hair back from her face. 'I can assure you I'm not joking.'

'You're a king, proposing marriage in a car lot when you've just had me up against the wall?'

'I'm a man asking a woman to marry me.'

'Aren't you being a little hasty?'

'Crazy things happen in car lots and this has been at the back of my mind for quite some time.'

'Only at the back,' she teased him as he helped her to sort out her clothes. And then she frowned. 'Are you really sure about this?'

'I'm not in the habit of making marriage proposals in car lots, or anywhere else, so, yes, I'm sure. But you're right—' Going down on one knee in the dirt, he asked the question again.

'You *are* sure,' she exclaimed. 'But how on earth will we make this work?'

'You and me can't solve this? Are you serious?'

'But—'

'But nothing,' he said. 'You can travel as I do. You can use the Internet. I don't have any trouble staying in touch.'

'And you run a country,' she mused.

'I'm only asking you to run my life.' He shrugged. 'How hard can that be?'

She gave him a crooked smile. 'I'd say that could be quite a challenge.'

'A challenge I hope you want to take on?' he said, holding her in front of him.

'Yes.'

'I'd be surprised if you'd said anything else,' he admitted, returning the grin as he brushed a kiss against her mouth.

'You arrogant—'

'Sheikhs are supposed to be arrogant,' he said, kissing her again. 'I'm only fulfilling my job description.'

'So I'd be staying here in Kareshi with you?'

'Living with me,' he corrected her. 'And running a very important project—with me, not for me. You'll be working for both our countries, alongside me. We'll be raising a family together, and you'll be my wife. But none of this will take place *here*, exactly. I did have somewhere a little better than a parking lot in mind.'

'What about the harem?'

'I'll tell them to go home.'

'I meant the tent.'

'We'll keep it for weekends. So? What's your answer, Britt?'

'I told you already. Yes. I accept your terms.'

'How about my love?'

'I accept that too—and most willingly,' she teased him, her eyes full of everything he wanted to see. 'I love you,' she shouted, making a flock of heavy-winged birds flap heavily up and away from the scaffolding. 'And I don't care who knows it.'

'And I love you too,' he said, and, drawing her into his arms, he kissed her again. 'I love you more than life itself, Britt Skavanga. Stay with me and help me build Kareshi into somewhere we can both be proud of. And I promise you that from now on there will be no secrets between us.'

But then she frowned again and asked the question he knew was coming.

'How can I ever leave Skavanga?'

'I'm not asking you to leave Skavanga. I'm asking you to be my wife, which will give you more freedom than you've ever dreamed of. You can work alongside me and raise a family. You can be a queen and a director of a company. You can head up charities and run my exchange programmes for me. You can recruit the brightest and the best of the students you've just met. I'm asking you to be my wife, the mother of my children, and my lover. The only restrictions will be those you impose on yourself, or that love imposes on you. You'll find a balance. I know it. And if you want more time—you've got it.'

They linked fingers as they walked back to Sharif's bike. They were close in every way. Her hand felt good in his. She felt good with this man. She felt safe. She felt warm inside. She felt complete.

EPILOGUE

'THERE'S JUST ONE thing missing,' Britt commented wistfully as her sister helped her to dress on her wedding day in her beautiful apartment at the citadel in Kareshi.

'Tyr,' Leila guessed as she lifted the cloud of cobweb-fine silk chiffon that would be attached to the sparkling diadem that would crown Britt's flowing golden hair.

'Have you heard anything? Has Sharif said anything to you about Tyr?' Eva demanded, her sharp tone mellowed somewhat by the hairpins she was holding in her mouth. 'After all, Tyr is a major player in the consortium now.'

'Nothing,' Britt admitted, turning to check her back view in the mirror. 'Sharif shares everything with me, but he won't share that. He says Tyr will return in his own good time, and that Tyr will explain his absence then, and that we must never think the worst of him, because Tyr is doing some wonderful work—'

'Righting wrongs everywhere but here,' Eva remarked.

'You know he's already done that—fighting with Sharif to free Kareshi. And I trust Sharif,' Britt said firmly. 'If he says Tyr will explain himself when he feels the time is right, then he will. And if Sharif has given his word to Tyr that he won't say anything, then he won't—not even to me.'

'So, I suppose we have to be satisfied with that,' Eva commented, standing back to admire her handiwork. 'And I must say those diamonds are fabulous.'

'I'm glad they distracted you,' Britt teased.

'Well, they would, wouldn't they?' Eva conceded. 'And this veil…'

'Eva, I do believe you're looking wistful,' Britt remarked with amusement as her sister reached for Britt's dress. 'Are you picturing yourself on your own wedding day?'

Eva sniffed. 'Don't be so ridiculous. There isn't a man alive I could be interested in.' Eva chose not to notice the look her sisters exchanged. 'Now, let's get this dress on you,' she said. 'The way Sharif runs you ragged with all those projects he's got you involved in, it will probably drop straight off you again.'

As Leila sighed even Eva was forced to give a pleased and surprised hum. 'Well… Who knew you could look so girlie?' she said with approval, standing back.

'Only a sister,' Britt muttered, throwing Eva a teasing fierce look while Leila tut-tutted at their exchange.

'Eva!' Leila complained where her two sisters settled down for a verbal sparring match. 'You can't get into a fight with Britt on her wedding day.'

'More's the pity,' Eva muttered, advancing with the veil.

'The dress fits like a dream,' Leila reassured Britt.

'Stand still, will you?' Eva ordered Britt. 'How am I supposed to fix this tiara to your head?'

'With a hammer and nails, in your present mood?' Britt suggested, exchanging a grin with Leila.

But Eva was right in one thing—the past six months

had been hectic. She had overseen so many exciting new schemes, as well as flying back to Skavanga to manage the ongoing work there. And as if that wasn't enough, she had insisted on having a hand in the organisation of her wedding at the citadel. Some people never knew when to relax the reins, Sharif had told her, with the type of smile that could distract her for quite a while. She wouldn't have it any other way, Britt reflected. Life had never been so rich, and when the baby came...

Tracing the outline of her stomach beneath the fairytale gown, she knew she would keep on working until Sharif tied her to the bed. Actually—

'Man alert,' Leila warned before Britt had chance to progress this delicious thought.

'Don't worry, I won't let him in,' Leila assured her.

'Stand back, I'll handle this,' Eva instructed her younger sister. Marching to the door, her red hair flying, Eva swung it open. 'Yes?'

There was silence for a moment and Britt turned to see who could possibly silence her combative middle sister.

'Ladies, please excuse me, but the bridegroom has asked me to deliver this gift to his beautiful bride.'

The voice was rich, dark chocolate, and even Britt could see that the man himself was just as tempting. Eva was still staring at him transfixed as Leila stepped forward to take the ruby red velvet box he was holding out.

'Thank you very much,' Britt said politely, taking another look at the man and then at Eva. Which one would blink first? she wondered.

'It is my pleasure,' he said, switching his attention back to Britt. 'Count Roman Quisvada at your service...'

He bowed? He bowed. 'And this is my sister, Leila,'

she said, remembering her manners. 'And Eva...' Who, of course, had to tip her stubborn little chin and glance meaningfully from the count to the door.

'I can see you're very busy,' the handsome Italian said, taking the hint, his dark eyes flashing with amusement. 'I hope to spend more time with you later.'

'Was he looking at me when he said that?' Eva demanded huffily, her cheeks an attractive shade of pink, Britt thought, as Eva closed the door behind the count with a flourish.

'There's no need to sound so peeved,' Leila pointed out. 'He's hot. And he's polite.'

'I do like a man who's polite in the bedroom,' Britt commented tongue in cheek.

'Wow, wow, wow,' Leila whispered as Britt opened the lid of the velvet box. 'And there's a note,' she added as the three Skavanga sisters stared awestruck at the blue-white diamond heart hanging from a finely worked platinum chain; the diamond flashing fire in all the colours of the rainbow.

Britt read the note while her sisters read over her shoulder: *I hope you enjoy wearing the first polished diamond to come from the Skavanga mine. It's as flawless as you are. Sharif.*

'Cheese-ee,' Eva commented. 'And he doesn't know you very well.'

Britt shook her head as the three sisters laughed.

When she walked down the red-carpeted steps towards him, the congregation in the grand ceremonial hall faded away, and there was only Britt— Beautiful Britt. His bride. But she was so much more than that and they were so much more together than they were apart.

'You look beautiful,' he murmured as her flame-haired sister and the young one, Leila, peeled away.

Now there were just the two of them he didn't dare to look at her or he'd carry her away and to hell with everyone. It took all he'd got to repeat the vows patiently and clearly when all the time his arms ached to hold her. Britt's darkening eyes said she felt the same, and as she held his gaze to tease him she knew how that would test him.

His control was definitely being severely tested, but that was one of the things he loved about Britt. She challenged him on every front and always had.

And long may it continue, he thought, teasing her back by staring fixedly ahead.

Sharif in heavy black silk robes perfumed with Sandalwood and edged with gold was a heady sight.

And he was her husband...

Her husband, Britt reflected, feeling a volcanic excitement rising inside her. Could she contain her lust? Sharif was refusing to look at her and it was only when they were declared man and wife that he finally turned.

Now she knew why he'd refused to look at her. The fire in his eyes was enough to melt her bones. How was she going to stand this? How was she going to sit through the wedding breakfast?

The food was delicious, but even that wasn't enough of a distraction. The setting was unparalleled, but nothing could take her mind off the main event. Candles flickered in golden sconces, casting a mellow glow over the jewel-coloured hangings, making golden plates and goblets flash as if they were on fire, while crystal glasses twinkled like fireflies dancing through the night. It was a voluptuous feast, prepared by world-renowned chefs, but she wondered if it would ever end, and was surprised when Sharif stood up.

'Ladies and gentlemen,' he began in the deep husky

voice Sharif could use to seduce to command. 'The evening is young, and I urge you to enjoy everything to the full. Thank you all for coming to help us celebrate this happiest of days, but now I must beg you to excuse us—'

She still didn't quite understand until Sharif whistled up his horse and held out his hand to her. His black stallion galloped into the hall. As *coup de théâtre* went, she had to admit this one was unparalleled. As their guests gasped the stallion skidded to a halt within inches of its master, and the next thing she knew Sharif was lifting her onto the saddle and holding her safely in front of him.

She gasped as the stallion reared, his silken mane flowing like liquid black diamonds, as his flashing ebony hooves clawed imperiously at the air.

The instant he touched down again, Sharif gave a command in the harsh tongue of Kareshi, and the horse took them galloping out of the hall into a starlit night, and a future that was sure to fulfil all their desires.

* * * * *

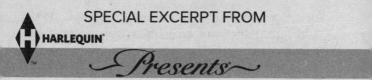
* * *

"I will not leave you again." It was a vow, accompanied by the slipping of the ring onto her finger.

Even though it was prompted by her pregnancy and the fact she now carried the heir to the Volyarus throne, the promise in his voice poured over the jagged edges of her heart with soothing warmth. The small weight of the metal band and diamonds on her finger was a source of more comfort than she would ever have believed possible.

She was not sure her heart would ever be whole again, but it did not have to hurt like it had for ten weeks.

"I won't leave you, either."

"I know." A small sound, almost a sigh, escaped his mouth. "Now we must convince your body that it still belongs to me."

"You have a very possessive side."

"This is nothing new."

"Actually, it kind of is." He'd shown indications of a possessive nature when they were dating, but he'd never been so primal about it before. "You're like a caveman."

His smile was predatory, his eyes burning with sensual intent. "You carry my child. It makes me feel *very* possessive, takes me back to the responses of my ancestors."

HPEXP0613-1

Air escaped her lungs in an unexpected whoosh. "Oh."

"I have read that some pregnant women desire sex more often than usual."

"I…" She wasn't sure what she felt in that department right now.

She always seemed to want him and could not imagine her hormones increasing that all too visceral need.

"However, I had not realized the pregnancy could impact the father in the same way." There was no mistaking his meaning.

Maks wanted her. And not in some casual, sex-as-physical-exercise way. The expression in his dark eyes said he wanted to devour her, the mother of his child, sexually.

Gillian shivered in response to that look.

"Cold?" he purred, pushing even closer. "Let me warm you."

"I'm not co—" But she wasn't allowed to finish the thought.

His mouth covered hers in a kiss that demanded full submission and reciprocation.

* * *

*Find out what happens when this powerful prince raises
the stakes of their marriage of convenience in
ONE NIGHT HEIR, out July 2013!*

*And don't miss the explosive second story,
PRINCE OF SECRETS, available August 2013.*

REQUEST YOUR FREE BOOKS!

◆HARLEQUIN *Presents*

PASSION GUARANTEED SEDUCTION

2 FREE NOVELS PLUS
2 FREE GIFTS!

YES! Please send me 2 FREE Harlequin Presents® novels and my 2 FREE gifts (gifts are worth about $10). After receiving them, if I don't wish to receive any more books, I can return the shipping statement marked "cancel." If I don't cancel, I will receive 6 brand-new novels every month and be billed just $4.30 per book in the U.S. or $4.99 per book in Canada. That's a saving of at least 14% off the cover price! It's quite a bargain! Shipping and handling is just 50¢ per book in the U.S. and 75¢ per book in Canada.* I understand that accepting the 2 free books and gifts places me under no obligation to buy anything. I can always return a shipment and cancel at any time. Even if I never buy another book, the two free books and gifts are mine to keep forever.

106/306 HDN FVRK

Name _____ (PLEASE PRINT)

Address _____ Apt. #

City _____ State/Prov. _____ Zip/Postal Code

Signature (if under 18, a parent or guardian must sign)

Mail to the **Harlequin® Reader Service:**
IN U.S.A.: P.O. Box 1867, Buffalo, NY 14240-1867
IN CANADA: P.O. Box 609, Fort Erie, Ontario L2A 5X3

**Are you a current subscriber to Harlequin Presents books
and want to receive the larger-print edition?
Call 1-800-873-8635 or visit www.ReaderService.com.**

* Terms and prices subject to change without notice. Prices do not include applicable taxes. Sales tax applicable in N.Y. Canadian residents will be charged applicable taxes. Offer not valid in Quebec. This offer is limited to one order per household. Not valid for current subscribers to Harlequin Presents books. All orders subject to credit approval. Credit or debit balances in a customer's account(s) may be offset by any other outstanding balance owed by or to the customer. Please allow 4 to 6 weeks for delivery. Offer available while quantities last.

Your Privacy—The Harlequin® Reader Service is committed to protecting your privacy. Our Privacy Policy is available online at www.ReaderService.com or upon request from the Harlequin Reader Service.

We make a portion of our mailing list available to reputable third parties that offer products we believe may interest you. If you prefer that we not exchange your name with third parties, or if you wish to clarify or modify your communication preferences, please visit us at www.ReaderService.com/consumerschoice or write to us at Harlequin Reader Service Preference Service, P.O. Box 9062, Buffalo, NY 14269. Include your complete name and address.

HPI3

#3153 HIS MOST EXQUISITE CONQUEST
The Legendary Finn Brothers
Emma Darcy

The vivacious Lucy Flippence has fallen prey to Michael Finn, whose reputation is legendary. She might be only a tick on his to-do list, but even the luxury lifestyle can't mask the feelings her secret has forced her to hide....

#3154 A SHADOW OF GUILT
Sicily's Corretti Dynasty
Abby Green

Valentina has always blamed Gio Corretti for her brother's death. But when she needs help, there's only one man she can turn to—the cold, inscrutable Gio, whose green eyes flash with guilt, regret and a passion that calls to her.

#3155 ONE NIGHT HEIR
By His Royal Decree
Lucy Monroe

Duty comes before desire for Prince Maksim. He knew that when he cut his ties to his mistress Gillian Harris. But when she gets pregnant this fierce royal Cossack must claim his heir and convince her to be his queen!

#3156 HIS BRAND OF PASSION
The Bryants: Powerful & Proud
Kate Hewitt

For billionaire Aaron Bryant, money usually solves everything, but he's not had a problem like this before. One unbridled night of passion with sassy Zoe Parker has left two little lines on a test—turning both their lives upside down.

You can find more information on upcoming Harlequin® titles, free excerpts and more at www.Harlequin.com.

#3157 THE COUPLE WHO FOOLED THE WORLD
Maisey Yates

Most women would kill to be on Ferro Calvaresi's arm. But Julia Anderson is not most women. When a major deal requires these two rivals to play nicely...*together*...is the world's hottest new couple beginning to believe their own lie?

#3158 THE RETURN OF HER PAST
Lindsay Armstrong

Housekeeper's daughter Mia Gardiner knew her feelings for multimillionaire Carlos O'Connor were foolish. Until she caught the ruthless playboy's eye. Even now, older and wiser, Mia has never forgotten the feel of his touch. Then, like a whirlwind, Carlos returns....

#3159 IN PETRAKIS'S POWER
Maggie Cox

To safeguard her family's future, Natalie makes a deal with the devil—Ludo Petrakis. She must travel to Greece—as his fiancée! But seeing the cracks in Ludo's unshakable control, she finds that it gets harder to resist the smoldering tension between them....

#3160 PROOF OF THEIR SIN
One Night with Consequences
Dani Collins

Lauren is pregnant and marriage is the only way to avoid scandal, but she still bears the scars from the first time she said "I do." Can she trust the powerful but guarded Paolo enough to reveal the truth?

HPCNM0613RB

Maisey Yates
brings readers another enticing story
The Couple Who Fooled the World

Most women would kill to be on Ferro Calvaresi's arm. The enigmatic Italian is one of the richest men in the world and at the top of his business game. Julia Anderson is not most women. She's as rich as Ferro and twice as hungry.

The only way to seal a major deal is for these two rivals to play nicely…together. Yet neither expects the media to soak up their ruse so quickly or so publicly! But when the deal is won, is the world's hottest new couple beginning to believe their own lie?

Find out this July

www.Harlequin.com

HP13163

"Are you my b[...] Stephanie aske[...]

Doug was not the least bit perturbed by her question. "What do you want me to say?"

"The truth, of course."

"Fine. That's what I had in mind. But for now, they'll be meaningless words. Because until you get to know me and learn to trust me, you'll question everything I say and do. You'll search for answers of your own to verify or contradict. That's human nature."

In the quietness that followed his words, Stephanie openly stared at him. "I'm sorry. I didn't mean to offend you." She dropped her gaze to the floor.

"Stephanie, look at me." He tilted her face to him. "I'm not avoiding your question. I'll always be open and honest with you, but it's your decision whether you choose to believe me."

"Okay. I'll try." But Stephanie was painfully aware that he still hadn't answered her question....

Dear Reader,

Fall is in full swing and so is Special Edition, with a very special lineup!

We begin this month with our THAT'S MY BABY! title for October. It's a lesson in instant motherhood for our heroine in *Mom for Hire*, the latest story from the popular Victoria Pade.

Three veteran authors will charm you with their miniseries this month. CUPID'S LITTLE HELPERS is the new series from Tracy Sinclair—don't miss book one, *Thank Heaven for Little Girls*. For fans of Elizabeth August, October is an extraspecial month—*The Husband* is the latest emotional and compelling title in her popular SMYTHESHIRE, MASSACHUSETTS series. This series began in Silhouette Romance and now it is coming to Special Edition for the very first time! And Pat Warren's REUNION series continues this month with *Keeping Kate*.

Helping to round out the month is *Not Before Marriage!* by Sandra Steffen—a compelling novel about waiting for Mr. Right. Finally, October is premiere month, where Special Edition brings you a new author. Debut author Julia Mozingo is one of our Women To Watch, and her title is *In a Family Way*.

I hope you enjoy this book, and all of the stories to come!

Sincerely,

Tara Gavin,
Senior Editor

Please address questions and book requests to:
Silhouette Reader Service
U.S.: 3010 Walden Ave., P.O. Box 1325, Buffalo, NY 14269
Canadian: P.O. Box 609, Fort Erie, Ont. L2A 5X3

JULIA MOZINGO

IN A FAMILY WAY

Published by Silhouette Books

America's Publisher of Contemporary Romance

To my husband and sons (Jim, Chris and Nick) for
giving me the freedom to spread my wings; OK-RWA
for encouragement during tough times; KLA for
believing in me; and APS, "where dreams grow."

 SILHOUETTE BOOKS

ISBN 0-373-24062-7

IN A FAMILY WAY

Copyright © 1996 by Julia Mozingo

Printed in U.S.A.

JULIA MOZINGO,

wife, mother and elementary teacher, lives in rural Oklahoma. Always looking for a way to be unique, she had her family first, then went to college, before she recognized and admitted to being a writer at heart and pursued that dream.

A Letter from the Author

Dear Reader,

Remember the song, "The Impossible Dream"? I'm proof that dreams *are* possible. I didn't grow up always wanting to be a writer, but somewhere along the line I acquired the desire.

Since that time, I longed to become a published novelist—a somewhat impossible dream—until I discovered the existence of writers' groups. I kid around about living "centrally dislocated" from everywhere, but in truth I wanted so much to be published that I willingly gave up my Saturdays for ten years to drive for hours to meet, interact with, listen to and learn from other writers. In effect, I realized my dream through hard work and never ever gave up hope. I'll admit, there were times when I was tempted.

Now you hold a part of my dream in your hands. *In a Family Way* is the beginning of my dream come true.

We all have aspirations, so I send a wish your way. May you maintain hope that your dreams can and will come true, too. As Eleanor Roosevelt once said, "The future belongs to those who believe in the beauty of their dreams."

Thank you for sharing your time and hard-earned money. Make yourself comfortable and allow me to entertain you as you journey through my first published novel. I hope you enjoy reading the story as much as I did writing it.

Sincerely,

Julia Mozingo

Chapter One

Muffled noises lured her from the sanctuary of darkness. Cool air drifted across her face; dryness scratched at her throat. Despite the heaviness tugging at her eyelids, she forced them open.

Darting her gaze around the room, she didn't recognize the surroundings—stark white walls, bright lights, a bed as hard as plywood, an antiseptic odor. She twitched her nose in protest. Various machines hovered at the head of the bed, their numerous umbilical cords linked to her. Where was she?

Her head ached, throbbing with each rhythmic pulse. With effort, she raked the long dark blond hair from her face and fingered the tenderness on her forehead. An enormous lump deformed the shape of her head.

"Welcome to Red Carpet Country, Oklahoma." A rugged, handsome man stood, entering her field of vision. Dressed in Western regalia, he was twisting a tan Stetson between his hands. "How do you feel, Stephanie?"

Stephanie? She dropped her gaze to her hands. She noticed a two-tone gold-and-silver ID bracelet on her wrist. The letters emblazoned on it read Stephanie. She swallowed her rising trepidation. "Uh, I'm fine. Just shaky."

"Do you know what happened?"

Forced to admit ignorance, she shook her head.

"You were in a wreck with my brother, Theodore."

Who was Theodore? Aloud, she asked, "How is he?"

At first she thought the stranger wasn't going to answer. Then, in a quiet voice, he said, "Not as fortunate as you." He fixed his gaze on her, dark brown eyes solemn. "He's dead."

At his calm announcement, hollowness settled in Stephanie's stomach. How awful! What should she say? She couldn't remember anything. "I'm sorry. It's difficult to lose a family member. Is there anything I can do to help ease your loss?"

"Get well."

Stephanie nodded. The silence in the room was kept at bay by the hum and beep of the machines near the head of the bed.

"A passerby pulled you both from the wreckage, seconds before it burst into flames. You'd fastened your seat belt. Theodore hadn't. You're the lucky one."

"Yeah, lucky." What kind of luck would rob her of her memory? Undoubtedly she was fortunate to be alive, though of course she was sad that another's life had been lost needlessly. Repeatedly she flexed her hands, alternately wadding the stiff white sheet and smoothing the wrinkles.

"The authorities recognized Theo and phoned immediately."

She stared at the man, seeking recognition—square jaw, thick, wavy light brown hair, dark brown eyes, weathered skin, naturally tan from outdoor work. Was she supposed to know him?

"Your purse was burned in the fire. Do you want me to call someone for you?"

Stephanie didn't offer a name or number. She couldn't. She didn't know either, or even her own last name.

His penetrating gaze unnerved her. She laced her fingers together to stop their fidgeting, and hedged. "I'll probably be up and gone before they can get here. I don't want to worry them or impose on you."

"I'm supposed to call a nurse as soon as you wake." He reached for the call button clipped to the pillowcase.

Her heart leaped to her throat. She grabbed his wrist; it was warm and hard, coated with wiry hair. "No, not yet. Give me a few minutes to settle my nerves."

Clearly skeptical, he eyed her, but withdrew his hand. "By the way, you haven't asked yet, but . . . your baby's fine."

"Baby?" How could she have forgotten that? Stephanie sat bolt upright. Pain shot through every pore. A groan of agony escaped her before she smothered the sound.

"Whoa! Take it easy." Gently clasping her shoulders, he eased her into a reclining position on the pillow. "Relax."

"Where's the baby? I want my baby." She darted her gaze around the room. Not seeing an infant, Stephanie stared at the tall stranger, her heart beating rapidly.

Scrutinizing her, he motioned toward her abdomen. "The baby's in your womb. You're two months pregnant, the doctor said."

Pregnant? Panic consumed Stephanie. She strangled on the next breath. Gingerly she coughed and pain flared through her battered body. She didn't try to hide the automatic moan that followed.

"Calm down. Try not to move around so much. You're causing yourself unnecessary pain." His hand dwarfing hers, he comforted her with a warm touch, "You didn't know about the baby?" He paused, shrewdly assessing her every action and reaction. "Or you don't remember?"

Movements carefully gauged to shield her from pain, Stephanie shrugged, desperate to control her rocketing emotions.

Probing, the astute man continued, "You don't know your name either, do you? Who Theodore was, or who I am?"

Stephanie's emotions were ragged; warm tears pooled in her eyes, blurring her vision, and spilled down her cheeks, leaving cold trails. "Please, don't tell anyone. I can't face questions right now. Give me a few days. I'll remember. I promise. You've got to help me."

"Why should I?"

Despite the pain it induced, Stephanie inhaled. She forced aside the feeling of helplessness. She relied on an inner strength she hadn't known she possessed. Hoping to successfully hide the internal turmoil, she intentionally calmed her voice. "Never mind. You don't owe me anything, Doug."

Wariness replaced sternness in his expression. "You called me Doug."

Surprised that the word had slipped so effortlessly from her, Stephanie experienced a measure of hope. "That's your name, isn't it?"

"Well, yes. Douglas Conrad Taylor. Do you remember?"

"I don't know." Valiantly searching her memory, Stephanie paused. In the quiet, the sounds of hospital activity drifted from the corridor. "I can't remember anything else."

"Here. This is yours."

He took her hand and pressed an engagement ring into her palm. The diamond solitaire sparkled. Bewildered, she stared at him. "Does this mean I'm not married?"

Before he could answer, an official-looking man in a white coat breezed through the door, a nurse flanking him, holding a shiny metal clipboard. He stopped at the foot of the bed. A wave of antiseptic odor emanated from him like a protective shield. "I see you're finally awake. How are you feeling?"

"Fine." Stephanie clutched the solitaire nervously.

"That's a nasty bump on your head." He picked a penlight from his pocket and strode to her side. Pinching open each lid alternately, he shone the light in her eyes, to his apparent satisfaction. "What's your name?"

"Stephanie."

"Do you have a last name, Stephanie?" He swung around to the nurse and muttered. She scribbled on the chart.

Stephanie took advantage of the respite to glance at Doug, then past him to the chair where he had previously sat. A magazine with the word *Oklahoma* in large letters on the front cover lay on the seat. The cover also featured a picture of a bison and displayed a slogan about the state, coupled with the symbol of a heart.

Out of the corner of her eye, Stephanie saw Doug shift his stance. She glanced at him and noticed his gaze drop to the magazine. Quickly she returned her attention to the physician, at the same time he swung his concentration back to her.

"Do you have a last name, Stephanie?" Repeating his question, the doctor smiled and waited.

Bravely she moistened dry lips. "Elkhart?" she said, at first hesitantly, trying out the sound of the name. Then in a stronger voice, she repeated, "Stephanie Elkhart." Immediately guilt assailed her at the dishonest response. "No. That's not right, but it could be. I'm not sure."

"Where are you from?" he asked next.

Stephanie glanced down, gripping the engagement ring so tightly it cut into the palm of her hand. "I was born in . . ."

"What's the address?"

She pressed her lips tightly together. Her heartbeat accelerated, as did the beeping on the monitor. Nervous, Stephanie fingered the bracelet, twisting it around her wrist until she viewed the script lettering. All the while, he waited for her answer. Stephanie stared up at the doctor. "I—I don't remember, but Doug tells me the baby's okay. Are you sure?"

"Yes. Everything appears fine. You seem healthy, except for that nasty bump on your head. Now, if you could just answer a few questions. Who's your next of kin?"

She raked her thumb across abrasive etching on the bracelet. She hazarded a glance at Doug. "I'm having difficulty remembering that, too."

The doctor lifted his eyebrows.

"I'm sure my forgetfulness is only temporary. It is, isn't it?" Stephanie stared hopefully at the doctor as she tried desperately to remember something...anything. "It seems like my parents aren't in the best of health. It's only a feeling, but I think I don't like to worry them unnecessarily."

"Of course, but we always notify next of kin before names are released to the local newspaper and radio."

Stephanie glanced through the window to the darkness outside, then dropped her gaze to the phone on the stand next to the bed. "I should be better by daybreak, after a little rest. I'll call my parents then. They'll be less upset speaking to me, rather than a stranger."

Displeased, the doctor shifted. "Miss, uh, Elkhart, or whatever—"

Doug broke in. "Damn it, Fred. Can't you see the poor girl's been traumatized? Give her a few hours' reprieve, or even a few days. Then, if necessary, we can put her picture in the local papers, both here and at home. Maybe someone will recognize her and come forward. What's it going to hurt? It's no big deal. Bend the procedures this time."

He sent Doug an icy glare. "I really shouldn't. A head injury with the possibility of amnesia is not to be taken lightly. But maybe a few hours' delay just this once won't hurt...only because *you* asked." Turning on his heel, he barked orders at the nurse. He marched from the room at a brisk pace, the nurse scurrying to keep up.

After the door closed behind them, relief filled Stephanie. Softness entered her voice. "Thank you. I don't know why you helped me. You didn't have to, but I appreciate the kindness."

Doug didn't reply. Honestly, he didn't know why he'd helped the poor girl, either, except that she looked so helpless.

Her words of gratitude hung in the quiet of the room.

As if her thanks embarrassed him, he pivoted away from her and retrieved the magazine. Sticking the publication in front of her face, he pointed to the animal on the cover. "That, my dear Stephanie, is a buffalo, not an elk."

A blanket of warmth descended with his words of endearment. The smile that slipped into place on her lips lightened the mood, if only for the moment. "I remember that much, *my dear Doug*, but honestly, would the doctor have believed Buffaloheart was my real name? Would you?"

Her response drew a chuckle from him. "Stick with Elkhart. Definitely sounds better, and less fabricated, than Stephanie Jane Doe."

As he tossed the magazine aside, Stephanie took the opportunity to examine the wide gold ring. The large diamond sparkled magnificently. Inside the band were the usual markings, but not the initials she had hoped to find. She slid the ring onto the third finger of her left hand—a perfect fit. Stephanie held her hand out for inspection. Just as naturally, she removed the ring and held it in the palm of her hand. "Does this mean Theodore and I were engaged?"

Doug shifted uncomfortably. "I was hoping you'd tell me."

Saturday morning, Doug returned to the hospital, intent on absolving the family of any legal responsibilities that might arise from the wreck. His attorney had advised him not to admit anything. Automatically he entered the elevator and pressed the button for *her* floor.

He didn't understand his own actions in championing the young injured woman the previous evening, but he couldn't let the matter lie. The sooner he cleaned up this mess of Theodore's, the better. How much would it cost this time?

Intent on his strategy, Doug followed the path to her room, oblivious of the activity around him. At Stephanie's half-closed door, he paused, the prepared speech and offer of a payoff on the tip of his tongue. Expecting her fully recovered and with legal counsel present, Doug shoved the door open and entered.

He met with the unexpected. The sight of the slight girl, her naked back peekabooing between the flaps of the hospital gown, stopped him dead in his tracks. His hormones alerted, a reminder of his masculinity rushed to the forefront, to be pushed aside as he assessed the situation.

The woman's shoulders shook as mournful sobs emanated from her. All his previous good intentions of ridding himself of possible problems fled, to be replaced by heartfelt pangs of human kindness and an urge to help someone in need.

To warn Stephanie of his presence and give her an opportunity to make herself presentable, he shoved his Stetson to the back of his head, braced his hands on his hips, then cleared his throat.

Immediately she rolled to face him, seemingly heedless of her red puffy eyes, tearstained face, and spiked wet lashes. Dark gold hair haloed her face and draped enticingly across the pillow. The discolored knot on her battered forehead combined with her woebegone look to instantly trap his sense of duty. He fought the instinct. "I take it no news is—"

"Horrible. Nerve-racking. Simply awful." She sniffled and tugged at the white sheet, mopping her face with the edge.

Doug strode to the bedside table and, yanking two tissues from the box, handed them to her. Uneasy, he waited as she noisily blew her nose.

Her predicament tore at his heartstrings, tightening the bands. All he wanted was to pay her off and get rid of her— to settle any liabilities. Yet here she was blubbering like a baby, appealing to his vulnerability, making him want to help solve her troubles and send the bad things away.

Consciously Doug avoided the inclination. "How are you feeling today, Stephanie?"

She sniffed and issued a weak "Fine."

"Sure. Just like last night." He flashed her a smile, encouraging her to expand on the declaration.

"Last night, I thought..." She hiccuped as she gained control over the sobs. "I thought I'd remember everything today, but I don't know any more than I did last night."

"What about your parents?"

Courageously she shifted her watery hazel eyes to meet his gaze. "What about them?"

"Did you phone?" At the negative shake of her head, he knew the answer to his next question before he asked it. "Why?"

"I don't even know who I am. How can I know who they are?" A single tear slid down her cheek. Pressing a hand over her eyes, she said, "If I didn't know better, I'd think the rescuers left my brain beside the road somewhere."

"Relax. You're trying too hard."

She dropped her hand from her face. Hope shone from within. "You really think so?"

Why did she have to look at him so trustingly? He offered her what little hope he could. "Last night you called me Doug. That's a beginning."

"Yeah, I guess so. I also found out I'm pregnant and I have amnesia. If I can't convince the man in the white coat I can take care of myself, how will I tend to an infant?" Tears once again filled her eyes, then spilled over the edges.

"Don't cry. We'll think of something." Genuine tears battered his defenses as no other ploy could. What if her baby was Theodore's? Doug pushed away the sudden thought, but it returned with more force. Was he truly free of his brother's escapades? "Have you remembered anything at all?"

Dabbing at her eyes, Stephanie shook her head.

In this case, Doug couldn't afford to play the odds. He had to know for sure how far his obligation extended to the woman. Only time would tell. Filled with conviction and a sense of duty, Doug recharted his course. "You don't have to face this alone. At least not right now. You can stay at my place."

Fear flashed in her eyes and her face hardened. "No. I'm not a charity case. You don't owe me anything."

Doug hadn't expected her resistance. He realigned his Stetson. "Okay, then. Where do you live?"

She sighed. "I don't know."

"Do you have any money?"

A fighting spirit fired her to life. "I'm not aware of any. Would it make a difference?"

Without answering her question, he continued, "Do you have a job, or hopes of one?"

"How could I? I'm stuck here in this hospital for I don't know how long." She glanced to the window. Bright sunlight filtered through the blinds. "Maybe being outside and walking around town would help."

"We know you were with Theodore. And the doctor won't release you until he's thoroughly checked your head injury and knows you have somewhere to go. So, let's plan for you to stay at the ranch." Doug hoped he didn't live to regret his impulsive decision. When Stephanie would have protested, he added, "Temporarily, until you recuperate."

"Do I have a choice?" She glared at him stubbornly, suddenly fearing dependence.

Doug looked around the room at the barren, stark white walls. He glanced back at Stephanie. "Obviously, not much of one."

Two days later, Stephanie stood in front of the small mirror in the hospital room, assessing what she could of her looks. The reflected image still appeared strange. Would she ever remember anything about her life?

Brush in hand, she swept a curtain of long blond hair forward to shield the discoloration on her forehead. But the hair blocked her vision, and she sure didn't need to stumble and bruise the other side of her face. In resignation, Stephanie flipped the brush in a backward stroke and repositioned the golden hair in a soft wave, more comfortably off her face.

Pitching down the brush, Stephanie once again studied her image in the mirror. An unfamiliar reflection stared back at her, pale and frightened. The stretchy dress that Doug had brought for her fit more like a sheath than a shift. The black sweater-knit dress's neckline plunged, accentuating the fullness of her breasts.

Feeling exposed, Stephanie tugged the neck higher and the shoulders inward—all without success. The moment she let go, the fabric sprang back into place, tightly cupping her half-naked white breasts. The contrast called attention to the dark bruise on her collarbone and made the discoloration more noticeable.

As a last resort, Stephanie wriggled her arms out of the narrow cap sleeves and twisted the shapeless dress so that the front was now the back. After slipping her arms in the sleeves, she smoothed the clingy fabric in place. Miraculously, Stephanie had a dress with a modest front neckline that concealed the bruise on her collarbone. The scoop back fit better.

This way, the dress seemed more appropriate for the funeral. What did one do at a funeral if she didn't remember her connection to the deceased? Doug had given her the choice of attending the ceremony or not. She'd chosen to go, hoping she'd remember something, anything.

With her index finger, Stephanie traced the newly aligned neck of the dress. Thankfully, the radiologist had determined that the injury to her collarbone was not significant enough to demand restrictive wrappings. Various cuts and bruises were sore and tender. Stephanie breathed deeply. In fact, she still ached all over, but at least she was alive, and so was her baby.

Stephanie pressed her hands over her stomach and molded them to the shape of her abdomen. Pivoting sideways, she peered at her silhouette in the mirror. Would anyone guess she was pregnant? Had she told anyone before the accident? Had she known? So many questions, so few answers.

Surprisingly, upon Stephanie's agreement, the doctor had consented to release her to Doug's care while she recuperated. She wondered why she knew him as Doug, when everyone else called him Conrad. Yes, she'd observed that much over the past couple of days. Yet there was so much more Stephanie didn't know.

Because of an unfortunate auto accident, she couldn't remember the father of her child, a man with whom she'd made love. Who was he? Was he the dead Theodore? Or could it be Doug, the ever-present rugged stranger who hovered like a mother hen and offered her a home when no one else had?

Stephanie hated depending upon a complete stranger, but was powerless to do otherwise. Vulnerable and at Doug's mercy, she didn't have much alternative other than to accept his hospitality.

Her breath caught in her throat. Tears threatened again for the umpteenth time. Bowing her head, she covered her face with her hands and searched for courage to meet her uncertain future.

"Are you ready to come home with me?"

Doug's softly spoken words caught her unawares. Stephanie hadn't heard him enter the room. Raising her head, she stared at his reflection in the mirror. He stood behind her, tall, commanding and confident in a beige suit and a chocolate-brown shirt, a shopping bag hanging from one hand.

He thumbed his Stetson to his crown. A shaft of unruly light brown hair sprang forward onto his forehead. Despite the stern, hard-as-granite set of his jaw, a gentleness entered his dark brown eyes, softening his appearance. "I brought you something." He held out the shopping bag.

Suddenly she doubted the wisdom of her decision to leave with this virtual stranger and live with him in his home. Now that the moment was upon her, Stephanie was tempted to change her mind. But where else could she go? Her choices were limited to the hospital or his ranch. She clasped her hands in front of her to still the jitters. "Can I trust you?"

An easy smile sprang to his lips. "I'm trustworthy, but you must decide whether or not *you* trust me." He pulled the contents from the plastic shopping bag. "I thought you could use a hat—it's more like a barrette with a black veil—to conceal that nasty-looking bruise on your forehead."

Ignoring the hat, she asked, "Why are you doing this? Are you my baby's father?"

Steadfastly, she waited for his answer.

Not the least bit perturbed by her question, he rested his hands on her shoulders. With a light touch, he guided her around to face him. "What do you want me to say?"

"The truth, of course."

"Fine. That's what I had in mind. But for now, they'll be meaningless words. Because until you get to know me and learn to trust me, you'll question everything I say and do."

When she would have interrupted with a protest, he pressed a finger across her lips. "No, don't deny it. Let me finish."

At her silent consent, he continued, "Regardless of my answer, you'll be suspicious of my actions and wonder if my words are just to fill a void or if they're the truth. You'll search for answers of your own to verify or contradict, whichever may be the case. That's human nature."

In the quiet that followed his words, Stephanie openly stared at him. How perceptive! She hadn't realized it until he voiced the words, but those were exactly her thoughts and feelings. "I'm sorry. I didn't mean to offend you, especially after you've been so kind and generous." She dropped her gaze to the floor and stared at the toes of his snakeskin boots. "Thank you for the clothes. Keep a tally. I intend to repay every cent you spend on my behalf."

"Stephanie, look at me." A hand beneath her chin, he tilted her face to him. "That's better. I'm not avoiding your question. I just thought it worth noting that I'll always be open and honest with you, but it's your decision whether or not you choose to believe me."

Encouraged by his words, she took a deep breath. "Okay. I'll try. But be patient."

Again Doug held out the wispy head covering. This time Stephanie took it and spun around to the mirror. She clipped the band in place and spread the soft nylon veil over her face. Perfect. She could easily see through the sheer fabric, yet it concealed the discoloration on her forehead from observers.

In the mirror, her gaze met Doug's. In the beige western suit, with his chocolate-brown shirt collar closed and a bolo tie in place, he was downright handsome. As he reached up to adjust his Stetson, Stephanie noticed that his fingers were bare of rings. Was he married? Single? Or spoken for?

He hadn't answered her earlier question. At least not to her satisfaction. Forget his persuasive speech about getting to know and learning to trust each other. She grappled with growing impatience and a need to know—now.

She was determined not to back down this time. Feeling as if she were stepping off a cliff, Stephanie took a deep breath and spun on her heel to combat him, head-on. "Doug, please, I've got to know. Are you the father of my child?"

Chapter Two

Doug barely knew this woman, yet he almost wished he could admit to being the father of her child. Why? Chalk it up to his wanting an heir, his biological clock ticking, or just the plain old-fashioned need to have someone he could call his own. A ready-made family was balanced on one word: *Yes.*

Stephanie approached him and casually laid one hand against his chest. "Doug, if you know anything at all, you've got to tell me. Not knowing is driving me crazy. I feel as though I don't exist, as if I'm nothing." She brought her other hand up to cup the side of his face. Tears gathered in her eyes. "Please, I beg you. Tell me. Are you my baby's father?"

On the brink of a milestone in his life, Doug teetered, first one way, then the other. In the end, his conscience won. How could he answer with anything less than the truth? Especially after his noble speech on trustworthiness.

"No, I'm not the father."

Withdrawing her warm touch, Stephanie shifted her gaze back and forth over him, evidently assessing the merits of his answer.

"Trust me. You have no choice at the present." He watched hope drain from her.

Bowing her head, she hid her face and swiped at the single tear that escaped. "Thank you for answering my question."

Why did he feel like a heel for telling the truth? He'd spent most of his life avoiding women who tried to snare him for his name, money and social position. Finally, he had to ask. "What would you have done if I'd said yes?"

She lifted her gaze to him. Several emotions flitted across her face, and then she shrugged. "Why didn't you?"

"Because it wouldn't be the truth. I'd just promised you that you could trust me. How could you, if I didn't tell the truth?"

His answer seemed to satisfy her, but her troubled hazel eyes held more questions. She voiced one. "If you're not the father, then why go out of your way to help? You could just as easily walk out of here and never come back."

"Yes, I could, and I probably should, except that's not my way of handling problems. I usually confront them head-on and take care of them, so they don't come back to haunt me."

"I have no past that I can remember. I plan to haunt every place I can to search for a trace of what I've lost." This time Stephanie picked up the plastic bag and stuffed her meager supply of personal items inside. "Is it possible I'm a ghost?"

He studied her in the mirror. "No, Stephanie, you're real."

Finished packing her hospital-issue toiletries, she was ready to leave the medical center. "Evidently you feel responsible for me. I admire you for that quality. In that way, you've earned part of my trust. But I won't become a weight around your neck. You don't owe me. I owe you for all this—the dress, shoes, stockings, underwear, and now the hat. I promise I'll pay you back, every penny, as soon as I can. I hereby absolve you of your self-imposed obligation."

She walked past him to the door. He caught up with her in two strides and grabbed her by the arm. "Whoa! Not so fast. Hospital procedure states you leave by wheelchair."

"Damn procedure."

Her headstrong attitude brought a smile to his lips. That had sounded like something he would say. In fact, he'd said as much a few days ago. While setting the Stetson forward on his head, he adjusted his grip on her arm to cup her elbow. Her skin was soft and smooth, made for stroking. Yet he resisted the impulse to do so. "At least let me escort you out."

They first stopped at the nurse's station for Stephanie to sign release forms. By the time they reached the front doors of the hospital, Doug had decided he wouldn't let this fragile-looking, headstrong woman go until he knew for sure that her child was not kin to him. "My car's two aisles over. Not far."

Stephanie hung back. "I'll wait here while you get it."

At first Doug thought the short trek had exhausted her, but then he recognized the look in her eye as one of independence. He didn't let on that he was aware. "Tired already?"

Stephanie offered him a weak smile.

He didn't argue. Instead, he swung her up in his arms, finding her much lighter than he anticipated.

She drew in a quick, agitated breath, alarm in her eyes. "Put me down."

Her breath, fanning the side of his face, brought to mind a warm summer breeze. As she struggled, inconspicuously, the heat of her exertions sent the clean scent of soap to assault his nostrils.

"Please, don't cause a scene."

"I won't if you won't." Her wiggles enticed him and his grip tightened. "Calm down and hold still before I drop you."

Intentionally he loosened his grasp to match his words. As anticipated, Stephanie hooked her slender arms around his neck. What he hadn't anticipated was that her simple action allowed her soft, full breast to press against his chest.

Doug strode to the car, not completely immune to the close contact. Lowering her to the ground, he unlocked the vehicle, keeping one arm around her slender waist. He swung open the door and motioned her inside.

Stubbornly she braced for battle. "You've been kind enough. I don't want to be further indebted."

Now what had he gotten himself into by volunteering to oversee her recovery? Fast losing patience with her sudden contrariness, Doug said, more harshly than he intended, "That's hogwash and you know it. We made a deal, and I'm going to hold you to it. After all, it's my reputation on the line. The doctor permitted your release only because you had a place to recuperate."

Her mutinous expression spoke volumes.

"Don't make this difficult." Doug hung his hands on his hips. Knowing he was opening himself to a possible lawsuit, but taking the chance, he presented his case. "You were with my brother at the time of the wreck. If you're carrying his child, then it's my relative. I have a vested interest to protect."

She glanced around the parking lot, seeking an alternate solution.

"Be reasonable." He stared down at her, prepared to intercept her flight, should she attempt one. "Where are you going? How will you pay? Life's not free in this day and age. The good Samaritans of old are rare. Besides, we've been through all this. The only sensible solution is to come home with me like we agreed."

She looked as skittish as a brand-new colt. "But..."

"I understand how you must feel, not having control over your life. Coming to my ranch doesn't mean I'm going to lock you inside or restrict your comings and goings. As you gain strength, we'll search for your past together. I want to know if that's my niece or nephew. Give me a chance to be a doting uncle."

The fight drained from her. Stephanie slumped against the side of the car. "All right. I'm not heartless. Or stupid. You present a good case." She smiled. "Are you by any chance a lawyer?"

"No way, lady. I'd rather deal with crops and cattle than people any day." Doug settled her inside the white luxury car and strapped the seat belt across her.

At first, tense and apprehensive, Stephanie scrupulously observed Doug's every move. As far as she knew, he could be driving them right off the face of the earth into oblivion, never to be heard from again.

Hoping for immediate recovery, she eagerly searched for recognizable bits of information—a sign, building or landmark—that would jog her memory. She twisted and turned, craning so as not to miss sight of anything that might prove significant.

All too soon, exhaustion crept into her battered body. A headache dominated, depleting her limited energy. She scooted down in the seat and positioned her head more comfortably against the headrest, watching the world pass by outside the windows of the moving car.

With Doug's expert driving, he swiftly maneuvered through the traffic in town, and before long they were cruising across flatland down a two-lane highway, the morning sun brightly shining as they headed west.

Flicking a lever, Doug rolled up the power windows. Afterward he adjusted the climate control until cool spring air infiltrated the car. Then he switched on the radio and fiddled with the buttons until he'd tuned in a classical music station. As the car ate up the miles, the rhythmic motion and soft orchestral music of Pachelbel's "Canon" soon lulled Stephanie into dreamless sleep.

Two hours later, the braking motion of the car woke her as Doug maneuvered the car through a town. Then they were back out on the open highway. But not for long, because Doug soon turned onto a smaller country road. Stephanie sat up and peered at her surroundings.

At distant intervals, dirt roads cut lines across the plains. The deep scratches in the earth's surface shone brightly with red clay. To Stephanie, there was something peculiar about the landscape. The tops of the few hills she'd seen were missing, as if someone or something had neatly sliced them off. Curiosity rising, she shot a glance at Doug. "What happened to the mountains? The tops are gone."

Her childish description brought a smile to his lips. This was a woman who'd keep him on his toes, challenge him in more ways than one. Checking the rearview mirror, he directed the car to the side of the road, slowing the speed even more. He brought the vehicle to a stop on the shoulder—an unnecessary precaution, because they were the only car on the crossroad. "You talking about those?" He pointed at the landform rising from the earth's surface. At her nod, he said, "We call them buttes."

"You mean they're supposed to be flat on top?"

"Yes. They're smaller than a mesa. When you feel better, I'll take you to see the Black Mesa, farther west in the panhandle. It extends into New Mexico and Colorado. Did you notice the plateau as we left Woodward this morning?"

Stephanie flashed a smile. "Plateau, butte, mesa... Sounds like a foreign language."

"Evidently you've never been to the Oklahoma panhandle."

"Either that, or I don't remember." Stephanie panned the view before her, noting the scope of the entire countryside. "There's not much out here, is there?"

"Much?" That had sounded like something his former wife would say. Doug reassessed Stephanie. "Depends on what you're looking for. That green wheat growing out there pays the bills and puts food on the table."

What kind of woman was he bringing into his life? Doug's mood altered. He didn't need another Constance. He'd better explain to Stephanie, up front, about the ranch's isolation.

The temperature inside the car dropped in relation to the cool tone of his voice. "If you're inclined to bright lights and city life, Guymon, back down the road—" he tipped his head to indicate the direction they'd come from "—with a population under eight thousand, is the closest you're going to find. Other than that, expect to drive hours and hundreds of miles to get somewhere."

With that information imparted, he pulled back onto the road. Gravel clattered beneath the car. A cloud of red dust swirled and settled behind them.

The acceleration jostled Stephanie against the seat. Instinctively her muscles tensed, aggravating their soreness. Heaviness pressed upon her chest, constricting her breathing. She became dizzy as an uncanny sense of panic seized her. Stephanie clasped her hands over her face to ward off the approaching darkness. She'd have to get used to riding in a car again, overcome her fear of another wreck.

Gradually she regained control of her physical reactions. A partial calmness replaced the former chaos.

Several miles down the road, Doug steered the car onto a narrow country lane. A half mile later, he halted in the center of the road. Stephanie hadn't seen another car since they'd left the state highway, so obviously it didn't matter.

He shed aloofness for pride and love. Yes, a woman knew when a man had the look of love in his eyes, and Doug did. Not for her, of course, but for the land that lay before them.

With a sweep of his arm, he motioned beyond the windshield. "Welcome to Triple T Estates."

A cast-iron entryway, sporting three elaborate *T*s across the top, opened onto a narrow gravel lane. All she saw for miles was rolling plains. She leaned forward in the seat.

Expecting Stephanie to comment on the vast nothingness again, Doug said, "Don't worry. You won't have to sleep outside in the open, under the stars. The house is on down the road, beyond view."

Relieved by his comment, Stephanie relaxed back in the seat. "I was beginning to wonder."

"We may not have much, but we have the essentials." Doug eased the car onto the ribbon of gravel that cut through the green wheat fields.

As they topped the first gentle slope, the homestead popped into view as a speck farther down the road. The closer they crept, the larger the cluster grew. It soon became apparent that the house was a traditional white two-story structure, clustered with a few trees and a nearby red barn.

The panorama delighted Stephanie. "Oh, what a lovely home! For a while, I thought we'd pitch tents."

"It serves its purpose. A place to hang your hat, rest your feet and eat a hot meal after a hard day's work."

Doug's matter-of-fact response earned a smile from Stephanie. "Just like a man. Not interested in aesthetics."

Lifting one eyebrow, he shot back, "Just like a woman. Preoccupied with outside appearances."

Doug sounded bitter toward women. Who had done this to him? "Are you talking about a particular woman?"

He pressed his lips into a straight line. "I'm talking about women in general."

"I take it you've known several." At his hooded glance, Stephanie realized she'd crossed the invisible line into snooping. "Never mind. I didn't mean to get personal."

"I've known a few women."

"Doug, I'm not prying. Honestly." Stephanie purposely stared straight ahead and clasped her hands loosely in her lap. She didn't want any more of his icy glares. "But you know as much about me as I do myself. I know nothing about you, except that you're Theodore's brother. And that you're kind enough to offer me a home while I recuperate."

He chastised himself. Doug knew better than to judge all women by his former wife, but there were times when he couldn't help it. Relenting, he asked, "What do you want to know?"

"What am I getting into by accepting your hospitality?" Stephanie gained enough courage to voice her trepidation. Her concern rushed out. "What should I expect? Who else lives in your house? Are you married? Do you have children?"

"No."

Another of his clipped, unexpansive answers. Stephanie raised her eyebrows. "No?"

"No, I don't have children, and no, I'm not married."

With sudden intuition, Stephanie added, "Don't worry, I'm not seeking the position."

A smile lifted the corner of Doug's mouth, softening his features. "Good, because I didn't ask."

Stephanie once again questioned the wisdom of her decision to come here. But it was too late for second-guessing.

Doug pulled the luxury car through the circular drive in front of the house, then followed a path that angled off to the side and around back. "Only company uses the front door."

After shutting off the engine, he added, "I have a woman who cooks and cleans. She lives in town, but has agreed to stay while you're here. Her name's Nadine Saddler."

"Don't go to any trouble because of me."

Admiration was reflected in his brown eyes. "You need rest and time to regain your health and strength."

That wasn't all she hoped to recover. The slamming of a screen door drew Stephanie's attention to the house. A large woman, dressed in a muumuu, waddled across the porch and eased down the steps, one at a time, making a beeline for them.

In the meantime, Doug climbed out of the car, walked around to Stephanie's side and opened the door. Together they met the woman halfway.

"I'd like you to meet Nadine Saddler," Doug said.

Extending her hand, Stephanie greeted the older woman. "How do you do?"

Nadine bypassed the offer of a handshake and hugged the younger woman instead. "Oh, you poor thing. Just call me Neddie. I'll take care of you."

Just as quickly, the woman set Stephanie at arm's length from her and, without preamble, lifted the veil, peeling it away from Stephanie's face. Two fingers beneath the younger girl's chin, she angled Stephanie's head first one way, then the other. "My, my, child, you're lucky to be alive. And thank goodness nothing happened to your little one."

Draping an arm around Stephanie, Neddie protectively led her to the house. She called over her shoulder to the forgotten Doug. "Put her things in the east corner room upstairs while I get her something to eat."

Doug caught up with them by the time they reached the porch. He aided Stephanie up the steps with a hand beneath her elbow. Springing ahead, he held the screen door open for them to enter.

"By the way," Neddie said to Doug, "ever since you left this morning, people have been bringing food."

Appreciating the local custom, Doug nodded. "We'll eat what we can, then freeze the rest before it spoils."

Stephanie stepped into a large, fully equipped kitchen laden with foil-wrapped and plastic-wrapped food. Not a bare spot remained on the U-shaped butcher-block counters.

To the left, beneath a bare window overlooking the backyard, was a double size stainless steel sink. A built-in range and cover dominated the center counter. The third wall of counters held a microwave and ended at a large side-by-side refrigerator before a double doorway opened into the living room.

In the middle of the kitchen, surrounded by four ladder-back chairs, a scarred oak pedestal table rose prominently. Two more chairs were shoved against the fourth wall on either side of another bare window.

Neddie steered Stephanie to the table and pressed her down in a chair. The older woman fluttered about the kitchen, unwrapping platters of meat, various casseroles, numerous side dishes and an array of desserts. When Stephanie thought the woman was finished, she pulled more food from the refrigerator, stacking salads and desserts on the sturdy round table.

Stephanie opened her eyes wider with each article added to the stash on the table. The so-called snack was a feast. "Don't go to any trouble on account of me."

"It's no bother. We can sample a bite or two of everything. Besides, we've got a couple of hours yet before the funeral."

During the ceremony, Stephanie hung back, observing from a nearby tree. A cool April breeze stirred the leaves above and ruffled her hair, sending a few strands across her face. Automatically she brushed them aside.

Even though she'd been invited, she felt like an interloper at the small gathering, about nine hundred yards from the house. She scanned the countryside. In every direction, miles and miles of flat farmland and grazing land stretched to the horizon without an ounce of familiarity, except for the clump designating the house.

Stephanie returned her attention to the small gathering of people. So these were the neighbors who'd brought mountains of food for the grieving family, which consisted entirely of Doug, as far as she could tell.

The site was apparently the family's private burial ground. She noticed six other markers. Theodore's made seven. But from the angle where she stood, Stephanie couldn't read the inscriptions on any of the headstones. She'd return another time, alone, to see whether the words brought any sense of recognition.

So far, the whole world seemed foreign to her. With any luck, given time and healing, the puzzle pieces would interlock and she'd find meaning and identity. But what if she didn't? What if she never remembered?

A cloak of sadness wrapped around Stephanie. This was Theodore's funeral. Shouldn't she be feeling something? A sense of loss? Grief? Evidently they'd been companions, but what else? Had they been engaged and in love? Had he fathered her child? Surely she'd remember loving someone, being intimate and sharing the routine of daily life with him. After all, he was the only person here who had known her. It wasn't fair that he should have died and left her clueless. Why couldn't she remember him?

A rising panic clawed at her for release. Automatically she sought Doug, the central and most commanding figure in the group. As if he'd detected her thoughts, he raised his head, peering in her direction.

His hooded gaze bored through her. Doug gripped the brim of his Stetson tighter as he held it in front of him. The poor girl, she looked so lost, standing there alone, her posture edged with panic. Compassion tugged at him. Yet, it wasn't smart to get involved. But how else would he learn any answers? And he wanted answers, every bit as much as she did. Besides, he was already involved. It was too late now.

He hoped this ceremony wasn't too much strain on Stephanie. After all, she'd been dismissed from the hospital only hours ago. He was harboring second thoughts about having invited her to the small funeral. But the gathering was an opportunity for her to remember.

How Stephanie wished she could remember something, anything, of the least little consequence. Her past was being buried along with this man, and she was helpless to prevent it. Why couldn't she remember him? What had he been to her?

Obviously, she should be shedding tears. But her mind was barren of recollections regarding Theodore, so any tears would be for herself, the life she'd lost and the one growing within. Automatically Stephanie crossed her wrists at her abdomen and shielded the unborn child.

Concealed behind the filmy veil, she observed each mourner's solemn face, hoping for a glimmer of recognition. Most seemed to be in their late thirties, around Doug's age. The men gave the impression that they were unaccustomed to suits and ties, tugging at their sleeves and running a finger around their collars. The wives dutifully hovered near their husbands' sides, prim and proper in Sunday dresses.

Returning her gaze to Doug, Stephanie noted that he seemed equally at home in his Western suit or in casual wear. A hint of sadness displayed itself in taut neck cords and a deepening crease near his mouth. Protectively she kept the shield of her arms in front of her abdomen. What was he thinking? Was he accusing her of wrongdoing, trying and convicting her on the spot? Agitation grew from her thoughts.

Again she fought the panicky instinct, trading it for outward composure. Stephanie sensed the contradictions within the man, despite the firm set of his jaw. Even from this distance, she imagined him calmly saying, "Relax, you're trying too hard. Give yourself time," the softness of his voice anomalous to his gruff demeanor.

All at once, the small ceremony was over, almost before it had begun. Each man in turn spoke a few quiet words of sympathy to Doug, then extended encouragement for the future. Stephanie intentionally hung back until the last goodbyes had been said.

"Ready? It's time we went home and put you to bed."

So lost was she in thought, Stephanie hadn't noticed they were alone. She glanced around. The last car disappeared in a cloud of dust down the narrow road. "Is it okay to walk back to the house?"

Doug hesitated, settling his tan Stetson on his head, before answering. "We could, but not today. After all, it's your first day home from the hospital. I don't want you to overdo it. As you gain your strength, you can walk anywhere you want."

Stephanie realized her strength was evaporating. She savored the sight of the countryside one last time before passively climbing in the car.

Beside her, Doug sighed. "I know. There's no place to go and nothing to do out here."

Surprised at his words, Stephanie asked, "Now, why would you say that? It's so peaceful, and beautiful, in its own quiet, understated way."

"I agree, but give yourself time. You may change your mind. Others have. Many don't see this place as having any draw." He circled the car and climbed in on the other side. Unhurried, he started the car and inched down the narrow road toward the white two-story house.

An uncanny sense of harmony with the area soothed Stephanie. Was the sensation familiarity? She hoped so.

Searching for clues to recovering her memory, she studied the surroundings, absorbing the sudden insight. "Something about the expanse of countryside gives me a certain comfort. The raw beauty of nature here soothes my soul. I feel like I belong." Excited, she twisted to Doug. "Have I been here before?"

"Yeah." He smiled. "This morning."

Stephanie couldn't help smiling at his teasing mood. "I know that. I mean another time."

"I can't answer that, because I don't know."

Stephanie's excitement evaporated as quickly as it arrived, dampened by his answer.

Encouragingly he smiled. "That doesn't mean much. You could have been in the area without my knowing."

Her hope wasn't completely doused. Inhaling a deep breath, Stephanie summoned up courage to ask something that had been bothering her. "Why do I know you as Doug, when the others call you Conrad?"

"That's what I'd like to know. Only family members—and Neddie, of course—call me Doug."

"Am I somehow family?"

"Not to my knowledge." Doug steered the car through the circular drive and around behind the large white house.

Was there another explanation? Stephanie debated whether or not she should ask. However, her need to know overshadowed pride. Looking straight ahead out the windshield, she purposely avoided eye contact with Doug. "Do we have any connection at all? Were we engaged?"

It shouldn't have been a difficult question to answer, but when Doug hesitated, Stephanie rationalized. "I know people change their minds or fall out of love. Maybe the baby was as much a surprise to you as it was to me."

"Whoa. Trust me. I'm not the father." Why hadn't he simply said yes the first time she'd asked? Yet, he knew the answer—because it wasn't the truth. And despite being an easy solution, the false admission would have created even more problems. Sadly Doug shook his head.

"I'm not trying to trap you." Bravely Stephanie glanced in his direction. "Or anyone else. I'm just trying to piece together my life. This not knowing drives me crazy. If only—"

"You're trying too hard to remember. Relax and let time be your companion."

"But—"

"Don't rush the process. You may do more harm than good. Give yourself a chance." He pulled the key from the ignition. "Perhaps you were with Theo enough that you picked up the name Doug from him."

She pondered that explanation. "Tell me about Theodore. What was he like?"

"He was five years younger than me. Lived in the fast lane. Kept the road hot under his feet." He glanced at Stephanie. "I wouldn't have thought him the settling-down type. Not yet, anyway, but possibly after he put on a few more years."

Stephanie challenged Doug's statement. "Maybe he changed. That happens."

"Or else someone—or some event—changed his life for him."

His words hurt, hinting as they did at entrapment. In her heart, Stephanie didn't believe that was the case. "Are you implying I, or perhaps my condition, had anything to do with—"

"I'm not implying a thing. I'm just telling you how I saw Theo. But how should I know what he was like? After all, I was only his interfering older brother, usually the last to know anything and the first to find fault. Some people act different around family than in public."

She detected the traces of a long-standing rivalry in his voice. "Was Theodore that type?"

"In some ways." Doug gauged her receptiveness before continuing. "Theo still had a lot of growing up to do. Our mother spoiled him as a child. It carried over into his adulthood."

"What about you? Did she spoil you?"

"Enough questions for now. You need to rest." Doug climbed out of the car, ending the conversation.

He seemed reluctant to talk about himself. Was he hiding something? Or was he naturally a private person who didn't like attention drawn to himself? Obligingly Stephanie refrained from asking more at this time, and followed Doug inside the house.

Because of her interrogation, he might have thought her prying. But she had so many unanswered questions bombarding her about her life, her existence, her connection to this man and his family, she naturally wanted to learn all she could. The slightest piece of information might trigger a switch in her mind to reveal her past, one that currently eluded her.

Chapter Three

Minutes later, alone in her upstairs bedroom, Stephanie had no trouble falling asleep. In fact, she slept through dinner and didn't wake until the next morning.

Bright sunlight filtered through the venetian blinds, forming a yellow-and-gray pattern on the ivory wall opposite.

Momentarily disoriented, Stephanie rose up on her elbows and assessed the room. It was utilitarian, with standard furnishings—dresser, chest, bed and nightstand. No visible traces of a previous occupant.

On the small table next to the bed sat a tray with a plate of shriveled peas, dried and cracked mashed potatoes, a curled slice of ham and a glass of what had once been iced tea but was now golden-brown liquid with a clear layer floating on top.

Then Stephanie remembered that she was in Doug Taylor's home and decided the room was austere and pristine, much like her host. She fell back on the bed and closed her eyes.

The smell of frying bacon penetrated the air, mingling with the aroma of freshly brewed coffee. Her stomach issued a growl of hungry protest.

Stephanie tossed aside the covers and crawled from the bed, clothed in her panties and bra. A round braided throw rug beside the bed kept her feet from the cold hardwood floor. Cautiously she stretched, feeling less achy than previous mornings. The long sleep had been good for her.

Too late, Stephanie realized she had nothing to wear except the black cotton knit shift she'd worn yesterday. She wished she'd taken time to hang up her dress; it lay in a crumpled heap on the floor.

Without a wardrobe to choose from, her selection was easy. She wiggled back into the black shift and smoothed the wrinkles as best she could. At the dresser, she bent at the waist and brushed her hair forward, then stood and flung it back over her shoulders with a certain amount of caution, so as not to cause pain from the decreasing knot on her forehead.

Half opening the door of her room, she poked her head into the hall and swept her gaze the length of the narrow passage. Not seeing anyone, she scampered to the bathroom, ill at ease and feeling as if she were trespassing. She wasn't yet at home in her new surroundings.

Once inside the bathroom, she quietly closed the door, not wanting to disturb anyone else. The enticing scent of Doug's after-shave tinged the air. A large, fluffy bath towel, tossed carelessly over the shower-curtain rod, was still damp from recent use. In the corner near the tub lay a small white heap that appeared to be Doug's discarded T-shirt and briefs.

The thought of sharing a bathroom with him sent a chill over her. It was almost too personal for comfort. Purposely she looked everywhere except at the male underwear.

Finished with her personal business, she washed her face and hands. Stephanie inched sideways as she reached for the hand towel. Her bare foot nudged the soft cottony fabric on the floor. Instinctively she recoiled, as though burned. How indecent to touch an article that had covered Doug so intimately!

Trying valiantly to ignore the tingling in her toes from the too-close contact, she padded barefoot downstairs to breakfast.

No one was in the kitchen. But on the counter beside the sink Stephanie saw a drip coffeemaker, the carafe half-full. A platter of bacon and biscuits sat on the stove in front of the oven vent. Still warm, they drew her irresistibly.

She ate a slice of bacon and started on a warm, fluffy baking-powder biscuit. With the initial sharpness of her hunger abated, Stephanie searched for a mug, starting with the cupboard above the coffeemaker, to the right of the sink.

Pausing in her search long enough to pop the last bite of her biscuit in her mouth, she licked crumbs from her fingers. A movement, almost out of sight, caught Stephanie's attention. She spun around to find Doug lounging against the doorjamb, adjusting his Stetson to the just-right position.

Stephanie felt like a kid caught with her hand in the cookie jar. The last bite lost its flavor. She wanted to get rid of it fast, but knew of only one way that wouldn't embarrass her.

That was when Doug noticed Stephanie. Since she was up and about, he thought she must be feeling better, but she was acting strangely. Was she all right? "Can I help you?" Doug asked, his face a bland expression.

She swallowed prematurely, the lump moving uncomfortably down her throat. "I wasn't snooping." When he raised his eyebrows, she added, "I was looking for a cup. I consider it rude to drink out of the carafe."

"I agree." At least she had a sense of humor. Doug relaxed. "Besides, we're civilized enough out here in the panhandle to have a few conventions. I'd never expect you to drink from the carafe—" his gaze dropped to her bare feet "—or your shoe," he added teasingly.

In a self-protective measure, Stephanie leaned against the counter and balanced one foot on top of the other. "A somewhat impossible task at this moment."

"So I see." Doug strode across the room and opened the cabinet to the left of the window, exposing bowls and cups. "Help yourself."

"Thanks." As she did so, Stephanie said the first words that popped in her head. "I've never seen a kitchen with so many cabinets. I could have searched all day and never found a mug."

"Eventually you would." He smiled. "Neddie has a peculiar order to the kitchen. She taught first grade twenty-nine years before she retired, so she's big on classifying and grouping. Anything used for cooking or baking will be found on that side of the kitchen." He motioned toward the area where the stove was located. "Near the refrigerator is food. I haven't figured out what order it's in this time. Over here are dishes, currently in alphabetical order—bowls, cups, glasses. Keep going. You'll eventually get to mugs and plates."

"A cup's fine." Smiling, Stephanie filled the container with hot, steaming coffee and gingerly sipped.

"Sugar or milk?" Doug asked, filling a mug with coffee for himself.

"Milk." Stephanie couldn't help but smile as she located the milk in the refrigerator and poured it generously into her coffee. "I guess grouping and classifying makes life interesting."

"Not if I can't figure out the name of the group."

She laughed at the image his words brought to mind. Stephanie pictured Doug left to his own devices, in the middle of the room, pondering where to find peanut butter. How many ways could one group a simple item? "Want some milk, while it's out?"

"No thanks. I've got to get to the fields. Have fun learning the many ways to group and classify today." He set his empty mug in the sink, then was out the door.

Stephanie watched through the window as he climbed into a late-model pickup and drove away. She didn't know what to think of the man. As far as she could determine, he was astute when it came to business, but a pushover in the kitchen, where Neddie took charge. He'd even been willing to take Stephanie, a virtual stranger, into his home at the mere suggestion that her child might be related to him.

How would she classify him? As a man of many facets.

Stephanie returned to the stove and helped herself to another piece of warm bacon.

At the slamming of the storm door, she spun around, bacon in hand, once again feeling caught in the act.

Neddie pitched an empty laundry basket to the floor and nudged it with her toe into the corner. "Hi, there. Glad to see you up and about. Guess you were plumb tuckered out after an eventful first day."

A smile perched on Stephanie's lips at the warm greeting. "I hadn't realized I was so tired until I lay down. Then I never knew a thing until I woke a few minutes ago. I'm sorry I didn't do your dinner justice."

"Nothing to worry about." Neddie waddled over to the sink and, with a squirt of dishwashing liquid, proceeded to wash the coffee mug Doug had left there. "I'd rather have food for you and you leave it than you go hungry for want of something to eat. Although leftovers aren't much to brag about."

"I'm not picky, Mrs. Saddler—"

"Please, just Neddie, or I'll think of you as one of my former students."

Neddie's warm demeanor easily brought another smile to Stephanie. "All right, Neddie. I don't want to be a burden, or cause you additional work on my account."

"Nonsense, child. You couldn't have picked a better place to stay during your convalescence. You're in the heart of Red Carpet Country, a place that prides itself on its warm hospitality." She dried the mug and her hands on the cup towel at the same time, in an efficient expenditure of motion that showed she was used to doing more than one task at a time.

After returning the mug to the shelf where it belonged, Neddie showered a bright smile on Stephanie. "Besides, I'm happiest when needed. And right now, you and Doug are the ones who need me most."

Neddie's warmth comforted Stephanie like a coat in winter. She trained her gaze out the kitchen window, where she'd last seen her host. "I'm curious about Doug."

"You and every other single female within shoutin' range." The older woman patted the younger one's hand. "Now, I didn't mean that the way it sounded. And I don't mean your curiosity isn't well-grounded. But Doug's had more than his share of fortune hunters, and nowadays he gives most predatory females a wide berth. Occasionally he gives one a second look, but he's mighty, mighty cautious. He's been burned too many times."

"I assumed that much by a few of his remarks." Stephanie pulled her gaze from the window and poured herself another cup of coffee. At the refrigerator, she topped the mug with a generous amount of milk. "I'm not here on any pretense at all. Right now, I don't have any other place to go until I regain my health or until I remember... I hope no one puts me in the category of husband hunter."

A cackle burst from Neddie. "Category? Now I know you've been talking to Doug. In my opinion, with you in your condition, expecting a little one and all, I'd expect you to be husband hunting. Although, nowadays, many pregnant single girls don't seem to be bothered about being unwed. Times have changed.''

"Right now I'm not sure of anything. But if it's any consolation, my inner instinct tells me I'm not the loose type. For all I know, I may already be married.''

"Oh, dear. Me and my big mouth.'' Neddie looped an arm around Stephanie's shoulders. "Now don't you worry none. I wasn't implying anything of the sort. I was merely making conversation.''

Stephanie blinked back quickly forming tears. "I'm sorry. I didn't mean to put you on the defensive. Just be yourself. I'm oversensitive right now. The least little thing makes me cry. I don't mean to get all teary-eyed.''

"Quit that apologizing this minute. Around this house, you can say and do as you please. No one's gonna judge you. While you're here, this is your home.''

"Thank you. That's nice to know. Everything's so strange. I feel lost, but I'm glad you're here.''

"Sit down, child. How about I fix you some eggs to go with the biscuits and bacon?'' Neddie poked her head inside the refrigerator.

"Don't bother.'' An uncomfortable sensation swelled in Stephanie's throat. Momentarily she pressed a hand to her mouth. "All of a sudden I feel queasy. I'm not sure the food I've already eaten is going to stay down.''

"No doubt it's a touch of morning sickness.''

Under Neddie's supervision, Stephanie returned to her room and lay on the bed with a cold, wet rag over her face.

After a couple hours of napping, then a shower, her stomach settled. She was more inclined to explore her new environment.

Neddie had scrounged through the chest and dresser and found sweat pants and a T-shirt for Stephanie to wear.

She also said she'd borrow some underwear and other items from her daughter Brenda, who was about Stephanie's size. Underwear was one of Brenda's penchants. She had it in every color and style, so much she hadn't even worn it all and wouldn't miss some.

Stephanie slid her feet into the black flats she'd worn here from the hospital and started her exploration with the hall.

"Feeling better?"

Neddie's voice from the end of the passage arrested her. Stephanie spun around. "Why, yes, thank you. I didn't see you there, Neddie."

"I'm just putting away clean linens. This is where you'll find sheets, towels and washcloths when you need them."

"Doug showed me yesterday."

"Good. I wasn't sure he remembered. It's so seldom he has company, except when Theodore came home."

At the mention of the younger brother's name, Stephanie postponed her tour of the house and neared the older woman. She couldn't resist conversing. "What was he like? Did he ever bring me here? Doug said I was in the car with Theodore when he wrecked, but I can't remember. What can you tell me?"

Neddie shoved a bunch of towels in Stephanie's arms. "Theodore came to visit Doug a few months ago. I can always tell—he leaves my linens in a mess. I bet he dumped them all on the floor and just stuffed them back any old way. I don't know how he took care of himself on his own. He was a messy kid, too, that one, quite opposite Doug."

Impatient, Stephanie asked, "Did Theodore mention my name? Was I with him when he came home last?"

"No, he came by himself. I do know the brothers argued and Theo tore out of here in a hurry." Neddie refolded a towel and then paused. "Do you suppose Doug's tired of these being grouped by items? I think I'll sort them by color this time, add a little spice to Doug's life. That one works from dawn to dark, all work and no play. Even as a kid, he was serious, never smiled much.''

Stephanie wanted to know about the brother, not Doug. "What about Theodore?"

"I didn't see him too often. Far as I know, he was all play. You'd have to ask someone who knew him better." Neddie took the rest of the towels from Stephanie and balanced them where they belonged. The new stacks were leaning towers of Pisa, sorted by color, but mismatched by size.

All finished, Neddie closed the door, hiding the waiting surprise for the next unsuspecting person, and picked up the empty laundry basket.

Figuring she'd learned all she could at this time about Theodore, Stephanie said, "Mind if I look around the house? I didn't take time to yesterday."

"Not at all, but let me tell you—" Neddie wagged a finger at Stephanie "—if you find any dust bunnies, don't blame them on me. There are times Doug refuses to let me clean some rooms, especially if he's got papers laying around." She waddled to the stairs and descended from view.

Wandering around upstairs, Stephanie found four bedrooms, in addition to the large bathroom, the one she'd showered in earlier.

Downstairs, of course, was the living room, complete with television and, off to the right through a double doorway, the kitchen. Beneath the stairs, she located a miniature hall that led to a bathroom, a laundry room and a bedroom, evidently Neddie's.

Stephanie returned to the living room. Along the far wall, she discovered a long, narrow room the width of the main structure that apparently served as a study. Inside the room, warm, rich paneling covered the walls, in contrast to the painted, textured Sheetrock in the rest of the house.

At the far end was an office with documents and photographs dotting the paneling. The area was furnished with a

large walnut desk in the middle and a tall swivel chair behind it, where the person seated could glide around and look
out the picture window. A barrel-shaped wooden chair sat
in front of the desk, and a computer system was arranged to
the user's right.

The other end of the room, the one closest to Stephanie,
appeared to be a library—an inviting couch, two easy chairs,
a stone fireplace, and an end wall totally covered with
shelves of books, ceiling to floor. The entire structure gave
the impression of being an add-on room, one that hadn't
originally been part of the house, but had been added at a
later date.

Automatically she browsed around the room, touching
objects—a brass coat rack, terra-cotta lamps, a coffee table
displaying the family Bible—until she came to the French
doors.

They opened onto a furnished patio complete with bar-
rels for flowers. The view of the wide open fields was magnificent, unhampered all the way to the horizon, giving one
a sense of authority, ownership and independence. The
sense of security touched her and warmed her soul. If only
she belonged somewhere.

Stephanie wandered over to the pictures on the wall of the
office area. She recognized Doug in one, shaking hands with
an official-looking man in a suit. They stood between the
American flag and the Oklahoma flag.

Scooting over, Stephanie studied the next photograph. It
was of a group of men posing on the steps in front of a
building. She couldn't see enough of the building to tell
what it was.

"That's the Guymon-area farmers at the state capitol,
rallying in support of the farm bill."

The male voice behind her startled Stephanie. She jumped
and spun around. "You surprised me. I didn't hear you
come in."

Doug hooked his thumbs in the front pockets of his jeans. "I didn't sneak up behind you on purpose."

"No, of course not." Stephanie motioned with a wave of her hand toward the frames on the wall. "I guess I was so engrossed in these photographs I didn't hear you. I was trying to familiarize myself with the layout of the house, and I was naturally curious about the pictures when I saw them, in case there was a face I remembered."

Doug pointed to the first photograph. "This is me with the governor, after the passage of the farm bill. He was thanking us for our support. I just happened to be spokesperson for the group you saw in the other picture."

She studied first one, then the other. Neither of the pictures stirred any recollections.

"Have you looked at those on the other side?" At the shake of Stephanie's head, he guided her around the desk to them. "This is a family photo. It was taken when Theo and I were kids. I think he was five here and I was ten."

Her interest piqued. Stephanie alternated her gaze between Doug and the photo. "I'm trying to picture what Theodore might have looked like older, as I compare the differences in age and appearance. The younger Doug and the older—"

"Don't say it. The years go by fast enough as it is. Sometimes too fast." He smiled.

She rephrased her observation. "All right, the more mature man you are today. Is that better?"

"Definitely." Doug pointed to the next picture. "Here's a later photo. Theo and me at his college graduation in Norman, at the University of Oklahoma, about ten years ago."

"Did you go to OU, too?"

"No, I went to an agriculture school, Oklahoma State University at Stillwater."

Stephanie studied the two brothers in the photo. "I can see the family resemblance. Same color hair, similar features. How old would Theodore have been here? Twenty-two?"

"Something like that."

"That would make him thirty-two now, and you thirty-seven." Stephanie glanced at Doug for confirmation.

"Close enough."

Tilting her head, Stephanie studied Doug's face. "You're not one of those guys that are sensitive about age, are you?"

"Not really, and not usually. Except I kinda get tired of everyone telling me it's time to settle down and have a houseful of kids so I'll have an heir."

"You need to do what's right for you, not what society deems proper and correct at a certain time in one's life." Stephanie acted on intuition. "You strike me as a man who does as he pleases and everyone else be hanged."

He peaked his eyebrows. "Am I as easy to read as a book?"

"No, not really. Uncanny as it sounds, I think I'm intuitive when it comes to judging people's character. With you and Neddie, my instincts tell me to relax and trust you."

"That's nice to know." Doug shoved his Stetson back on his head. "Listen, I can't stay. I only came back to the house to pick up some papers."

Reaching across the desktop, Doug rummaged through scattered papers until he pulled out a sealed envelope buried in the pile. "Tell Neddie not to wait dinner. I'll be late tonight."

"Okay." Suddenly shy, and already missing the warm interaction of a few minutes ago, Stephanie glanced everywhere except at Doug. "I hope you don't mind my coming in here. Neddie warned me some rooms were off-limits, but—"

"Some rooms *are* off-limits." Doug tucked the envelope in his shirt pocket as he straightened.

"I didn't mean to invade your privacy. I'm sorry if I intruded." Stephanie cast her gaze downward, and would have brushed past Doug, but he waylaid her with a hand on her forearm.

"You're not intruding. Especially if you take *the* solemn oath." Laughter filled his voice.

Puzzled, Stephanie lifted her gaze. She stared him in the eye and met his challenge. "What's *the* solemn oath?"

"Raise your right hand," he instructed.

She did as ordered.

"You, Stephanie...uh, Elkhart, do solemnly promise..." He paused for her to repeat after him.

Her response was slow, wary as she was about the unorthodox proceedings. "I, Stephanie Elkhart, do solemnly promise..."

"Not to group, organize or otherwise rearrange anything in this room, whether it be *ABC* order, backward alphabetical order, out of order or seemingly in no order at all, and will return all borrowed objects to the place where they were found." His eyes sparkled with mischief, and his face was contorted with his effort to keep his laughter under control.

Stephanie had no such constraints. Laughter burst from her. She quickly slapped a hand to her mouth to restrict the flow. After gaining control of her spontaneous eruption, she said, "You're serious, aren't you?"

"I'm dead serious. I won't be able to live with two Neddies in the house. Someone will have to leave, and it won't be me. It's as easy as that. What's your decision?"

"I'll make the ultimate sacrifice and force myself to abide by the rules." Laughter clung to her voice.

He furrowed his brow and sent her a stern expression. "Be absolutely certain, because I'm an ogre on this one point, and intend to hold you to it."

"All right. I don't feel any inclinations toward that particular characteristic, especially after I witnessed one of those attacks this morning." She paused, debating whether to say anything more. In the end, she continued, "I'll warn you. Beware of the upstairs linen closet when you open the door.''

Doug shot his gaze in the direction of the living room.

"Yes, Neddie struck again." Neddie-like, Stephanie wagged a finger at him. "Don't say you weren't fore-warned."

He braced his hands on his hips. "You know, it might be kind of handy having a spy in the house. What do you say? Are you applying for the position?"

Stephanie folded an arm at her waist and supported the opposite elbow. She tapped a finger to her cheek. "How about the job of arbitrator or peacemaker? Do you have an opening for either of those?"

"You know, Steph, that might just be the best idea yet. It'd be similar to being a king's taster before he eats, wouldn't it?" A smile wreathed his face. "I like your sug-gestion."

"I'm not so sure I agree with this king business. I was thinking more of soothing the lion before he roared."

Laughter rang out from Doug. "I knew I liked you for some reason. It's your honesty and willingness to face that lion."

His approval coated her with a blanket of warmth and lent her strength. Stephanie offer her hand. "Do we have a deal?"

He clasped his large, warm fingers around hers. "Deal."

By the end of a month, Stephanie had regained her health and stamina, but not her memory. Oh, there were sudden momentary flashes and glimmers, but they were too brief and too elusive for her to put her finger on them and draw out her past for examination.

During the month of May, Stephanie had also begun as-sisting Neddie with daily housekeeping and cooking chores; though the older woman protested, it seemed to please her.

This evening they cooked homemade fried chicken with mashed potatoes and cream gravy that deserved to be eaten hot, fresh from the stovetop, followed by warm cherry pie topped with vanilla ice cream.

The living room clock chimed six times as they sat down for dinner. But no sooner had they settled than Neddie popped up, first for one thing, then another—salt and pepper, bread and butter, finally napkins.

"Neddie," Doug said, "if you don't sit down and eat, you're going to give everyone indigestion with your bouncing around like a basketball."

The older woman returned to the table and dealt out the paper napkins before seating herself once again. "Just you eat, and never mind me. Seldom do you eat a fresh-hot-from-the-stove meal. You're usually late. Isn't that right, Stephanie?"

Suddenly caught in the middle of the conversation, the younger woman paused, her hand in midair, spooning mashed potatoes onto her plate. Diplomatically she said, "I've never observed Doug's eating habits. I really can't say."

"That's all right, child. Take my word for it. I know."

Stephanie sneaked a peek at Doug from beneath her lashes. He sent her a wink. Or was he blinking, and she just thought it was a wink? She ducked her head and attended to filling her plate.

Neddie chattered on, not noticing that the conversation was one-sided, changing from one subject to another without drawing a breath, yet eating around the words. "Speaking of Stephanie, just look at the poor girl."

Stephanie straightened her posture and locked gazes with Doug, curious about Neddie's next tangent.

"Why, you ought to be ashamed of yourself, Doug. She doesn't have a thing to wear except old T-shirts and sweats I scrounged from you boys' closets, and a few of Brenda's secondhand clothes."

Relaxing, Stephanie returned her attention to eating, and scooped up a bite of potatoes and gravy.

"She probably has to sleep nude because she doesn't have a nightgown."

Heat crawled up Stephanie's neck. "It's all right, Neddie."

"Sure," Doug chimed in. "Not everyone sleeps in clothes. They're too confining."

"What difference does it make how I sleep?" Stephanie was blushing. "But if you must know, I sleep in a T-shirt. I find it quite comfortable. Thank you for your concern."

Concentrating on eating, Stephanie tore off another bite of chicken, all the while wishing—or rather hoping and praying—that Neddie would change subjects again.

"What about her underwear, then?"

How embarrassing! The bite of meat lodged in Stephanie's throat. She coughed in protest, tensing uncomfortably.

"What about it?" Doug raised one eyebrow in jest.

"She's only got one new pair. The others I borrowed from Brenda. Haven't you noticed all she wears is hand-me-downs? Don't you think she deserves a few new things? It's not like you can't afford it. I know you can."

Where was the nearest rug to hide under? The closest place to curl up and die? Valiantly Stephanie worked to empty her mouth of food without embarrassing herself further. Even though mortified, she once again tried to ease out of the humiliating predicament.

Displaying a forced outer calm worthy of an Emmy award, Stephanie carefully laid down her fork and wiped her mouth with the napkin, her appetite suddenly displaced. She stared openly at Doug, wondering if he, too, was uncomfortable. "Personally, I don't mind wearing hand-me-downs. They're really quite comfortable. Besides, I don't want to be deeper in debt than I am already. After all, I'm not attending the governor's ball, the president's inauguration, or even my own wedding.''

"That's an interesting idea." Neddie cocked her head sideways. "Just never you mind, honey. You're a respectable person, even courageous in your situation. As such, I insist that you have some new belongings to call your own. I'll settle for clothes this time. But eventually I'd like to find you a husband to take care of you and your little one."

The older woman directed her gaze at Doug. "And a wife to take proper care of this here lonesome cowboy."

Chapter Four

The next day, after delegating routine chores he usually took care of himself, Doug returned to the house and holed up in his office for an hour, preparing to face the inevitable. He swiveled his high-backed leather chair around and stared out the picture window with unseeing eyes.

What kind of host was he, that he blindly ignored the comfort of his guest? He hadn't done it on purpose. He guessed it had been too long since he'd last entertained or taken responsibility for another human, apart from Theodore. And Theo was the exception. Being family, Doug had cleaned up after him and covered his tracks, not provided for his basic needs.

Jeesh! He treated his cattle better than he did Stephanie. Water, food and shelter were easily provided. But clothing? What kind of monster did she consider him?

On the other hand, why hadn't she mentioned anything earlier? There had been ample opportunity. Sure. All she needed to do was lasso and hog-tie him.

He'd purposely avoided her like a dreaded disease since that day a month ago in the study, when she'd asked about the photos on the wall. She'd seemed so open, warm, vulnerable and, as a result, so dangerous to his peace of mind.

Granted, it must be hard starting over, and even more so as an adult—a pregnant one, at that—with no memory of a past, without a sense of belonging, and lacking resources.

Well, like it or not, Doug had willingly asked for this responsibility. He'd practically begged Stephanie to live at the ranch. And her child—yes, he'd noticed the slight bulge to her stomach recently, especially when she wore that damn black knit dress that fit like a sock.

Against his will, Doug's imagination took flight. Yes, he'd noticed the acre of ivory skin exposed at the neckline in the back, and the way the fabric cupped the soft curve of her rounded behind, the hem working higher with each graceful step she took. Doug raked a hand across his eyes, but the action didn't erase the image of her ample breasts enlarging and pulling a ripple across the front of the dress as her body prepared for the child.

Shifting in the leather chair, Doug knew he had no one else to blame but himself. After all, he was the one who'd bought the damn black dress. Only when he bought the garment, it had been shapeless, and that had suited him just fine.

When Neddie took it upon herself to ransack his closet and dresser to outfit Stephanie after she arrived at the ranch, he should have done something about her wardrobe. Neddie shouldn't have to borrow from her daughter to clothe Stephanie. Right off, he'd noticed how small she was. His shirts hung from her jutting breasts, leaving the rest of her to his imagination.

Over and over again, Doug had replayed the day he'd carried Stephanie to his car in the hospital parking lot, the feel of her in his arms, her hands clasped around his neck, her soft, full breast pressed against his chest. She had no idea that her innocent wiggling against him had unleashed his longing for a woman—not just a female to fulfill his physical needs, but a woman of his own, to share his life and his dreams.

But from experience, he knew most women of his acquaintance always wanted and asked for more. They weren't satisfied with the quiet life of a rancher's wife. No, they wanted the material things his wealth could provide. Yet Stephanie never asked.

Even a month ago, when they talked in this very room, Doug had suspected her presence in his life would create turmoil for his peace of mind. That was why he'd purposely avoided her ever since.

"Doug?"

The musical sound of his name on Stephanie's lips arrested Doug's thoughts. He spun the swivel chair around and leaned forward, forearms on the desk.

"Neddie said you wanted me."

"Yes." He wanted her in more ways than he was willing to admit. Doug swallowed and shuffled papers on the desktop. "We're going out today. I phoned the doctor's office and made an appointment for your monthly checkup."

"But I feel fine."

The mild protest drew Doug's gaze to her for the first time since she'd walked into the room. Immediately he noticed that she'd missed fastening the button between her breasts. He glanced at the desk, the wall, the room behind her, anywhere except at the shirtfront that was peeping open, exposing her creamy cleavage. "I didn't say you weren't feeling fine. It's routine to see the doctor every month while you're pregnant, to make sure the baby is okay and your pregnancy is progressing normally."

"Oh. I've never been pregnant before. I didn't know."

"Now you do. Besides, it will be a good opportunity to buy you clothes."

Fear, underscored by face-saving anger, glared from her hazel eyes. She braced her hands on the desk and leaned across it, closing the gap between Doug and her.

Her action accentuated the opening in the shirtfront and gave him an unhampered view of her ivory breasts, cupped in lacy black fabric.

"I told you last night—these clothes are fine. I don't want to be indebted to you any more than I am already. What if I can't repay you? Aren't you afraid of that?"

"No!" He was more afraid of involvement with her. "Button your shirt, Steph."

Red suffused Stephanie's face. She glanced down, then popped upright, away from the desk, and fastened the button.

He changed the subject. "Can you be ready in an hour?"

Unaccustomed to asking for favors, Stephanie ventured, "Can we look around while we're in town, search for clues to my past?"

Doug nodded. "I'll drive up and down every street. We'll not leave a rock unturned."

Stephanie's eyes were sparkling with excitement now, and her fear and anger disappeared, to be replaced with a smile of anticipation. "In that case, I'll be ready in less than an hour."

Two hours later, after Doug's helpful intervention on her behalf regarding the medical history required from new patients, the nurse recorded her pulse, temperature and blood pressure. Shortly thereafter, the doctor examined Stephanie.

When he'd finished charting his notes, the general practitioner scrawled illegibly on a prescription pad, tore off the sheet and handed it to Stephanie. He walked her to Doug, who was waiting outside the door of the examining room. "Get this prescription filled for prenatal vitamins. Meanwhile, I'll send for a copy of your accident records from the Woodward hospital.''

"That doctor called it retrograde amnesia," Stephanie offered, hoping for a quick solution. "But so much was happening I don't remember everything he said."

The older physician explained more fully. "It's the type where you retain most of what you've learned during your life, but have a gap surrounding the time of the accident. You function normally regarding speech and motor skills."

Speaking quietly, he continued, "Don't worry. You're healthy, and the pregnancy's progressing fine. Regaining your memory will take time." He smiled. "We can't rush Mother Nature in either instance."

Stephanie grew impatient with the prognosis. "But I thought after a week, and surely now after a month, my memory would return and everything would be back to normal."

"Give yourself time," the doctor told her comfortingly. "Not to alarm you, but occasionally amnesia has been known to last for weeks, months, or even years."

His announcement dismayed Stephanie. "No. There's got to be another way, a faster method than waiting."

"Yes, there's medication as an alternative."

Stephanie glanced at the silent Doug, then back to the doctor. "Well, why not at least try it?"

The physician sighed and answered patiently, "Nowadays we live in a society based on instant gratification, I know, but there are times when old-fashioned remedies work best. In my professional opinion, this is one of those times. Because I don't want to prescribe any drugs that might harm the fetus, my advice is to wait and see what happens."

Agitated, Stephanie pleaded, "Doug, do something. There's got to be a way we can speed up the process."

"Calm down, Steph." Placing his hands on her shoulders, he squeezed gently. "Dr. Perryman knows what he's talking about. You'll only make matters worse by getting upset."

Clearing his throat, the general practitioner thought for a moment. Finally he conceded, "There is one thing you can do."

Bereft of words, Stephanie held her breath in anticipation.

"What's that?" Doug asked.

"The method may be slow and time-consuming." He paused.

"We'll make time," Doug assured him, and Stephanie, as well.

Dr. Perryman shifted his gaze between the two of them. "The idea is to entice recall and recognition by searching for an associative thread that will lead the way back to the return of the memory."

"How do I do that?" Stephanie asked.

"Observe occupational skills, read events in the newspaper, listen for familiar songs on the radio, search an area on the map, or even try word association." Dr. Perryman smiled encouragingly. "Once you find a clue, you'll gradually begin piecing together your identity."

Hope once again rising, Stephanie steepled her hands together in front of her mouth, offering a silent entreaty. Aspiration brought warm, moist tears that blurred her sight. She blinked them away.

Doug scrutinized Stephanie's profile as, shielding her eyes against the bright sunlight, she peered up and down the street, oblivious of his intense inspection.

The raising of her arms tugged the black knit dress even tighter, molding it indecently around her full breasts and slim rib cage. Running his gaze lower still, he noticed that the dress cupped every inch of her softly rounded behind. The hem inched even higher with her innocent action, exposing more leg than he cared to think of at this moment.

He shifted his attention away from Stephanie and noticed the gawks male passersby sent in her direction. An intense reaction spiraled within, and suddenly, without consideration, Doug decided he didn't like other men looking too long or too hard at Stephanie.

"Where to?" she asked, spinning around to him, and dropping her arms to unsuccessfully tug the hem of her dress lower.

"I don't care. Anywhere. Let's just get off the street and get the shopping done." Threatened by his discovery, Doug spoke more harshly than he'd intended.

Stephanie flashed a curious glance in his direction.

He took her by the elbow and ushered her inside the car.

After driving to Main Street, Doug parked in front of a shop. "What about here?"

"But this place looks too expensive," she protested.

"Don't worry about cost. Get what you need." He climbed out of the car and escorted her inside.

At Stephanie's hesitation, he said, "Go ahead. Wander around. I'll wait here while you shop." Doug hooked his thumbs in his jeans pockets and turned around to stare out the plate-glass front window.

After twenty minutes, Doug hooked a glance over his shoulder at Stephanie, assessing her progress. She was examining a red pair of string bikini panties without enough fabric in them to hold their lace in position. She traded them for a pair of sky-blue low-top, high-cut-leg see-through panties free of lace. Another time she held up a pair of full-cut traditional white panties and stretched the waist before inspecting the inside.

That did it for Doug. He jammed his Stetson down hard on his head, pulling the brim low over his eyes. Women! Why couldn't they just grab what they needed that served the purpose and be on their way? It wasn't as if they'd parade undergarments in public every time they left home.

"Excuse me, Doug. How should I pay for these?"

Stephanie's soft musical voice at his side interrupted his thoughts. He glanced at her and noticed the small rainbow-colored bundle clutched against her. "Is that all? You didn't get very much."

"It's enough. They'll launder. Besides, the other things weren't quite my style." She smiled hesitantly, plainly uncomfortable with the whole situation.

Doug shrugged. He wasn't going to force her to buy out the store, as other women in his past acquaintance would have done if he was paying. Secretly, though, Doug had noticed her giving the price tags more attention than the garments, and he'd decided that cost had more to do with her leaving the shop than style.

A short time later, they were back out on the sidewalk. Doug gave Stephanie free rein and told her to lead the way. Soon she paused at the window of another boutique. At Doug's urging, they went inside.

After observing Stephanie trying on several outfits, Doug realized that everything looked good on her, from body-hugging stirrup pants to loose-fitting, softly swaying skirts and dresses. He hadn't seen anything that wasn't her style. Yet she only purchased three polyester warm-up suits, in fuchsia, smoky blue and forest green.

As Stephanie approached him, she said, "This is enough here. Let's try somewhere else. Is there a discount store nearby?"

"Just down the road."

"I get the feeling I'd be more comfortable shopping there than in places like this. Not that the merchandise isn't nice, but I can't justify spending a small fortune when I'll need maternity clothes before long."

Shoving the small sack of underwear inside the larger bag of warm-up suits, Doug consolidated Stephanie's purchases to one easier-to-carry package.

They walked outside, into the bright sunlight, and continued down the sidewalk and across the intersection to the next block.

"Quit worrying about cost," Doug urged, "and get what you need. I'm not limiting your budget."

A storefront sign farther along caught Stephanie's eye. She pointed. "Let's go there."

Before Doug could take her elbow, she sprinted ahead, leaving him to trail behind. She halted in front of the display window exhibiting a sewing machine, bolts of fabric, patterns and sewing notions.

Stephanie stood there so long, Doug at first thought something was wrong. "What is it, Steph? Are you feeling okay?"

She didn't answer, just stood motionless, staring through the plate-glass window, oblivious of her surroundings. Covering her mouth with trembling fingers, Stephanie closed her eyes and leaned her forehead against the window.

Doug's concern grew. "Are you all right?"

Rubbing her temples with both hands, Stephanie again didn't answer. She stood entranced, ignoring everything.

"Damn it, Stephanie, answer me." Doug gripped her by the upper arm and spun her to him.

Her eyes popped open, sparkling brightly with unshed tears. "I know how to sew. I remember that much. When I saw the sewing machine, an image flashed in my mind of me sewing. But nothing else. Let's go inside. Maybe I'll remember more."

Once inside, Stephanie moved through the store reverently, like a kid in a candy store with too many selections to choose from. This time Doug followed in her shadow, not letting her out of his sight. He watched as she filled her senses.

She leaned closer to the fabric bolts and sniffed. Personally, he didn't like the odor of the sizing in new fabrics. They all smelled alike to him.

Gingerly Stephanie opened the fold of fabric and slid her palm over the surface. Close beside her, Doug followed suit with feigned interest, finding the silky fabrics, cool and slick. The few calluses on his hand from work caught and pricked the fabric. Denim and broadcloth met with more resistance. He noticed that they were stiffer and rougher than the silky ones, absorbing the heat of his hand.

He'd never consciously paid attention to the properties of fabric before, but instantly he imagined the feel of them draped over Stephanie's curves, her softness hidden beneath.

Something on the other side of the store caught Stephanie's attention. She did a U-turn in the narrow aisle and brushed past him in a hurry to examine her findings.

Doug clenched his fist and dropped it to his side. What was wrong with him? It wasn't like him to covet an unavailable woman. And Stephanie was definitely unavailable. She was pregnant, and possibly had belonged to his brother. So what if his brother was no longer living? It was Doug's duty to oversee his brother's unfinished business. Right now, that was Stephanie.

Impatient with himself for the direction of his earlier thoughts, Doug followed close behind and lashed out at Stephanie. "How long does it take to shop in a fabric store? There's nothing to try on."

"Oh, Doug." She chuckled. "How typically male you are! Use your imagination, like when you plant a crop and look forward to a plentiful harvest." She draped first one, then another, length of fabric across her chest. "Look at the possibilities."

That was the problem. He was viewing too much. "It's not a lack of imagination. Sometimes one has too vivid an imagination." He pulled his Stetson down low over his eyes.

"Ha-ha. Very funny. I have yet to meet a man who appreciates aesthetics the way a woman does."

"Ah, Steph. Don't stereotype me as if I were one of Neddie's items to be grouped and labeled. Someday I'll show you just how much I appreciate aesthetics, and in what form."

"Do you have a sewing machine?" Stephanie waited for his answer.

"There should be one in the attic. It hasn't been used in years, though."

Stephanie glanced up at him. "Do you mind if I clean it and use it?"

"I don't even know if it still works. By today's standards, it's a dinosaur, because it doesn't zigzag or make buttonholes."

Tapping a forefinger to her cheek, Stephanie contemplated her choices. "For what it's worth, I can make clothes cheaper than buying them ready-made."

"Don't worry. Money's not a problem."

"But I'd rather make them. Sewing would be therapy. I could think while I'm sewing. And who knows, maybe being engaged in a familiar activity would entice my memory to return sooner?"

"Let's look at the new models." Doug traipsed to the back of the store, where various machines were displayed. He glanced over his shoulder. "Which one would you suggest?"

After methodically checking the cost of each machine, Stephanie stopped in front of Doug. "Does Guymon have a pawnshop?"

Now what? Doug shrugged. "Yeah, I guess so. Why?"

Stephanie's independent spirit asserted itself. "Since I intend to pay back every cent you spend on me, I don't want to be in hock too deep."

Exasperation setting in, Doug sighed. "How many times do I have to tell you? Money's no big deal, Steph."

"It is to me, until I know more about myself. A used sewing machine will be a fraction of the cost of a new one."

"You don't have to do this."

"I know, you've told me, but I *want* to make my clothes."

Maybe she wasn't as good a seamstress as she thought. However, it might be a good idea to let her make the clothes. Hopefully, they'd all be shapeless tents and parachutes. That would suit him just fine. "Whatever."

"Thanks for the vote of confidence," she said, her words dripping sarcasm.

She marched over to the pattern books and thumbed the pages until she found a couple of patterns she wanted. Then she returned to the aisles of fabrics and selected several bolts. With the salesclerk's help, Stephanie soon had a sackful of fabric and notions.

The pawnshop beckoned next.

Less than an hour later, back in the car, with the used sewing machine she'd purchased stowed in the trunk, Stephanie asked, "What's next on the agenda?"

"That's about it, as far as I'm concerned." The sooner he got her back home and out of his presence, the more comfortable he'd be. She was unsettling him too much. The fact that she had more than likely been Theo's lover put Doug at a disadvantage. He felt honor-bound to see her through a healthy pregnancy, and guilty for thinking of her in ways other than the platonic.

Stephanie studied the surroundings. "Before we head back to the ranch, could we drive around town?"

He supposed that would be a good idea. After all, he'd said they would, and the sooner she recovered, the sooner his life could return to normal. "Where to first?"

"I don't know. Just anywhere. I'd like a good look around. Maybe I'll recognize something else. I'm excited about the prospects. Just out of the blue, the connection with sewing came about. Who knows? Maybe I'll remem-

ber everything. Then I could return home." Excited,
Stephanie gawked in all directions, unable to sit still.

Her wiggling worked the hem of her skirt up even more.
Why couldn't he just keep his mind on the business of driving and think of her as a younger sister? Because she was a
woman in every way—nothing about her seemed particularly young or innocent. In his estimation, she appeared to
be in her early thirties.

By the time Doug had circled through neighborhoods and
past schools in various parts of town, Stephanie's restless
excitement had changed to disappointment. She wanted
desperately to recapture her elusive past, and he wanted it
for her—not to mention for his peace of mind—but apparently her complete recovery wasn't to be, at least not today.

In the days that followed, Doug kept to himself, oversee-
ing the daily operations of his three businesses—natural-gas
wells, wheat farming and cattle-raising.

Interestingly enough, Stephanie proved to be an adept
seamstress. Doug observed with curiosity as she magically
created, from shapeless lengths of fabric and tissue-paper
patterns, a wardrobe worthy of the time and effort spent.

He had to admit, she was good, really good. He wouldn't
have believed it, had he not witnessed the entire process
from start to finish.

This creative woman was indeed full of surprises, and not
unpleasant ones, either, which was more unsettling for Doug
the man than for Doug the responsible brother. So, in the
interest of self-preservation, Doug kept his distance from
Stephanie. It was a more difficult task with every passing
day.

"Ah!" Doug added a curse to the exclamation, and the
word echoed through the hollowness of the barn. If he'd
had his mind on the business at hand, instead of thinking
about Stephanie, the accident wouldn't have happened.

Automatically he grabbed his side, where the stinging sensation grew. Warm stickiness spread rapidly. He pressed his left hand against the bright red splotch spreading on the left side of his shirt and threw down the chisel with the other hand.

Not knowing the seriousness of his injury, Doug yanked the tail of his shirt out of his jeans and unbuttoned the garment. He whipped it open, but saw only the large smear of blood on his ribs. His hands were too black with grease for him to examine the wound more closely.

Doug strode to the corner of the barn and, scooping up a blob of hand cleaner, proceeded to cleanse his hands. He rinsed them at the outside faucet. Then, cupping his hands, he pitched cold water against the wound on his left side, drenching the waist of his jeans.

Upon further examination, the wound appeared to be more of a scrape than a puncture, which he'd first feared. In search of gauze, he returned to the barn and located the first-aid kit. No gauze. He was supposed to have replaced that weeks ago, but with the advent of the wreck and the ensuing obligations, he'd completely forgotten.

No big deal. There was more gauze at the house. Tightly clasping his shirt against his side, he strode in that direction.

Minutes later, Doug marched through the kitchen, parading past a startled Stephanie. Without a word, he charged through the living room and up the stairs, taking them two at a time, to the bathroom. He stripped off his shirt and dropped it to the floor.

Automatically he rummaged through the medicine cabinet. By the time he located the gauze, Stephanie stood at the door, a hand over her mouth, her face colorless. "What happened?"

"It's just a scrape," he said in an attempt to reassure her. He was still angry with himself over his carelessness, and his words came out harsher than he intended. "Where are the blasted scissors? I can't find them."

"I don't know. I'll get the ones from the kitchen."

Stephanie returned so quickly, Doug hardly knew she'd left.

Boldly she joined him in the bathroom, determined to help. Taking charge, she grabbed a washcloth. She soaked it with cold water, then gently bathed the area around the wound.

The floral scent of her shampoo assaulted his nostrils, while her warm breath fanned his bare chest. Her gentle ministrations sabotaged his restraints and encouraged thoughts he'd previously chased away. The sudden close proximity aroused his male instincts despite his injury.

Self-preservation demanded action. He grabbed her wrist. "Steph, for heaven's sake, this is the bathroom. Can't a man have some privacy? Get out and let me tend to my own business."

When she tilted her head up to him, mere inches separated their mouths. His wound momentarily forgotten, Stephanie parted her moist full lips. It was an invitation, as far as he was concerned.

Chapter Five

Stephanie stared at Doug. She was only trying to help. His intense scrutiny, inches from her, unnerved her. Parting her lips, she started to speak, then changed her mind. Instead, she dropped her gaze, breaking eye contact. A mistake—a big one indeed! Acres of tanned bare chest rippling with taut muscles and pelted with dark hair filled her vision.

Her fingers itched with the impulse to glide them over the expanse. To avoid the inclination, she gripped the washcloth more tightly, while her gaze traveled downward, to where the dark hair below Doug's navel disappeared into the waist of his jeans.

"You're hurt. Let me help." Intuitively Stephanie thought Doug would kiss her—if he didn't bite her head off first. To cover up the jittery feeling the thought instigated, she gingerly dabbed the cold, wet cloth below the wound, despite his previous dismissal.

Doug sucked in his stomach.

Was his reaction to the chill or to her touch?

"I'm capable of taking care of myself."

"I know you are, but since I'm here, be quiet and accept a little help." She rinsed the cloth and wrung out the excess cold water. Pressing the washcloth against the wound, she said, "Hold this tight to stop the bleeding, while I find something to put on the wound."

Doug peeked under the cloth. "It's not too bad—it could have been worse."

"Be thankful it's not. I imagine stitches in the stomach aren't very pleasant." Stephanie spun to the medicine chest and rummaged through its contents until she found a tube of antibiotic ointment. "Here, hold this."

She slapped the tube into Doug's palm. "Even though the wound doesn't need stitches, it needs a thorough cleaning. Where do you keep the antiseptic?"

"Under the sink. There's a bag of cotton balls, too."

Stooping, Stephanie opened the door beneath the sink and easily spotted the indicated items. After saturating several cotton balls, she took the wet cloth from Doug and tossed it in the sink. She dabbed the wound several times and watched the white bubbles fizz before squeezing on a generous amount of ointment.

While the antibiotic soaked in, she cut a length of gauze and folded it to fit the area. She centered a white strip over the wound, her cool fingers contacting Doug's warm skin.

A shudder pulsed through him. His breath hissed through his firmly set teeth.

His reaction unnerved Stephanie. "Hold this while I cut the tape." Successfully she hid the tremor in her hands that the slight contact produced. Steeling herself against further contact, she added several strips of tape to the bandage, more roughly than she should have.

Doug shoved her hands away. "That's enough. I'll never survive the removal of the tape."

"It's not sticking very well, because of your natural fur coat. Just a couple more pieces," she urged.

"No. If it doesn't stick, that's too bad. You've already made me look like a tic-tac-toe board." Doug strode from the small, confining bathroom without even an attempt at a thank-you-so-very-much.

Sounds of movement in his room, next door, filtered into the bathroom, followed by the echo of his footsteps as he lumbered downstairs and outside, the screen door slamming behind him.

Spying the discarded Western shirt lying on the floor, Stephanie picked it up and rinsed the worst of the blood-stain from it in cold running water at the sink. She left it and the washcloth soaking while she went in search of salt to finish drawing out the stain.

How did she know to use salt? The reaction was automatic and natural—just as it was her nature to help another person in need.

It was nearing seven o'clock the next evening, and Stephanie sat at the kitchen table in front of the sewing machine. Totally engrossed in the delicate procedure of machine blind-stitching the hem of a dress, she carefully guided the edge of the folded fabric through the feeder foot close to the needle. Noticing a pucker in the making, she moistened her forefinger and deftly eased the excess fabric in front of the needle into alignment.

Unexpectedly the screen door slammed, startling Stephanie. She jumped, her forefinger moving into the path of the descending needle. The needle penetrated the fleshy edge of her finger. Jerking her hand away, she hollered, "Ow!"

The machine stopped with a clink and a thud. Immediately Stephanie withdrew her foot from the power-control pedal. With a swipe of her other hand, she brushed strands of dark blond hair off her face that had worked loose from the ponytail at the nape of her neck. She held the injured finger close to her face and leaned toward the light.

"What happened?" Doug asked, striding to Stephanie's side.

"Nothing," she replied automatically, before fully assessing the situation. "I just stitched my finger and broke a needle."

Doug leaned closer to inspect the injury, carrying with him the fresh scent of outdoors.

His warm breath was a kiss of comfort to Stephanie's injured finger, making her squirm under his scrutiny. "I'm all right."

"Like hell! You've got the broken needle lodged in your finger." He grasped her wrist and held up the injured finger for his inspection, rotating it for a view of all sides.

The action brought Stephanie closer to him, and that was far more disturbing than the needle poking through her finger. She tugged unsuccessfully against his warm, work-roughened touch. "It's not the first time, and probably won't be the last."

Doug ignored Stephanie's resistance and glanced around the kitchen. He yanked open three drawers before he found the one he was looking for. He pawed through what appeared to be a catchall drawer and soon unearthed a pair of pliers.

Swinging back around to Stephanie, Doug cautioned, "Don't watch, if you're squeamish."

"I'm fine. Just hurry. The feeling's returning, and along with it, a dull pain."

After a glance at Stephanie, he trained his attention on her wound. Carefully he nosed the cold pliers against her flesh, grasped the protruding end and gingerly pulled out the offending piece of steel. "All right?"

Stephanie nodded and released the pent-up breath she hadn't realized she'd held since traipsing across the room with Doug. A throb stirred in her finger. A bright red bead formed on the tip.

Doug squeezed to induce bleeding. "Need to get out all the germs."

Next he towed a tongue-tied Stephanie to the sink and rinsed the injured appendage under cold water. However, the cold water did nothing to lower the heated awareness she experienced at his tender ministrations.

Still bereft of words, Stephanie watched mutely as Doug jerked a paper towel from the roll at the windowsill and blotted dry her hand and injured finger. She forced words through stiff lips. "Thanks. That already feels better."

"Not just yet." Doug lifted her hand and kissed it tenderly before releasing his hold on her. "Now how does it feel? My mother taught me always to kiss it better."

Stephanie wasn't sure which one of them was more surprised. Nervous, she pulled her T-shirt down, stretching it tight across her rounded abdomen.

A silly grin climbed up one side of his face. "What do mothers know? You'd be better off to play it safe and put antiseptic on it."

His boyish demeanor sent Stephanie into a tailspin. She couldn't think of anything intelligent to say. "It's funny that we've both been accident-prone lately."

"Do you suppose it's contagious?"

Stephanie opened her eyes wider. "I surely hope not."

Doug lifted an eyebrow. "Why? Are you afraid of what Mother's remedy might be?" He edged closer to Stephanie.

This side of Doug was totally foreign to her, and dangerous to her equilibrium. Stammering, she backed against the chair she'd recently vacated. Grabbing it to help maintain her balance, she mumbled, "Yeah, sure. I mean, no, of course not. I'd better go put some antiseptic on my finger right now."

Giving up on sensible speech, Stephanie clasped her injured hand to her chest and darted from the room as if the devil himself were after her. She sprinted upstairs to the bathroom and, when she was safely inside, slammed the door behind her.

She leaned back against the door, her heartbeat racing and pounding deafeningly in her ears. Her finger burned, not from the injury, but from the touch of Doug's warm lips pursed against the appendage, offering comfort, yet unsettling her. She touched the fingertip to her lips, pondering the most recent moments and wondering about those in her past that she couldn't yet retrieve.

In the kitchen the next evening, while helping Neddie prepare dinner, Stephanie asked, "Why does Doug avoid me most of the time? I feel as though I'm highly contagious. To my knowledge, neither amnesia nor pregnancy is communicable."

She sought confirmation from Neddie, while continuing to tear lettuce for a tossed salad. "If I'm imposing, I'll gladly alter the situation—that is, I would, if I had any idea of where to go or what to do. This waiting day after day for my memory to return is unnerving. I'm sure it bothers Doug as much as it does me. Probably you, too." Stephanie smiled ruefully before moving on to the task of chopping carrots and celery for the salad.

"Nah. Don't you worry none." Neddie crossed the kitchen after stirring the pot of chicken and rice. She patted Stephanie's arm, then burst out with a chuckle. "It's not the amnesia, nor the pregnancy. I've got a feeling it has more to do with having a pretty lady around the house day and night, glowing on the threshold of motherhood. That's hard on a man, especially a single one."

Stephanie blushed at the implied intimacy between a man and woman that Neddie hinted at, one that her physical condition bolstered, though it still eluded her memory.

The older woman continued, "It's been a long time since Doug shared living quarters with anyone."

Returning the remaining lettuce, carrots and celery to the refrigerator, Stephanie retrieved a tomato and a cucumber. She didn't know how to respond to Neddie's last statement about sharing living arrangements with Doug. "What can I do to make the situation easier on everyone?"

"Nothing, child." Neddie paused thoughtfully. "Doug has some problems from the past he needs to work out. He's never completely forgiven himself for something that was beyond his control. Time heals all wounds. Give him space to work out his troubles. And when the time is right, you'll know. I'll go so far as to guarantee it."

Hearing that someone other than herself had problems comforted Stephanie, made her feel more normal, more accepting of her plight. "Is there anything I can do to help Doug?"

Neddie shook her head negatively. "Just be yourself, and always be honest. Truth and trust can mend many a fence."

Stephanie paused, her attention drawn from the task at hand. "I'm curious. Does Doug have a lady friend?"

Stooped over the dishwasher, loading dirty dishes, the older woman straightened. "Why do you ask?"

Nervous, feeling she'd stepped over one of the invisible boundaries she constantly found in this household, Stephanie shrugged. "No special reason. It just seems odd for a man like Doug to be without a female companion. In some circumstances, he acts like a totally different person from the withdrawn man I see most of the time."

"I'll admit Doug's not much of a socializer. Not anymore."

Stephanie raised an eyebrow. "Oh? That strikes me as odd. He's nice-looking, and appears well established in his business. It's hard to believe he's not involved with someone."

On her high horse now, Neddie waved her wooden stirring spoon at Stephanie. "Some of his more recent associations with so-called ladies have made him more cautious.

They've done him wrong. He's very selective now. I just wish I were a few years younger."

Embarrassed at her own intense interest in Doug's private life, Stephanie covered up her lapse in good manners. "How did we ever get on this topic of conversation in the first place? All I wanted to know was what Doug does all day, every day, to keep busy while he's actively avoiding me."

The dreaminess left Neddie's voice. She focused once again on stirring dinner. "Well, why didn't you say that in the first place? He single-handedly runs three extremely successful businesses—cattle, wheat and natural-gas operations." She smiled, pride beaming from her. "In fact, he's the leading notable in this part of the state."

"I didn't mean to pry," Stephanie said apologetically, and went on to explain. "I was just trying to understand Doug. I can't figure out much about myself, so I thought I'd look elsewhere for answers. Doug happened to be the next person I thought about." She tossed a smile in Neddie's direction. "My generous benefactor is somewhat of an enigma."

"Not if you know the real Doug."

"And just who is the real Doug?" Stephanie asked, intrigued.

"He's a man who's been hurt time and time again, by women, both financially and emotionally." Neddie spared a glance for Stephanie, to see if she was listening. "When Doug loves, he loves deeply and wholeheartedly, without any reservations. But when one's been hurt as many times as he has by women wanting him for his money, his social position, and the material things he can give them, it's no wonder he steers clear of the opposite sex."

"But, Neddie, I'm not like that. I'm not husband-hunting, looking for a date or anything else from Doug. I'm not even looking for a father for my baby, at least not yet. All I want is to find myself first, who I am and where I belong on this earth. I want my memory back. I want everything normal again. I want to be my own person, responsible for myself, not dependent upon anyone. Tell me what I can do to achieve that.''

"Patience, my dear. Patience. Both you and Doug need it, in abundant supplies. The best things in life come when they're least expected. Don't expect too much of yourself right now, or of Doug. Time is the best companion right now, for both of you.''

Were she and Doug alike in some ways? Stephanie hadn't contemplated that prospect.

The slamming of the door jarred her from reverie. Stephanie glanced in the direction of the noise. Doug was home in time for dinner. Automatically she flashed him a welcoming smile. His gaze caught and held hers. Warmth suffused Stephanie; self-consciously she lowered her gaze. "Dinner will be ready in five minutes.''

Doug glanced down at himself. "That should give me enough time to wash and put on a clean shirt.''

The pictures Stephanie's mind conjured up of his bare chest softly pelted with dark hair sent another wave of warmth surging through her.

Lately Stephanie was unable to ignore the womanly responses she often experienced in Doug's presence. She'd worked hard to justify the awareness as being caused by the highly emotional state due to her pregnant condition.

Intuitively Stephanie knew otherwise. The condition was a classic case of body chemistry—a woman drawn to an attractive man, pure and simple animal magnetism. Nothing to worry about. Or was it?

Doug reappeared downstairs as Stephanie finished setting the table. As usual when he appeared for dinner, Neddie supplied the conversation for them, flitting from one topic to another without ever finishing the previous one.

At the ringing of the phone on the wall, Neddie never ceased her chatter. She just simply changed topics again.

"Now who could that be? Can't a family have a decent meal without a body disturbing them while they're eating?"

Unperturbed, Doug glanced up. "No law says we have to answer it right now. If it's important, they'll leave a message or call back."

By the fourth ring, Doug hadn't moved a muscle toward the phone. Neddie couldn't stand the incessant ringing. "Well, if you're not going to answer, then I am. I'll tell them a thing or two about manners, and decent times to call."

Neddie scooted her chair from the table, hefted herself up, then waddled to the phone, mumbling all the while, "Hold yer britches. I'm a-coming as fast as my old legs'll carry me."

Flicking her gaze from Neddie to Doug, Stephanie detected a humorous twinkle in his eye. The smile he sent her arrested her next thought and quickened her pulse.

He shook his head. "I never did understand why one has to answer the phone just because it rings. I consider it a tool for my convenience, not a hoop I have to jump through."

"I guess when one lives out in the country, a phone has its merits." Stephanie couldn't believe she and Doug were sitting here discussing the pros and cons of subscribing to the telephone service.

Out of the corner of her eye, she saw Neddie returning. Thank goodness! There was no telling what she and Doug would have discussed next. Evidently they were both deficient in conversational skills, apparently having gotten through school without taking and passing Conversation 101.

Neddie bustled up to the table. "That was Brenda. She's at the hospital. Jason—that's my grandson," Neddie explained for Stephanie's benefit, "fell off his bike and bumped his elbow pretty hard. Brenda gets rattled easily, especially when her husband's out of town. She's having his arm X-rayed."

"Don't worry about the kitchen or the table. I'll clean up," Stephanie offered. "Go be with Brenda and Jason."

"Get your purse, Neddie. I'll drive you over." Shoving back from the dinner table, Doug stood.

"I won't hear of such a thing. I'm plenty capable of driving myself. You two finish dinner as if I was sitting right there with you. Be sure and eat all your vegetables."

A smiled jumped to Doug's lips. He winked at Stephanie. "If I don't, I won't grow up to be big and strong like my daddy. Or something akin to that?"

"'Bout time you learned."

Doug smiled indulgently, sitting down again. "Go ahead, Neddie. I'm sure we're old enough to be left on our own for a few hours."

The older woman was already out of sight before Doug finished speaking. She returned with a few last instructions before departing. "Don't forget to lock the windows and doors before you go to bed."

"Yes, ma'am."

From the tone of his voice, Stephanie wouldn't have been surprised if Doug saluted. Indeed, she found his rapport with the older woman admirable. By the time Neddie was out of earshot, Stephanie was bursting with curiosity. "You let her talk to you like that?"

Doug leaned back in his chair and smiled rakishly. "What can I say? Neddie's Neddie. She's one of the joys in my life. You either accept her as she is or stay out of her way."

"Well, I'll be..." Doug's tolerance of the older woman amazed Stephanie. "You're a kitten when it comes to Neddie."

"Don't tell her. You'll spoil her fun." Crinkles formed at the corners of Doug's eyes when he smiled.

This side of Doug intrigued Stephanie. He had more facets than a diamond, each more appealing than the one he usually presented to her—withdrawn, guarded, and hardened.

"Finished with dinner?" Stephanie asked.

"Yeah."

For now, they were back to their monosyllabic conversations. Stephanie stood and stretched across the table to get Neddie's abandoned plate of food. She experienced the warmth of Doug's gaze upon her, but refused to acknowledge it. Maintaining her composure, she set the plate atop hers while gathering the used utensils. Then, hands laden with dirty dishes, Stephanie crossed the room to the sink.

Doug's unbridled scrutiny ignited the flame of awareness inside Stephanie once again. Hands unsteady, she removed the trash can from beneath the sink and scraped the plates. "By the way, Neddie left so quickly I don't think she mentioned that the dishwasher broke this morning."

"She told me at lunch. I phoned the repairman and he promised he'd be here tomorrow to fix it. I'll wash if you'll dry."

"Deal. I'm not self-sacrificing enough to turn down an offer like that. You're stuck, buddy."

Side by side they worked, with limited conversation. When they had finished the chore and were drying their hands on opposite ends of the same towel, Stephanie decided to confront Doug. Whatever this uncomfortable feeling between them was, it needed dispensing with before real problems developed. "This is the first time we've been alone in ages."

At the lifting of Doug's eyebrows, Stephanie amended her statement. "This is the first chance we've had to talk in a while. Doug, I don't know what's going on, but I wish you'd communicate with me. I get the feeling that you're constantly avoiding me."

Crossing his arms, Doug leaned a hip against the counter, staring out the kitchen window.

"See, you're doing it now. Purposely trying to ignore me."

Doug shifted his gaze and peered down his patrician nose at Stephanie.

The tightening of his jaw muscles alerted her to his displeasure. "It's not that I need your undivided attention, but this attitude you display toward me makes me uncomfortable."

His voice deadly quiet, Doug finally spoke more than one word. "Me too, lady."

Of late, his stubborn refusal to address her by name had irritated Stephanie. She stamped a foot and curled her fists. "Quit calling me that. My name's Stephanie."

"Okay, Steph. I'm listening. Say what's on your mind."

Determined to settle this once and for all, Stephanie faced Doug and spoke with a controlled voice. "I'm not here at the ranch because *I* want to be—" she hooked a thumb at herself, then jabbed a finger in his chest "—but because *you* invited me."

Without acknowledging a word of what she said, Doug stared unflinchingly.

She poked him again with her finger. "If I've overstayed my welcome, tell me. I'll leave. I don't care where I have to go. You got that, buddy?"

He swiped a hand from its resting place across his chest and captured her hand, flattening the palm against him. "The name's Doug, not buddy. And the problem's mine, not yours."

Compassion, resulting from the hints Neddie had dropped earlier relating to Doug's troubled past, motivated Stephanie to cup her free hand against the side of Doug's face. Beneath her other hand, his heartbeat raced, as her own did. She fought against the moisture filling her eyes. The strength of her voice evaporated to a mere whisper. "I'll never ask for more than you want to give. I don't want anything material from you. If we're going to live together for a short time, let's at least be friends."

"My home's your home. I've told you."

"Then why treat me like I've got a communicable disease? I can't live this way—as though I'm unwanted garbage."

"Unwanted—? Believe me, Steph, that's not the case at all. In fact, quite the opposite." Tilting his head, Doug planted his lips across Stephanie's without warning.

Unhurried, his touch lingered. The longing Stephanie experienced captured her breath, drawing strength from her, weakening her knees.

When Doug withdrew, his expression spoke volumes. His action had surprised both of them.

At a loss for words, Stephanie stared, wide-eyed, full of unanswered questions.

"I'm the one who should be sorry." Doug sighed heavily, his breath fanning out to encompass them both in the golden glow from the light above the sink. "There's no need for you to leave, Steph. We'll work this out."

Chapter Six

Disaster! There was no other word to describe what had happened when Stephanie confronted Doug about his avoidance of her and received a kiss for her effort. Her emotions teeter-tottered first one way, then the other. Up and down, down and up, back and forth. The dizzying effect was driving her mad. What was she going to do? What could she do?

Hugging her arms to her waist, Stephanie spun on her heel and paced in the opposite direction. The dim, honey-colored glow from the small bedside lamp chased away the inky black of night and guided her around the bedroom.

Alone in her room in the middle of the night, she had nowhere else to go and nothing else she could do at this hour to remedy what she considered a total disaster.

Stephanie halted in front of the maple dresser. Instead of staring helplessly at her bedraggled appearance in the mirror, she focused on the single item in the wooden valet centered on top of the dresser—the solitaire engagement ring.

Long moments passed before she reached out and picked up the ring. She hadn't given it much thought since she'd left the Woodward hospital two months earlier. Now the wide gold band with the multifaceted stone sparkling in the dim light consumed her thoughts.

To Stephanie's knowledge, no matching wedding band had been found, so evidently she wasn't married. But the authorities had found the ring clutched in her hand. Had Theodore just given it to her? Or had she been returning it? Had Theodore aided in her escape from someone? Had Theodore been the messenger for someone else—like Doug?

No, of course not. Doug had denied that. He'd even gone so far as to promise he wouldn't lie to her, ever. And Neddie had never given any indication otherwise. Knowing Neddie, Stephanie thought she'd have said something if the situation warranted it.

Was it all wishful thinking on Stephanie's part? She wanted so desperately to belong somewhere, anywhere. No, she evidently had no prior association with Doug, but the way she felt about him of late, she wouldn't mind if they had a linked past.

Since they hadn't been involved before, why did she feel such a strong connection to him?

Stephanie clasped her fist around the ring and held it to her chest, between her breasts. Eyes closed, she purposely blanked out all thoughts and concentrated on receiving images induced by the ring.

The memory of Doug swooping down and unhurriedly claiming her lips with warm moistness overshadowed everything, even her sensibilities. Why hadn't she dodged or resisted? The way he'd pressed her palm flat against his chest to sense his increased heartbeat should have been indication enough of what he'd intended.

Stephanie had to admit that she'd wanted that kiss every bit as much as Doug had.

What was so wrong about a man wanting a woman or, for that matter, a woman wanting a man? Absolutely nothing at all, unless one of them wasn't free to do so.

According to Neddie, Doug was footloose and fancy-free—well, at least eligible. But did Neddie know that for a fact? As for Stephanie, she didn't know herself or her own status, so how could anyone else?

Stephanie pressed a palm to her aching head. Why wouldn't her brain allow her access to the information trapped within that would reveal her past? What was so horrible that she should be denied the present, or a future, because of not knowing what had gone before?

Totally exhausted, yet no closer to the answers she sought, Stephanie returned to bed, the ring still clasped tightly to her chest, and curled into a ball on her side. What was it like to love someone so much you willingly shared your body and agreed to share your life?

During the rest of June and into July, Doug observed from a distance as Stephanie blossomed into motherhood and her fifth month of pregnancy. Her satiny complexion glowed. Her long golden hair trapped the sunlight, shining as though the ball of light were housed there permanently. And her womanly dips and curves shaped the loose fabric of her clothes in the most interesting places.

Hiding in the study, Doug swung the high-backed leather chair around from the desk to face the large window. Thoughts of Stephanie, and that one kiss, plagued him. He wasn't getting any paperwork done this morning. He might as well call it quits for now.

Even though he purposely kept an emotional distance, Doug tried not to let his avoidance of Stephanie be as noticeable as before. Yet most of the time he purposely avoided her, because he couldn't emotionally afford an entanglement with her, or anyone else, for that matter.

In the past, all his dealings with women, including those with his wife, had been disastrous for him, either financially or emotionally. Only someone with money would understand the problems brought by wealth.

After several years and many burns and scorches, he'd thought he'd finally learned his lesson. Although in a weak moment Doug had succumbed to physical need and kissed Stephanie, he'd be danged sure it didn't happen again. Thank goodness Neddie was there to act as buffer between Stephanie and himself.

A knock sounded at the study door. He spun the chair from the window to the desk. "Come in."

The door opened. Neddie entered and approached the desk. "I thought I'd let you know you've got a problem."

Doug raised his eyebrows. "Oh? And what might that be?"

"Stephanie's got a doctor's appointment this afternoon, but Brenda needs me to watch the grandkids while she drives to Amarillo to pick up her husband at the airport. You're gonna have to take Stephanie to her doctor's appointment this time. That is, unless you want her driving your car. But we don't even know if she can drive or not. So I don't think it's a good idea to let her have the car and make her own way to town. Of course, if you want to ask a farmhand to do the job, then it's not my place to tell you what to do, because it's up to you the way you want to handle the situation, you being the boss and all. But if you want my opinion—"

"Whoa!" Doug threw up a hand to halt the rush of words. "That's enough. I get the idea. You tend to your grandchildren, and I'll take responsibility for Stephanie."

"Good. I thought you'd see it my way, especially after I explained all the details to you. I knew I could trust you to do the right thing."

Doug vacated his chair and rounded the desk to go to Neddie's side. She talked the whole time, without pausing between sentences or noticing he'd changed positions. With a hand beneath her elbow, he guided Neddie in the direction of the door.

She never skipped a beat, giving no indication of realizing that she'd been dismissed. "I shouldn't have worried myself over the whole ordeal. I even said as much to Brenda over the phone. I told her Doug would understand how blood's thicker than water and that grandchildren are important to grandmothers."

"Have fun. Go be a grandmother." He nudged her through the doorway as she took off on another tangent. Gently Doug closed the door behind her as she waddled across the living room, talking more to herself than to him.

He couldn't help but chuckle at the lovable Neddie, until the realization of her mission slammed into him full force. He'd agreed to take full responsibility for getting Stephanie to and from town for her monthly doctor's appointment. That meant the two of them alone together in the small confines of a car.

Sheesh! Why had he bothered to worry earlier this morning?

Unable to concentrate long enough to read a magazine in Dr. Perryman's office, Doug tossed the periodical down, careful that it missed his upturned Stetson, and stood. He lumbered across the room, hooked his thumbs in the back pockets of his jeans and stared out the window, heedless of the happenings outside, on the sidewalk and the street.

Neddie and Stephanie were total opposites. Neddie could talk a person to death, whereas Stephanie used the deadly silence routine. Both were effective weapons, as far as Doug was concerned.

"I'm finished."

Stephanie's softly spoken words behind him sent Doug spinning in her direction. "That didn't take long. Did you already make the appointment for next month?"

At her nod, Doug walked across the room, retrieved his Stetson and jammed it on his head. Following her outside, he couldn't help but notice the tantalizing wiggle to her backside as she walked and the way the once loose sweat-pants tightly cupped her hips, forming wrinkles as the fab-ric stretched to accommodate her expanding abdomen. Every few steps, the T-shirt inched up over her hips, expos-ing the softly rounded contours of her backside. Looking self-conscious, she continually tugged it back down.

"Steph."

Hearing him call her name, she paused, waiting for him to draw up next to her.

"Would you like to pick up more fabric while we're in town?"

"Yes, definitely." Relief shone in her eyes as she lifted a hand to brush back the dark golden tendrils the Oklahoma breeze scooted across her face.

"I'll arrange for you to have charge accounts around town. That way, if you need something when you're in town with Neddie, it'll be easy enough for you to pick it up."

"Thanks." She glanced down and pressed a hand to her abdomen, a secretive smile curling across her face. "My baby thanks you, too."

Doug dropped his gaze to her hand at her belly.

"I just found out from Dr. Perryman that what I thought were gas pains are really the baby's kicking and moving." She slid her hand to a different spot on her abdomen.

Excitement sparkled from her eyes. Her gaze met and held Doug's. "I detect a lump beneath the surface, moving slowly, as though he—" at the lifting of Doug's eyebrows, Stephanie amended her statement "—or she, is changing positions."

As still as a statue, she contemplated the happening. "I don't know if it's a foot or an elbow or what, but I defi-nitely feel the knot and pressure both from the inside and out. Do you want to feel?"

Lady, have you lost your ever loving mind? His voice pitched high, Doug asked, "Here?"

Stephanie glanced around and grinned. "I guess a public sidewalk in town is not the best place in the world to ask a man to touch my stomach."

Tugging his Stetson low over his eyes, Doug took hold of her elbow and propelled her in the direction of the car. "I hope you don't ask all the men you meet to fondle your stomach."

"Well, of course not," Stephanie snapped, jerking her arm from his grasp. "I usually hang a sign around my neck and charge for the privilege."

"Look, Steph," Doug said, halting in the middle of the sidewalk, sliding his hands in his hip pockets. "I didn't mean to offend you, but you can't just walk around town asking strange men to fondle you."

"For your information, I didn't issue a blanket invitation to just any strange man walking by. I asked only you." Bristling with anger, Stephanie pitched her voice louder. "And I didn't ask you to *fondle* me."

A lady passing by turned and openly stared, faltering on a crack in the sidewalk with her next step.

Doug pasted a smile on his face. "A lovers' spat."

The lady's eyes bugged out as she raked her gaze up and down Stephanie.

He hooked his arm around Stephanie and escorted her to the car. His words were intentionally loud enough for the eavesdropper to hear. "Come along, dear. This definitely is not the place to kiss and make up."

The woman continued down the sidewalk, shaking her head.

Stephanie shoved from Doug's hold. "I'm not kissing and making up, and I'm not your dear."

"All right. Calm down. I'm sorry."

Waiting for him to unlock the car door, Stephanie glared at him across the hood. "I thought we were going to the fabric store—or did you change your mind?"

He punched a button inside the driver's door and released the automatic lock. "Get in."

Minutes later, Doug parked the car downtown in front of the fabric shop. When they climbed from the car, he suggested to Stephanie, "Go ahead. I'll catch up. I thought of something I need to do. It won't take long."

Doug had determined that it was best to put a little distance between them while he could. Impulsively he angled across the street to the barbershop. It wasn't that he needed a haircut, but the shop was as good a place as any for a reprieve.

"Hey, Conrad," Ray called from the barber chair. "You lost?"

"No. I was in town, so I decided to drop in and let you clean the fuzz off my neck." Rubbing a hand at the back edge of his collar, Doug stopped in front of the barber.

Ray guffawed and slapped a hand against his thigh. "Since when did a little fuzz bother you?"

Doug bristled. "You want my business or not?"

"Sure. Come on over and rest yourself here." Ray climbed down from the hydraulic chair and patted the vinyl seat. "In all these years I've been cutting your hair, you've never set foot in here more than once a month. Your style's more like every six weeks to two months."

"Maybe my style's changing as I get older." Doug removed the Stetson from his head and, upturning it on the counter, levered into the chair. "Besides, I never heard you holler about a fellow spending money in your shop before."

Ten minutes later, Stetson in place atop his head, Doug was back on the street, ambling in the direction of the fabric store.

Once there, he shoved open the door and stepped inside. Pausing, he surveyed the shop for Stephanie. After locating her in a narrow aisle, her dark golden head bent close to a bolt of fabric, Doug cut a path to her.

When he stopped near her side, Stephanie straightened, her face wreathed in smiles. "Look at what I've found. Seersucker."

"Is it supposed to be puckered and wrinkled like that?"

"That's the beauty of the way it's made. It doesn't have to be ironed." She spun around and, farther down the aisle, dislodged a bolt of fabric from between two others. After unwinding two rounds, she held up the length. "Will you look at this? Flannel. Feel it."

Without waiting for Doug to respond, Stephanie stroked the edge of the fabric against Doug's temple and cheekbone. "All soft and velvety. Won't these fabrics make darling baby gowns and diaper shirts?"

Scratching his head, Doug eased the Stetson back to his crown, his light brown hair springing onto his forehead in a wave. "I thought diapers went on the other end."

"Not diapers, silly, diaper shirts." Stephanie chuckled, then patiently explained. "Short shirts a baby wears on the top half."

"But we don't even know yet if it's a boy or a girl."

Stephanie selected several fabrics, pulling out the bolts and stacking them on top. "It really doesn't matter. Many of the colors and prints, as well as the styles, are suitable for both males and females."

Automatically Doug picked up the fabric bolts and stuffed them under his arm, as though they were nothing more than schoolbooks. "Wouldn't it be easier to buy the things you need?"

"Yes, I'm sure it would. Out of necessity, I'll buy some things, because I can't make everything. But the shirts and gowns will be easy to sew." Stephanie smiled and shrugged. "Besides, sewing will keep me busy."

As Doug followed Stephanie to the front counter, he thought of plenty of activities to keep her busy, all requiring his help. And he'd willingly lend his assistance, especially when she beamed that smile in his direction.

Offhand, Doug was at a loss to understand how Stephanie derived so much pleasure from creating something from almost nothing. But if she stayed busy, she was apparently content.

For some reason, he possessed the uncanny desire to always keep her this animated. "Whatever makes you happy."

The drive from town to the ranch wasn't the ordeal Doug had imagined. In fact, it proved to be quite the opposite. Stephanie's excitement glowed in every word, in every deed. Her curiosity about her surroundings demonstrated childlike wonder as she took pleasure in learning what nature offered in the Red Carpet Country.

By the time they reached the Triple T Estates, Doug's staunch resolve to avoid Stephanie had weakened a notch. He actually found himself enjoying her company on the return trip as he introduced her to his world, sharing information about what he loved most—his ranch and the hidden beauty of this part of the country.

Stephanie's enthusiasm softened his mood, granting him tolerance toward her presence at the ranch and in his life.

Doug arrived home in a more peaceful state of mind than he'd experienced since Stephanie's appearance at the ranch. He switched off the car engine. "I don't know about you, but today seems to have turned out better than it started."

"Definitely. Today's been—" Stephanie halted in midsentence with a soft gasp.

Concerned, Doug twisted in her direction. Without warning she grabbed his hands and placed them on her rounded abdomen. She beamed him one of those heartstopping smiles of hers, eyes full of sparkles, and held his hands tightly against her. A hardened knot moved beneath his touch, and then her entire belly jumped.

"The baby's got the hiccups. Did you feel him—"

"Or her," Doug put in.

"—or her, jump?"

"Is that what that was? The hiccups?"

"Can you believe it?"

Doug couldn't believe he was sitting here with his hands cupped around Stephanie's belly as if he possessed some special right to do so.

She parted her soft, full lips in anticipation of his response.

Another vision filled his mind, that of his wife full with child, his hand on her stomach. Constance's angry words echoed in his head. *It's you who wants this child, not me. Just feel the torture my body must endure.*

Doug's heart skipped a beat. He trained his gaze on Stephanie. "Does it hurt? The baby moving like this?"

"No, of course not. This baby gives me a reason to go on living day after day. Without this child to occupy my thoughts, I'd go stark raving mad, dwelling on who I am and where I came from. Chalk it up to motherly instinct, but this baby means more to me than life itself."

Jolted by her declaration, Doug stared. "You're serious, aren't you? You actually mean every word of what you said?"

"Of course I do. It's a totally natural and honest response. Name a mother who wouldn't gladly lay down her life for her child." Full of innocence, the look in Stephanie's eyes verified the truth of her softly spoken words.

Doug could name one such mother, but he refused to do so. Instead, he climbed from the car, his day spoiled by the haunting thoughts of his dead wife and child.

At times, her crude laughter and harsh words still reverberated in his ears as a cruel reminder of reality. *Not your money or anything you own, Conrad, can keep me here at this godforsaken ranch, not even your child.*

*   *   *

Later that afternoon, without conscious thought, Doug wandered around the house. He stopped on the second-floor landing and stared at the door leading to the attic.

With memories of feeling Stephanie's baby move fresh on his mind, he opened the door and flipped the switch, flooding the stairs with light. He climbed the stairs and, using the glow from the stairwell light, cautiously picked his way to the center of the room. He pulled the dangling chain, and a once dark bulb lit the room.

Pivoting slowly, Doug glanced around until he found what he sought—the solid oak cradle he'd built ten years ago, in anticipation of his child. In the end, he'd packed the cradle away without its ever having been used.

A few minutes later, Doug succeeded in digging the cradle out from beneath a pile of boxes. What would Stephanie think? Would she even want to use it?

As though his thoughts had conjured her up from nowhere, Doug heard her calling his name. Soon the sound was stronger as her voice echoed up the stairwell into the attic.

"Doug, are you up there?"

He didn't answer, but he didn't have to, because Stephanie rose into view as she climbed the stairs. When she reached the top, he called out, "Be careful up here. Watch your step. You don't want to fall."

Her gaze lit on Doug. She halted on the top step. "You had a phone call. When I couldn't find you, I took a message and said you'd phone back later."

"Thanks."

Stephanie surveyed the room. "What a roomful of treasures! I love antiques."

Doug straightened and, stuffing his hands in his hip pockets, glanced around the room. "This stuff? It's mostly junk that found its way up here when someone got tired of looking at it or no longer needed it downstairs.''

"Maybe to you, but I'm sure it was all bought for a reason and holds sentimental value. Just imagine the interesting stories tucked away up here, all part of someone's life.''

"Yeah, I guess so.'' Doug nudged the cradle with the toe of his boot. Though slight, the poke sent the crib rocking back and forth.

The movement caught Stephanie's eye. "What's that?''

Doug lowered his gaze to the object of discussion. "A dusty old cradle I thought you might use if I brought it downstairs and cleaned it up.''

"I want to see.'' Stephanie picked a path across the room to where Doug stood. Kneeling, she touched the side with one finger and set the cradle in motion once again. "This is wonderful! I can't wait to use it.''

Doug reached out and dusted it with his hand. "Looks like it needs a good cleaning.''

Stephanie ran a hand across the edge to the end and examined the design. "This is beautifully crafted. It looks handcarved.''

"It is.''

Her gaze shot to him. "Did you make it?''

Doug didn't know why, but he was tempted to say no. However, as was his custom, he told the truth. "Yeah.''

"I didn't know you could do anything like that.''

"There's a lot about me you don't know. Consider yourself lucky.'' Her penetrating stare made him uncomfortable. Doug glanced around to ease the tense moment. "See anything else you can use?''

Stephanie stood and glanced around. "I don't know. What all's up here?''

Hooking his thumbs in his front pockets, Doug shrugged. "A little bit of this, a whole lot of that. Basically junk.''

"Treasures," Stephanie countered, then sent him one of her heart-stopping smiles.

A flame of awareness shot to life inside him. He really wished she wouldn't do that. Emotions carefully guarded, he glanced down. "Whatever."

"Yoo-hoo!" Neddie's voice carried up the stairs.

"We're in the attic," Doug called out.

"Dinner's ready. Don't let it get cold."

"We'll be right there." While Stephanie dallied, Doug picked up the cradle and carried it downstairs, to the second-floor landing. He returned to the top of the stairs. "You heard Neddie. Dinner's waiting."

Regretfully Stephanie glanced around the room one last time. "Can I come back up here another time and see if there's anything else I can use?"

"Sure. Suit yourself."

With a pull of the chain, Stephanie switched off the light and inched her way to where Doug stood. As she neared him, she stumbled in the semidarkness and pitched forward.

Automatically Doug shot out his arms to break her fall and shield her with his body. She flailed her arms, causing him to catch her in an awkward grasp. Despite the awkwardness, he bent his arms to absorb the force of the fall.

Stephanie twisted to regain her balance. One of her breasts settled in Doug's hand. With their two bodies together, her gyrations stilled, trapping his hand between them.

The female softness against him stirred Doug. Each throb of his pulse magnified his need.

In Doug's embrace, Stephanie melted against him.

Neither moved to shatter the moment of intense awareness.

To Doug, it seemed natural to have Stephanie in his arms. His fingers twitched with the temptation to caress the soft, full breast filling his hand, but Doug resisted. Instinctively he pressed his need into her softness. However, his fingers remained motionless, allowing Stephanie the prerogative of choosing what happened next.

Chapter Seven

When Doug rescued Stephanie from the fall, everything happened so fast, she relied more on instinct than on thought. But instinct created chaos for her.

As she stilled, Stephanie realized that Doug had wrapped one arm around her. His other hand was trapped between them. Her gyration to regain her balance resulted in his hand being firmly planted upon her breast. Doug didn't take advantage of the position. Yet the stillness of his fingers on her breast enticed Stephanie more than if he'd clutched at her.

The remembrance of their one kiss bounded to the forefront of her memory. Would he kiss her again? Did she want him to?

Shaken from the ordeal, Stephanie relaxed against him, safe and secure. Sadly, she couldn't even remember the kisses of her baby's father. More of Doug's kisses would only complicate matters. Yet she couldn't bear to leave the shelter of his arms after such a short while.

She rested her head on his chest, snuggling against him. Their heartbeats raced in unison. A gentle nudge from Doug made her fully aware of his arousal. Sudden desire to experience with him what she'd previously experienced with her baby's father and lost to amnesia fanned to life the flame of desire within her. Knowing Doug wanted her triggered an impulse toward reckless, wanton abandonment.

Stephanie rocked against him. Buckling his knees, he fitted himself against her. The warmth of his hard presence incited desire. She eased up on her toes.

In response, Doug kneaded her soft, full breast while lifting her with his other arm. He positioned her more firmly against him. Her weight nestled upon him, Stephanie held on to his shoulders and tilted her face to him.

The indecision in Doug's eyes thwarted Stephanie's impetuous response. Immediately lucidity returned, closely followed by humiliation.

How could she have practically begged him to take her, here and now? There was no excuse for such imprudent behavior. A hot wave of embarrassment rushed up her neck and exploded, tingling her hair at the roots.

Pushing away from him, Stephanie self-consciously slid down Doug to stand on the floor. Quickly she stepped backward on wobbly legs. "Uh…thanks for supporting me while I regained my footing. I didn't mean to throw myself in your arms. I can stand on my own now."

Without waiting for Doug's response, Stephanie spun on her heel and bolted down the stairs.

For days after his lapse in gentlemanly behavior in the attic, Doug wrestled with his conscience. Alone in the study, elbows on the desk, he pressed the heels of his hands into his eyes. How could he have been so bold as to take advantage of Stephanie when she tripped?

One minute she'd been standing there talking, the next he'd been groping her breast and thrusting at her as though he had a right to do so. He wouldn't blame her if she never set foot in the same room with him again, much less spoke another word to him.

How would they get along the next four months? In the past three, they'd gone from bad to worse. He'd bullied her into staying when she hinted at leaving. He'd grudgingly taken her shopping, and then he'd avoided her. But he found it impossible to resist her. He couldn't remain unaffected by an attractive woman in his home, day after day, week after week, month after month.

A light rapping sounded at the door to the study. Doug glanced up.

The door edged opened, and Stephanie entered with a feather duster. She stopped in the middle of the room. "Oh, I'm sorry. I didn't know you were here. When there wasn't an answer, I thought the room was empty. I'll come back later."

Doug caught Stephanie's gaze and held it. An uncomfortable silence impregnated the room. "No. It's all right. You won't bother me." That was a lie, and Doug knew it the second the words left his mouth. Her presence was a distraction—although not an altogether unpleasant one.

Quietly she moved about the room, waving the feather duster. Unable to do otherwise, Doug followed her progress with his gaze. Stephanie now wore maternity clothes, but they were far from the shapeless tents he had anticipated. Even though full and flowing, the dress she wore today draped attractively around her enlarged breasts and blossoming stomach.

As she stretched to reach the top shelves, the dress climbed higher to give him a view of her shapely bare thighs. When she stooped to dust the lower shelves and occasional tables, the fullness of the dress fell forward, offering glimpses of her cleavage.

Angry at himself for becoming distracted, Doug spun his tall leather chair to face the picture window. He raked a hand across his face to erase the images of her seductive body.

For heaven's sake, this was more than likely his brother's lady. She had been branded by Theodore, or some man, and was carrying a child. He couldn't covet a woman who belonged to his own brother. She'd be almost like family. That is, *if* Stephanie was indeed the girl Theodore had spoken of in his last letter.

Momentarily Doug swung around to the desk and, purposely keeping his gaze off Stephanie, dug through the mess of papers in the shallow center drawer until he located the last two letters from Theodore. Checking the postmarks, he chose the more recent one and spun back around to the picture window.

Keeping the letter hidden low on his lap, Doug carefully removed the pages from the envelope and unfolded them.

Just as he'd remembered—no name given to the girl of Theo's dreams, no identifying facts, no information that could be traced. He'd said he'd met a girl. She'd made a difference in his life, given him hope, and a reason to believe in himself. When she could get away from work, he'd bring her home to meet Doug.

Theo hadn't mentioned what line of work she was in, or where or how they met. He hadn't even mentioned his sudden decision to marry, after being so adamantly against the institution of marriage only two months earlier, during a weekend visit. Doug wondered whether Theo's motives would be low enough to— No, surely not. Only a desperate person would—

A movement out of the corner of his eye made him return the letter to its envelope. He swung his chair around and tucked the letter at the back of the drawer, at the bottom.

"Would you like me to dust the desktop?" Stephanie asked, standing to the right of the desk, after dusting the photographs and frames hanging on the wall. "I can come back later, when you're not here."

"No, go ahead and do it now." Doug stood and rolled his chair backward, out of her way, to give her a wide berth.

After a few deft strokes across the computer and the desk, Stephanie moved to the other side of the desk and the pictures on the opposite wall.

Should he or shouldn't he? Doug harbored a moral obligation to Theo, Stephanie and himself to do what was honorable and right. He'd put off the unpleasant task until now. But for some reason, the time seemed more right now than it had before. On impulse, he made his decision. "Steph?"

The one word halted her motion. She hooked a glance over her shoulder and waited.

"I have some business to tend to in Oklahoma City." He tried to avoid looking at her, but couldn't resist noting her reaction to what he had to say. He focused on her hazel eyes. "Would you—and Neddie, of course—want to come along?"

"When?"

"Be ready to leave bright and early tomorrow morning, and pack an overnight bag."

The drive from the ranch to Oklahoma City took more than half a day. By late afternoon, after several rest stops along the way for Stephanie's benefit, they pulled into a parking lot at an apartment complex not far from the interstate.

Without explanation, Doug climbed from the car and indicated that the two women should do the same. Mutely Stephanie followed in the procession and waited silently while Doug opened the door to a second-floor residence. Gripping the rail, she looked down on the grassy inner court; there was a swimming pool to one side.

"Steph, you coming inside?" Doug asked, holding the door open behind Neddie.

After a moment's hesitation, Stephanie pivoted in the direction of the apartment. "Yes, of course."

Doug closed the door securely behind them.

Evidently the person who lived there hadn't expected company. Clutter littered the room—magazines, clothing, drinking glasses and a couple of coffee mugs. In fact, from the looks of them, the glasses had been there a while, the contents evaporated to a thick layer of crust.

As Stephanie walked around, a putrid odor caught her attention. She easily located the source, a plastic cup from a fast-food establishment, half-full of what had once been milk, now curdled and coated with fuzzy green-gray mold.

She turned around, seeking Doug and Neddie. They were nowhere in sight, but undertones of their voices carried from what appeared to be the bedroom. Not waiting for permission, Stephanie gingerly picked up the offending cup and made her way to the kitchen. Stopping in the center of the room, she found similar disarray there.

A quick search of the area yielded a trash can under the sink, filled to capacity. Her nose curled in protest. The odor from the trash can also indicated rotting and decayed matter. Fresh out of alternatives, Stephanie set the plastic cup on the counter, next to the sink.

As she passed by the table again, she noticed mail scattered about. Curious, she stepped closer. None was personal; most was addressed to Occupant or Resident.

When she would have left, a colorful mail-order catalog caught her attention. She flipped through a few pages, then, losing interest, folded the magazine shut. The name on the outside left no further doubt as to whose apartment this was. In bold lettering was the name Mr. Theodore Taylor.

Her legs weakened at her discovery. Stephanie gripped the back of the chair for support. Suddenly she viewed everything in a different perspective. Chances were, part of her past was hidden somewhere in this apartment.

Trembling with both excitement and apprehension, Stephanie lowered herself into the chair. She glanced to the doorway. What was going on here? Was this some kind of test? Was she supposed to pass or fail?

With more interest, Stephanie shuffled through the mail, one item at a time, stacking it to the side afterward. She found no other indication of the occupant's personal life. All she knew was his name and that he was on several mailing lists that were electronic in nature. Nothing important.

Elbows propped on the table, Stephanie lowered her face to her hands. Why couldn't she remember anything? What had he looked like? Had they dated often? For how long?

She needed answers, and she needed them now. Summoning up strength and courage, she pushed up from the table and made her way, shakily, back through the living room to the bedroom. Leaning against the door, she observed Doug and Neddie, without them knowing she was there.

Neddie was methodically removing clothes from the dresser, folding them and stacking them on the bed. A stack of suits, hangers and all, lay across the foot of the bed. Probably two dozen or more shirts, on hangers, were stacked nearby.

"Did you find anything?" Doug called from the closet, where he was emptying the top shelf's contents on the floor.

"Nothing," Neddie answered.

"Me either," Stephanie said.

At the sound of her voice, both Doug and Neddie spun in her direction, their activity ceasing.

"Well, I found the dinner table scattered with mail, and discovered that this is, or was, Theodore's apartment. Why didn't you tell me?"

Neddie squirmed underneath Stephanie's accusing gaze and silently appealed to Doug to answer the question.

He strode out of the closet and faced Stephanie. He tucked his thumbs in his hip pockets. "I'd hoped coming here would jar your memory."

"It jarred me, all right, but not my memory." Warm tears moistened her eyes. She reined them in, struggling to regain her composure. Still reeling from her shock, and angry that he hadn't given her any forewarning, Stephanie lashed out at Doug with harsh words. "Are you trying to trip me—I mean, trick me?"

At her Freudian slip, the memory of their time in the attic together rushed to the forefront of her mind. Was Doug thinking of that moment, too? The remembrance of her wanton behavior silenced Stephanie with lingering embarrassment.

Doug curled his fingers into a fist. His flaring nostrils indicated that her words had struck home. She'd been as much to blame as he for the ordeal, if not more so. Being angry at herself for lacking inhibition was no reason for Stephanie to take stabs at Doug.

She spun on her heel and retreated to the living room. Following close behind, Doug stopped when she halted. "I'm sorry, Steph. Maybe I was wrong not to tell you we were coming here, but I honestly didn't know what to do." Behind her, he clasped her shoulders with both hands.

Stephanie shrugged from his touch and spun to face him. "Were you afraid I'd have time to concoct a story and hide my initial response?"

"No."

"You think I'm faking, don't you? You don't actually believe I have real amnesia, because it's so rare. Do you think I'm another one of those women who are only after what I can get from you?" Stephanie hid her face in her hands, hoping desperately to control the tears.

"No, of course not." His words faded away to nothing.

As the silence lengthened, Stephanie conquered the need to shed tears.

"Steph, look at me," Doug commanded with softly spoken words. "Please."

That one word had the strength to shatter her resolve. Stephanie bit her lips to still their trembling, then lowered her hands from her face and met Doug's gaze.

Regret hovered in his dark brown eyes. "I was tempted to tell you where we were coming. I wanted to, but I decided against it."

"Why?" Stephanie desperately wanted to understand his reasoning.

"I didn't want you to worry yourself sick before we got here about what might or might not happen." He shrugged. "And if you don't remember anything, then it's no big deal. On the other hand, if being here brings back your memory, then it will have been worth the extra caution."

She contemplated what Doug said.

Doug ducked his head and rubbed a hand across the back of his neck. "Besides, I wasn't sure how I'd react upon seeing Theo's belongings. But regardless of whether or not you decided to come here with me today, I had to clean out his personal things. There's no sense renewing the lease on this apartment."

Stephanie glanced around. "It's going to need a good cleaning."

"Don't worry about it. I'll hire professionals to come in after we get what we want. In fact, I don't see that there's much to keep. I'll probably donate his stuff to Goodwill, or the Salvation Army."

At the raising of Stephanie's eyebrows, Doug hastily added, "The furniture's all rented, anyway."

"Oh."

"I'd better get back to helping Neddie before she thinks I deserted her." At the doorway to the bedroom, Doug swung back around. "Check things out. See if there's anything that brings an air of familiarity. Holler if you need me."

* * *

In the middle of the night, Stephanie's hollers and screams shattered the silent darkness. She bolted to a sitting position and, staring into the inky blackness, hugged her knees to her chest.

A pounding sounded at the motel door. "Steph, are you all right? Open up." Panic threaded Doug's voice. "Open up, or I'll bust the door down."

Stephanie didn't answer.

"Do you hear me?"

She sat on the bed, rocking back and forth in a curled position.

"You've got until the count of three. One. Two."

Catapulting from the bed, Stephanie dashed to the door. Quickly she unlatched the dead bolt and safety chain, then flung the door wide open.

"Three," Doug said, standing half-naked in the doorway, hands braced on his hips. Without so much as a word, he stalked in and searched the room. Cautiously he checked behind the drapes, peeked under the bed and glanced in the closet.

Then, barefoot, he made a quick trip through the bathroom, shifting the shower curtain, before he stopped in front of Stephanie, his jeans gaping open at the waist having been hastily retrieved. Acres of bare, muscled chest heaved with his deep breaths of exertion. "There's no one here. What happened?"

"I had a nightmare." Without looking at him, Stephanie ran her hands up and down her upper arms to chase away the chill of apprehension. "It was a wreck. I couldn't see the driver, because it was too dark. We were going too fast. The car kept swerving off the edge of the road. I was scared and wanted out, but couldn't get out. He—I don't know who, just that it was a man—he wouldn't let me out."

Stephanie squeezed her eyes tightly shut, attempting to recall the dream. Hard as she tried, the image eluded her.

"It's all right. You've had a long drive in the car today." Doug wrapped his arms loosely around her, comforting her. "Get back in bed and try to get some sleep."

Putting off the inevitable return to bed, Stephanie said, "I hope I didn't wake Neddie."

"I wouldn't worry about it," Doug told her. "Nothing wakes Neddie."

An arm draped loosely around Stephanie's shoulders, he walked with her to the door. "I'd tuck you in bed, but then you wouldn't have anyone to latch the door behind me."

She wanted to ask him to stay, wanted the security of having another human near, but she knew she couldn't and wouldn't.

Had the shock of finding herself in Theo's apartment earlier this afternoon loosened the restraints on her memory? Were her dreams an indication she was beginning to remember things? Stephanie could only hope for the best.

July drew to an end and August moved in, hot and dry. Doug realized how his and Stephanie's lives had molded together since her arrival at the Triple T Estates four months ago. His bachelor life-style had somehow evolved into a makeshift family unit.

He'd mellowed since their trip to Oklahoma City to clean out Theodore's apartment. He'd grown used to having Stephanie around. Now he couldn't imagine life without her. What was more, he didn't want to.

He was used to the constant hum of the sewing machine, enjoyed having home-cooked meals most evenings, and was accustomed to sharing his space. He'd learned the kind of person Stephanie was, and he could be alone with her without harboring thoughts that she had ulterior motives.

He no longer suspected the situation with the amnesia had been engineered for her personal gain. She wasn't that kind of person. She was as she appeared—truthful to the point of being frank at times, creative, resourceful, courageous and nurturing. All admirable qualities, and to his mind, it was rare that they were all bundled into one living breathing person. All this endeared Stephanie to him that much more. From what he could tell, she was going to be a great mother, and would make some lucky guy a great wife and helpmeet.

He wondered if that lucky man could be him. But he knew that was just a silly dream. He'd treated her so poorly from the beginning, she'd never look at him twice, much less learn to love him. Why was he sitting here yearning for something he couldn't have?

Doug had learned long ago that he wasn't, and never would be, husband or father material. He'd proved that ten years ago. Now he accepted that he was meant to be alone. That was his lot in life, always to be a caretaker, never to be cared for.

And because he wasn't a kid anymore, he knew better than to dream about such things. He was grown, and because he was, he knew life wasn't fair and couldn't be expected to be otherwise. The fulfillment of his needs would have to come from working the land, not from the kind of gratification only a woman could give.

Why was he sitting here torturing himself this way? He knew his place in life was to pick up after Theo, always had been, always would be. It would be unthinkable for Doug to do otherwise. So, as was expected of him, he'd take care of his brother's—what? Girlfriend? Lover? Child? At least for now, that seemed to be the case.

The opening of the study door broke Doug's reverie.

Stephanie strolled to the center of the room. "Brenda called and asked Neddie to baby-sit the grandkids while she accompanied her husband on a short business trip. She left while you were out. They're supposed to be back late this evening sometime, no later than midnight."

When he didn't comment, Stephanie continued, "As far as dinner goes, I can cook, or we can have leftovers. It's your choice. What do you want?"

Want? His choice? A wife and family to call his own. Doug closed his eyes and groaned. "To be honest, I wasn't even thinking about dinner."

Curiosity piqued, Stephanie lifted her eyebrows. "Oh? And what's that supposed to mean?"

Doug gulped. Suddenly an idea came to him—one that might keep Stephanie in his life. He'd prove to her how entertaining he could be, that he'd make a great uncle for her kid. Maybe she'd consider staying after the baby came. The ranch would be a great place to raise a child. Then he wouldn't be so alone.

Grasping at the first thought that offered salvation for both Stephanie and him, Doug blurted out, "How would you like to go out for the afternoon and observe the workings of the ranch?"

He leaned back in the chair and, crossing his arms over his chest, watched as she toyed with the offer, hoping against hope that his inner turmoil was once again repressed, even if temporarily.

Stephanie wavered, rubbing her hand in a slow circular motion on her swollen stomach. "I'm not sure climbing on a horse in my condition is a good idea. After all, I don't even know if I can ride or not."

Doug decided for her. "You don't have to ride a horse in this day and age."

Surprised, Stephanie blinked. "This I've got to see."

"Right this way."

Grabbing his Stetson as he left the house, Doug led Stephanie to the back of the barn, where the Jeep was parked. "Meet Hector, my loyal mount."

A smile stretched across her face. "You've got to be kidding. You actually name your vehicles?"

"Sure, some of them. Especially the hardworking ones. Ain't that right, old boy?" Doug reached out and patted the hood affectionately. "Ol' Hector may not be much to look at, but he does a heck of a good job getting me around where I need to go, when we don't always have a road to follow."

Stephanie's skepticism showed through in her words as reticence. "I'm not sure about this."

Doug was sure. He definitely was not hanging around the house all day, with only the two of them there. Perhaps playful banter would win her over. "Come on. What will a couple of hours playing hooky from housework and sewing hurt? I promise not to tell the boss."

A smile worked its way across her face. "Oh, you know him, too, huh?"

"Yeah, he can be a real pain sometimes, but don't tell him I said so." Doug waggled his brows at her.

"Okay. You talked me into it." Stephanie hiked a foot into the Jeep and, with Doug's assistance, climbed aboard Hector. "How can I turn down an offer like that?"

"You can't."

She slid a glance his way. "You think you know me pretty well, don't you, mister?"

He stuck the key in the ignition and switched on the engine. "Fasten your seat belt, lady, and hush your yapping. You're going for the ride of your life."

Conscious of Stephanie's condition, Doug cautiously pulled out onto the dirt trail that cut through the fields of wheat stubble at the back of the house. At a snail's pace, he kept the jolting to a minimum.

The fields close to the ranch were tamer—manicured wheat stubble being plowed under. But the farther out one traveled, the wilder the countryside became—natural grassland unhampered by man.

During the hot August afternoon, they spotted a couple of farmhands mending a fence and spoke briefly with them.

Stephanie thrilled at having the wind in her hair. She couldn't get over the beauty that surrounded them. They rode for a time in silence, enjoying the natural landscape.

Near the time they should have started their return journey to the house, Stephanie saw a herd of cattle at a distance and pointed. "Are those your critters over there?"

His gaze followed the direction she indicated. "Part of them. You want a close up look?"

At her nod, he steered Hector the Jeep across the grassland to a better vantage point.

Stephanie watched with interest as the cattle milled around, chewing grass. Unfastening her seat belt, she stood in the open vehicle, holding on to the windshield frame for support.

Doug shifted the gear lever to neutral, then set the hand brake. He scooted up to sit on the top edge of the seatback and admire the view nature presented, one that never bored him.

Stephanie pointed to the herd. "What's that spot on the rear of some of the cows?"

"Cattle," Doug corrected. "Because they're not all cows."

"Okay, cattle. What is it?" She glanced at Doug. "It looks like a birthmark or a tattoo."

Curious, Stephanie climbed out of the Jeep without waiting for his response and walked to the fence for a closer look.

"Careful," Doug said, strolling up behind her. The Oklahoma wind flung strands of her dark golden hair, scented with apple shampoo, across his face. He swiped at the tickling corn silk, only to have the wind tangle the tresses around his hand. Doug released his fingers from the golden snare.

Squinting against the bright sun, Stephanie gathered her hair in a hand-held ponytail and glanced over her shoulder at Doug. "Is that a monogram?"

Before he could answer, she laughed. It was the first he'd heard her laugh in a while. The sound reminded him of a wind chime.

"Don't tell me these animals are gourmet delights, contracted by special order, a sort of exclusive brand name."

Doug grinned at her description. "No, they're just ordinary cattle, and that so-called spot is a brand. It's a rancher's way of putting his name on livestock. A brand shows ownership."

"How come they all don't have brands?"

"They do. You just can't see them. The homegrown animals—the ones born and bred here at the Triple T—are branded on their ribs. The others are marked on the left hip, simply because it's easier to do so as they go through the chute."

"The brands are like a code, then."

"Yeah, I guess you could say that. Not all ranchers brand this way, but it works for me."

At that moment a clap of thunder, totally unexpected, sounded overhead and shook the ground beneath them.

Shielding his eyes with one hand, Doug squinted up at the sky. "Sorry, Steph. Oftentimes we don't have much warning before a storm hits this part of the country." He grabbed her by the elbow. "Quick. Let's hop in the Jeep. Maybe I can get us somewhere before we get drenched."

As he steered the Jeep in a U-turn, Doug spouted instructions over the increasing howl of the wind. "Watch for lightning, then count slow—one thousand one, one thousand two—until the thunder sounds. Divide the number by five. That'll help us estimate how long before the storm hits."

An expert driver, Doug drove as fast as he dared, but he didn't drive as fast as he would've had he been alone. In her condition, Stephanie wouldn't be able to tolerate the harsh jostling. He wouldn't do anything to jeopardize her health, or that of the baby.

Lightning shot across the sky. Stephanie counted, loud and clear. By the time the thunder echoed, she'd counted to fifteen.

Not much time to seek shelter, much less time enough to reach the house, Doug thought. Impulsively he redirected the Jeep to a deserted dugout—a cavelike shelter dug in the side of a hill—on the other side of the range. It was closer than the house, but not nearly as clean and definitely not as warm.

Chapter Eight

Doug raced ahead and, as he neared the shelter, pulled the Jeep to a skidding stop at the deserted dugout—none too soon. They were already wet, but not dripping. He hopped from the Jeep and dashed around the front of it to Stephanie. He assisted her climbing down to the ground.

Together they darted to the entrance, which was partially concealed by tall prairie grass. Holding aside the tall grass, Doug opened a path so that they could enter. He stepped across the broken doorjamb into the interior; Stephanie followed close behind. Inside, the earthen room was cool and damp.

For a while, they stood and looked outside, watching the rain fall to the ground.

"If it's any consolation," Doug said, "rainstorms such as this don't usually last too long."

"Good." Stephanie spoke between stiff lips, hugging her arms around her, staring out into the rain.

Before long, Doug grew restless, and cold from his wet clothing. Jamming his hands in his pockets, seeking warmth, he prowled around the cavern.

Their temporary abode wasn't too bad. At least he didn't find any rattlesnakes. However, spiderwebs were plentiful. Walking up behind Stephanie, he stopped. "It's hard to believe entire families lived in a space this size—equivalent to one of our modern-day rooms. Why, it's no larger than the smallest bedroom at the house."

Stiffly Stephanie glanced at Doug. "Can you start a fire?"

"I don't have any matches." Tired of standing, Doug moved to the back of the cavity and sat against the hard dirt wall.

Without anything else to do, Doug was free to observe Stephanie. She was freezing, but determinedly trying not to show her discomfort. "You might want to move away from the opening," Doug suggested. "It's by no means warm back here, but it seems warmer without the rain spraying in."

Stephanie took him at his word, but instead of sitting, she paced back and forth in front of him, across the narrow space.

Doug drew up the length of his legs and rested his arms atop his knees. Closing his eyes, he tried to forget that they were alone and confined. That is, until her teeth began chattering.

Opening his eyes, Doug followed Stephanie with his gaze. When she neared him, he stuck out a leg, blocking her path. "Sit down and let me help you get warm."

Her hazel eyes grew round. Undecided, she stared.

"Come on. We'll warm each other." When he thought she'd refuse, he said, "Either that or we stay cold. It's your choice."

Stephanie knelt in front of Doug.

Spreading his legs, he gathered her to him. Shudders racked her body. He drew her close and wrapped his arms around her in an attempt to make the shivers abate. Arms curled between their bodies, she buried her face in his neck and snuggled close, her cold nose nuzzling him.

Deliberately Doug trained his thoughts elsewhere; it was his only means of survival.

When the worst of the chill had passed, Stephanie stirred. She uncurled her hands, splaying them on Doug's chest. His heartbeat quickened uncontrollably.

Without considering the hazards, Doug drew a deep breath. His lungs filled with the scent of her. Struggling to maintain his ironclad control, he released his pent-up breath in a gradual, steady stream.

Wiggling again, Stephanie reached up and picked damp hair strands off her face. She hooked them behind one ear. Then, with unhurried movements, she trailed her touch back across his chest. She repeatedly traced circles around the nearest button of his shirt with a restless finger.

Intent on stilling her distracting activity, Doug clasped a hand over her fidgety one.

As she warmed, Stephanie sought a more comfortable position on her side. Jutting her hip against Doug's crotch, Stephanie looped her other arm around his torso. Her innocent action pressed a soft, full breast to his ribs.

Instant desire pulsed to life at the core of his being, his body a staunch opponent of his resolve. Unable to prevent the automatic physical reaction, Doug moaned. Gruffness in his voice, he rasped, "Sit still, Steph. Please."

"I'm trying, but the baby's restless." She sighed and, freeing her clasped hand, caressed her abdomen with circular strokes.

Then, as though it were the most natural thing in the world, Stephanie sought Doug's hand and, upon finding it, unselfconsciously placed it upon her swollen stomach. Her hand covering his, she guided his touch to different areas of her abdomen as the baby moved.

Tracking the movement of a hard knot, which could easily have been either the infant's elbow or its foot, Stephanie moved Doug's palm lower and lower, until the tips of his fingers fell into the juncture of her thighs.

Unable to help himself, Doug perceptibly tightened his fingers on her. His grip prevented her moving his hand any farther, into a position that might easily be his undoing. "Steph, do you know what you're doing?"

"I'm sharing this unique moment with you." Her voice full of wonder, Stephanie said, "I still can't believe I'm pregnant, and that this wiggly little thing inside of me is a baby—my baby." She eased up, tilting her head so that she could see him, eyes full of innocence. "Isn't it wonderful? Especially when everything else in my life is such a disaster right now."

Disaster was right. No other word described the situation better, as her full, moist lips filled his vision and invited his kiss. What could one kiss hurt?

Gradually relinquishing control, Doug released his last coherent thought to freedom as he closed his eyes and surrendered, conceding to defeat. He covered her mouth with his, tasting, probing, experiencing.

Clutching a handful of his shirt, Stephanie responded, returning his kiss in full.

Even though he'd promised himself only one kiss, Doug was unable to resist a second helping, this time plunging his tongue inside her mouth, sampling the sweetness there. Her response was immediate and wholehearted, holding back nothing.

When he would have pulled away, Stephanie demanded more. She pressed his hand to her guarded womanhood and trapped it between her legs, squeezing. Then, boldly, she found the proof of his arousal and traced its length through the thickness of denim, offering him a glimpse of heaven with her gentle ministrations.

The last thread of his self-control fast disintegrating, Doug devoured her hot moist lips. Instinctively, and without meeting resistance, he moved his hand beneath the outer coverings. He marveled at the soft delicacy of her warm flesh. Their kisses grew more demanding, their tongues mating, leading the way for their bodies.

Without conscious thought, Doug took what Stephanie offered. He edged his hand along the path of silken, bare skin in further exploration. Enticed by her acceptance of his touch, he inched his finger inside her womanhood, finding her slick with wetness.

His heart convulsed. Dared he hope that this woman was his alone? And wanted him as he wanted her? A warm shudder pulsed through him.

Stephanie released the button at his waist. If Doug hadn't known better, he'd have thought he was dreaming. The denim fabric gave way as she unhurriedly toyed with the zipper pull, slowly lowering it, blazing a trail of agonizing delight.

Drugged as they were with each other, their kisses escalated in intensity.

When Stephanie's cool fingertips danced against his heated skin, Doug caught and held his breath. Finally, his angel of mercy freed him. She caressed the length of him with a boldness that surprised him.

Before the last thread of his control was totally and completely severed, Doug's ever-present conscience nudged him. He cringed at its timing and groaned at the implications. Oh, how he wanted to ignore the prompting. What would one time hurt?

A wrestling match with his conscience ensued.

But, as usual, he couldn't and wouldn't shove aside what he knew in his heart to be right. Because he had to live with himself the rest of his life.

Reluctantly and painfully, Doug slowly withdrew his hand from its warm shelter inside Stephanie's garments. "Steph, wait a minute."

He leaned his forehead against hers. Shaking with need and desire, he gritted his teeth, searching for words that were difficult to find in his state of arousal.

"Are you sure this is what you want?"

Stephanie rained kisses on his face. "I want to know what a man feels like inside me. Here I am pregnant, and I don't even know, because I can't remember."

Anguish and desperation rang out in her words.

A knife twisted in Doug's gut. He wouldn't make love to her simply as an experiment! "Listen to me. I'm by no means a saint, but for your sake, it's not too late to quit."

"I don't want to stop."

Doug sighed. "I don't, either." Despite his words, he experienced a subtle shift in attitude. He leaned back against the hard, cold dirt wall. Was each of them in a different way, using the other, she to experience a man and he to find gratification with a woman? Was this all physical, without a touch of the wonderful, elusive emotion called love? Had he once again been fooled?

"Don't be mad."

He shouldn't be, but he was, mostly at himself. At his age, Doug should know the difference between lust and love. But he was totally befuddled this time. What was this between Stephanie and him? Lust or love?

Honestly, he didn't know. When he thought he did, she threw him a curveball and knocked him off balance. Confusion set in, along with self-loathing. Doug couldn't honestly look Stephanie in the eye, not with the disgust he directed toward himself.

A small whimpering escaped from Stephanie. In a quiet, broken voice, her words followed, haltingly. "I...I...I'm sorry. I shouldn't have... Please forgive me, for taking advantage of you—"

"What?" His head shot up with a jolt, and he met her gaze.

"I have no right to ask for your forgiveness, especially after you've so kindly provided a home and food for me. But I thought I'd—"

Doug sucked in a quick breath and totally withdrew his touch from Stephanie. Icy foreboding clamped around his heart. "Is that what this is all about? You feel like you owe me? Well, lady, you owe me nothing." Briskly he knocked her hands away and rearranged his clothes.

Stephanie wiped a hand across her face and moaned. "That's not it at all. I owe you an explanation." Folding her legs underneath her, Stephanie sat back on her heels. "I'll admit I'm attracted to you. All these feelings and emotions overwhelm me. At this moment, I don't remember any other man in my life, except what I've experienced with you."

When Doug would have said something, she laid her cool fingers against his lips to silence him.

Glancing at him from beneath long, dark lashes, she drew a breath, renewing her courage. "I have a responsibility to this baby and an obligation to the father, whoever he is. I know I must have cared deeply for him, or I never could have been intimate with him. In my heart I know I'm not the kind of woman to be free with my body where a man is concerned."

She moistened her lips and pressed them into a straight line before continuing. "Because I feel what we have between us is special, I don't want to jeopardize it. But, in all honesty, I can't continue. It was unfair of me to respond without thinking first. I admit I was wrong. I'll take all the blame."

A deep sigh emerged from Doug. How did everything get so complicated? "No, Steph. I'm the one who's wrong. I knew better than to allow this to happen in the first place."

He wiped a hand across his face, wishing he could blot out this whole episode. "Go ahead, blame the whole thing on me. I'll accept full responsibility. After all, you're still recovering. But I haven't any excuse, except poor judgment."

Lines of worry disappeared from Stephanie's brow. A smile graced her face. "We're equally to blame. I realize I can't be intimate with you—or anyone, for that matter—until I learn more about my past and whether there's a man waiting for me, trusting me to be faithful. Please try to understand."

Stephanie offered her right hand. "Friends?"

Yes, common sense told him they were only meant to be friends, even though his body was opposed to the idea, wanting and needing more. Gallantly Doug accepted her proffered hand, steeling himself against its delicacy inside his larger, callus-roughened palm, especially now, when he was aware of the magic she held in her fingers.

Common sense fully in charge, Doug stood. Gently he tugged Stephanie's arm, assisting her to her feet. "It's quit raining."

Hand in hand, they walked to the door of the dugout and paused to admire the double rainbows arched across the clear blue Oklahoma sky. Droplets of fresh-fallen rain sparkled like jewels in the golden wheat stubble, releasing the sweet, clean fragrance of rural life.

The days passed, and Stephanie entered her sixth month of pregnancy. She and Doug religiously maintained the standard they'd outlined that day in the dugout for their continued relationship. They were bound by a new understanding of each other, and they knew the price they paid for friendship.

So one day, after helping Neddie clear the dining table of lunch paraphernalia, Stephanie once again spread out her sewing. She dumped a tissue-paper pattern out of its envelope and separated the pieces, setting aside the ones she intended to use.

As she unfolded the fragile tissue-paper pieces, ragged from numerous uses, Stephanie smoothed out the wrinkles with the palms of her hands. Despite her caution, she accidently tore one of the flimsy pieces.

Requiring Neddie's assistance, she searched for and found the older woman in the laundry room. "I tore a pattern piece. Is there a roll of tape around the house anywhere?"

"Check the desk in the study—the long, shallow drawer in the center, I believe. You might have to dig a bit to find it, because Doug refuses to let me straighten up the desk for him. In fact, he won't let me anywhere near."

"Thanks."

Stephanie traipsed through the house to the study. Moving around to the front of the desk, she sat down in Doug's large leather swivel chair to hunt her prey. She slid open the drawer and rummaged through the front of it. Not finding the tape, she pulled the drawer all the way out, until it stopped.

Shuffling aside the many envelopes and papers, she continued looking, without any luck. Finally she took out handfuls of the contents and began sorting them into two stacks, one for envelopes, one for papers. As she neared the back of the drawer, she located the tape. However, she was so close to having finished straightening the drawer, Stephanie chose to finish before returning to her sewing.

Pulling the last of the contents from the drawer, she sorted it into her two piles. She hadn't paid any attention to the others, but one envelope caught her eye. In the corner for the return address she read Theodore's name. The postmark was almost indecipherable. Although curious, Stephanie laid it atop the stack.

To fit everything back in the drawer, she broke the size of her piles into smaller stacks and began replacing the papers and envelopes. She saved the handful of envelopes containing Theodore's until last. Stephanie stuffed the whole stack, including Theo's letter, in the drawer and slid the drawer closed.

Picking up the tape, she strolled to the door. However, before she reached the door, she made a U-turn and returned to the desk. She dropped down to the leather chair and stared at the closed center drawer.

No, she couldn't. And really, she shouldn't. But, on the other hand, what would it hurt? Toying with the idea, Stephanie glanced around the room to ensure that she was alone. Cautious, she listened intently. When she determined that the coast was clear, Stephanie opened the drawer a mere six inches. The letter from Theodore lay on top, beckoning her. Staring at it for a long time, Stephanie sat there, transfixed, before making the final decision.

Using two fingers, she slid the enticing envelope from the drawer and laid it on the desktop. She stared at it. In the end, unable to withstand her curiosity, Stephanie eased the sheets of paper from the envelope.

It was a letter from Theo, all right. She checked the signature on the last page first. Returning to the first page, Stephanie began reading.

In the letter, Theo asked Doug to help him get out of debt. He wanted to start again with a clean slate, he said. He promised to be more careful with his finances in the future. Knowing he had no right to ask Doug for more than he'd already given him, Theo asked anyway. He wanted to make it on his own away from the ranch.

In stilted language, with many words marked out and awkwardly rewritten, Theodore apologized by saying he wasn't cut out for ranching and farming. Desperately he pleaded for understanding from his older brother. He promised never to ask for another penny that wasn't due him.

Then he implored Doug not to force him to drastic measures.

I'm fully aware of the terms of my trust fund. I know about the clause which forbids me the money before age thirty-five if I leave the family business. You made sure I heard of that. Still, the lure of money didn't keep me there. However, you didn't tell me I'd get the money before thirty-five if I married and needed to support a family. Hey, brother, I think I'm getting wedding fever. Ha! Ha! I'm not as dumb as you think. I'm just abiding by the rules. Now, mind you, this isn't a threat, but understand that I have no qualms about doing what I have to do.

Without warning, Doug snatched the letter from Stephanie's hands. "What are you doing with this?"

Stunned, Stephanie stared at him from the other side of the desk, then lunged from her seated position across the desk and grabbed for the letter. "Give me that!"

At six feet, next to her five foot three, Doug easily held the pages out of reach. "This doesn't concern you. It's none of your business. I consider it a private family affair."

Stephanie braced her hands on her hips. "I beg to differ with you. I can read between the lines. Put Stephanie and Theodore in a car together. Make sure she's pregnant. Add one engagement ring. Presto! Instant wealth from trust fund before age thirty-five."

The expression on Doug's face hardened. "You've got it all wrong."

"Oh, yeah?" How gullible did he think she was?

"That's enough." His gaze impaled her. "Calm down, Steph. You don't know what you're talking about. You're jumping to conclusions. You don't have all the facts."

"Then give me the facts." She spread her hands, signaling her willingness to listen. "What else do you know that you haven't seen fit to tell me? Did you think you could just pat Stephanie on the head, give her a bone to chew on, and maybe she'd go away?"

Irritation flared Doug's nostrils. "It wasn't like that. Trust me. I don't want to give you false hope."

"Start talking." Stephanie folded her arms across her chest. "You've got a lot of explaining to do. If you know anything at all, then why not tell me? Are you afraid of what I might do?"

Doug stiffened his posture. "I'm not afraid of anything."

Stephanie slammed a fist down on the desk between them. "Then prove it. Tell me everything you know. You know more about this than you're letting on. You know who I am and where I came from. Don't you? Tell me! Tell me this instant!"

He sighed. "I honestly don't know."

"I don't believe you. Prove it."

"Why won't you trust me?" When she didn't answer, Doug strode around the desk and scrounged through the center drawer. By the time he found what he was searching for, the drawer was no neater than before Stephanie had straightened it. He pulled out an envelope bearing a business logo, but addressed in the same handwriting as the letter he'd taken from her moments before. Impatient, Doug yanked the letter out, tearing the envelope.

"Look." He shoved the pages in Stephanie's face. "Take a close look. It's dated a month *after* the other one."

Before Stephanie could read the contents, he yanked the letter back and scanned the pages, summarizing for Stephanie's benefit. "He says he found his mate, a girl who brings out the best in him."

He read part of the letter aloud. "'She believes in me and has renewed my self-confidence. Doug, she loves unconditionally, loves me for myself, not for who I am, what I have, or who I'm kin to. You've got to meet her. She's heaven on earth. I know you'll approve. As soon as she can arrange for time off work, I'll bring her home to meet you.' Then Theo signs the letter, but he adds a P.S. 'No hard feelings, brother.'" Doug tossed the pages on the desk.

Stephanie leaned over the desk and picked up the letter. "Why haven't you told me all this sooner?"

"It's all circumstantial. There's no real proof he's talking about you. See for yourself. Theo never mentions the girl's name, or any clues that lead me to believe it could be you. It could be anybody."

"But I was in the car with him when the wreck occurred."

"That doesn't mean you're the same girl mentioned in the letter. Maybe he was giving you a lift somewhere."

"What about the engagement ring?"

"What about it?"

"Doesn't that prove anything?"

"Not a thing, as far as I'm concerned. You could've been engaged to someone else and had a spat. A ring wouldn't keep Theo from doing you a favor by taking you somewhere." Doug paused, sending her an uncomfortable stare. "Why are you so insistent that Theo is the father of your child?"

Stephanie shrugged. "I'm not, but right now that's the only lead I have to my identity and where I came from."

"Whether or not Theo is the father is not the main issue. We can always run a test to determine that." Sometime in these past weeks, Doug's attitude had shifted. He hadn't even realized it until this minute. His words reflected the change.

"The primary concern is that you take care of yourself and the baby. You suffered a severe trauma in the wreck. You don't need any more major upsets before your child is born. Why torture yourself with conjectures that may not be true?" Relaxing his stance, he smiled and walked closer. He halted in front of Stephanie.

She dropped her gaze to the desktop and the letter. He was right. Everything was circumstantial. Another thread of hope regarding her past had been severed. Bitter disappointment claimed her. Biting her lips to forestall the imminent tears, Stephanie bowed her head.

Doug's large hands settled on her shoulders and began kneading the tight muscles. "Relax. You're wound too tight. All this emotional upheaval can't be good for you, or the baby."

His kindness and concern, after all the mean things she'd said to him, released the flood of hot tears. Stephanie hid her face in her hands.

At Doug's urging, she turned to him and found a haven in his embrace.

"Don't make the situation harder on you than it is already. Until you remember, we can only speculate."

Stephanie didn't want to theorize. She wanted truths, answers regarding her past, and she wanted them now. Why wouldn't her memory allow her access to the knowledge? Had something so horrible happened that it was best forgotten?

Chapter Nine

In the days that followed, Stephanie took solace in venturing farther and farther away from the house on her daily exercise walks, as long as the weather permitted.

On one particularly nice afternoon, lost in thought, she walked farther than intended and discovered that she'd walked all the way to the family burial plot without realizing she'd gone so far. Since she was there, she took advantage of the opportunity for a rest and a look around before she returned.

Leaving the side of the roadway, Stephanie carefully picked her way across the tall grass and uneven ground to the headstones beneath the trees. As expected, two were the Taylor grandparents', and two the parents'. Of course, one was Theodore's. It was the two remaining headstones that captured her interest.

Etched on one stone was the name Constance Taylor. From the dates listed on the marker, Stephanie calculated her age to have been twenty-two when she died. The last headstone indicated an infant, Baby Tyler Taylor, born and died the same day.

Stephanie hooked her arms around her swollen abdomen and hugged her unborn child to her. What would she do if her baby died at birth? The thought distressed her.

The sound of an approaching vehicle diverted her attention. She glanced up in time to see Doug veer the Jeep off the roadway and bring it to a stop in the tall grass. He climbed out and strode in her direction. "Hi."

"Hi." Her heart somersaulted as she openly admired him. More and more of late, she yearned for him, reliving their few kisses and the time they'd briefly explored each other's bodies without fulfillment. But she kept the thoughts to herself, knowing it was useless to pine for something she couldn't have.

Doug stopped a couple of feet away from her and hooked his thumbs in his front pockets. His heart pounded in reaction to the anxious moments he experienced as he observed Stephanie from afar. Had he gotten here in time? "Are you all right?"

"I'm fine." She smiled.

"From a distance, I saw you grab your stomach. I thought you might be going into labor earlier than anticipated."

"No." Stephanie glanced at the headstone marking the grave of the infant, then back to Doug. "I was just hoping and praying my child didn't die at birth."

Doug stared at the infant's headstone, clenching his jaw, his concern for Stephanie overshadowed by unhappy memories from the past. "He didn't have a chance."

"What happened?" When Stephanie thought Doug wasn't going to answer, she said, "Maybe I shouldn't have asked. It's none of my business. You don't have to answer."

Sighing, Doug pondered the toes of his snakeskin boots. "In a fit of temper, his mother went horseback riding, even though she knew she shouldn't. The horse was too spirited for her to handle. She knew that, too, and purposely took him. He threw her, but not without cause. Afterward, I examined the horse and found marks that indicated she'd used a whip on him.''

Doug stared off into the distance, as though he were remembering, painfully. Various emotions flickered across his face—torment, disgust, anger, sorrow. Then, just as suddenly, his face was a closed book, that chapter finished. ''The fall broke her neck and sent her into early labor. By the time we found her and got her to the hospital, it was too late to save either of them.''

The cloak Doug wore disguised his true emotions, but Stephanie had witnessed the depth of his sorrow. It touched her. Her heart went out to Doug. ''Was she your sister?''

Valiantly, he looked Stephanie in the eye. He hadn't wanted to discuss it, but she might as well know. ''My wife.''

His announcement took her breath away. Stephanie was at a loss for words. Uncomfortable with Doug's disclosure, she dropped her gaze. In the ensuing silence, the significance of his admission hit her. She jerked her head up and fixed him with her gaze, seeking confirmation. ''Then the baby was your child.''

He never even had a chance to be a father. Doug grappled with the old hurts, the ache renewed. Grudgingly he nodded.

The pain of Doug's loss stabbed at Stephanie. She knew the aching emptiness she'd feel if it were her child buried in the grave. Her throat constricted. Quietly she said, ''I'm sorry, Doug. I didn't know.''

Not wanting her pity, Doug wished he hadn't told her. He shrugged off the dismal mood. ''It was a long time ago, and it's best forgotten.''

Stephanie reached out and, taking his hand, entwined her fingers with his. ''We don't ever forget those we love.''

Or those we hate. He shot a piercing glare at her and clenched his jaw.

Noting his reaction, Stephanie knew she'd said the wrong thing. Again.

Doug tucked Stephanie's hand inside the crook of his elbow. "Come on. I'll give you a ride back to the house."

She flashed him a weak smile. "Thank you. I'd appreciate it. I walked farther than I intended."

Attentive to her every need, Doug helped Stephanie climb in the Jeep. He assisted with fastening the seat belt, positioning the lap portion low across her abdomen and the shoulder strap between her breasts, angling it around her bulging stomach, always mindful of Stephanie's pregnant condition. His tender ministrations generated an ache of loss in her heart.

Later that same afternoon, while assisting Neddie in putting clean sheets on the bed in Stephanie's room, Stephanie seized the opportunity to interrogate the older woman for more information than Doug had offered. "What was Constance like?"

Neddie stood upright. "Oh, Lordy, how did you hear about her?"

"Doug mentioned that she'd been his wife, and they'd had a child together, but both died in a freak accident."

Bending back down to the mattress, Neddie continued with the task at hand. "That wasn't no accident, honey. She killed herself and that baby on purpose, just as sure as I stand here. She never wanted the baby, not once the whole time she was pregnant."

Finished tucking the fitted sheet around the corners of the mattress on her side, Neddie unfolded to a standing position. "Grab that top sheet and toss it across here."

Stephanie did as asked. She found it difficult to understand a mother not wanting her own child. "But why would a woman not want her own child, especially if she had a home and a husband?"

"She was quite a bit younger than Doug, about the same difference in age as you and he. Mind you, I'm not excusing her youth. I think she liked being Mrs. Taylor, the prominent social position and all, but she wasn't ready to settle down. She kept nagging Doug to go here and go there. She tried to talk him into moving to the city."

"But why? His livelihood is here."

"She figured as long as they were rich, she could do as she pleased, without a worry as to how they made the money."

"Didn't she understand it came from working the land and tending to the cattle?"

"I guess not. Or rather she didn't want to think about it. To her it was dirty and smelly. But she liked the riches it afforded them. The end result was all that mattered."

"What did Doug think about her wanting to move?"

"He was willing to do anything to make and keep her happy— except *that*. He was a rancher when they married, and had no intentions of changing. My goodness, how would he make a living if they moved away?"

"He couldn't."

"That's right. Or at least not in a way that made him happy and content. Why on earth he couldn't see that she only wanted his money and social position before they married, I'll never know."

Stephanie experienced a desire to protect Doug. "Well, you know that old saying about love being blind."

"Yeah, but it doesn't have to be stupid. I think once Doug realized the situation, he didn't want to admit they'd made a mistake. He figured with maturity she'd change, but she didn't. If anything, the situation got worse." Finished making the bed in Stephanie's room, Neddie grabbed the laundry basket and lumbered downstairs.

Stephanie followed while Neddie chattered on. "The more she nagged, the longer hours he worked. She must have manipulated their bedroom activities to try and persuade him to get her own way, and one day she ended up pregnant. Oooeee, was she ever mad! She stomped around here like an old wet hen.''

Outside at the clothesline, the two women retrieved the sheets for Doug's bed. The basket between them, Stephanie took hold of a handle to help Neddie carry the clean laundry inside.

But Neddie paid Stephanie no mind. As if in a trance, she carried on with her story. "But I'll tell you, I never saw a happier man in my life. He thought for sure a baby would keep her occupied and take her mind off moving, convert her into a good woman."

Neddie stooped for the handle and lifted her side of the basket. She waddled toward the house, but stopped in mid-stride and sighed, putting down the basket. "If ever I saw a man who was in need of a good woman, it's Doug. He's never had a woman love him as deeply as he's loved. Now I think he's given up the search. Too many of them have caused him too much trouble, always more concerned with the money than the man. He's been burned so often he doesn't want any type of close relationship anymore. I think that because he couldn't make Constance happy, he feels like a failure, and is not willing to try marriage again."

Standing like a statue in the middle of the backyard, Neddie talked more to herself than Stephanie. "But, you know, I don't think he regrets not having given in and moved. He'd die without the soil to work. It's in his blood, and it was in his daddy's too. But Theodore, he was more like Constance. The isolation and quiet created a restlessness in him. He'd prowl like a caged animal until he could get to town."

Realizing they were still standing outside, Neddie once again lifted her side of the basket and trudged back inside the house. "Oh, well. I guess that shouldn't be my concern."

Back upstairs they went, with Neddie hardly drawing a breath the whole time. "Now where was I? Oh, yeah, Constance and her excuses. If anything, she used the pregnancy to try and sway Doug into changing his mind about moving. The baby would have to ride the bus to school, poor thing. He wouldn't have anyone living close by to play with. He wouldn't have the opportunities found in the city to develop a well-rounded personality. On and on and on she nagged—how deprived the child would be and how it was Doug's obligation as a potential father to think of all these things ahead of time."

In Doug's room, they coaxed the fitted sheet onto the king-size bed. Next Stephanie picked up the top sheet and, holding on to one side, parachuted the remaining fabric to Neddie on the other side of the bed. "I shouldn't take sides, but her reasoning sounds like a weak excuse to me. I've always thought city kids were the deprived ones, because they miss all the fun of being close to nature—eating fresh fruits and vegetables, being around animals, skinny-dipping, running through an open field."

Suddenly Stephanie released her grip on the sheet, the fabric on her side folding with pockets of air and floating to the middle of the bed. She stood momentarily immobilized, staring into empty space.

"Hon, are you okay? Is it the baby?" Neddie's words came from far away, gradually moving closer as the older lady made her way around the large bed to Stephanie's side. "Come, sit down for a minute. You'll feel better if you get off your feet and rest a bit."

Neddie coaxed Stephanie to the bed. "What is it? Tell Neddie, so I can help. I won't know what it is if you don't tell me."

Unwilling to speak, Stephanie beseeched Neddie with a shake of her head. She stared past the older woman with unseeing eyes, but it was too late. The vision was gone. It evaporated as quickly as it appeared.

Concerned, Neddie pressed a hand to the younger girl's shoulder and touched the other hand to her forehead, checking for a fever. "Better now? Your color's coming back. For a minute there, you turned so white I thought you'd seen a ghost and were gonna faint to the floor. I couldn't allow that to happen. You might hurt yourself, or that baby of yours."

Taking hold of Neddie's hand, Stephanie implored her with her gaze. "I remembered when I was younger I always wanted to live on a farm. I was jealous of my classmates who did. They always thought I was lucky, living in the city, but to me they were the more fortunate."

Stephanie stared at Neddie. "The memory was simply a flash, as quick as lightning, and then it was gone. I wanted it to stay. I tried to make it stay, but it wouldn't. It was so sudden and unexpected, it startled me. That was all, just a fleeting second. Why wouldn't it stay?"

"Calm down. You're all right now. Maybe your memory's trying to come back." She prodded Stephanie to her feet and led her to her bedroom across the hall. "Why don't you lie down for a while? Take a nap. You'll feel better, and maybe you'll remember more, especially since your mind seems to be trying to break through your amnesia and open up. It certainly won't hurt to give it a try."

Hands on Stephanie's shoulders, Neddie guided the younger woman down on the bed and pressed her into a reclining position. She removed Stephanie's shoes and dropped them on the floor next to the bed. "Don't you worry none. Just you take it easy. I'll check back on you later."

The older woman waddled out, partially closing the door as she left. Stephanie rolled onto her side and, stuffing the second pillow under her belly and between her legs, snuggled into the welcoming bed.

Unable to fall into a deep sleep, Stephanie wrestled with the fleeting pictures flashing before her mind's eye—a car wreck, a horse-riding accident, a dead man, a lifeless woman, a baby's grave, each in a different locale. Then came showers of gifts, a diamond solitaire, and a man's arms around her.

None of the persons who peopled her dreams had faces. All were blank, featureless, like store mannequins. And none of the scenes seemed related. Disjointed as they were, they didn't make sense to Stephanie.

Neither did the phone call from the hospital which came the next day. Brenda called Neddie and said she'd broken her leg while in-line skating with the kids.

Neddie went on a rampage. "Why on earth would a grown woman act like a kid in the first place and show off without having practiced in years, even if she was teaching the youngsters to skate, or whatever they call it nowadays? It's inexcusable!"

The older woman muttered the whole time she was packing to stay with her recovering daughter, all the way to the car and then some, until she was so far down the road she could no longer be heard.

Stephanie smiled to herself. One couldn't help but like Neddie. She kept their lives interesting, what with her incessant chattering and her obsessive organizing.

From the time she received the phone call until she was lost from sight in the cloud of billowing dust along the road, Neddie rattled instructions to Stephanie. The younger woman wasn't sure she'd remember them all, much less carry them out. But Stephanie had confidence that she and Doug would survive the ordeal, and hopefully without any misfortune of their own.

In the days that followed, Stephanie took over full responsibility for the household chores and cooking. Doug didn't seem to mind. He didn't encourage or discourage her.

One cool day, she experienced a charge of creativity and experimented in the kitchen for dinner that evening, ending up with her own concoctions for vegetable soup and corn bread, as well as apple crumb pie for dessert. The prepared dinner was ready and waiting when Doug arrived home.

"Where did you come up with these recipes?" Doug asked as he ladled more soup into his once again empty bowl.

Stephanie glanced up. "What's wrong? Don't you like it?"

"No, quite the contrary." He smiled. "I wouldn't be eating my third bowlful if I didn't like it."

"Oh, thank you, I guess, if you're giving a backhanded compliment. I stirred up something and kept tasting until it seemed right." Stephanie resumed eating.

Doug smiled. "My own resident Goldilocks, huh?"

Did he really think of her as his own? She doubted it.

"Steph, how much of your memory is returning nowadays? I know you've experienced some flashes, because Neddie told me before she left, with instructions to keep an eye on you."

She laid down her spoon and, elbows on the table, tented her fingers over her bowl. "Not as much nor as fast as I'd like. Several days ago, before Neddie left, I remembered I was raised as a city kid, not a farm kid. Then, today, I felt so restless I spent the pent-up energy cooking."

Restless? Was she bored with country life and ready to return to the city? Doug should have known that would happen. He didn't say anything. He didn't eat, didn't drink, didn't do a thing except stare into the bowl of soup. After a lengthy pause, he laid down his spoon.

"I appreciate the effort. You turned out a good meal. Reminds me of my mom's cooking. It's been years since I've eaten sweetened corn bread. I wasn't even sure anyone made it anymore."

"To tell the truth," Stephanie said, "I don't know why I did it that way, except I seemed to be on autopilot and followed my instincts. It just happened."

As he thought of Stephanie's restlessness, Doug's appetite waned. He quit eating.

Noticing that Doug was finished with his meal, Stephanie scooted the dessert over. She cut a wedge and set it on a small plate in front of him. "Here's a piece of apple crumb pie, still warm from the oven. I didn't want my cooking compared to Neddie's cherry pie, so I fixed something different."

Not willing to hurt her feelings, Doug forced down the pie, despite his lack of appetite.

While Doug ate, Stephanie carried the soiled dishes to the sink. She rinsed them and stacked them in the dishwasher. Standing at the kitchen sink, she watched the setting sun. Salmon-pink rays blanketed the horizon and deepened in color as the sun dropped from view. The underbellies of the gray clouds caught and reflected the color-charged display.

Finished eating his pie, Doug brought his dish and fork to the sink. He stuck them in the dishwasher and then, standing behind Stephanie, admired the view she was sighing over.

She hooked a glance over her shoulder at him. "Isn't it beautiful? I just love the sunsets and sunrises here at your ranch. I can't ever remember seeing such vivid ones before." Aware too late of her wording, she rolled her eyes back in her head. "Well, that's kind of an understatement, isn't it?"

Doug moved to stand beside her, resting a hip against the kitchen counter. He folded his arms across his chest. "Just how much are you remembering?"

Stephanie turned sideways to face him. "Not much. Mainly that incident before Neddie left, the cooking today, and the restless creative energy I feel when I'm not sewing." She shrugged. "That's it."

There was that word again—*restless*. A premonition warned Doug to exercise caution.

Recalling her fitful sleep at night on occasions, Stephanie added, "Oh, and sometimes I experience disjointed dreams, more like nightmares." Resignation crept into her voice. "Never enough of anything to say this is who I am and where I came from, or this is where I belong."

"It's funny, Steph, but people can live someplace all their life and never really feel like they belong. For instance, I know I belong on the land here, doing the work I do, but I'm also a loner. I've found out the hard way, I don't belong with people. Money sets one apart. You can't ever know whether you're loved for yourself or for what you've got, no matter how careful you are in choosing your relationships."

Did she dare ask? Curious, she chanced it. "Tell me about Constance."

"What's there to tell?" Constance had also been restless. Must he admit it?

"I've heard Neddie's version of the story, but I want to hear yours."

For what reason? Did she enjoy inflicting pain on him? "That was a long time ago, and it's a long story."

"I'm in no hurry to go anywhere. I've got time to listen."

Why not tell? To Doug, Stephanie's interest seemed genuine. "She was young, really too young, now that I look back at when we married. Fresh out of high school, she hadn't even had her eighteenth birthday yet. I was still footloose and fancy-free, without any cares or worries. We hit it off great. Or so I thought. I fell head over heels for her."

Doug pushed away from the counter and hooked his thumbs in his hip pockets, his blue plaid western shirt pulling tight across his wide chest. "About that same time, Dad fell sick and died. That meant it was up to me to take over the businesses."

Hurtful memories returned. Bitterness entered Doug's voice. "All Constance saw were dollar signs."

Forcing a change of attitude, he shoved aside the hurt and bitterness with a shrug of acceptance. "I really can't cast all the blame on her for our ruined relationship. I was pretty much the playboy one day—" he flashed her an embarrassed grin "—and a nerd the next. I took my new responsibilities seriously. I knew it fell on my shoulders whether the Triple T survived or went belly-up. I guess I grew up overnight and Constance didn't."

Stephanie ached to relieve the pain and suffering she witnessed in his eyes. "Fate directs our lives. We have to accept it and go on, for better or for worse. Some people handle change better than others, and I believe change offers opportunities that the status quo doesn't. However, I guess many people don't see it that way."

"Constance didn't. She only saw the opportunity to party the rest of her life. Then, when she got pregnant, I thought she'd change and grow up overnight, like I'd had to do." Sadly he shook his head. "No such luck. I can see now she used her condition as leverage to get practically anything she wanted."

Doug walked over to the door and looked out at the freshly plowed fields. "I say practically because the one thing I wouldn't give in on was moving to the city. I couldn't farm and ranch if I commuted. The days are too long and hard for that, the daylight hours too precious to waste on the road, getting there and coming back. I wanted to put in my hours and come home to a loving family as soon as possible, without traveling another hour or so to get there. Was that too much to ask?"

Stephanie walked over to stand beside Doug at the door. "You shouldn't have to ask. It's a universal truth, recognized by most, that home is where the heart is, or in this case where the work is."

At Stephanie's gentle prompting, Doug was finding that talking about the past was therapeutic. Words long sealed inside fell from Doug's lips. "She didn't want the baby, even threatened to get rid of it if I didn't meet her demands. I also found out during that time that she didn't even want me anymore, just my money and the respect of the position as Mrs. Taylor. She abused that in the way she treated others around town."

Doug's agony pierced Stephanie's heart. In that moment, she knew she'd spent the past months falling in love with him. She couldn't help herself, despite the fact that she didn't even know whether she was free to do so or not.

Closing the gap between them, she curled her arms around his torso and hugged him close. When he would have withdrawn from her embrace, she peeked up at him. "Let me hold you. Nothing more—I promise. I need to be held. That's all." She rested her head against his chest and heard his heartbeat accelerate. His arms came around her in a tender moment of oneness and unity of souls.

"I guess I just haven't got what it takes to be a husband and father," he confessed, admitting more than he'd planned to. "In my case, it's not meant to be." Wistfully Doug sighed, his breath ruffling the top of her hair. "Life deals us some hard blows at times."

Stephanie snuggled against him, rubbing the side of her face on his cotton shirt. "Yeah, I got knocked on the head."

Her humor eased the awkwardness of the confession and the embrace. Doug chuckled. "Oh, Steph, what'll I do when you're no longer around to put life in perspective for me?" The laughter drained from him as another thought slammed into him. Would Stephanie leave as soon as her memory returned?

She leaned back in the circle of his arms and peered up at him. Studying his face sent her pulse into a wild gallop. He had so much love and tenderness to offer the right woman, but so much hurt and disappointment to resolve first.

Stephanie ached for him, heartbroken that he'd chosen to be alone rather than search for someone special to share his life and love. She longed to kiss his hurt away and make it all better for him.

Stephanie moistened her dry lips and pressed them together. She could hold back no longer. "Doug?"

"Hmm?" He pierced her inner being with his dark brown puppy eyes.

"I'm sorry. I lied."

What did she mean? He opened his eyes wide. "About what?"

Unable to meet his stare, Stephanie lowered her gaze to his shirtfront and traced a finger along the topstitching. "I'm going to break my promise about not wanting anything more than being held."

She refocused her gaze on his face. "Call the need mother instinct, if you have to give it a name, because I remember you told me an old remedy of your mother's. Something about a kiss would make the hurt go away, right? And I want to send your hurt away—far, far away."

Wasn't she adorable? The corner of his mouth twitched before curling into a smile. "That's right."

Lifting a finger to his lips, Stephanie traced the outline of his mouth. So smooth. So gentle. "Do you believe in home remedies? Will they work?"

"I don't know if they do or not." Doug's heart skipped a beat in anticipation. He dropped his gaze to her lips. "I guess we could try. Sorta like an experiment."

Somewhat surprised, Stephanie asked, "You won't mind?"

Pulse racing, Doug bent closer. "Not if you don't."

His warm breath fanned her face. Stephanie braced her hands on his chest, preparing for the impact of their lips coming together. Standing on tiptoe, she met his lips halfway, grazing them with a tentative contact.

Doug brushed his lips against hers, testing the fit. So soft. So welcoming. So sweet. So innocent. Repeatedly they came together, ever so gently, then broke the delicate contact and met again with feathery touches, cautious about disturbing the fragile communication.

Stephanie slid her hands up Doug's muscled chest, curling her arms around his neck.

Willingly he accepted the embrace. What wonder it would be to love and be loved unconditionally! His arms tightened around her, bringing her protruding abdomen more firmly against him.

This time, when they matched their lips together, Doug and Stephanie clung longer before releasing. With warm, moist lips, they experimented again. Each time they kissed, Stephanie found it more difficult to let him go.

However, before the point of no return tempted them beyond control, Stephanie loosened her hold around Doug's neck and levered herself away.

Regretfully he released her and let her go, experiencing a sense of loss.

She smiled. "Well, what's the verdict? Does Mother know best?"

"I'm inclined to believe she does." Cocking an eyebrow, Doug tweaked her on the tip of the nose, the closeness of the moment still warming his heart. "Mother also told me not to play with fire, or I'd get burned."

In a playful mood, Stephanie batted her eyelashes. "And do you always do what Mother says?"

The shadows of pain that flickered in his eyes contradicted his impish grin. A hint of vulnerability replaced the pain and was reflected in the depths of his brown eyes. "No. I reckon that's why I get burned so often. And at my age, I should know better. You'd think I'd learn from experience, but I guess I'm a slow learner. Either that, or you can't teach an old dog new tricks."

Chapter Ten

Alone in the study the next day, Doug contemplated the scene from the night before. Today's distance from the situation gave him a more objective outlook than he'd had last night. He had no regrets.

Overall, he considered the evening a pleasant one. In some ways, it had been an eye-opener. His and Stephanie's talk had aired a lot of baggage he'd carried around for years. He clearly saw the past as an episode in his life that was over and done with, not to be repeated.

The peculiar thing about last night was the peace he'd experienced just holding Stephanie in his arms. The kisses had held their own healing elixir. Who would ever have thought it was possible for plain, simple kisses and hugs to affect healing? Stephanie's unadulterated, spontaneous request for kisses and hugs shed new light on the power of mothers' generations-old home remedies.

What was he going to do with Stephanie? Better yet, what would he do when it came time, as it would eventually, for her to leave his domain? Doug didn't want to think about that happening, not yet. He was quickly becoming attached to his ward. It wasn't that he wanted to, but there was a quality about her that drew out his protective instincts.

Although he'd never been one to procrastinate, where Stephanie's leaving was concerned, he refused to consider any decisions at this time. He'd call the shots when they needed to be called, and not before then. Hopefully, time would be on his side.

A knock sounded at the door to the study. Doug rallied his thoughts. Where had the morning gone? The door was pushed open, and Stephanie popped her head in. He motioned her inside.

She stopped at the desk, shuffling from one foot to the other. "I'm sorry to have to bother you, but I forgot to mention that I have another doctor's appointment today. With Neddie gone, I need to make arrangements for a ride to town. Or I guess I could call and change the day, if I need to."

"No. That's all right. I'll give you a lift. A run to town will give me break. What time do you need to be there?"

"Two."

It was ten-thirty now. "We'll leave right after lunch. That should get us there in plenty of time."

"Thanks."

When she didn't immediately disappear from the room, as she usually did, he raised his brow. "Is there anything else?"

"I feel like I'm always asking favors or imposing on someone."

He smiled. "You shouldn't have to ask, but since I don't seem to think of these things on my own, without prompting from you or Neddie, go ahead. I'm open for suggestions."

"Neddie's been letting me drive some, between here and the main road. I haven't experienced any problems so far, and I seem to know what to do. Apparently I've driven in my past." Even though her hands were fidgety, she boldly met his look with her hazel eyes. "Perhaps it would be easier for everyone if I got a driver's license. Then I wouldn't have to beg a ride when I needed to go somewhere. That is, if you don't object to me driving one of your vehicles."

Why hadn't he thought of that? "It's a darn good idea. We'll check on it while we're in town."

Three o'clock that September afternoon, Stephanie exited the patient examining room. Dr. Perryman walked with her as far as the waiting room. Seeing them approach, Doug met them at the door.

"Stephanie," Dr. Perryman said quietly, laying a hand on her shoulder for reassurance, "I had hoped your amnesia would be behind you by now, because the condition is usually temporary. Although it doesn't happen often, it can occasionally last for years. Very rarely is it permanent, if that's any consolation. At this point, I don't exactly know what to tell you."

He patted her forearm. "My first inclination leads me to believe there's been serious brain damage, but I know that's out of the question. You've been thoroughly examined and tested, with all results indicating normal functioning."

Scratching his head, he glanced at Doug, then back to Stephanie. "The only other speculation is basic organic amnesia that has overlapped with psychogenic memory loss. It follows a head injury and is coupled with an urge to escape from a hurtful situation. The inability to remember is used as a defense to help someone dodge a specific situation that produced unbearable anxiety and distress. We refer to it as selected or motivated forgetting. If that's the case, you may experience a sudden and complete recovery.

"Other than that—" he shrugged "—I don't know what else to tell you, except don't fret about it. Face the prospects head-on, and take advantage of the opportunity to build a satisfying life in your new location."

Upon hearing the prognosis, Stephanie bravely glued an artificial smile on her face. All the while, her heart was breaking. "Thank you, Doctor," she said graciously, and politely extended her hand for a shake.

Dr. Perryman's advice was anything but good news. She wasn't ready to retire her hope for a return to her previous life. Yet, if she was honest, Stephanie had to admit she wasn't totally unhappy being with Doug at his ranch.

As quickly as she could, before she burst into tears in front of the occupants of the waiting room, Stephanie charged out the door and onto the sidewalk. She dropped the facade of acceptance and stood, gulping in deep breaths, hoping to chase away the dreary outlook for her speedy recovery. She clamped her teeth on her lips to forestall the tears that threatened.

Doug caught up with her. "Where to next?"

Unable to speak just yet, Stephanie shrugged and brushed away the moisture gathering in her eyes.

"Chin up, Steph. The main thing is that you and the baby are both healthy." Then, despite their being on the sidewalk, in open view, Doug drew her to him and wrapped his arms around her. "We'll face this together. I don't care what happened in the past to chase your memory away. You're here now, and you're welcome to stay as long as you want."

Want? Not need? At this moment, she wanted to stay forever. The security of knowing she had Doug's support lent her strength. Sniffling, she momentarily closed her eyes and returned his hug. Taking advantage of his nearness, she feathered a kiss on his cheek. "Thanks. You don't know how much that means to me—" she laid a hand on her extended abdomen "—and my baby."

Momentarily his gaze met and held hers. "Ready to try your hand at passing a driving test?"

Since the doctor's recent announcement, her enthusiasm had waned. "It doesn't matter."

"Maybe not right this minute, but it eventually will, though." With a hand to her elbow, he urged her in the direction of the car. "Having your license will give you more independence. Then, when you feel restless and cooped up at the ranch, you can run to town, or if you feel so inclined, you can run errands for Neddie."

"Never mind," Stephanie said in resignation. "It was a dumb idea. The authorities won't issue me a driver's license, because I don't have any ID and haven't hopes of getting it any time soon."

Doug stopped at the car and turned Stephanie to face him. "You just concentrate on passing the driving test. I'll take care of the rest. It's time I called in a favor. Don't worry, I won't do anything illegal, you understand. And don't get your hopes too high. More than likely you'll only be able to have a temporary permit." He shrugged. "But I guess that will be better than none at all."

Surprising them both, Stephanie passed her test with flying colors the first time. She drove home from town.

In the days that followed, Stephanie and Doug settled into a comfortable routine. Neddie extended her stay at Brenda's indefinitely to help with the children during her daughter's convalescence. Not knowing when the older woman would return, Stephanie and Doug interacted more, weaving a tighter bond and strengthening their relationship.

One evening in late September, after dinner, while enjoying the view of a blazing Oklahoma sunset from the picture window in the study, Doug and Stephanie stood side by side.

Fidgety, Doug shuffled his weight from one foot to the other. He hooked his thumbs in his front jeans pockets, but not for long. Changing positions, he stuffed his hands in his hip pockets. He cast sideways glances at Stephanie.

Uncomfortable with his restlessness, Stephanie opened her mouth, intent on questioning him regarding his disquiet.

At the same time, Doug plunged in headlong, while staring out the window. "Steph, I've been thinking about what Dr. Perryman said, and everything else, too. You've been here nearly five months now. Perhaps we should take some steps to secure your future, and that of the baby." He glanced in her direction. "Does that make sense?"

"Kind of." Puzzled, Stephanie stared at Doug. "What are you trying to say?"

He impaled her with his gaze. "Maybe we ought to consider getting married."

A bombshell couldn't have surprised her more. Marriage? Her and him? Together? Were her ears deceiving her?

Doug shrugged. "It doesn't have to be a real marriage, unless you want it to be. A ceremony would help stabilize your life. You wouldn't have to wonder if I was going to wake up some morning and throw you and the baby out." He grinned.

In total shock, Stephanie was unable to do anything but stare. Finally she asked, "What about a marriage license? I don't even know my own name, much less my social security number."

"Don't worry. I'll check the legalities. It may be as simple as getting a sworn statement from Dr. Perryman."

Her mouth dropped open.

A finger to her chin, Doug lifted. "We wouldn't be the first couple to enter into a marriage of convenience. I'm sure others have done the same. Just think how sensible it would be. Marriage will give your baby a name and you a home."

Sensible? Nothing was making sense right now.

"We get along okay. I'd go so far as to say we're compatible. At times we're even fond of each other, judging from our actions—you know, a little kiss or hug, here and there. What do you say?" Doug held his breath.

Stephanie didn't know what to say. He'd taken her totally and completely by surprise. "What if later I regain my memory, and we discover there's another man in my life?"

He released his pent-up breath. "I guess that would be up to you. We could stay married, or we could dissolve the marriage."

No matter what she really wanted, she had to examine every side of the issue. "What if the father of my child comes looking for the baby? He might file a paternity suit."

Doug shrugged. "So, let him. I won't keep him from his child if he wants parental rights. I'll willingly waive all rights, when and if you request such."

His unselfishness baffled her. Her defenses weakened. "Why are you doing this? What's in it for you?"

"Nothing." Looking down at the toes of his boots, Doug rocked forward. His pride and vulnerability wouldn't allow total honesty, wouldn't let him tell her that he thought he was falling in love with her and wanted to keep her with him forever. "It just so happens I enjoy your company, and think this is a situation we—you, me, and the baby—could all benefit from. We'd be a family of sorts, look out for each other, depend on one another to a certain degree."

This thing was snowballing. She had to slow it down, reverse it. Do something! Anything! "What about the cost?"

Unperturbed, he smiled. "I'm not worried about cost. I can afford to feed another mouth or two." He hesitated. "Or more, if you want additional children."

The thought of having a child with him sent Stephanie's heart racing. "Doug, this is insane. It doesn't make a bit of sense. In fact, it's totally senseless."

He tilted his head, eyeing her from the vantage point of his height. Could he convince her to accept what he was offering? "No, Steph. It's logical. Everything can be spelled out in black and white, like a business deal. In fact, I've noticed you're so good at your sewing that I'll even let you decorate the house, if you want. You can have a free hand—

curtains, upholstery, wall hangings, paint, furnishings, the works.''

How was decorating the ranch part of a marriage proposal? Doug's quick responses to her every objection threw Stephanie into a tailspin that was dizzying in effect. Totally overwhelmed by this fast-moving deal, she spoke facetiously. ''What if I want to paint the walls purple and hang psychedelic lights?''

Dared he hope? Doug opened his eyes wide. ''Does that mean we have a deal?''

Throwing up her hands, Stephanie spun around in exasperation. ''It means I don't even know myself. How could you?''

Hope brightened for Doug. ''Ah, but I do. I know the person you've been these past five months. I know what you've been through, what you've suffered, and how far you've come.''

When she didn't refute him, Doug felt he had a chance of winning her over. ''I also know you were with my brother when he wrecked. Because of that, I owe you, Steph. How can I ever repay what he took from you? Since that time, we've created our own little world. Tell me it's not so bad, Steph.''

At that moment, he looked so vulnerable, so afraid of losing something of great value that belonged to him. How could she deny him? Especially when Stephanie knew she loved Doug and wanted to stay here with him the rest of her life. He was offering her what she wanted most—a home and a life with him, forever. No strings attached. The deal sounded too good to be true.

She studied his dark brown eyes. ''You don't have to do this, you know. It's not too late to change your mind.''

He knew what he wanted. His decision was made. Doug stood a little taller. ''I'm not changing my mind. The offer still stands. Take it or leave it.''

Leave behind an opportunity she'd willingly die for? "Are you sure this is what you want?"

"I'm sure, Steph." He stared her straight in the eyes, standing firm in his resolve. "The question is, what do you want?"

Stephanie couldn't believe she was standing here wavering. Doug had just asked her to marry him, and all she could do was shoot down his reasoning and ask questions in return.

He hadn't said anything about love. Maybe Doug had difficulty expressing his deepest feelings, especially since he'd been hurt before. She opened her mouth to say the words, but they wouldn't come.

She licked her dry lips and tried again. When she finally spoke, her voice was squeaky. "Okay. I agree. I'll do it. We'll do it. Let's get married."

Smiling in relief, Doug offered a hand to seal their agreement with a shake, but Stephanie had other ideas.

"This is how you seal a deal." She raised up on tiptoe and kissed him firmly on the lips. When she would have drawn away, he brought his arms around her and held her in place. That was all the prompting Stephanie needed. Hands on his shoulders to steady her balance, she urged his mouth back down to hers.

Bending, Doug complied. Relief drained away his tension to be replaced with nervous excitement. Hope shot through him. This woman in his arms was his.

Stephanie folded her arms around his neck and kissed him again. Automatically she touched her tongue to his lips.

Jeesh! This woman knew how to push all his buttons. Maintaining control, he at first kept his lips sealed. He didn't want to frighten her with an unleashed response.

When she drew one of his lips between her teeth and laved her tongue over the tender inner skin, Doug's control slipped a notch. He shuddered beneath her provocative touch.

Empowered by her own boldness, Stephanie slid her tongue past his teeth and flicked the tip against his warm moist tongue, then quickly withdrew.

From deep in his throat, a moan broke free. She was effectively assaulting his better judgment. Doug tightened his hold around Stephanie, molding their shapes together. He held her to him, unable to control his natural response.

Stephanie's awareness of Doug's need aroused a desire of her own. Once fanned to life, the desire was enhanced by her love for him.

Doug and Stephanie explored each other's mouth with their tongues—tasting, feeling, sensitizing. In and out, nibbling, dueling, dancing, mating. Slow, precise movements, tapping the hot, wet sweetness housed within.

With an overpowering need to touch, they sent their hands exploring. Stephanie flattened one hand on Doug's chest, spreading her fingers, feeling his muscles. What freedom to hold this man she loved in her arms and touch him without reservation! Stephanie sent her other hand over his back in large circular motions. Rising and falling, she moved it over the rippled muscles of his back, pressing him closer still.

In response to the snug fit, she twisted, angling her protruding belly to a more comfortable fit against her love.

With a sense of homecoming, she suddenly wanted all their newfound life and love offered. She didn't want the proffered marriage of convenience. She wanted the real thing.

Emboldened by her sense of security and longing, Stephanie rocked against Doug, signaling him that she wanted all of him.

Doug shivered. Had fate finally sent a woman without ulterior motives, one especially for him? He slid a hand to the small of her back and applied pressure as he smoothed his fingers down to cup the curve of her hips.

Stephanie wiggled suggestively against him and nipped his earlobe. Sensations long forgotten surged through Doug with added urgency. With his other hand, Doug found a soft, full breast, and lifted its heaviness with a caressing touch. Running teasing circles around the tip with the pad of his thumb, he toyed with the hardened peak.

His tender, almost reverent touch thrilled Stephanie. Doug left a wet trail of kisses down the column of her neck. When he came up for air, Stephanie nibbled at the velvety smoothness of the lobe of his ear. She couldn't get close enough to Doug. She tugged his shirt and T-shirt from his jeans. What freedom to touch him at will!

Diving her hands beneath his clothing, she ran her cool fingers over his heated bare torso, luxuriating in his firmness. She couldn't touch him enough. Experiencing a moment of bold discovery, she inched the tips of her fingers into the waistband of his jeans.

Doug was fast losing control. Did she want him as much as he wanted her? Was it possible? The mere presence of her fingertips against his bare skin unleased his dearest fantasy. He shivered beneath her touch. A groan escaped. "Oh, Steph . . . I can't take much more."

"It's all right, Doug. You don't have to," she assured him. "This is what I want." She withdrew her hands from him long enough to unbutton her maternity top and shove it aside to offer herself to him. "Oh, please—touch me, and let me touch you."

The smoldering in Doug erupted into a full flame.

Stephanie cupped her hands around his face and kissed him hard on the lips. Leaving no doubts as to her desires, she boldly guided him to her bareness.

Doug needed no further tutoring. He flicked his tongue against the silky skin of her chest and forged downward to the valley between her mountainous peaks. Oh, how he'd dreamed of touching her like this.

All too soon, the scalloped, lacy trim of her undergarment stopped his descent. With his tongue, he traced the line where her soft fullness disappeared into the flimsy covering.

Doug left behind a trail of wetness that cooled the minute the air made contact. Goose bumps rose on Stephanie's flesh. In amazement at their newfound communication, Stephanie ran her fingers through his thick, wavy light brown hair, ruffling it. The front wave sprang forward onto his forehead.

Aching for more of his touch against her bare skin, Stephanie shimmied out of her blouse. With one deft movement of her hand, she peeled her undergarment off, freeing her breasts to him.

Doug paused to admire her nakedness, his wanting fully apparent. "Steph, you're beautiful, so beautiful, even more so than I imagined," he said, his voice full of awe.

Thrilled at his response, she said, "I'm all yours." She smiled. "Why don't we get you a little more comfortable?" She reached out and unsnapped the fasteners on his Western-style shirt. Laying it open, she slid the shirt from Doug's shoulders and arms, then waited while he peeled off his cotton T-shirt.

Afterward, he touched the tips of her naked, rosy peaks, his cool fingers trembling. Gingerly he weighed the fullness of her in each hand. Ducking his head, he laved one rosy peak, then took it fully in his mouth. When he withdrew his warmth, the air-cooled wetness brought her to a hardened pucker. He moved his mouth to her other breast giving it equal attention and titillation. Doug drew back for another view of the glorious sight before him.

Seizing the opportunity, Stephanie encircled him with her arms and rubbed her taut peaks over him, pressing her nakedness against him. Bare male skin against bare feminine skin set off a series of dominolike reactions, all escalating toward release and fulfillment.

Unable to resist, Stephanie nuzzled Doug's chest, covered with coarse, curly hair. Leaving a trail of wet kisses, she nibbled her way to one hardened button. Gently taking the nub between her teeth, Stephanie tantalized him with her tongue. She opened her mouth over the entire disk, then caressed the velvety area with her tongue. Mischief in her eyes, she smiled up at him, fully aware of the exquisite sensations she was bringing to life for him.

"Steph, you witch. If you think you're going to get off scot-free after torturing me like this, then think again." Doug swooped down and captured her mouth. He swirled his tongue on her lips, but not inside, giving back some of her own teasing.

She longed for the taste of him. Without waiting for him to come to her, Stephanie chased his tongue with hers.

Playfully Doug avoided her, teasing her, enticing her, yet withdrawing when she attempted to mate their tongues. "Oh, Steph, you're priceless."

"You talk too much. Shut up and kiss me." She rocked against him, rubbing her nakedness on his bareness.

"Just you wait. I'm going to get you for that. You're not home free yet." Doug clamped his mouth over hers, his tongue rhythmically stroking in and out, mating, then withdrawing, then mating again.

Stephanie matched him stroke for stroke. Taking, then giving. Giving, then taking. Her need for more intimate contact with him consumed her. She cupped her hand to the denim housing Doug's treasures.

He tensed and separated their mouths. Bringing his forehead against her, he closed his eyes. "Careful, Steph. I can only stand so much. You might get more than you bargained for."

"Don't you understand? I want it all, Doug." Gliding her fingers along the bulge in his jeans, she traced the shape of him. "You said it was my choice as to whether or not I wanted a real marriage. I'm telling you now—I want a real marriage. By real, I mean making love to you.''

Doug's heart leaped into his throat, nearly choking him. ''You sure know how to tell a man what he wants to hear, don't you.'' Overwhelmed, he clasped her to his trembling body, weakened with desire and, very possibly, love.

Tilting her smiling face to him, Stephanie said, ''Better yet, why don't I show you?'' Boldly she unbuttoned and unzipped his jeans. After folding back the opening, she leaned over and kissed his hair-roughened stomach.

Automatically he sucked in his belly. Sheer wonder engulfed him. What had he unleashed?

Stephanie traced a fingertip along the top edge of his briefs before inching her cool fingers inside to touch and caress him.

His ironclad control slipped. A man could stand only so much. Nearly out of his mind with rocketing sensations, he hesitated. His hesitation cost him dearly.

Tugging down the remaining covering, Stephanie bared him. The heaviness of his desire fell into her hand. Wonder shone in her face. In awe, she gently stroked the velvety skin.

Was she real, or was he dreaming? His voice came out a mere rasp. ''It's all yours, Steph.'' The real test was yet to come. Which choice would she make?

Stephanie wrapped an arm around his waist. ''Let's go upstairs. My bed is more to my liking than the floor or the desk, or even the couch.''

Picking up their discarded clothing to take with them, Stephanie and Doug climbed the stairs, arm in arm, slowing long enough to exchange heated kisses that couldn't wait.

Inside her room, Stephanie switched on the bedside lamp, instead of the overhead fixture. The small glow bathed the head of the bed with golden light, while the rest of the room fell away to darkness.

Suddenly shy, Stephanie watched as Doug removed his remaining clothes, admiring his physique. Self-consciously she wriggled out of her remaining clothes, as well, and left them on the floor. A draft of cool air sent goose bumps scurrying over her skin. Nervous, she crossed to the double bed and peeled back the covers.

Having second thoughts, she twisted around to search out Doug. She needed reassurance. Was she doing the right thing?

He stood a couple of feet away, watching and waiting, leaving the final decision to her.

What an unselfish man! What a magnificent man to have as her very own! Beyond a doubt, Stephanie knew she loved this man and always would, no matter what.

Her indecision abated, she slid between the cool sheets and scooted over. She motioned for Doug to join her. Her voice shaky, she said, "I'm waiting. It's lonesome over here. Care to join me?"

Doug shifted his gaze back and forth between his clothes and the bed. Indecision weighed heavily. This was what he'd fantasized about for weeks, even months. Why was he floundering, especially when she was the one issuing the invitation?

Was he simply taking advantage of a situation of his own making? What about that magnanimous speech he'd given only moments ago, allowing Stephanie to choose whether or not she wanted a real or a convenient marriage? Apparently she'd chosen.

Now it was his turn to answer her invitation, to fulfill his part of the bargain, and to bury the last of his doubts.

Doug crawled into the bed and stretched out next to Stephanie, cool flesh against warm flesh, feminine softness next to male hardness.

Doug slid a callus-roughened palm over her abdomen with reverence, caressing her fullness with unhurried movements. Then, curling his arms around her, he brought

Stephanie closer. Lying on his side, he pressed against her while he captured her mouth.

She cupped her hands to his face and opened to him, accepting his tongue and the sweetness within.

His need pulsed against her. Primarily concerned with Stephanie's delicate condition, Doug maintained his iron-clad restraint, despite his own personal suffering. "What about the baby? Are you sure it's all right to do this? It's not too late. I understand your condition."

"I'm fine. The baby's fine. It's okay...or will be if you'll just shut up and let nature have its way." Despite her swollen abdomen, Stephanie maneuvered into a position that immediately threatened the last of Doug's control.

He had to be certain there would be no reason to regret later what could be avoided now. Twisting his head, Doug separated his mouth from hers. His voice hoarse and rasping, he exercised his last hold on his better judgment. "Steph, forgive me. I want to, but I... We c-can't...."

She laid cool fingers across his forehead, erasing the wrinkles the stress of the moment caused. Her voice soft and coaxing, she reassured him. "It's all right, Doug. I can and I will. Trust me. The baby will be fine. It's okay."

Without further discourse, she altered her position and gave herself to him.

Doug shuddered uncontrollably with need and released his last tenuous hold on sanity. He covered Stephanie's mouth with his. The intensity of his kisses increased, much as if he were a starving man partaking of his first meal in weeks.

Kisses had never been sweeter, or more devouring. Breath mingling, their mouths melded with an intensity unknown before. They were locked in an embrace of total possession, their love promising new hope for the future.

Together they ventured across that threshold as Doug throbbed at her entrance, then, ever so gently, probed and prodded, easing into her welcoming warmth. At first, he jutted cautiously, in consideration of Stephanie's condition. But, impatient for total bliss with the one she loved, Stephanie gyrated to his rhythm with insatiable hunger, accepting all of him.

Her wild urging rocketed them to an unexplored plane of delight. They soared, absorbing the wonder of their latest discovery. Then, all too soon, with sudden light flashing where once there had been total darkness, their love exploded with unexpected force.

Locked in each other's embrace, they parachuted back to earth, spiraling down to a mind-boggling landing, falling limp and motionless, panting, waiting for their vital signs to return to normal.

As logic returned, Doug felt the first inklings of guilt. Had he come on too strong, forcing Stephanie into a commitment she wasn't yet ready for? He lay quietly for a while, assessing the situation. Why did he act first and ask questions later?

With Stephanie still trapped in his embrace, he twisted his head and separated his mouth from hers with a peck of a kiss. He hugged her to him and planted a kiss on her forehead.

The foreboding didn't go away. When finally he gathered enough courage to speak, his voice sounded hoarse and rasping. "I'm sorry, Steph. I shouldn't have... Forgive me. We should have waited. I wanted to make it good for you, but I..."

"Shhh..." Stephanie reached out to him, laying a finger across his lips, suppressing her own ragged emotions to comfort him. She cuddled against his side, purring. "It was good, Doug, the absolute best. Don't worry. We'll have other times together."

He smoothed a hand up and down her arm, offering comfort. "Did I hurt you? I didn't mean to, so help me."

A satiated smile tilted her lips upward. Closing her eyes in exhaustion, almost dozing, she shook her head. "I'm fine, really. The baby's fine. It was wonderful. You were wonderful. Don't worry. Just let's sleep for a while.''

Despite her reassurances, Doug was still concerned. If he pushed Stephanie too fast and hard for this marriage commitment, she might bolt. Then he'd never see her again. Had he already pushed her too hard for a decision? He couldn't afford any mistakes. He didn't want to lose her.

He shoved out of Stephanie's arms, unintentionally rejecting her, intent on undoing any harm he might have already caused. He rolled away from her and sat on the side of the bed. Elbows on knees, he dropped his head into his hands.

How could he have taken someone else's woman? He had badgered her into submission. Earlier, in the study, he wouldn't take no for a answer. He'd deftly shot down every defense she offered. She hadn't had a chance to exercise her own free will. He was as subtle as a bulldozer. How could he have been so primitive?

Sleepy, Stephanie sat up behind Doug. Folding her legs beneath her, she clasped her arms around him and lay her head on his shoulder. She snuggled against him and nuzzled him, dropping a series of kisses on his back. "Come to bed. Let's sleep for a while.''

"Stop, Stephanie. Just stop. Can't you see I ruined everything?'' Doug stood up from the bed and, snatching his clothes from the floor where he'd discarded them, left the room without so much as a backward glance.

Chapter Eleven

Entering his own room, Doug kicked the door, slamming it shut, totally disgusted with himself. He threw the wad of clothes clasped in his arms to the floor and strode to the window. Planting his feet firmly on the floor, he braced his hands on his hips and, stark naked, stared through the blinds at the moonlit fields before him.

Why, of all times, had his conscience chosen now to haunt him? The answer was easy. Until they were totally free of Stephanie's past, he shouldn't take advantage of her, especially if she had been with his brother and her child was his niece or nephew. To Doug, that was too near to home, akin to committing adultery.

As for the offer of marriage, he wouldn't change his mind. A corner of his heart wouldn't let him allow her to walk out of his life a woman alone, with child and with no place to go or anyone to turn to.

Respect for his brother's territory wouldn't allow him to have her without guilt, yet neither was he free to send her on her way, totally defenseless.

Maybe, given more time to adjust to the idea of marriage to Stephanie and after going through the legal ceremony, his sense of right and wrong would accept their coming together more freely. After all, Doug had given her the right to choose whether or not she wanted their marriage to be a real one. It wasn't as if he'd forced himself on her.

He supposed only time would tell what the future had in store.

Sitting stark naked in the middle of her bed, Stephanie stared after Doug. His speedy departure had left the door to her room standing open. The slamming of his bedroom door echoed loudly through the nighttime quiet.

With sleep no longer a possibility, Stephanie lay down and rolled over on her side, pulling the covers over her to ward off the cold that Doug's exodus left behind. She didn't close the door, in case he changed his mind. A closed door would make it seem that he wasn't welcome in her room. She didn't want to give that impression at all.

Tears gushed to the surface. What had she done wrong? One minute Doug had been kissing her and making love to her, the next he'd been running from her. Did her shape make her undesirable? He'd been rubbing his hand over her fullness, feeling her swollen shape, and then . . . then all of a sudden, within a span of a few minutes, he'd been finished and hadn't wanted anything else to do with her.

Disappointment shot through her. To have been so close one minute with someone she loved and hoped desired her, and then to have it all taken away the next moment, in the blink of an eye, was devastating.

No, devastation would have been losing her life in the car wreck and not experiencing this newfound love with Doug.

Disappointments were minor when compared to life and death.

Stephanie hugged the life within her, thankful she had not lost the child in the wreck and thankful destiny had sent Doug her way. She loved him, and somehow she'd find a way to convince him they belonged together.

Hope didn't abandon her. The strength of her love would help them overcome any difficulties they met. Stephanie halted her thoughts in midstream. Now why had she said *her* love? Why not *their* love?

She searched her recollections. To her knowledge, Doug had never—not once—mentioned anything about love. She was the one who'd instigated their sealing the deal with actions other than a handshake. The catastrophe was all her fault.

But then, he hadn't seemed opposed to her recommendation. He'd kissed her as much as she kissed him. Doug had willingly accompanied her to her room. She hadn't forced him.

He had said they were fond of each other. If he was fond of her, did that mean he respected Stephanie enough not to want to consummate their relationship until after the ceremony, even though his body was more than willing and ready? That would mean that, against his better judgment, Stephanie had coaxed him into doing so anyway. Had that made him feel worse?

Relieved by her deduction and discovery, Stephanie relaxed and accepted the incident as her mistake for crossing the line that Doug had evidently established for both their sakes.

Reverting to their earlier camaraderie, Doug and Stephanie resumed daily life as though nothing had happened. The next day, she sought him out. She found him in the barn, repairing a piece of equipment.

"Doug?" Stephanie called to him. When he didn't answer, she stepped closer and called again, a little louder, "Doug?"

Looking up, he peeked around a support post. "Yeah. I'm over here. Watch your step."

Carefully picking her way across the straw-covered floor, Stephanie closed the distance between them. "I'd like to borrow the car to go into town. You said it was all right to decorate, hang a few curtains and add some accessories, didn't you?"

"Sure. Go ahead. But..." Doug didn't finish whatever he was going to say. He stood.

"But what? Don't buy purple, and forget about the psychedelic lights?"

He grinned. "Something like that. Only be careful and come back all in one piece."

"What's wrong? Afraid I'm going to dent your precious car?" Stephanie planted her hands on her hips. "Don't you trust my driving?"

Serious, he admitted, "It's the other drivers I don't trust."

"Meaning?"

Doug stood from his crouched position and glanced down at the toes of his boots. "I don't want you hurt again. Or worse."

She hadn't been wrong. He did care. Stephanie closed the gap between them. Hooking an arm around his neck, she urged his head down to hers and kissed him on the cheek. "Thanks. I'll be careful."

"See that you are." He tweaked her nose affectionately.

Surprised, yet pleased, Stephanie accepted what he offered, warmed by his spontaneous act. "Now that we've got that settled, where do I find the keys?"

A smile stretched across his face. "Right here in my front right pocket. But you're going to have to dig them out. My hands are too dirty."

Stephanie's heart leaped at the prospect. She opened her eyes wide in anticipation.

Doug intercepted her thoughts. "No funny business. You hear me?"

Fingers tingling in awareness, Steph slid her hand down into his pocket; the fit was snug enough that the back of her hand contacted his body. She groped around for the keys.

"Careful, Steph. Watch what you're doing."

His warm breath fanned across her face. She stilled her fingers and stared up at him innocently.

He focused his gaze on her lips. "You do like to play dangerous, don't you?"

"No, I don't." Stephanie jerked back, her hand still trapped in his pocket. "I promise. I'll behave."

"You'd better."

"Okay. Just please stand still, and I'll get this over with as quick as I can, as painlessly as possible—" she glanced up at him "—for both of us."

The tips of her fingers made contact with the warm metal of the keys. Hooking a finger through the ring, she tugged them up. Not releasing the keys, his pocket bunched into a wad. With her other hand, she pinched the bottom edge of the pocket, her knuckles grazing the front of his jeans.

He groaned.

Stephanie pulled the keys free at last. She dropped her hold on the front of his jeans. Relieved, she held what she'd procured, dangling the ring of keys from one finger, the metal jangling together, and smiled. "See there I got them."

"Thank goodness. Get more keys made while you're in town, so we'll each have a set."

Knowing for sure that Doug hadn't rejected her the night before, Stephanie gave him a quick hug and pecked him on the cheek. "Get your mind on something else—like fixing whatever it was you were fixing—and I'll see you later. Bye."

* * *

Entering town thirty minutes later, Stephanie couldn't find a parking place in front of the fabric shop, so she circled a few blocks. When she passed the public library, her first inclination was to go inside and research everything she could find regarding the wreck with Theodore, but she ignored the prompting.

Eventually she found parking near the fabric store and took her time with her selections. Afterward she drove to the local Wal-Mart to complete her shopping. There she purchased flat sheets to make curtains, then strode to the fabric department for fabrics and notions to make throw pillows and valances with.

After she stashed her purchases in the trunk of the car, the thought of the public library once again beckoned Stephanie. On impulse, she postponed her return trip to the ranch for a mission that was long overdue. She drove to the library and soon entered. Once inside, she paused to get her bearings.

A librarian stood at the front counter, stamping books for a series of customers. To one side was the children's section, complete with a large area rug and bolsters, so that the young patrons could read sitting or lying on the floor.

Swinging her gaze in the other direction, Stephanie saw the card catalog, a reference section and an adult reading area. She headed for the reading area first.

Wooden shelves displayed current periodicals and newspapers. Her pulse quickened. That was what she'd hoped to find. Perusing the shelves she noted several newspapers—the *New York Times,* the *Daily Oklahoman,* the Tulsa paper and a small local newspaper. That answered one of her questions.

Stephanie returned to the front desk, in hopes of finding back issues and more answers. Although anxious, she waited patiently for her turn. When it came, she asked the librarian, "Do you have a Woodward newspaper?"

"Afraid not." The librarian resumed the task of checking in books.

Just as Stephanie thought. "Okay, let me have a week's worth of the local one and the *Daily Oklahoman,* issues about six months old."

"They're probably already on microfiche. Usually after three months or so we save space by putting them on film." She pointed to a nook on her left, set away from the card catalog. "Go around there. The *Daily Oklahoman* will be in that gray cabinet on the back wall. The ends of the drawers are marked by date. The smaller wooden cabinet next to it holds the microfiche for the local paper. Let me know if you need any help."

After several hours of sitting in front of the microfiche reader, Stephanie bowed her head and rubbed her eyes. No luck. But had she really expected any? There had been only an off chance that she'd find any clues to her identity in the back papers, but she wouldn't have known if she hadn't tried.

The Guymon paper had run a front-page picture of Theodore and a sizable article that told Stephanie nothing she didn't already know from Doug or her conversations with Neddie. They'd also run an "Anyone Know Stephanie?" article about her, but apparently all to no avail.

Doug had told her the same information had been posted in the Woodward paper.

She'd learned next to nothing from the Oklahoma City paper, except that Theo's death had been news to the ranching industry, as well as the natural-gas business, since he'd been one of the Taylors of the Triple T.

Momentarily, Stephanie pressed her fingers to her tired eyes. All her efforts had been without success. What next?

"Getting along okay? Need any help?"

Upon hearing the librarian's voice at her side, Stephanie sat up straight in the chair, casting a glance over her shoul-

der. "My eyes are tired from reading off the screen so long.
I guess I should come back another time."

When she exited the library, Stephanie noticed Doug
leaning against the car she'd borrowed. Had something
happened at the ranch? Or to Neddie?

In three strides, he was at her side. "What happened?"

"What do you mean, what happened?" Stephanie asked.
"That's what I was going to ask you." She propped her
hands on her hips.

Doug mirrored Stephanie's stance. "Where have you
been?"

"Right where I said I was going. I went to the fabric shop.
Then I went to Wal-Mart. Afterward, I stopped in the library for a while." Snatching a quick breath, Stephanie
squirmed beneath his scrutiny. "I'm not sure how long. I
lost track of time. I guess it was a couple of hours."

In a moment of repentance, Stephanie added, "I'm sorry.
I forgot about the time. It didn't seem important."

"Then you don't know what time it is?" Doug asked.

"Well, no." Stephanie admitted sheepishly.

Doug shoved his Stetson back on his head. "It's nearly
dinnertime."

His quizzing her every move irritated Stephanie. She
spewed out her anger. "What's that supposed to mean?"

"I phoned the newspaper about our plans—"

"You mean the wedding?"

He nodded. "Not the exact date, but the announcement
at least. I made an appointment at the photographer's, and
was hoping you'd be able to buy something new and get
your hair styled, but—"

"We only decided last night." Everything was moving too
fast. Panic attacked Stephanie. "I acted irresponsibly by
staying gone so long, and now I've ruined everything. It's all
my fault."

"It's not that, Steph. I can reschedule the appointment."
Sighing, Doug relaxed his defensive stance. "You've been

gone for hours. When you didn't come back, I thought you weren't... Well, I thought maybe you had car trouble. I imagined you in early labor, and stranded all by yourself, without help. Then, when I didn't find the car broke down along the road anywhere, I couldn't imagine what had happened.''

Vulnerability dented his armor. He glanced down at the toes of his snakeskin boots, then back at Stephanie. Laying pride aside, he confessed, ''Well, I imagined what might have happened, but I didn't think you'd leave without telling me.''

At that moment, standing there on the sidewalk, looking so vulnerable, Doug shot Stephanie's anger to pieces. He actually cared. Maybe this marriage of convenience wasn't as coldhearted as he'd led her to believe. She wilted against him, wrapping her arms around him, and kissed his neck where it disappeared into his collar.

Hating that he'd admitted a weakness, Doug stiffened beneath her touch, keeping his arms at his sides.

Contrite, Stephanie pulled back and stared up at him. ''I'm sorry. I guess I should have called, or come back sooner.'' She cupped a hand against his whisker-roughened jaw. ''Honestly, I had no idea it was so late. Forgive me. Okay?'' She smiled into his eyes.

''Are you hungry?''

Discouraged by Doug's ignoring her hug and her question, Stephanie released him and drew away. ''Why, yes, I am.''

''Excuse me, Mr. Taylor.''

They turned toward the voice. A young man with a camera extended his hand to Doug and shook hands. ''Good evening, sir. I take it this lovely lady is the bride-to-be.''

At Doug's nod, he continued, ''I'm the reporter you spoke to earlier in the day, when you phoned the newspaper. Boy! Have I had a time chasing you down! I wonder, could I have a candid shot to run with the announcement?

I'm trying to work myself into a better position with the paper, and a scoop like this for the front page would sure help.''

Doug and Stephanie glanced at each other. She shrugged in answer to his unvoiced question.

"Don't worry, ma'am," the reporter directed to her. "This is really big news in this town. I'm sure the society editor will be more than happy to run a full-length, formal article, with a professional photograph and all the trimmings, later.''

Doug answered for the two of them. "All right, son. Take your picture.''

Stephanie turned to Doug and smiled shyly up into his eyes.

A camera flashed in their faces, temporarily blinding the pair.

"Thank you, ma'am. Thank you, sir," the young man said, full of excitement. Then he rushed away.

After a fried-chicken meal at the colonel's punctuated with stilted conversation, they headed home, Stephanie driving the car, Doug following in the pickup.

When they arrived at the house, Doug climbed out, slammed the door and, without conversation, carried Stephanie's packages as far as the kitchen table.

Alone in his dark room upstairs, Doug adjusted the miniblinds and peered out at the dark night.

He was acting like a horse's behind and he knew it, but he couldn't help himself. Today, during all his worrying and fretting about her safety and welfare, Doug had realized just how much he cared for this woman who'd taken up residence in his home. What made him mad was that he cared for her and didn't have any right to care.

The last time he cared for someone, she'd killed herself and their unborn child. It had taken him years to erect this wall of self-preservation around himself, and he didn't intend to give it up so easily.

Last night, when he asked her to marry him and presented his airtight case to persuade her, he'd actually believed the whole proposition was a business transaction—that is, until she showed him how to seal a bargain.

Even this morning, in the light of day, he'd refused to believe otherwise—but then she'd disappeared for hours on end. Then he'd known just how firmly their lives were entwined.

Doug also kept persuading himself with the same arguments he'd used on her, that this business deal, or marriage of convenience, as he'd referred to it, would benefit them all. Logically, that was so. However, deep down, Doug knew he was simply setting himself up once again for the agony of hurt.

Was it too late to stop this whole thing snowballing? Did he really want to stop it? Doug deliberately refused to acknowledge the answer to that question.

But evidently he'd known the truth all along, because earlier in the morning, before he ever went to town today, he'd phoned the local newspaper. Pointedly Doug had told the reporter the announcement of the engagement was for immediate release. It was too late to change his mind now.

Doug turned from the window, only to be swallowed up by the darkness of the room. If the truth be known, he didn't want to stop what he'd already set in motion.

He just wasn't sure which was dictating his actions—his head or his heart.

Chapter Twelve

The next evening, when Stephanie walked to the road and retrieved the newspaper, along with the mail, she came face-to-face with a picture of Doug and herself splashed across the front page. The angle of the camera shot had caught them from the shoulders up, with the library in the background.

In the picture, she was smiling up into Doug's eyes. He was staring down at her, the expression on his face full of serious thought. The headline read Roll out the red carpet—wedding bells are chiming.

What would Doug say?

Before moving from the spot, Stephanie read every word of the article. She stared at the candid shot again. Apparently Doug had said plenty. They'd quoted him.

The ceremony would take place as soon as they could make the appropriate arrangements. Following the ceremony, the couple would make their home at the Triple T Estates.

Well, if nothing else, she at least knew he was serious about his proposal—serious enough that he'd announced their plans to the world. She didn't have to worry that this was some cruel joke that would evaporate the next time she woke up. There would be a permanence in her life that she desperately wanted and needed.

Slowly Stephanie walked back up the graveled road to the house. Disbelieving, she read the article again, even more carefully this time.

By the time she reached the front door of the house, climbed the few steps and walked inside, the telephone was ringing. Stephanie made a beeline for the instrument and answered it. "Hello."

"Stephanie, dear, what have you and Doug been up to while I've been gone? Never mind, you don't have to answer that. I can see with my own eyes, if I look at the newspaper that just came. My goodness! A body can't turn her back for a minute. Can she?"

Neddie. As usual, she wasn't giving anyone else a chance for a word edgewise. Stephanie couldn't help the smile that sprang to her face. She missed that dear woman, chatter and all.

When Neddie finally stopped long enough to draw a second breath, Stephanie jumped in. "Of course, you'll come to the wedding, won't you? I wouldn't dream of getting married without you, especially after all you've done for me during these past five months."

Patiently Stephanie answered the barrage of questions which followed. "Guaranteed, you'll be one of the first to know, as soon as we've set the date."

Over the course of the next week, as September faded into October, Stephanie answered an endless barrage of phone calls. In fact, she wouldn't have been surprised if the receiver sprouted roots in her ear. However, despite the continual interruptions, she accomplished a vast amount of sewing.

Elegant valances and simple curtains took shape before her eyes. She swept flowing curtains back in graceful lines and held them in place with matching tiebacks. Next she covered toss pillows in accent colors and trimmed them with ruffles and piping to match the curtains.

Using leftover fabric, Stephanie created matching doilies, scarves and armrest covers for the furniture by edging the scraps with scallops and zigzag stitching to prevent raveling.

Talk about making something out of nothing. She felt she'd performed a miracle when she dressed the various rooms of the house with her creations. Stephanie didn't leave a single room untouched in her attempt to remake Doug's house into a home—their home. Overall, she was more than pleased with her efforts.

Then, one afternoon during the first week of October, as Stephanie cleaned up her sewing mess at the kitchen table in preparation for cooking dinner, the phone rang. The shrill sound shattered the quiet of the house.

By the third ring, she'd emptied her hands and picked up the receiver. "Hello."

"Is this the residence of Douglas Conrad Taylor of the Triple T Estates?" a woman asked.

Alert, Stephanie answered with caution. "Yes, it is. How may I help you?"

"I'm trying to locate a Miss Stephanie, uh...Elkhart."

Premonition forewarned Stephanie. She gripped the receiver tighter than usual. "This is she."

"This is Evelyn Lankford—" the woman paused, before continuing "—of the Creative Designs home interior sewing shop in Tulsa, Oklahoma."

Sighing, Stephanie relaxed. They'd been inundated with phone solicitations since the wedding announcement. "I'm sorry. We're not interested."

"But—"

"Ma'am, we don't need whatever it is you're selling."

"You don't understand. I'm—"

"Ms. Lankford, you're the one who doesn't understand. I appreciate you taking time to phone and all, but we're not interested in purchasing anything at present. Thank you for calling. Goodbye." Stephanie hung up the receiver without waiting for a response. She'd learned to be assertive of late, because of the deluge of calls, most soliciting them to purchase one thing or another.

However, she'd no sooner hung up than the phone rang again. This time Stephanie was tempted not to answer, but she did, her voice full of impatience. "Hello."

"Steph, don't hang up. I've called practically every Taylor in the book trying to find you. This is Evie, your business partner in Tulsa."

The words sucked the life from Stephanie. Nothing else the woman said penetrated. In total shock, Stephanie stared at the phone as though it had a life of its own. She gripped the receiver tighter than was necessary, every muscle in her body hardening with tension.

Somehow finding strength to speak, Stephanie forced words through a constricted throat. Her voice deadly quiet, she said, "Excuse me. I think we have a poor connection. I didn't hear you very well. Would you repeat what you just said?"

"This is Evie, Evelyn Lankford, your business partner in Tulsa. We're co-owners of Creative Designs, a home interior sewing shop."

That explained why Stephanie knew how to sew.

When she didn't respond, the woman said, "You are the Stephanie that is in the picture with Conrad Taylor and is reportedly engaged to him, aren't you?"

"Yes."

"Then why are you calling yourself Stephanie Elkhart instead of your real name, Stephanie Garrison? You're not in some kind of trouble with the law, are you?"

"No, of course not. Why would you think that?"

"You left one day about five and a half months ago to personally work on a big job we had in Oklahoma City. As you got busier with the final stages of the project, your phone calls were less frequent."

The more the woman talked, the more familiar her voice sounded.

"I knew you planned to take time off afterward, for a short vacation. But we'd had so many inquiries about our services, I called to ask you to delay your vacation and check about expanding our design business there. When I couldn't get you, I phoned the client you'd been working with. She said you'd finished the job and left on vacation."

Like a parched desert, Stephanie absorbed every word, trying hard at the same time to remember.

"Only thing is, you never came back, and you never phoned or wrote or anything. Tell me what's going on. I feel I have a right to know."

Even though more and more questions flooded her mind, Stephanie patiently asked one at a time. "Did you fill out a missing-person's report?"

The woman hesitated before answering. "Not right away."

"Why not?"

Evelyn sighed. "I thought you'd come back."

"Of course I would have, if I'd been able."

"I waited another two weeks after I spoke to the client, before I finally decided you weren't on an ordinary vacation. By that time, I was worried sick. That's when I reported you missing." Evelyn's voice held a hint of regret. "By then it was too late to find out anything. Too much time had passed. Your trail was cold."

So many questions to ask. Stephanie hardly knew where to begin. "What about my parents? Weren't they worried? Did I live alone? Was there a man in my life? Am I already married?"

Evelyn made a funny noise. "What odd questions! Why do you ask?"

"About five and a half months ago, I was in a bad car wreck. The man in the car with me died. My purse and belongings all burned. I suffered a head injury and have had amnesia ever since." Stephanie paused, remembering when she'd woken up in the hospital.

She shook off the encroaching depression. "Oh, I have a few flashes of memories occasionally, but never enough to string together that I can remember who I am or where I came from." Her voice broke. Striving for composure, Stephanie stopped.

"Oh, how awful! That must be a nightmare!"

Crying silently, tears running down her face, Stephanie nodded. Then, realizing the caller couldn't see her, she struggled for composure. "It was. It still is at times. Evie, I have so many questions to ask you, I don't even know where to begin." A fresh wave of tears assaulted Stephanie.

"Don't cry, Steph."

Evie's voice calmed Stephanie. Still, she couldn't speak.

"Everything's going to work out okay. Please settle down, or you're going to have me crying, too. Then we'll never understand each other, with both of us blubbering."

Her words brought a smile to Stephanie. Just knowing Evie was out there somewhere, and that she finally had a past life she could explore, comforted her, but she couldn't curtail the onslaught of tears. They fell freely.

"I'm sorry I've fallen apart like this on the telephone." Stephanie hiccuped between sobs. "Give me your phone number. I'll call you back later this evening, when I've settled down and gotten control of myself. We'll have a good long chat and get reacquainted."

Hours later, when Doug returned home for the evening, Stephanie stayed curled up on the couch in front of the fireplace in the study with a box of tissue and waited for him to find her.

She still suffered occasional bouts of weepiness and was sure her eyes were swollen and red. Hugging a decorative pillow, she stared at the dying yellow-orange flames in the fireplace. The logs' crackling and popping broke the silence of the room. Totally impervious to the wads of used tissue surrounding her, Stephanie stared, mesmerized and lost in deep thought.

"Steph," Doug called.

But she didn't answer.

Minutes later, he strolled into the study. "Oh, there you are. Did you want to eat out tonight? I'll—" Seeing the litter of tissue, he halted in midsentence. "Steph, what is it? What's happened?"

After blowing her nose and mopping her eyes once again, she focused on Doug. "I'm Stephanie Garrison from Tulsa."

The color drained from his face. Foreboding clenched his heart. He dropped into the nearest chair. "You remembered!"

Slowly she shook her head. "No. I received a phone call this afternoon from Evelyn Lankford in Tulsa. She saw our picture and wedding announcement in the Tulsa paper."

"I didn't put it in the Tulsa paper," Doug was quick to answer.

But Stephanie had a ready response. "You being an important person in this part of the state probably gave them reason enough to pick up the story and run it for their circulation."

Stephanie dabbed at her leaking eyes with a fresh tissue. "Anyway, she said we co-own a home interior sewing shop called Creative Designs."

A sinking feeling pulled at Doug. He grabbed his first thought and voiced it. "You believed her without any proof?"

"Why not? Just look at all the sewing I've been doing. Plus, she told me that I left about five and a half months ago to finish a big decorating project in Oklahoma City and take a vacation afterward. But I never returned."

Common sense threw Doug's logic into overdrive. Easily he combated each statement with a plausible rebuttal. "She could have found out those facts from any news report. It sounds pretty vague to me."

"Why are you so skeptical?" Not believing he would squelch an opportunity for her to regain her memory, Stephanie stared at Doug. "Don't you want me to find out who I am or where I come from?"

"Of course I do." He leaned forward, placing his elbows on his knees and clasping his hands together. "But, Steph, when you're in my position, you've got to be cautious."

Stephanie's voice gained strength and firmness. "That's just it. I'm not in your position. I'm my own person."

"You're engaged to me." He pierced her with a hardened gaze, his fear mounting with each declaration Stephanie made. "That implies plenty. When we marry, you'll share equally in my assets."

She sighed. "I'm not marrying you for your wealth."

Doug bowed his head to his hands. How hard was he willing to fight to keep Stephanie? Was he being fair? "That's not the point. You can't trust every Tom, Dick, or Harry—or in this case, every Jane Doe or Evelyn Lankford—that comes along, especially if there might be money involved."

Irritated by Doug's refusal to acknowledge this lead that might unlock her memory, Stephanie glared at him. "Who said anything about any money? Besides, Evie seemed to know what she was talking about."

Standing, Doug towered over her. Anger at her stubbornness and refusal to trust his judgment replaced his fear. "All con artists know what they're talking about, but then, that's their livelihood. It's a racket. They read about a variety of misfortune in the newspaper, then prey on the victims. It's all coldhearted and calculated. People like this con innocent, unsuspecting people like you, and bleed them dry."

Ready to battle, Stephanie also stood. "But surely not Evie. You're mistaken on this. Don't spoil—"

"Trust me on this, Steph." He glanced at her. "Lay low for a few days while I have this woman checked out and her claims verified. I'll call a private investigator first thing tomorrow morning."

"What if I don't want to wait?"

Doug sighed. "Be sensible. You've already waited five and a half months. What's a few more days gonna matter?"

His caution provoked Stephanie to anger. "I'm telling you, I don't want to wait."

Stephanie's arguing irritated Doug. He wasn't used to anyone challenging his opinion, and especially not a woman. Raising his voice, he said, "I say you're going to wait a little longer. We can't take the chance on this being a fraud."

Near tears again, Stephanie asked, "Don't you want me to regain my memory?"

He softened his voice. "Of course I do, Steph. But not at the expense of more heartache. It's for your own good."

Still angry, Stephanie shot back, "How can you know what's good for me, when I don't even know myself?"

"Calm down, Steph. You're getting too worked up over this. The upheaval can't be good for you, or the baby." Doug pulled her into the circle of his arms.

She struggled free. "Leave me alone." Stephanie turned her back on him and, crossing her arms over her chest, stared into the glowing embers of the fireplace.

Closing the gap that separated them, Doug moved until he stood behind Stephanie. Tenderly he massaged her tense shoulder and neck muscles. "Relax. I'll go fix soup and grilled cheese sandwiches for dinner. When you calm down, come and eat something. I'll have it ready and waiting."

Doug's footfalls echoed across the hardwood floor as he left the room.

At the click of the closing door, Stephanie glanced over her shoulder. She was indeed alone in the room. She didn't like arguing with Doug. Arguing with him left a bitter taste in her mouth. Yes, she loved him and thought he cared for her in return. But sometimes he was just too darn bossy to suit her.

Was she balking at his controlling manner? Or was she convinced enough by Evelyn Lankford's phone call to believe what the woman said to be the truth? Both, it seemed.

While her mind replayed the events of the past few hours, Stephanie mechanically moved around the room, gathering up the wads of used tissue. She strode across the room, behind the desk, to the wastebasket in the corner, where she emptied her hands.

At the picture window, she observed the setting sun. Reddish-orange rays blazed across the clear blue evening sky. With each passing minute, the golden ball of light dipped lower in the sky, until it dropped from sight, spreading a fiery blanket over the horizon.

The beauty of an Oklahoma sunset against the flattened prairie, unhampered by man-made concrete buildings, never ceased to amaze her. If only she could stay here the rest of her life, she'd want for nothing else.

But before she could do that, guilt-free, she had to lay to rest the ghosts of her past.

Stephanie cupped her swollen abdomen. If nothing else, she at least owed her baby a sense of identity—her family history, her past and, hopefully, the father's name. She had a responsibility to this child, one she would not relinquish easily.

She had six weeks until her delivery date. After that, her activity would be restricted for a few more weeks. In her estimation, the weeks added up to months of waiting before she'd be able to go to Tulsa to explore Evelyn Lankford's claims.

If only she could meet Evie, talk with her in person, see the sewing shop and visit a few familiar haunts, surely her memory would return.

Excitement mounting within, Stephanie plotted what she needed to do. She had to act immediately. She didn't have time to spare. In her estimation, even tomorrow was too late, but she couldn't see how she could possibly leave any sooner, especially without risking being seen. If that happened, Doug would probably hog-tie her and lock her inside the house. Then she wouldn't be able to assuage her curiosity for weeks or even months. And that was too depressing to even consider.

Was this type of secrecy characteristic for her? Evie had said she'd left Tulsa without telling her what she intended to do on her vacation. Did Stephanie only do this when she felt she had no alternative? When she felt the situation warranted a measure of privacy? After all, she was an adult. And adults could do as they darn well pleased. Couldn't they?

In the end, she wouldn't hurt or endanger anyone. She surely didn't consider her actions life-threatening. Otherwise, she'd never attempt the journey.

If she remembered correctly, Doug had once mentioned Tulsa being about three hundred and fifty miles away, an easy day's drive under normal circumstances. But in her pregnant condition, Stephanie would need several rest stops to keep the circulation moving in her legs and prevent back discomfort and muscle strain.

Even at that, Stephanie could make the trip easily in a day—probably a long day, but still one day. She'd be gone three days, four at the most—one day to drive over, one day to drive back, and one, possibly two, days visiting and poking around. She'd leave as early as she could, just as soon as Doug was out of the house and gone to the fields.

With that concern out of the way, Stephanie traipsed to the kitchen for her temporary farewell meal with Doug, her step lighter than it had been in ages.

The next morning, after staying up late the night before, packing by the golden glow of the small bedside lamp and composing a convincing note to Doug explaining why she felt compelled to go against his wishes—or rather his demands—Stephanie was ready to leave Triple T Estates. She didn't really want to steal away like a common thief, but after witnessing Doug's objections the previous evening, Stephanie felt she had no choice at present.

As a last-minute decision, she walked to the dresser, picked up the solitaire engagement ring and slid it on the third finger of her left hand. Technically, she was an engaged woman. Why not show that to the outside world, subtly announce that she belonged to someone of her very own.

Stephanie considered it a moot point that Doug hadn't yet bought her a ring. They'd more than likely go shopping together one day in the near future and pick one out. Although Doug might just as easily have an heirloom ring in a safe-deposit box somewhere.

For now, she felt compelled to wear the solitaire the rescuer had found her gripping at the time of the wreck. After all, the presence of the jewel as a constant reminder might make for a speedier recovery. As far as Stephanie was concerned, it couldn't hurt.

Squaring her shoulders, she left her room and descended the stairs in search of her morning cup of coffee, acting as though she hadn't a worry in the world.

In the kitchen, Stephanie found coffee already brewed. That meant Doug was up ahead of her. Hopefully, that was an indication he'd leave the house early today.

As was her customary habit, Stephanie located a coffee mug and filled it two-thirds full with coffee, then topped it off with milk. Instead of cooking, this morning, she opted for a breakfast consisting of orange juice, buttered toast and sweetened cold cereal. Anxious to get on the road early, she quickly rinsed the dishes, including Doug's, which were in the sink, and stacked them all in the dishwasher.

Turning on the faucet, Stephanie dampened the dishcloth beneath the warm running water. She squeezed out the excess moisture. At the table, she made short work of wiping off the crumbs. Spinning on her heel, she ran smack-dab into Doug. "Oh! Sorry! I didn't see you there. Did I hurt your toe?"

When he shook his head, she said, "What are you doing sneaking up on a person, anyway?"

"I didn't sneak up on you."

"You did, too, and you scared me to death." Stephanie's palms were growing clammy, and not because she was holding the damp dishcloth, either.

"What are you so jumpy about, this early in the morning?"

"I'm not jumpy," she said, too quickly. "You just startled me. I didn't expect you to come creeping up behind me."

"I wasn't creeping around. Jeesh! Can't a guy move around freely in his own home without being accused of underhandedness?"

At the mention of the word *underhandedness,* a pang of guilt shot through Stephanie regarding her premeditated excursion to Tulsa. Contrite, she gave in to the need to confess all to Doug. "I'm sorry. I should explain. Last night, I..." No, she couldn't. She must remain firm on her decision. She had to discover who she was, where she came from, and whether or not another man had a claim to her and the child. It was only right. Stephanie owed that much to Doug before they exchanged wedding vows.

Now more than ever, she desperately wanted and needed to give her baby a sense of identity. With the newfound information from Evie, she had a chance, possibly her only chance. Stephanie wasn't going to turn down that opportunity, at least not without a fight.

She met his gaze, a hint of a smile trembling at her lips. "I was so upset last night, I didn't sleep well. I guess I'm a little on edge, after all that happened yesterday. I didn't mean to snap. I'm sorry." Stephanie dropped her gaze to the floor.

A thumb and finger on her chin, Doug tilted her face up. An uncanny fear was mounting inside him with each passing minute. He planted a kiss on her lips. "How about I stay with you today, and we do something special? Just the two of us."

Stephanie's eyes shot wide open with surprise. "No! I mean... I'm okay. That's not necessary."

He grinned. Maybe he was being oversensitive, but he needed some reassurance after their spat last night. Being with her would help his sudden insecurity. "I know it's not necessary, but I want to."

"But you'll get behind in all that work you have to do."

Curious, he stared at her. Why was she giving him the brush-off? "Steph, you act like you don't want me around today."

"Not at all. It's just..." Clutching at the first convincing thought that came to mind, she cupped her left hand to Doug's cheek. "I really need to finish some sewing today. Besides, I thought you'd still be mad about last night. I don't like arguing with you."

"I don't like arguing with you, either." Doug twisted his face to her hand and kissed her fingers, his mouth meeting with metal. Why was she wearing the ring from the accident? He grasped her hand and studied it.

Stephanie tugged her hand away from his tight hold.

Hooking his arms around her, Doug drew her to him until her swollen belly pressed against him. A cold finger of dread eased around his heart. Had he already lost her? "What do you say we kiss and make up?"

She pecked him on the cheek. "There, it's better now. All's forgiven."

Twisting from his hold, Stephanie stepped away from Doug. She laid a hand on her protruding stomach and glanced around the room, anywhere except at Doug, to keep him from reading what was in her heart. She wanted him, but she also needed to leave without telling him.

Doug wasn't exactly sure what was going on here, but an uneasy feeling cut deep to his core, sending a chill throughout his being. He chuckled halfheartedly in an attempt to throw off the ominous sense of foreboding. "Steph, you're priceless. I think you're still mad at me about last night and don't want to admit it."

His cocksure attitude ruffled her feathers. She stamped a foot. "I'm telling you the truth." Well, at least partially. "It's your own fault if you won't believe me."

He smiled. "See there? I told you so. I knew you were still mad at me."

Stephanie raised her voice for emphasis. "I am not."

"You are, too. See you're yelling at me." He tweaked her nose.

She brushed his hand away and lowered her voice. "I wasn't before, but I am now." Crossing her arms over her chest, Stephanie smiled sweetly. "I hope you get stuck in a rainstorm by yourself somewhere. You deserve a little discomfort."

No closer to discovering the cause for his uneasiness, Doug dismissed the inkling as a carryover from last night's disagreement. He stuck out his lower lip in a little-boy pout. "Now you're being mean."

"No, I'm not." Unable to resist his playfulness, she smiled. "Okay, I am being mean, but if you really want to know what mean is, come here for a minute." She crooked her index finger, motioning him to her.

At his approach, she said, "Give me a big goodbye kiss to remember you by all day long, you lug, then go to work."

The kiss started warm and gentle, nipping and teasing. All too soon, comfortable in each other's embrace, Doug and Stephanie planted their mouths firmly together and deepened the kiss. Their tongues met and mated, in and out, back and forth, exchanging sweet elixir. Eventually they broke the bond, but, unable to sever the contact, they touched their foreheads together, breathing heavily.

In time, their pulses returned to normal.

Doug pulled back. "Now, Steph, that's really mean."

Unable to suppress the words, she said, "I told you so."

He smiled. "I hope I meet with that cold rain shower you wished on me sooner, instead of later."

Chapter Thirteen

Stephanie switched the car's wiper blades from low to high. Still, the falling sheets of cold October rain obscured her view of the highway. Why hadn't she thought to check the weather forecast before she left the Triple T Estates for Tulsa?

There was no turning back now. She was more than two-thirds of the way there. She'd taken a rest stop at Woodward, and most recently at Enid. Pushing onward, Stephanie fantasized about regaining her memory at the end of her journey to Tulsa.

All too soon, her thoughts wandered to her biggest fear—car trouble. She was in no shape to change a tire or hitch a ride—not now that she was seven and a half months pregnant.

Stephanie kept telling herself she hadn't stolen the car, even though her conscience told her otherwise. She was simply running an errand, as on any other day, except that the errand happened to be more than three hundred and fifty miles away and required her to spend the night.

Other worries surfaced. She assuaged her conscience by reminding herself that she'd left the note on the bed in Doug's room, in plain sight, where he would easily find it. He'd be hurt that she'd disobeyed him, but hopefully he'd understand the importance of her mission and that would outweigh his wrath.

In order to drown out the nagging voice within, Stephanie turned on the radio. The interior of the car flooded with the crackly sound of static electricity. Repeatedly she pressed the seek button, sending the radio tuner on an automatic search for the strongest radio signals nearby. After settling on a National Public Radio broadcast station, she relaxed back in the seat as best she could and let the automobile fill with classical music.

Arriving in Tulsa after dark frightened Stephanie almost as much as the threat of car trouble, especially since the streets and landmarks appeared so foreign and strange to her. However, Stephanie kept a cool head. After exiting the interstate onto Lewis Avenue, she located a pay phone and called Evelyn.

"Stephanie, are you really here in Tulsa? Tonight?" Surprise threaded through Evelyn's voice.

For the first time in a long time, Stephanie laughed spontaneously. "Yes. I wouldn't tease about something as important as this."

"I can't believe it—and all so soon. Wow!" Evelyn giggled with her.

"Okay, I'm just north of the intersection at the interstate and Lewis Place, at a convenience store. Tell me again how to find your place." Carefully Stephanie listened, taking meticulous notes. "Okay, I got it. See you in a few minutes."

After balancing the receiver in its cradle, Stephanie rolled up the window on the driver's side, then eased the car away from the pay phone and into a gap in the oncoming traffic. Anxious to be at the end of her journey, Stephanie pressed the accelerator. The powerful engine surged beneath her touch.

In no time at all, she steered the car into a narrow drive beside a private residence and pulled up behind a blue Ford Escort. She shut off the engine. Stephanie sat quietly for a moment to settle her nerves.

A porch light popped on, bathing her in a yellow glow. By the time Stephanie climbed from the car, a woman of about the same age as her bounced out the door and down three steps to the sidewalk.

"Steph, is that really you, after all this time?"

The minute the woman spoke, Stephanie recognized the voice as belonging to the person she'd spoken with on the phone moments ago, and twice yesterday at Doug's ranch.

"Yes, it's me."

Stephanie took hold of the woman's extended hands. "Evelyn, you look so nice. I don't know what I expected, but it wasn't anything close to reality."

The women hugged each other. When Evelyn butted up against Stephanie's protruding stomach, she drew away and glanced down. Her eyes grew round. "My, oh, my! You didn't tell me you were expecting. When did this happen?"

Stephanie ran a hand over the fullness of her stomach. "Apparently about two months before the wreck."

Evelyn's eyes widened, their enlarged size engulfing her face. "That means you're due..."

"In six weeks," Stephanie finished for her.

"I can't believe you drove all that way by yourself, and in your condition." She tugged on Stephanie's arm. "Let's get you inside before you get cold."

Stopping, Stephanie turned back to the car. "Just a minute. Let me grab my overnight bag from the back seat."

After Stephanie retrieved the bag, Evie took it from her and urged her on ahead of her into the warm house.

Once inside the dwelling, Evie led Stephanie to the kitchen and prepared them each a cup of hot instant decaffeinated coffee in the microwave. "I remember how you used to love lots of milk in your coffee. Do you still use milk?"

At Stephanie's nod, Evie continued, "I thought of you when I found these recently. Try one." She offered Stephanie a choice of designer creamers to flavor her beverage. Evelyn smiled. "Pick your own poison. I'm already addicted. Will it be Irish cream, mocha almond, French vanilla royale or Amaretto?"

Stephanie clapped gleefully. "Yes, but I can't."

"Yes, but no?" Perplexed, Evelyn stared at her.

"I'd love to, but I don't think it best for the baby." She cupped a hand lovingly to her abdomen.

"Why not?" Evie continued with her preparations, not taking no for an answer.

"I'm not taking any chances. Alcohol's not good for a baby."

"I wouldn't put your baby at risk. You know me better than that." Evie paused. "No, I guess you don't. You've forgotten." She smiled. "Put your mind at ease. These are the nonalcoholic variety."

Relieved, Stephanie shrugged. "In that case, I want to try them all, but I'll probably have to do it tomorrow. It's already late tonight, so I'll have an amaretto, please."

"Please? Since when did you get so polite with me? This is Evie. We're not strangers, you know. We used to be best friends." She patted Stephanie on the shoulder. "But I'm sure it will take time for you to become accustomed to the idea, especially since you more than likely feel you barely know me."

Emptying the creamer into her coffee, Stephanie smiled weakly. "I'm sorry."

"No, don't be sorry. I'm the one who should apologize to you. I shouldn't be so pushy. Drink up."

The hot coffee soothed Stephanie's pent-up emotions after the stressful day and relaxed her tired muscles. "Now, tell me everything you know about me. Am I married? Who's the father of my baby? Do I have any relatives?" Stephanie stifled a yawn.

"It's already so late, and you've had such a long, eventful day. I can see you're exhausted. Wouldn't you rather wait? We'll have plenty of time to chat tomorrow." She patted Stephanie's arm. "Let's get you in bed for a good night's sleep."

"No, Evie." Stephanie shook her head, more to clear the exhaustion than to give a negative reply. "This is important to me. I've got to know now."

"Where do you want me to begin?"

"Anywhere. I want every crumb of information I can get. I'm desperate."

Over the next hour, Stephanie fought hard to keep her eyes open and her attention alert, so as not to miss anything. Evie told her about their business alliance and their shop. She mentioned that Stephanie's parents had wanderlust and were having a ball traveling around in their motor home to various places.

Stephanie actually dozed off during the discourse. She jerked herself awake in time to hear Evie admit that she hadn't exactly informed Stephanie's parents that their daughter was missing.

"I didn't want to worry them, even though I was worried sick myself." Evie smiled. "Now, as it all turned out, I won't have to tell them anything. You'll want to tell them. You don't know what a big relief that is."

"Thank goodness they haven't worried themselves sick." Stephanie rubbed her eyes.

"Steph, you've got to get in bed. Exhaustion isn't good for you or the baby."

"I know, but I so desperately want to find out everything tonight." She covered another yawn.

"Please, Steph, go to bed. We can talk more tomorrow." Evie rinsed their cups at the sink. "Besides, I've got to get up and go to work tomorrow. If I stay up much later, I won't be able to get up, much less go to work."

"I'm sorry." Yawning, Stephanie stood and rubbed her lower back, greatly disappointed, and fully aware that she hadn't discovered that which was most important to her— the name of her child's father. "I didn't mean to impose, especially after you've been so kind."

Evie led the way to the guest room. "Quit being so polite and apologetic. Relax and have a good night's sleep."

Stephanie halted in the doorway. "Will you answer one more question?"

"Not tonight, hon. You've been too tired to comprehend a word I've said for the past half hour. There'll be plenty of time tomorrow."

Disappointed that she hadn't learned more, Stephanie fell into an exhausted sleep the second her head hit the pillow.

When Doug returned to the house later in the evening, he told himself not to panic and run to town, as he had last time. All he'd accomplished then was to make a fool of himself. So to keep busy and while away the hours until Stephanie returned home from town and, undoubtedly, a shopping spree to assuage her hurt pride, he went to the study and worked on long overdue paperwork.

However, Doug couldn't keep his mind on the tasks at hand. He constantly kept one eye on the clock. The more hours that came and went, the more uptight he grew. She was probably staying out late on purpose, because she knew the action would needle Doug, especially after the last time.

Already he could predict that their life together would be a rocky road, but evidently they'd both decided it worth the chance to marry. Both of them had walked into this proposition with their eyes wide open.

Doug's main concern was how he would overcome his conscience with regard to Stephanie as Theodore's territory. Would he ever be free to make love to her as he wanted? Hopefully, when they'd married and Doug knew he had the legal right to make love to her, the knowledge would free him from guilt. How soon would that be?

Grabbing the calendar from the desk, Doug studied it. He calculated the earliest date to be sometime next week, five weeks before the baby was due to be born. Would Stephanie agree? If not, she could pick the date.

Glancing at the clock, he noted that nine o'clock had come and gone. Doug busied himself so as not to go raving mad. When the clock chimed ten and there was still no Stephanie, Doug scoured the house once again. She was nowhere to be found.

As the time neared eleven, Doug admitted he was worried. Stephanie was not a stay-up-late person, but he wasn't sure what she would do in a fit of temper. Surely she wasn't so mad that she'd stay out most of the night just to show him she had a mind of her own and could darn well do as she pleased.

By midnight, Doug forgot about being reasonable. He drove the pickup the thirty-mile distance into town and scoured the streets for the car. Block after city block, he crept up and down the roads, business district and residential areas alike. He even shone the beam of a flashlight into yards and at times onto porches when he glimpsed a movement, a person or car that could have been Stephanie or her car.

At five o'clock in the morning, his resources depleted, Doug inched back home, once again scouring the roads on his way to the ranch. Doug thought he knew all the hiding places in town and between town and the ranch, but Stephanie and the car were nowhere to be found.

Had he been too heavy-handed with her, as he had with Theo and Constance? Had he made her hate rural life? Had she, too, decided to leave the quiet confines of the ranch for the hustle and bustle of city life?

After returning home past six in the morning, Doug phoned the hospital as a last resort. No, they didn't have a patient admitted in the past twenty-four hours by the name of Stephanie Elkhart, or Stephanie anything, for that matter.

Doug shrugged out of his heavy sheepskin-and-suede jacket. Stepping outside, on to the patio off the study, he walked to the edge and peered toward the road. He looked in all directions. Not a light or movement or car in sight.

For an hour and a half longer he stood there, watching and waiting, numbness creeping into him from the cold. Hands shoved deep in his pockets, Doug wondered where he had gone wrong.

During the time Stephanie had lived in his home, he'd given her all the material things she needed or wanted, which wasn't very much. He'd opened charge accounts around town for her to use, but she hadn't overspent by any means. In fact, he'd been surprised at how little she spent in order to do what she did with that sewing machine. As if by magic, she created beautiful window dressings, wall hangings and matching accessories from a little of nothing, with no shape or form to begin with. He'd allowed her a free hand in decorating, and he had to admit she'd done a heck of a good job transforming the house from a cold, barren abode into a warm, welcoming home.

Now his home and heart seemed empty without her.

Before long, reddish-orange fingers of sunlight stretched across the eastern horizon, loosening darkness's hold on the land. Midnight blue gave way to orange, then yellow against a clear blue morning sky.

The shrill ringing of the phone pulled Doug inside. In the study, he answered on the fifth ring. "Hello."

"Doug—"

"Steph, is that you?" His stomach flipped over at his own name in her soft voice.

"Just listen and let me explain."

Nightmarish scenes flashed before Doug. "Are you all right?"

She sighed. "I'm fine, but be quiet and—"

"Where are you?" She wasn't giving him the facts fast enough to suit him.

"Didn't you find my note?"

"What note?"

"The one I left on your bed?"

"I haven't even been to my room." Doug tensed, hoping against hope, attempting to change the reality of the situation, his dread building as he talked, "Tell me where you are. Did the car break down? I'll come and get you."

Her voice came stronger, irritation at the forefront. "If you don't shut up and listen, I'll hang up, and then you sure enough won't know until you read the note." She paused.

At her threat, Doug kept silent, biting his tongue the whole time, impatient with her slow speed in relating what he wanted to know.

Taking his silence for agreement, she went on. "Doug, I don't want you to worry. That's why I'm phoning. I would have phoned sooner, but it was late when I arrived at Evelyn's in Tulsa—"

"Tulsa!" His silence slipped. "Are you out of your mind? The baby's due in less than two months. You should stay close to home, not be out gallivanting around the whole countryside like you haven't a worry in the world."

"Doug, please, just listen."

At the uncommon firmness in her voice, he curtailed his rush of words.

"I couldn't rest easy after Evie called. If I don't take the opportunity now, before the baby's born, to learn my past, it will be at least three months before I'll be able to come here. I *have* to find out who I am, where I came from, and what I was before we met." She paused, her breath whispering over the phone line.

When Doug didn't say anything, she continued. "Please understand that I *have* to find out who the other man in my life was, the one who fathered my child, and what promises, if any, we made to each other, before I'll be free to come back to the ranch."

The pain of loss clamped a fist around Doug's heart. He'd known better than to become too involved with another woman. Always his fate was the same, to be alone with his first love—his precious ranch. How long before he learned his lesson?

"Doug, are you still there?"

Soft whimpers carried across the line, piercing his heart. "Yes," he answered between stiff lips.

"Say something—" Her voice broke.

Doug hardened his response, determined not to let her know the effect she had on him. "I'm listening. Go ahead. Say what you called to say."

"Today I..."

Strain was evident in her voice. This ordeal wasn't easy for Stephanie, either.

"I plan to spend the day with Evie at the sewing store. I hope that being here in Tulsa and in the shop will force me to remember everything. Combating this amnesia head-on has got to be better than waiting around there at the ranch, hoping for a recovery that may never come."

A catch in her voice indicated that she was close to tears.

"Please understand, this is something I *have* to do. Not knowing is driving me mad, especially since learning I have this opportunity to recover what I've lost. I desperately need to give this baby a sense of identity before it's born."

Hearing her heartache, Doug drew in a ragged breath. Stephanie's suffering was as hard on him as it was on her. He steadied his voice. "Do what you have to do. You know where to find me, if you need anything."

Now, she openly cried. "I want to remember everything today and be on my way home tomorrow."

Home? Stephanie had actually referred to him and the ranch as home! "Steph, what if your plan doesn't work?" He owed that much to them both—to play devil's advocate. Every situation had two sides, a good one and a not-so-good one.

Audibly she gasped. "Don't say that. Don't even think it. The plan has to work. This is my last chance, my last hope to regain my memory."

Unable to take much more of listening to how much this ordeal was upsetting Stephanie, Doug gave her an easy out, though his heart was breaking into a billion pieces. "Stay in touch, Steph."

"I will," she whispered.

Doug cleared his throat. "Keep me posted on your progress."

A whimper mewed across the phone line. "Doug, it's only going to be one day. I plan to be home tomorrow night. Honest."

"Whatever you say, Steph." Disbelief colored his words.

For a moment, she didn't say a word. Soft sobs pulsed through the connection. Finally her weepy voice drifted across the line. "You talk like this is goodbye."

"In a way, it is." Finding it necessary to keep his voice clear and firm, Doug paused to compose himself and gather strength. "You won't ever be the same as I know you now, no matter what happens. Have a good life, Steph." Doug hung up, breaking the connection, before she even said goodbye. Stupid pride! He hadn't even asked for a phone number or an address.

Angry with himself, Doug strode back to the patio door and stared out into the clear morning sky. Once again his ranch had won out over the love of a woman. Love? Ha! Neither he nor she had ever mentioned the word or the emotion. *Convenient cohabitation* was a better term. And now living together was no longer convenient. Well, they wouldn't be the first couple to admit they'd made a mistake. Much better now than later.

Stephanie sat down on the edge of the bed in Evelyn's master bedroom. Slowly she replaced the receiver in the cradle of the phone. That click had sounded so final, like the severing of a lifeline—hers and Doug's. Had she been so wrong in coming to Tulsa without his blessing? On the other hand, Stephanie knew she'd never have gotten it, especially not with her due date drawing nearer. Couldn't he understand that she wasn't Constance? She wouldn't do anything stupid where her baby was concerned.

"Steph, are you about ready to leave?" Evelyn's voice carried to her from the living room. "I've got the car all warmed up for you. I parked yours by the curb. We'll go in my car." She appeared at the bedroom door, bundled up in a coat and scarf.

Smiling weakly, Stephanie stood and shrugged into her own coat, then wrapped a knit scarf around her neck and face. "I'm ready to face the dragon."

"Come on, slugger. Grab your fire extinguisher. Your chariot awaits. I don't think it would be advisable for you to mount a white horse in your condition."

Stephanie couldn't resist the smile Evelyn's words brought. How warm and friendly the woman seemed, more than willing and ready to mother Stephanie.

Forty-five minutes later, after crossing town in the midst of morning traffic, Evelyn steered her Ford Escort onto a side street. She pulled into a strip mall, circled around behind the business establishments, then parked beneath a posted sign reserving three spaces for Creative Designs employees.

With bated breath, Stephanie waited while Evelyn unlocked the back door, then followed her into their shop. The back room housed boxes of thread spools and several types of sewing machines—a serger, industrial-strength, a free-arm, a basic model, and a computerized model for custom-made embroidered designs.

Through the wide double door, in the front portion of the shop, shelves and tables bulged with every style, shape, size and color of trims, bindings and decorations imaginable. Various displays of miniature windows and finished products, grouped in a rainbow of coordinated colors, lined the walls. Numerous accessories filled several tables to overflowing. Throughout the shop, bolts of fabric stood side by side, library-book-fashion, on rows of tables, allowing the shopper to easily select the textile of her choice.

Evelyn led Stephanie to a cozy corner near the front of the shop, where a couch and a stuffed chair sat in an arrangement demonstrating how a finished room might look with their additions. An oak unit bolted to the wall boasted shelves lined with large D-ring binders and swatch books.

One of the binders lay open on the coffee table in front of the couch, swatches spread beside it. Quickly leafing through the notebook, Evelyn showed Stephanie clear plastic page protectors filled with eight-by-ten professional color photographs documenting their work over the years. "Steph, why don't you start here? Study the photos, and see if they bring back memories. Meanwhile, I'll go put on a pot of coffee—the real thing this morning."

Stephanie glanced at the retreating Evelyn. "Do you by chance have—"

"Flavored coffee creamers here, too." Evelyn hooked a glance over her shoulder and finished Stephanie's question. "Wouldn't be without them, especially now that you're here to share them with me." Evie disappeared into the back room.

As Stephanie flipped the pages, an inkling nagged at her. Instead of forming, the impression swam elusively, wavering in and out of her consciousness. An awareness tugged at the back of her mind. The photographs held a familiarity, but she couldn't quite put her finger on exactly what caused the sensation. Seeking confirmation of her suspicions, Stephanie thumbed through the rest of the notebook, her gaze searching the many pictures.

Becoming restless, she wandered around the shop, studying the different displays. Repeatedly Stephanie returned to the notebook of photographs, fixing her gaze on them, as if in a trance. Then, in the next few minutes, she inched back to the displays, drawn to them in some unfathomable way.

Back and forth, back and forth, she paced, repeating the action, using the identical path, in exactly the same way, over and over. Just barely out of reach, the clue she sought hovered. If only she could grasp what was hiding within, begging for release.

Suddenly the relevance she was seeking burst forth from her subconscious, full-blown. The significance of the discovery sent a weakness through her, buckling her legs. Breathing heavily, she sat down on the couch, hands and knees trembling.

The curtains and throw pillows—that was it. The ones she'd made for Doug's home were mirror images of the ones on display and the ones exhibited in the pictures. Even though of different fabrics, the style, with pinched-pleat needlework at each of the corners, was the same, unique to the Creative Designs sewing shop, more or less a signature or trademark.

Warm tears pooled in Stephanie's eyes, spilling over the bottom edge of the lids. Yes, her presence was stamped here, as well as in Doug's home. The artistic expression in sewing was definitely characteristic of her, this store a part of her past as much as Doug's home held and foretold of her future.

The aroma of fresh-brewed coffee drifted to the front of the store, where Stephanie was perched on the edge of the couch. Unable to resist any longer, she brushed away the tears, shoved aside the binder and made her way to the back of the store.

At a cluttered desk, Evelyn sat discussing the details of a job with a customer over the phone. She rolled her eyeballs back in her head, indicating that she'd be glad when the call was over. Pointing an index finger, she directed Stephanie to the coffeepot.

By the time Stephanie had prepared two servings of coffee and returned to the desk with both mugs in hand, Evelyn was placing the receiver on the cradle.

"Ugh!" She made a face. "Why did we ever decide we wanted to work for the public? Some of them can be so nit-picky and indecisive, constantly changing their minds about the least little detail. They make you want to scream in total frustration and tell them to take their business elsewhere."

Stephanie shoved a mug of hot mocha-almond-flavored coffee her way. "Here, you look like you could use this."

Taking a sip, Evelyn relaxed back in the chair. "Mm . . . I needed that. Thanks."

Glancing around, Evelyn spotted a straight-backed chair not far away, beneath a stack of papers. She set her mug on the corner of the desk, then, traipsing across the room, dropped the papers to the floor and pulled the chair close to the desk. "Here, have a seat, partner. Let me fill you in on what's going on—what's hot and what's not. Get your feet wet again and hopefully jog that hard head of yours into remembering that sewing and decorating aren't a piece of cake, all fun and games."

"I never said they were." Stephanie smiled, blinking away the warmth of fresh tears. "Besides, I'm not opposed to a hard day's work for my wages."

Evie laughed. "You'd better not have second thoughts and think you'd rather turn tail and run. Remember, I found you once. I'll find you again. That's a promise, lady."

"Thank goodness you did. Or no telling when I'd have shown up to claim my share of all the riches." She eyed the shop.

"Yeah, sure. Rich and famous designers." Evelyn pointed to the stack of papers in the floor. "That's only the most recent of the bills. I never was particularly adept at keeping up with the paperwork. That was supposed to be your job. A little behind, aren't you?"

Stephanie smiled. "Only about five and a half months. Too bad I didn't choose a partner with more business sense and less creativity."

"Gee, thanks." Evelyn offered a fake pout. "Here I am working my buns off to keep the shop's head above water, while you go off on an *extended* vacation, my sweet. So much for all the thanks I hoped to get."

"I guess we both have our strengths and weaknesses." Stephanie waggled her eyebrows. "And right now, mine is another cup of that wonderful coffee. How about seconds?"

"You twisted my arm." Evelyn finished the last of her coffee and shoved her mug in Stephanie's direction, while at the same time straightening the desktop. "I plead no contest."

Afraid of bursting into tears, Stephanie stared at the toes of her black flats, keeping track of Evelyn's actions from the corner of her eye. "Evie, thanks for caring enough to call, and for persisting when I slammed the receiver down in your ear the first time."

"No thanks needed, hon. Just keep that coffee coming." Evelyn glanced in Stephanie's direction. She halted her desk cleaning attempt. "Do I detect tears in those hazel eyes?"

Stephanie redirected her gaze to Evelyn. "I recognized the style of curtains and pillows. The ones here in the shop and in the notebook pictures are identical to those I recently made for Doug's home."

"So you're willing to accept that I'm telling the truth? That you're partners with me in this business?"

Nodding, Stephanie conceded. "But nothing else is clear. Who was I dating? Who fathered my child? Where did I live?"

"I'm sorry, Steph. I can't answer all your questions, because that was a busy time for both of us. We were passing each other coming and going." Evelyn shrugged. "However, if it helps any, just before you left we hired several part-time seamstresses to help with minor sewing construction jobs to free us for consultation and custom work. In fact, that's how you arranged to be gone on that Oklahoma City project for a while without it causing undue hardship for the business."

"And now?" Stephanie asked.

"I have . . . I mean, we have three girls that sew regularly for us, each with a sewing station of her own." Evelyn pointed out the three designated areas. "The business has managed to continue generating enough profit that I deposit your share each month to an account in your name—minus your monthly expenses, of course."

Stephanie thought for a moment, then asked, "What monthly expenses do I incur?"

"The answer to that also answers one of your original questions. You bought a small two-bedroom house four months before you left. We'd established the business well enough you felt you could invest in a lifelong dream—a house of your own, with a backyard. You said you were tired of living in apartments with no outdoor space to call your own."

A moment of panic seized Stephanie. "Was it repossessed while I was gone?"

"Heavens, no!" Evelyn spoke as though the idea were pure nonsense. "I wouldn't let anyone take away your dream that easily. I've kept up all your payments and utilities. The place is just like you left it five and half months ago. I haven't touched a thing, except to take out the trash and empty the perishables out of the refrigerator, so you wouldn't have to come home to a stinking mess."

Dreamily Stephanie smiled. "A house of my very own."

"Yes." Evelyn's eyes sparkled at Stephanie's enjoyment.

A foreign feeling of excitement claimed Stephanie. "How soon can I go there?"

"Now, if you like. We always kept an extra key to each other's homes, in case either of us got locked out." Evelyn dug the key out of a small zippered compartment in her purse. "I can't go with you right now, but there's no reason you can't go on your own. We'll phone for a cab to take you over, then I'll stop by and get you when I leave here this evening. You will be all right, won't you?" She slapped the warm key in Stephanie's palm.

Stephanie stared at the key. What secrets would it unlock?

"Steph?"

Evelyn's voice halted Stephanie's musings. She glanced up, astounded by the implications this news brought. "Yes, of course I'll be fine. It's quite a surprise to find I'm a homeowner. That's all."

In the taxi on her way to the small house, Stephanie wondered how Doug would accept the news of another home, in Tulsa. What would he say when she shared the findings of the first day there? With the initial day having been so productive, maybe a second day, or even a few more days in residence in Tulsa would help even more. A longer stay than originally planned surely couldn't hurt. Could it?

Chapter Fourteen

After paying the taxi driver, Stephanie stood at the curb and stared at the small two-bedroom house that belonged to her. This side of the street was banked, making the house look as if it rested on a hill. Hers was white, with a steep gray shingle roof. Forest-green shutters flanked the windows, and a matching green rail outlined the large covered porch.

On shaky legs, Stephanie walked up the narrow drive and followed the sidewalk to the three steps that led up to the concrete porch and front door. She opened the storm door and, while holding it with her body, fit the key in the deadbolt lock. Her fingers were so jittery, she tried twice before she finally unlatched the lock and flung open the door.

She stepped into a long, narrow living room with a fake fireplace and mantel, sparsely furnished, with a rose-colored sectional couch partitioning the room. When she adjusted the blinds at the double window, enough sunlight filtered in to adequately light the pale green room.

A small portable TV was angled across the corner to face the couch. Farther along the fireplace wall, she found a radio on a small side table near the door to the kitchen.

Briefly peeking into the kitchen, she saw that the walls were sky blue and the countertop sunshine yellow. Although small and compact, the kitchen was equipped with all the necessary appliances—even a dishwasher. A door led to the yard out back. Counters on either side, like narrow breakfast bars, separated the kitchen from the dining area.

Retracing her steps to the living room, Stephanie passed through the third door in the living room to a small hallway. Off the hall, across from the living room, was the bathroom, with pink ceramic tile halfway up the wall and trimmed with blue tiles. Blue diamond-shaped tiles also accented the pink tiles in a precise pattern repeated every few tiles.

The room doubled as a laundry room, with the washer beside the sink and a dryer along the opposite wall, partially hidden behind the open door.

Being an older home, the house had an inset at the end of the hall for the telephone. Twin doors bracketed the telephone inset, each opening into a bedroom—the master bedroom on the left, the front side of the house and the guest room on the right, the back of the house.

Apparently Evie stopped by often, tending to her mail and bills and discarding junk mail, because nothing seemed out of place. There weren't any stacks of dirty dishes or piles of mail like the ones she'd witnessed at Theodore's apartment.

Stephanie stepped into the master bedroom and turned a circle, not knowing where to begin or what to do first. Everything seemed so foreign, as though she were in a stranger's house instead of her own home.

Unexpectedly, the phone rang, startling her. She walked to the hallway and stared at the instrument, wondering who would be calling her. After four rings, she picked up the receiver. "Hello."

"Hi, Steph, this is Evie. I was just checking to make sure you arrived safe and sound."

"Yeah, but I feel weird. It's as if I've walked into another person's home and am invading her privacy. I'm a stranger in my own home. So far nothing's familiar."

"How about I buy carryout Chinese food for dinner and we eat there, more or less to celebrate your homecoming?"

"That sounds like fun. Plus, it will give me time to reacquaint myself with my home."

"Okay, see you later."

Stephanie spent the remainder of the day plundering through drawers and closets. Digging deep, she eventually unearthed a picture album and a high school yearbook.

The people in the yearbook brought no recognition, their young faces several years removed from the present. Would she recognize any of these people as they were now—older?

Hoping for more clues in the photo album, Stephanie put aside the yearbook and turned to it. However, to her disappointment, she found very few pictures of real consequence. She had evidently started it with high school graduation, because the first entries were photos of her by herself or with a younger-looking Evie, both of them wearing mortarboards.

Other pictures were with an older couple, apparently her parents. Stephanie studied them. She had her father's nose and hairline, her mother's eyes and smile. She'd inherited her hair coloring from her mother, but the waves evidently came from her father. Judging from the photos in comparison to her, neither of her parents was particularly tall, but then, neither was she. The family resemblance could be seen easily.

Grazing her fingertips across the photos, Stephanie wished she remembered her parents, but, regrettably, she didn't. Not yet, anyway.

A few other pictures lay loose inside the album. They showed landscapes, perhaps places she'd visited on vacation, or maybe places her parents had traveled to in their excursions. At any rate, they held no meaning today.

She also found pictures of room treatments, as though she'd photographed them at a furniture store or a trade show in preparation for new decorating schemes. Maybe she'd spent time with her parents on one of their many expeditions and taken these while there.

Stephanie thumbed through the remaining pages. She discovered clippings of room interiors and snippets of fabrics, obviously photos collected from decorating magazines, judging by the slick paper and perfect look to the rooms. She fingered the swatches of fabric. No memories bounced to the forefront. She guessed she'd had ideas to use these fabrics in treatments similar to those in the pictures. Who knew?

With more searching, Stephanie found three boxes of old tax records and wondered how much she could piece together of her life from receipts and past billing statements. Not very visual, but factual—places she'd shopped and things she'd bought.

Other than the album, high school yearbook and tax records she found very little with which to rebuild her past and identify her old life. Evidently when she moved she'd thrown out most of her memorabilia. Hence the barrenness of the house.

That was nice for keeping the house neat and clean, but not the least bit helpful when it came to sneaking a peek at her former life or reconstructing it from scratch.

All too soon, the afternoon had passed, with her digging through drawers and closets, hoping for more disclosures about her past. Before Stephanie realized how late the time was, Evelyn's knock sounded at the front door, announcing her entry. The opening and closing of the storm door, followed by footsteps, indicated that she'd walked inside without waiting to be invited.

"Yoo-hoo! I'm here with dinner. Are you hungry?" Evelyn paused. "Where are you, Steph?"

"I'm in here," Stephanie hollered from the master bedroom. "Come on back."

Evelyn soon appeared at the doorway, her arms laden with a sack full of delicious-smelling Chinese food.

"Mm..." Stephanie said from the center of the room. "I didn't realize how hungry I was until I got a whiff of that. Let's eat. I've already set each of us a place."

In the kitchen, Stephanie retrieved a pitcher of iced tea from the refrigerator, then joined Evelyn at the table. She poured a glassful of the amber liquid for each of them.

"Well, how did your day go?" Evelyn asked.

A shrug to her shoulders, Stephanie said, "Okay, I guess. I haven't made any personal connections here at the house, like I did at the store. I guess I was hoping for too much."

Evelyn waved her fork at Stephanie. "It could be you didn't live here long enough to settle in and consider it home."

Those few words brightened Stephanie's attitude. "That's a possibility I didn't think of. I explored drawers, closets, and all likely hiding places. I found very few keepsakes. In fact, nothing I felt a special affinity toward."

Patting Stephanie's arm, Evelyn comforted her. "Don't worry too much. You've done enough for one day. Rome wasn't built in twenty-four hours, and neither was Tulsa or your life."

On impulse, Stephanie made a declaration that had been forming all afternoon. "Evie, I want to spend the night here, in this house."

Evelyn's face contorted with apprehension. "Will you be all right?"

Feeling confident, Stephanie brushed aside Evie's concern. "Sure. I'll be fine."

Not fully persuaded, Evelyn suggested, "I'll leave my number beside the phone, in case you need me."

Later in the evening, after returning home with her car, Stephanie debated whether or not to phone Doug. A bit hesitant about how she'd explain her change of plans, she wavered until she'd worked it out in her head. Before she could change her mind, she dialed Doug's number at the Triple T ranch.

In the study, catching up on paperwork, Doug busied himself so that he wouldn't dwell on the quietness of the house. Funny, he'd noticed how quiet the dwelling was until after Stephanie left. Never before had the quiet bothered him. But the arrival of the amnesiac woman into his life had changed him without his even being aware of the transformation.

The sudden shrill ringing of the telephone shattered the quiet. Even though he didn't feel much like talking to anyone and was tempted not to answer, Doug picked up the receiver after the fourth ring. "Hello."

"Hi, it's me." Stephanie's soft voice carried over the line.

Doug's insides twisted with a sense of premonition. "And..."

"Do you miss me?"

He wasn't about to admit anything. She already held more power to hurt him than anyone else ever had. He hardened his heart. "Is answering that question a prerequisite for this conversation?"

Coolness entered her voice. "Well, no, not exactly."

Not knowing why, Doug sought any excuse to end the conversation—what little there had been of it. Maybe he didn't want to face the bleakness of a future without Stephanie. If he didn't listen to her, he could avoid looking reality in the face for a while longer, and he could hang on to his last thread of hope for a future with her. "Look, I'm kind of busy right now. What do you need?"

Why was he shoving her away? Had he changed his mind about the wedding? When next Stephanie spoke, anger tinged her voice. "I thought I'd give you a report on my first day's findings."

"First day," he repeated, premonition overriding his stranglehold on hope. "That has implications." His attitude sickened even him. Doug wouldn't have blamed Stephanie if she hung up and never called back. Why was he doing this?

Couldn't he be happy that Stephanie was piecing together her past so that they could have a future? Hurt crept into her voice. She spoke louder. "Yes, *first*. I, just this very minute, decided to extend my visit. Originally, I planned to return tomorrow, but while I was at the shop today, I confirmed that sewing was definitely my line of work before the accident."

Her thoughts somersaulting, Stephanie rattled on to Doug, confused by his chilly telephone reception. Didn't he want to know that she knew she was different from the person she'd been before the accident, that even if there was another man in her life, it was Doug she loved now? Didn't he care that she was doing all this for them, so that they could be free of her past?

She drew in a quick breath. "As far as my personal life or the house goes, I haven't had as much luck remembering anything else." Hurt as she was by his aloof attitude, sarcasm coated her words. "But a longer stay should remedy that. Don't you agree?"

Even as he willed the impending pain to go away, a fresh ache entered Doug's heart. He'd known all along that this was what would happen. No woman in her right mind would willingly stay on a ranch out in the middle of nowhere, isolated day in and day out. Stephanie had a right to her life in the city. Doug fought off his hurt with biting words. "Of course. Stay as long as you want. It's your life, and your prerogative to do as you please. Whatever you decide is of no concern to me."

By the time they'd disconnected, Doug was disappointed that they'd argued again. Although their words skirted the main concern, emotions had clouded the issues and driven the conversation. Just like his first wife, Constance, Stephanie had already tired of rural life, although he had to admit it had been much quicker than with Constance. Maybe she had less grit than he'd thought. He'd thought she was different.

All things considered, it was better that they discovered this discontent, before the ceremony, rather than afterward. Ties were more easily broken before a wedding than later.

The severing of their souls was bound to happen. But why did it have to hurt so badly? Doug's only recourse was to bury himself so deep in work that he wouldn't feel a thing.

With each passing day, Stephanie hoped her memory would return. Just one more day, she repeatedly told herself. One day soon became three. A few soon slid into a week. Before she found all her answers, time slipped away into two weeks, then three. By the time five weeks had passed and her baby was due in less than a week, Stephanie had pieced together most of her past, but was no closer to retrieving her memory concerning the few weeks before the accident—the weeks that would tell her who was the father of her child. Much to her consternation, she hadn't experienced any additional flashes of insight.

During that five weeks Stephanie couldn't pass a phone without staring at the inanimate object. What had happened? Somehow, all the words had gotten twisted between her phone and Doug's.

"Steph, what's wrong?" Evelyn finally questioned her late one Friday afternoon at work. "You used to talk to me. Whatever it is, you don't need to carry the burden alone. Let me help."

Stephanie shifted her gaze between the phone and Evie. When she would have refused to answer, Evelyn hustled her into a quiet corner of the office and forced a confrontation. "I'm concerned about you. You look exhausted."

Immediately Stephanie put a hand to her distended abdomen, ready to offer the standard excuse.

Before she could speak, Evelyn continued, "I know you're due in less than a week. That's something else we need to talk about. But what I want to know is why you're still here in Tulsa, when you should be home with your rancher, preparing for a wedding and your baby's arrival."

"Don't worry." Tears pooled in Stephanie's eyes and threatened to spill over. As always, she struggled to keep them at bay when her thoughts turned to Doug. "I'm seeing a doctor here in Tulsa now. Everything's fine."

"Everything is not fine. If you tell me that one more time, I'm going to scream." She shoved Stephanie down into the nearest chair and pulled up another for herself. "Out with it, now."

Fidgeting with her fingers, keeping her eyes downcast, Stephanie hesitated only a moment before the dam of words burst. "A simple courtesy call—merely to let him know I was staying another day or two longer before returning home to the ranch, so he wouldn't worry—suddenly escalated into a full-blown argument."

"By him, I assume you mean Doug."

Stephanie nodded. "He implied there was no reason for me to return to the ranch. I think he changed his mind about wanting to get married."

"You love him, don't you?" At Stephanie's nod, Evelyn continued. "Doesn't that count for anything?"

"Actually, I thought he cared for me, too." Stephanie raised her gaze to meet Evelyn's. "Evidently I was wrong."

Evelyn laid a hand over Stephanie's. "Could be he's had problems at the ranch. Have you thought about calling him again?"

Stephanie glanced at the phone. "I would have phoned back and apologized that very day, if I'd thought the gesture would help matters any, but in the dark mood Doug was in, I didn't think he'd even speak to me again so soon. And the longer I waited, the more difficult it became. Now it's too late."

"Nonsense." Evelyn stood and paced the small area, in concentrated thought. She stopped in front of Stephanie. "Evidently you don't know men. Doug may have been hurt by your going against his wishes—"

"Orders," Stephanie interjected.

"Details!" Evelyn rolled her eyes back and shrugged. "Okay, orders—and coming to Tulsa at what he considered to be an inopportune time, near the end of your pregnancy."

"But I feel fine, am in good health, and have had a trouble-free pregnancy. I saw absolutely no reason to cut my visit short like I originally planned." Tears pricked her eyes as she once again replayed the phone conversation in her mind. "I also got a bit miffed and said words I shouldn't have. So it wasn't all Doug's fault."

Evie stared Stephanie in the eye. "But now you've stayed too long and shouldn't make such a long trip by yourself."

"Something like that." Stephanie ducked her head, ashamed of her childish behavior. "I hoped time would heal the hurts of our rash words. After all, I love Doug, and know a few ill-chosen words will never change that fact."

"Have you spoken to him since then?" At the shake of Stephanie's head, Evelyn sighed. "In that case, Steph, I want you to promise me something."

Stephanie pinned her gaze on Evie.

"Don't let pride stand in your way. Go home tonight and phone Doug. Try to work it out. True love is too precious to throw away."

Later that Friday evening, in her cozy home, with the cold November wind howling outside, Stephanie concentrated on the positive. She earned a good living, worked at a job she enjoyed and owned a home. What else could a person want?

Always when she asked herself that question Stephanie's thoughts drifted to Doug. She loved him and wanted him to love her in return. But evidently it was not to be.

He hadn't called. But neither had she. He'd avoided her since their last exchange of words. To Stephanie's way of thinking, that meant he wanted her out of his life and was possibly regretting his rash behavior in asking her to marry him, even if it was only a marriage of convenience.

Evie was right. Stephanie had exhausted herself worrying and wrestling with the whole ordeal. After this afternoon's confrontation with Evie and much thought and deliberation over the past five weeks—and without having heard another peep from Doug—Stephanie had to make a decision. With less than a week until her baby was due, she couldn't return to the ranch. That added another dimension to her decision.

Weighing the odds, Stephanie decided it was in her best interests—and the baby's—to forget all about Doug and go on living here, as though nothing had happened, because evidently nothing had, just the exchange of a few kisses and—that was all. She would let him off the hook, since that was what he apparently wanted.

In order to clear her conscience and add closure to that chapter of her life so that she could get on with living, Stephanie concluded it was time she erased the slate and started fresh. She'd make it perfectly clear to Doug that this was what she wanted and that he was in no way obligated to her.

Her mind made up when she went to bed that Friday night, Stephanie phoned him early Saturday morning, thinking she'd catch him before he left the house at the crack of dawn. She saw no reason to further delay the inevitable.

She lifted the receiver and pressed the buttons for his number, fingers trembling all the while. Why she'd thought today would be any different, she didn't know, but she had to do something, even if it was just leaving a final message for him to find. This walking around in limbo was driving her crazy.

The answering machine picked up on the fifth ring. After the beep, Stephanie swallowed the lump in her throat and acted on her convictions in a strong, clear voice. "Doug, this is Stephanie. For all I know, you may be sitting there this very minute, listening. Please, if you're there, pick up the phone. Don't refuse to talk to me."

Stephanie paused, but as she'd expected, Doug didn't pick up the receiver. "I've thought this through, and no matter which angle I view the situation from, I arrive at the same conclusion each time. The time has come for us to get on with our lives."

Alone at the ranch house, in the study that seemed empty without Stephanie, Doug listened to her soft voice transmitted over the line. He turned from the picture window and the colorful sunrise to the phone. When her voice stopped, he grabbed up the receiver, hoping to catch her before she disconnected.

"Hey, Steph, I'm here." He wanted to add *waiting for you to come home,* but he didn't.

"Oh, hi. I don't want to keep you, so just let me say my piece and get it over with." Stephanie swallowed her rising trepidation, before continuing her recitation. "The word *love* was never mentioned between us, so there's no emotional stake involved. We had a business deal which no longer seems to benefit either of us."

The longer Stephanie talked, the harder the words were to get out. It would be so much easier just to hang up and not give Doug an explanation, but that would also be the coward's way out. She didn't consider herself a coward.

Dong wanted to tell her he loved her, wanted to explain his awful behavior. When Stephanie paused, he said, "But, Steph, I...I..." The words wouldn't come. His voice trailed off to nothing.

Difficult though the words were, Stephanie said what had to be said. "I realize there's a possibility my baby may be your brother's child, and as such the only heir to the Triple T Estates. It's possible that's the only reason you've asked us to stay."

Her words cut Doug to the core. He had no one to blame but himself. She'd evidently listened to all the excuses he'd offered as to why they should marry—all but the real reason, which he hadn't given and had only recently recognized and admitted. He couldn't stifle a groan.

Stephanie's words flowed on. "No, don't feel bad, if that's the case. You've acted on your convictions and sense of fair play. But since we have no proof, I'm not willing to take the chance and submit my child to the responsibilities that inheritance entails."

Self-loathing tortured Doug's soul. Why couldn't he share his true feelings with this woman? He opened his mouth to speak, but again, no words came. All he could do was listen to her musical voice as her words sliced him to pieces.

With her admission out of the way, words flooded Stephanie's mind and spilled forth. "In addition, I appreciate you sharing the story of your wife and child. Though loss is difficult for anyone to bear, the amount of your loss has been magnified, in that you've lost your parents and brother, as well as your wife and child, in a relatively short period of time."

Yes, those were losses, but none were as great as losing Stephanie. "I'm not good with words, but I'm sorry, Steph."

She drew a quick intake of breath. "I'm sorry, too. Our deal was convenient, and would allow my child and me to step into those empty places, as more or less a surrogate wife and child to you. Reliving the past is not fair to you, either, dredging up hurt and filling the void left by something that is irreplaceable."

Unbearable pain was strangling Doug's heart. The only past he was reliving now was the past months and weeks spent in Stephanie's company. Who would fill the void she'd leave in his life? "I wasn't asking you to take someone else's place. You've made your own place in my life."

Noisily Stephanie sucked in more air. "Doug, I know you're a responsible person, and I commend you on acting on your sense of responsibility for what you feel right and just compensation for the baby and me, even if there is no blood relation.

"Just because I was in the wreck with Theodore, I don't want you to feel you owe it to me to repay that which was taken from me. I don't blame you or your family. The wreck could have happened to anybody. It wasn't anyone's fault. The accident just happened, and I accept that I happened to be in the wrong place at the wrong time."

Doug wondered how she could possibly say that. She'd been in the right place at the right time for their two paths to cross.

"I can relieve you of the guilt and obligation you feel toward us. I'll sign the necessary release forms required by you or your lawyer or your insurance company to relieve any implied liability. Consider it a gift."

What was she talking about? Did she think he'd try to take the baby away from her? He wanted them both. "That won't be necessary, Steph. I'd rather give you a gift."

Stephanie sighed. "That's not necessary. I have to be honest, because I have to live with myself the rest of my life. As I learn more about myself every day, I know I'm the type who must respect myself in order to live happily and guilt-free. Wealth cannot and will not buy my happiness. I must have love in my life, not just possess things."

She offered a stilted laugh. "So, I'm idealistic. I can't change that about me, but on the other hand, I don't know that I really want to change. Have a good life, Doug."

The tension drained from Stephanie. She relaxed, her voice softening. "I know my past lies here in Tulsa, so don't worry about me. I'll be fine. I have a house, and I have a job that provides an adequate living for my baby and me. I'm able to meet my basic needs, with some leftovers for occasional splurges. In the long run, that's all that really matters."

"No, it's not."

Stephanie closed her eyes and leaned her forehead against the cool wall. "Please forgive me for rattling on so long. But this all needed to be said. I just wish I could have told you in person. However, you realize I'm not in any shape to travel right now."

Her last words fell away to a whisper. "All of this is to say the engagement's off, and the wedding's off. I hereby give you your freedom. Enjoy your life, and live it to the fullest. You deserve happiness—hopefully not too late in your life for you to make the best of it. Goodbye, my dear Doug, and good luck."

Releasing the tight grasp she'd unconsciously been holding on the phone, Stephanie removed the receiver from her ear, unable to hold back the flood of emotion any longer. Bursting into tears, she gently replaced the receiver in the cradle, severing the final link to Doug and her last contact with him forever.

Behind the desk in the study, Doug sat as still as stone, listening as Stephanie delivered her closing words. The cry of anguish he heard just before the soft click of disconnection tore at his heartstrings, shattering his final resistance. Swallowing his pride, Doug said, "Steph! Stephanie, don't hang up. I... I'm sorry. Oh, baby, you don't know how sorry. I was wrong. I'll make it right."

Damn! He was too late. The dial tone buzzed deafeningly in his ear. For long moments, he held the noisy receiver.

How could he have been so stubborn? So stupid and so blind? He slammed the receiver down on the phone. This was his own fault. He couldn't blame a soul except himself.

But this was the way he'd wanted it from the beginning. He'd wanted Stephanie out of his life, or so he'd thought. Without her, his life would be easy. He wouldn't think about her and wouldn't worry about her. He wouldn't fuss when they differed in opinion. And he wouldn't have to endure the endless wanting, or the guilt that came when he thought of Theo and her together.

In fact, removing her from his life would make things easier all around. She wouldn't kiss him every time she walked by, wouldn't place his hands on her belly so that he could feel the child within. She wouldn't slide her small hands inside his clothes and caress him with her dancing fingers. And she wouldn't mate her tongue with his. No, she wouldn't do any of those things. And that would make his life easier all around, wouldn't it?

Doug stood and stared out the large picture window. Endless tilled fields of newly planted wheat stretched as far as the eye could see. In that moment, the ranch didn't hold a candle to Stephanie. His life would be empty and meaningless without her. As far as he was concerned, not worth living.

Returning to his seat, Doug rolled the chair up to the desk. He picked up the phone. The only thing he could do was to eat crow—and plenty of it.

He pondered the situation. He had two possible courses of action.

One, he could call her. However, if he did that, she'd probably refuse to talk to him, especially since he'd done the very same thing to her. He couldn't really blame her if she did. In addition, was he strong enough and sure enough of himself to argue with her over a long-distance line?

No, definitely not. The least hesitation on her part could easily give him the wrong impression. And at this time in their relationship, they certainly didn't need any more falsehoods.

The other recourse would be to face her and observe firsthand her reactions to him. Even though she might evade the issue with her words, or go so far as to tell him an outright lie, he'd know from her body language, and especially her eyes, whether or not she answered him truthfully. But if she did that, as he fully expected her to, did he have enough courage in the face of defeat to persuade her to believe what he knew to be the truth? That he...he... Damn, it was hard to admit, but it was the honest-to-goodness truth. He actually loved her.

There, he'd finally admitted it to himself. And—Doug glanced around the room—the roof hadn't fallen in, the walls hadn't crumbled around him, and his heart had swelled with pride at the admission. Yes, honestly, Douglas

Conrad Taylor loved Stephanie Elkhart—no, the last name was Garrison—Stephanie Garrison with all his heart.

If the world thought he'd let matters lie, it had another thought coming. As soon as he could grab a few articles of clothing, he'd be on the road to reclaim their love and their hopes of a lifetime together.

Doug bolted for the staircase and his room to make good on his most recent discovery.

Now, all he had to do was arrive in Tulsa lickety-split, locate the Creative Designs shop before they closed for the day, and possibly the entire weekend, and convince Miss Stephanie Garrison of the sincerity and genuineness of his love—more than likely the most difficult accomplishment Doug would ever achieve in his life.

Dared he hope for the best? What if he failed?

Chapter Fifteen

Saturday afternoon, Doug arrived in Tulsa, battling a cold north wind. He pulled off the highway into a convenience-store parking lot and went inside. There he asked to borrow the phone book. After locating and writing down the address of Creative Designs, he purchased a city map and left.

Forty minutes later, Doug parked in front of the shop. What would he do if Stephanie wasn't inside?

Glancing around the parking area of the strip mall, he located his car. Okay, that meant chances were she was there. Now all Doug needed to do was to trust the instincts that told him he was doing the right thing.

For a few minutes, he watched the storefront. He didn't see her through the plate-glass window, and only a few customers walked in and out. Good! That meant he had a chance of talking to her privately. If not, he was prepared to shout his declaration of love at the top of his lungs in front of everybody, if that was what it took to get her attention.

Slowly Doug climbed from the truck, his heart in his hands, and walked up to the store. He hesitated while he got a better grip on his courage before entering.

Almost immediately, a woman, similar in age to Stephanie, walked from the back room and approached him with a smile on her face. "May I help you, sir?"

Automatically, from habit, Doug shifted the Stetson to the crown of his head. The light brown wave sprang forward onto his forehead. "Stephanie Elkhart—er, Garrison—please."

"I'm Evelyn Lankford, co-owner. Perhaps I could help."

Doug shook his head. "No, I'd rather talk to Steph. This is personal business."

Evelyn gave him a wary once-over. "Who shall I say is asking for her?"

His answer came in one clipped syllable. "Doug."

Evelyn's eyebrows shot up. "No last name."

"She'll know who I am."

Turning to leave, Evelyn halted and spun back around. "You're not by chance Douglas Conrad Taylor of the Triple T Estates, are you?"

Self-conscious, Doug smiled. "I'm afraid so."

"Oh, Lordy." Evelyn rushed to the back of the store without another word.

"Stephanie!" Evelyn hurried through the double door that separated the front of the store from the sewing room in the back. She stopped in front of Stephanie, all excited. "He's here!"

Puzzled, Stephanie looked up from her bent position at the cutting table. "Who's here?"

"That Doug fellow. You know, the one from the Triple T. And he's asking for you."

Stephanie straightened, her hands automatically going to her lower back to ease the muscle strain there. What did he want? Immediately she thought of his car, parked out front

Taking her time, Stephanie walked over to the file cabinet in the corner.

The unflappable Evie was suddenly everywhere Stephanie was. "He's waiting. Will you hurry?"

"What's the rush?" Stephanie dug through her shoulder bag until she located the keys. Gripping them in her hand, she closed the file cabinet drawer and turned to the excited Evelyn. "Calm down. It's no big deal. He probably just wants his car, since I'm not going back to the ranch."

When she reached the double door, Stephanie hooked a glance over her shoulder. "Come on. I'll introduce you."

Evelyn followed on Stephanie's heels as she wound her way through the maze of tables to the front of the store, where Doug was studying the displays on the wall. She imprinted the sight of him standing there on her memory, stashing it away to have for later. "Doug."

At the sound of his name, he spun around. Automatically his gaze lit on Stephanie, then momentarily flickered to the woman beside her.

"Doug, I'd like you to meet my business partner, Evelyn Lankford." Turning slightly, Stephanie said, "Evie, this is Doug Taylor of the Triple T, the man who provided a home for me during my convalescence."

Evelyn offered a hand in greeting. "Nice to meet you."

Ignoring her offer of a handshake, Doug nodded. "Likewise." Turning his attention back to Stephanie, he said, "We need to talk, preferably alone."

"Oh, don't mind me. I've got plenty to do." Evelyn retreated to the counter where the cash register sat and busied herself with the sales tickets on the spindle.

Stephanie returned her attention to Doug. She held out her hand. "Here are your keys. I'd like to thank you for the loan of the car, and all you've done for me. Just as soon as I can, I'll pay back every penny I owe you."

Doug stared at her extended hand, but didn't take the proffered keys.

Two ladies entered the store and made a beeline for the notebook on the coffee table. They seated themselves on the couch near Doug and Stephanie, chattering all the while.

Glancing around the store, Doug returned his gaze to Stephanie. "Look, can we go somewhere less public and more quiet to talk?"

"We can go to the back room of the store, but there are three girls sewing, so I'm not sure how quiet it will be."

"Let's go somewhere in the car. Take the rest of the afternoon off. It's only a couple of hours until closing time, anyhow."

"I can't just up and leave."

Doug's impatience grew. "Why not? I'm sure Evelyn's closed the store many times without your help."

Another customer entered and began browsing. To Stephanie, it looked as though the customer would soon be working her way closer to where they stood. "Oh, all right. Let me tell Evie and get my purse. I'll meet you at the front door." She pressed the keys into his warm hand.

A couple of minutes later, Doug and Stephanie were in the car, with him driving and her giving directions and pointing the way. Despite its being late afternoon on Saturday, traffic was heavy around them. Cars whipped in and out of lanes, speeding faster than the posted limit.

Stephanie tensed. Maybe it would be better to direct him to the interstate. Hopefully, the traffic would thin out there.

When Doug stopped for a red light at an intersection, he turned to Stephanie. "How much farther?"

"Not far. Maybe a half-dozen more blocks, until you turn right at the doughnut shop. Then we'll be out of the worst of the traffic. From there it will be easy enough to get on the freeway."

The light changed, and Doug followed Stephanie's instructions. For a while, the traffic cleared, but then it thickened again. Noticeably anxious to be at their destination, Doug drove faster. Cars veered in and out of lanes, each driver searching for the quickest route through the traffic.

"Where are we going?" Doug asked, sliding a glance in her direction.

She directed her attention to him. "Does it matter?"

He shrugged. "I guess not. Just so it's someplace we can talk without interruptions. Be sure to let me know ahead of time when I need to change lanes."

A horn blared beside Stephanie. She whipped around in time to see a car cut in front of an eighteen-wheeler in the lane to her right. Smoke spewed from the tires as the truck swerved toward them.

Her heart leaping into her throat, Stephanie gripped the armrest. Fear paralyzed her.

Reacting quickly, Doug accelerated to give the trucker the room he needed to avoid catastrophe.

The force of the acceleration jolted Stephanie back against the seat.

As the traffic moved faster and faster, cars shifting from one lane to another, scenes flashed before Stephanie. Speechless, she stared at Doug. In her mind, the interior of the car dimmed to nighttime darkness. Headlights from the oncoming traffic flung the silhouette of a male driver before her. Inky blackness hid his identity. As quick as the vision came, it disappeared.

Adrenaline shot through Stephanie's veins. Her heart beat rapidly, its force seemingly strong enough to crack her ribs and loud as a resounding kettledrum in her ears. A cold sweat drenched her. Fear robbed her of speech.

Doug reduced his speed to meld back with the flow of traffic. Then, from out of nowhere, a car cut from his left

across their lane to the lane on the right. The same car that
had forced its way in front of the eighteen-wheeler shot
through the narrow opening between the two cars and
forced its way in front of Doug.

Expertly Doug maneuvered the car to the now empty right
lane, avoiding a collision.

The sound of squealing tires, breaking glass and crunch-
ing metal echoed in Stephanie's ears, tossed up from the
depths of her memory. She threw her hands up in front of
her face and shrieked with terror.

Immediately Doug signaled and steered to the shoulder of
the highway, where he slowed to a stop. Slamming the gear
shift lever into park, he twisted in the seat and grabbed
Stephanie by the shoulders.

She flailed at him with her arms.

He dodged the blows, yet maintained his grip upon her.
"Steph, what is it? What's wrong?"

With unseeing eyes, she stared at him, mute, her face
colorless.

Her pallor frightened him. Hands gripping her upper
arms tighter, he shook her. "You can't faint now. Don't do
this."

A strange voice from the past echoed in Stephanie's ears.
"No, don't do this. You can't. Not now."

Automatically Stephanie repeated the words she heard her
own voice saying. "I want out. Stop the car this instant."

Stephanie succumbed to an onslaught of trembling as the
force of a tornado ripped the locked door of her mind from
its hinges and sent it sailing across time. Pent-up memories
from her past were bottlenecked at the small, unexpected
opening before the abrupt release suddenly allowed them to
burst through into the wide open void to freedom.

The tide of memories, like water from a ruptured dam,
gushed out to fill all the cracks and crevices of the abyss, the
torrents seeking and finding an equalizing level. There the

contents rested comfortably, lapping against the walls of her mind, her senses absorbing the return of information, much like a parched dessert receiving a long-awaited flooding rain.

Panic gripped Doug. He cupped Stephanie's face in a tender hold. His voice softened to a coaxing tone. "The car is stopped. Why do you want out?"

The gentleness in his hands, along with his soothing voice, pulled Stephanie out of her stupor. The quaking in her muscles subsided. Relaxing, she glanced in all directions, assessing the situation and gaining her bearings. "Steph, look around. See for yourself. The car is stopped," Doug patiently repeated. "Why do you want out?"

Finally accepting his statement as true, she trained her gaze on him. "Doug?"

Fingers shaking, he smoothed her dark blond hair back from her damp face. "Yes, I'm here."

Tentatively she touched her fingers to the side of his face, which was prickly with day-old stubble. "Are we all right?"

A smile, shaky with relief, inched across his face. He swallowed. "It was close, but we're fine."

"M-m-my memory. It's back. I remember everything." She stared at Doug, drinking in the sight of him. "The night of the wreck—I was with Theodore. We were on our way to the ranch."

Staring off into space, she backtracked. "We met while I was working on a design project in Oklahoma City. I'd only known him for a short while, less than three months—but in that time he swept me off my feet. I'd never had so much attention in all my life. He made me feel beautiful and desirable. I couldn't resist his fun-loving attitude and carefree life-style. For months I'd worked too hard. I needed a change of pace, some fun in my life and someone to care."

She glanced at Doug. "As much as I hate to admit it, I'm not a very social person when it comes to parties, but we hung out together at various dinner parties. Our being there was supposed to be beneficial to his job and provide good contacts for mine. Evie and I were considering expanding to the Oklahoma City area."

Embarrassed, Stephanie stared down at her fidgeting hands. "Later, when I looked back at that night, he was so attentive, so considerate, as though I was the only thing of importance. He talked about how important family was to a person."

She glanced up at Doug. "Theo missed having you nearby. He said his family had always doted on him. In a way, I think he was sorry about the rift he'd caused."

Stephanie trained her gaze straight ahead, out the windshield. "I never had much family, just Mom and Dad. We moved around a lot, that is until I got a place of my own, after graduation. Even now, they travel around in a motor home, not staying in any one place too long. I wanted roots, a family and a home, a place to belong—somewhere I'd never have to leave."

Doug's gentle touch, his forefinger tracing her jawbone, drew her attention to him.

"No, don't stop." He tendered a kiss on her forehead. "Talk it all out. Remember everything there is to remember."

"Theodore offered those things to me. By the time we got to my place, our dreams fused into one, or so I thought. Theo seemed excited at the prospects, too.

"His promises to fulfill my dream overwhelmed me and made me love him that much more. In fact, I loved him more than I'd ever loved anyone before. I guess I was weak in judgment that night, and...well..." She shrugged. "One thing led to another. We were careful and used protection—at least the first time."

Doug kissed her on the tip of the nose. "There's no need to blush. It's just me. I'm not passing judgment."

Stephanie continued, "Anyhow, to make a long story short, I—no, we both wanted a baby and knew we'd marry as soon as possible. However, we were both so busy with work it was hard to find time to make any definite plans or even a trip to the Triple T to tell you."

Sensitive to Stephanie's discomfort, Doug clasped her hands. "You don't have to tell me all this. It's in the past and can't be changed."

"I know, but I want you to know. That way, there won't be any secrets between us." Boldly she met his stare.

He nodded his understanding.

Stephanie continued. "As soon as I found out I was pregnant, I couldn't wait to tell Theo about the baby. We were already planning to be married, so it was a matter of information, not for entrapment purposes or financial gain, or any of those things. All my life I've wanted a baby." She caressed her swollen abdomen with loving strokes.

"Theo wasn't averse to me being pregnant." Stephanie smiled as she thought back. "Really quite the opposite. He said he never knew what it was to want to settle down until we met. We made plans immediately to go to the Triple T, so that I could meet you and we could share our news."

Stephanie peered at Doug from beneath her lashes. "You were his idol, you know. He talked about you constantly. I think in some ways he was disappointed in himself, because he wasn't happy at the ranch and couldn't be a rancher like was expected of him. He so wanted to please."

A smile of understanding crossed Doug's face. "Don't we all, at one time or another in our life?"

"Yes, I guess so." Stephanie pressed a hand to her engorged abdomen and momentarily held her breath as a tightening sensation hardened her stomach. She soon released her pent-up breath and stroked her stomach with both hands in circular motions, hoping to relieve her discomfort. "Remember the engagement ring from the accident?"

Doug nodded, and suddenly realized she was no longer wearing it, as she had the morning she left the ranch. "Do you?"

"Yes." Stephanie didn't immediately elaborate, but before long she did. "Theo handed me the ring without much preamble. He said something to the effect of 'Since we're getting married, I guess you ought to wear this.' He never formally proposed."

Stephanie clasped her stomach and sat up straighter, gradually drawing in a deep breath, then releasing it slowly. The periodic waves of discomfort and intensity were increasing with time. After a couple of minutes, she relaxed back into the seat.

"Go ahead, finish your story. I'm listening," Doug coaxed.

"I accepted the ring without any qualms. But now that I think back, I can see that after I was pregnant, Theo wasn't as attentive as he had been. I thought he was preoccupied with work..." Her voice trailed off as she remembered. She turned to Doug. "That is, until Theo said I couldn't have planned things better."

Doug raised his eyebrows. "Oh, really?"

"Yeah, that's what I thought, too. I didn't fully understand at first." Finding courage, Stephanie explained, "He said 'your baby'—not our baby, mind you, but 'your baby,' meaning my baby—was his ticket to freedom, to gaining his inheritance. When I questioned him and asked for an explanation, he laughed and tried to retract his words, saying they sounded harsher than he meant. He was just so enamored with his good luck that nothing else counted."

Stephanie momentarily stared out the windshield at the passing traffic, massaging her abdomen, hoping the stomachache would dissipate. "I didn't immediately confront

Theo, but the more I thought about his slip of the tongue on the drive to the ranch, the more I rejected the idea of marrying for money—at least it seemed like he was marrying so he could have his money. Suddenly, I couldn't foresee anything but trouble ahead. Marriage meant more to me than money.''

She shrugged, avoiding eye contact with Doug. "Needless to say, I told Theo to stop the car, that I'd changed my mind about going to the Triple T and about getting married. He wouldn't hear of it. He accused me of being selfish, thinking only of myself. We argued.''

Sadness crept into Stephanie's voice. "Theo changed that night, right before my eyes. Instead of stopping and letting me out, he took his anger out in speed. He thought I'd buckle to his wishes out of fear. The longer I refused to bow to his wishes, the faster he drove. I was determined not to let any man have that kind of power over me, no matter the consequences.''

Releasing a low whistle, Doug adjusted his Stetson. "Steph, you were so brave.''

She smiled. "I wasn't brave. It was just a matter of principle, and not letting someone else control my destiny.''

"For what it's worth, I thought that crazy driver awhile ago had ended it for both of us." Doug sighed. "I didn't realize what I had until it was almost taken from me. In fact, when you decided not to come back to the ranch, I realized my loss at that time, and recognized it was up to me to straighten things out. I'll admit at first I thought you were like Constance, and Theo, too, preferring city life to rural life.''

Shaking her head, she smiled. "Not at all. I found a peace and sense of belonging at the Triple T that I've never before experienced. It's a wonderful place to live and raise a family.''

"Would you?''

Stephanie opened her mouth to speak.

"No, don't answer yet. Let me say what I came here to say. If we had wrecked back there and you had died, I would have died with you, because without you I have no reason to go on living. I think I fell in love with you that first time you opened your eyes in the hospital and didn't know who you were or where you were from and confronted the consequences anyway." A smile climbed upon Doug's face. "You were brave then, too."

His dark brown gaze latched on to Stephanie. "I'm not much good with words, but what I'm trying to say is I love you, Steph, more than life itself. I can't live without you."

Valiantly Stephanie stifled a gasp and clasped her swollen abdomen, as it once again tightened and hardened, this time more forcibly. She clenched her teeth to hide her discomfort.

Worry clouded Doug's eyes. "Whether or not you believe me is up to you, but it's the honest-to-goodness truth. I didn't want to love you, Steph. I fought it long and hard, always thinking in the back of my mind that you belonged to Theo and that I was pretty sorry for wanting you for myself. But now I see how wrong I was."

Doug leaned over and gently kissed Stephanie on the lips. "I love you, Steph, forever and always. I want both you and your baby, for no other reason than to love and protect you. I don't know how you feel, but I can't live without you. I know I'm beginning to sound like a broken record, but I can't help it. I almost lost you once because of my stupid pride, and I don't want to lose you again."

Her contractions relaxing, Stephanie stared at him. "What about more children?"

"Lady, I'd like making babies with you. In fact, I'm all for a large family—the more the merrier. No child should be raised alone."

A smile tugged at her mouth. "I hoped you'd feel that way."

"Don't tempt me. I'm almost at the end of my endurance now." Doug smiled in return. "Does this mean you're saying yes?"

Coyly Stephanie looked at him through her lashes. "I don't know. I haven't been asked yet."

"Egad, Steph. You sure make it hard on a man." Doug brought her hand to his lips and kissed her palm. "Stephanie Elkhart Garrison, or whatever your name is, will you do me the honor of becoming my bride?"

"Yes," Stephanie said on an audible gasp, grabbing at her fiercely contracting abdomen. "But the ceremony's going to have to wait, because this baby won't. Get me to the hospital quick. This baby's coming *now*."

Epilogue

Six weeks later, on the brink of the New Year, Stephanie stared out a cabin window at Black Mesa State Park overlooking a moonlit lake. The silence at the resort was a stark contrast to the baby's crying, which usually happened around ten o'clock each night—the last feeding before the early-morning wails at six o'clock.

A booted footfall behind her alerted Stephanie to Doug's approach. He threaded his arms around her waist and drew her back against him. "We just got here, and already you're thinking about her again, aren't you?"

Stephanie relaxed against him. "I'm sorry. I can't help it. She's so little and dependent."

Tenderly Doug kissed her on the neck with a series of nibbles. "Would it make you feel better to phone Neddie and check on Deena?"

"No, I'll be fine." Stephanie turned in the circle of Doug's arms to face him. "It's only for one night."

"That was your choice, not mine. We could have brought her. In fact, I encouraged you to do just that."

"I know, but she's six weeks old now, and one night without us won't harm her." Stephanie ran the pad of her thumb across his eyebrow in a gentle caress, then kissed him on the tip of the chin. "I'm not regretting the decision. It's just hard, this first time away from her for any length of time."

"Do you want me to take you back home? It's only an hour's drive." At the shake of her head, he asked, "Do you want to go get her and bring her here with us for the night?"

"No. Let her get acquainted with her grandparents tonight. I want you all to myself on our wedding night." Stephanie ducked her head and kissed the hollow at the base of his neck. With her tongue, she traced the U-shaped indention in the bone structure.

Alone at last, Doug relaxed his guard. Stephanie's warm, gentle touches and damp kisses ignited a desire too long denied. "Try not to think about Deena for a little while, then."

Doug unbuttoned the front of Stephanie's blouse, his knuckles grazing the swell of her creamy flesh. A series of goose bumps rose on her skin. He lowered his head and kissed the exposed area, following her fullness to the edge, where she disappeared into the lacy undergarment.

Once there, he trailed the tip of his tongue along the line of the barrier. Impatient, he bowed his head and drew the hardened tip of one jutting feminine curve into his mouth, silky fabric and all.

A purring sound escaped from deep in Stephanie's throat. Her words slurred. "Hmm... Deena. You don't think Neddie minded that we named the baby after her, do you? I'm trying not to worry too much."

Releasing the hardened nub of her peak, Doug straightened. "Good. Then quit worrying, because I plan to keep you occupied with other thoughts and deeds this one night we have alone.''

Still preoccupied with thoughts of the baby, Stephanie couldn't yet give her full attention to Doug. ''I can't believe she's already six weeks old. My, how time flies when—''

''You're having fun,'' Doug finished for her. He placed his forehead against hers and sighed, his warm, minty breath drifting across her face. ''Well, this isn't much fun, lady, without your cooperation. You're going to make a saint out of me yet, Steph. After all this time, how can you stand here ignoring me?''

''I'm not ignoring you. Far from it.'' She patted him on the side of the face. ''I'm teaching you patience. And along with patience automatically comes sainthood.''

Shaking his head, Doug said, ''See. What did I tell you?''

Stephanie hooked her arms around his torso, bringing their bodies together. She rocked against him seductively. ''Come here, Saint Doug, and kiss me.''

Anxious, he shifted against her, nudging and prodding. ''I'm going to do more than kiss you this time, you witch.''

Stephanie leaned away from him, yet remained in the circle of his arms. ''Here I thought I was an angel of mercy on a mission assigned to put you out of your misery.''

''Stop talking.'' Doug covered her mouth with his and flicked his tongue against hers.

Any comeback was lost in the deep, moist caverns where their tongues dueled.

Doug strained against her.

Wedging her fingers inside the back of his waistband, Stephanie pressed him to her.

Their tongues stroked and parted. They tangled, then withdrew. In and out, searching and testing, meeting and mating.

Unable to stand the separation any longer, Stephanie withdrew her hands from their warm resting place and explored the feel of her husband beneath her fingers.

At the same time, Doug luxuriated in the discovery of Stephanie. His hands spanned her waist, then flared over her hips, cupping her roundedness and impaling her more firmly on his need.

She ran her hands up the taut muscles of his back and down again, over his trim hips, kneading him to a quivering mass beneath her touch. Next she trailed them to the front, edging her fingers between them, and possessively grazed the shape of his need.

Her touches sent him rocketing with desperate want of her, a yearning too long denied. Doug's patience was running thin. Without hesitation, he proceeded with the reverent expedition of the disrobing ceremony.

Stephanie followed suit. Releasing him first, she delighted in his velvety softness before pressing against him. The heat of his need permeated her thin, silky, half-slip. An answering rush of warm moisture prepared her for him.

Once again Doug captured her mouth while they completed the disrobing ceremony, his honeyed kisses totally distracting her from her mission. When finally they discarded the last strips of clothing, nakedness roamed freely against nakedness, at first cool, then heated with desperation and need.

Doug bent and, with an arm beneath Stephanie's knees, scooped her up into his arms. Leaving the small lamp burning golden in the corner of the cozy living room, he strode to the beckoning darkened bedroom, stealing numerous moist kisses along the way.

Once at their destination, Doug lowered her to a standing position beside the bed, where she waited impatiently while he peeled back the covers. Together they slid between cool, starched sheets, then stretched out side by side, rolling to face one another.

Stephanie combed her fingers through the coarse fur of chest hair to the tender flesh beneath. In awe, she meandered her hands up his firm chest in exploration and across the broad, muscled width of his shoulders, marveling at the man who was now her husband.

Briefly recalling the last time they'd lain in a bed together, Stephanie sought to comfort Doug. "I love you with all my heart. Nothing will ever change the way I feel about you. Heaven knows we didn't pursue this avenue—if anything, we fought it—but fate intervened and granted us a love more perfect than I ever imagined possible."

In the darkly shadowed room, Doug smiled into her eyes. "I fought the attraction from day one. What a battle it was, believing you belonged to my brother, yet wanting you for myself. But in the end, my loss was our gain. Destiny knew better than either of us that our fates would be intertwined."

She traced the heated, kiss-swollen bow of his lips with her forefinger and smiled. "Just so you know I love you, my dear Doug."

He kissed her fingertip. "And I love you, my dear Stephanie."

Tenderly Doug joined his lips to Stephanie's in unhurried exploration and passion. With near reverence, they touched each other, tentatively at first, then more possessively, as they accustomed themselves to touching and being touched. Eagerly they accepted each other's loving caresses.

Without restraint, Doug and Stephanie both gave freely gently pleasing and inflaming each other's needs and desires, until soon they were ready to claim the rights and privileges the wedding ceremony had bestowed upon them.

Wrapped in a loving embrace, they rolled until Stephanie rested on her back, Doug covering her. The heat of his desire pulsated between them. Gently he nudged her to fulfill the promise of their love. In compliance and anticipation, Stephanie parted her limbs welcoming him. Doug settled into her, nestling in her cradle.

Fiercely Stephanie clung to him, this man who was hers in the eyes of God and the law. Then, impatient, she gently gyrated beneath him, urging him to enter her.

Doug's heart swelled at Stephanie's unspoken language. He shifted, positioning himself against her entrance.

A fleeting sense of apprehension arrested him.

Stephanie recognized his hesitancy as expectation and fear of the nagging guilt he'd felt before. Her voice husky, she reassured him. "I want only you, Doug, and no other. Our love was destined from day one. We're meant to be together. Theodore's death gave us that freedom. The ceremony guaranteed it."

To lend impetus to her words, Stephanie trailed her hands down his back to his hips and urged him to fulfillment with a bold nudge. She fastened her mouth on Doug's and laved him with her tongue. Further encouraging him, she mated her tongue with his to reclaim their love.

When she did, his last thread of insecurity fell away. Unable to resist that which was inevitable, Doug plunged himself deep within Stephanie and held on for dear life. Trembling with need, he partially withdrew, then penetrated again.

In a frenzy of love and physical need, they united, discovering their own unique rhythm, that which proved perfect for them.

Paradise was theirs at last. They feasted on the once forbidden fruit with insatiable hunger. Because of their long abstinence, the sharpness of their initial appetites sliced through all barriers to the core of their love and erupted.

Doug shuddered against Stephanie, releasing her long-pent-up love to flow freely.

Possessively he held her within the circle of his arms and sealed their fate with an all-encompassing kiss.

Their love had finally found a home—a true love that, despite the odds, had waited for its own time to be realized.

*   *   *   *   *

Continuing in October from Silhouette Books...

This exciting new cross-line continuity series unites five of your favorite authors as they weave five connected novels about love, marriage—and Daddy's unexpected need for a baby carriage!

You loved

THE BABY NOTION by Dixie Browning
(Desire 7/96)

BABY IN A BASKET by Helen R. Myers
(Romance 8/96)

MARRIED...WITH TWINS! by Jennifer Mikels
(Special Edition 9/96)

And the romance in New Hope, Texas, continues with:

HOW TO HOOK A HUSBAND (AND A BABY)
by Carolyn Zane (Yours Truly 10/96)

She vowed to get hitched by her thirtieth birthday. But plain-Jane Wendy Wilcox didn't have a clue how to catch herself a husband—until Travis, her sexy neighbor, offered to teach her what a man really wants in a wife....

And look for the thrilling conclusion to the series in:

DISCOVERED: DADDY
by Marilyn Pappano (Intimate Moments 11/96)

DADDY KNOWS LAST continues each month...
only in ▼ *Silhouette*®

DKL-YT

The Calhoun Saga continues...

in November
New York Times bestselling author

NORA ROBERTS

takes us back to the Towers and introduces us to
the newest addition to the Calhoun household,
sister-in-law Megan O'Riley in

MEGAN'S MATE
(Intimate Moments #745)

And in December
look in retail stores for the special collectors'
trade-size edition of

THE
Calhoun
Women

containing all four fabulous Calhoun series books:
COURTING CATHERINE,
A MAN FOR AMANDA, FOR THE LOVE OF LILAH
and *SUZANNA'S SURRENDER.*
Available wherever books are sold.

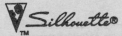

FORTUNE'S Children™

Bestselling Author

BARBARA BOSWELL

Continues the twelve-book series—FORTUNE'S CHILDREN—
in **October 1996** with Book Four

STAND-IN BRIDE

When Fortune Company executive Michael Fortune needed help
warding off female admirers after being named one of the ten most
eligible bachelors in the United States, he turned to his faithful
assistant, Julia Chandler. Julia agreed to a pretend engagement, but
what starts as a charade produces an unexpected Fortune heir....

MEET THE FORTUNES—a family whose legacy is greater than riches.
Because where there's a will...there's a *wedding!*

"Ms. Boswell is one of those rare treasures who combines humor
and romance into sheer magic."
—*Rave Reviews*

*A CASTING CALL TO
ALL FORTUNE'S CHILDREN FANS!*
If you are truly one of the fortunate
you may win a trip to
Los Angeles to audition for
Wheel of Fortune®. Look for
details in all retail Fortune's Children titles!

Look us up on-line at: http://www.romance.net   FC-4-C

This October, be the first to read these wonderful authors as they make their dazzling debuts!

Women to Watch

THE WEDDING KISS by Robin Wells
(Silhouette Romance #1185)
A reluctant bachelor rescues the woman he loves from the man she's about to marry—and turns into a willing groom himself!

THE SEX TEST by Patty Salier
(Silhouette Desire #1032)
A pretty professor learns there's more to making love than meets the eye when she takes lessons from a sexy stranger.

IN A FAMILY WAY by Julia Mozingo
(Special Edition #1062)
A woman without a past finds shelter in the arms of a handsome rancher. Can she trust him to protect her unborn child?

UNDER COVER OF THE NIGHT by Roberta Tobeck
(Intimate Moments #744)
A rugged government agent encounters the woman he has always loved. But past secrets could threaten their future.

DATELESS IN DALLAS by Samantha Carter
(Yours Truly)
A hapless reporter investigates how to find the perfect mate—and winds up falling for her handsome rival!

Don't miss the brightest stars of tomorrow!

Only from Silhouette®

"Just call me Dr. Mom....

I know everything there is to know about birthing *everyone else's* babies. I'd love to have one of my own, so I've taken on the job as nanny to three motherless tots and their very sexy single dad, Gib Harden. True, I'm no expert, and he's more handy at changing diapers than I—but I have a feeling that what this family really needs is the tender loving care of someone like me...."

MOM FOR HIRE
by
Victoria Pade
(SE #1057)

In October, Silhouette Special Edition brings you

THAT'S MY BABY!
Sometimes bringing up baby can bring surprises...
and showers of love.

There's nothing quite like a family

REUNION

HANNAH MICHAEL KATE

The new miniseries by
Pat Warren

Three siblings are about to be reunited.
And each finds love along the way....

HANNAH
Her life is about to change now that she's met
the irresistible Joel Merrick in HOME FOR HANNAH
(Special Edition #1048, August 1996).

MICHAEL
He's been on his own all his life. Now he's
going to take a risk on love...and
take part in the reunion he's been
waiting for in MICHAEL'S HOUSE
(Intimate Moments #737, September 1996).

KATE
A job as a nanny leads her to Aaron Carver,
his adorable baby daughter and the
fulfillment of her dreams in KEEPING KATE
(Special Edition #1060, October 1996).

Meet these three siblings from

Silhouette SPECIAL EDITION®
and

▼INTIMATE MOMENTS®
™ *Silhouette*

Look us up on-line at: http://www.romance.net